Copyright © 2019 by Dar

All rights reserved. No ...ed, transmitted, downloaded ... red in, or introduced into any ..., in any form or by any me... ow known, hereinafter inven...., ..., ... of the publisher. For permission requests, write to the publisher, addressed "Attention: Permissions Coordinator," at the address below.

Typewriter Pub, an imprint of Blvnp Incorporated
A Nevada Corporation
1887 Whitney Mesa DR #2002
Henderson, NV 89014
www.typewriterpub.com/info@typewriterpub.com

ISBN: **978-1-64434-049-3**

DISCLAIMER

This book is a work of fiction. The characters, incidents, and dialogue are drawn from the author's imagination and are not to be construed as real. While references might be made to actual historical events or existing locations, the names, characters, places, and incidents are either products of the author's imagination or are used fictitiously, and any resemblance to actual persons living or dead, business establishments, events or locales is entirely coincidental.

THE FORBIDDEN

DANTE CULLEN

type
writer
pub

To my Wattpad *followers who inspire me every day.*

BLUE MOON SERIES • BOOK ONE

all it took was one look

T. LANAY

CHAPTER ONE

ZAC

"I'm sorry Zac, it's just...it's no longer working out between us."

He'd said those words—finally. I should have been happy, but I wasn't. I should have been angry, but I couldn't even muster that. They say anger is easier than happiness, and that people are more inclined to show anger than happiness.

But not me.

At that moment, I surprisingly didn't feel anything. I didn't do anything either. I just stood there, looking at the guy whom I'd given my heart to.

"Zac, say something," he said, almost pleading.

What did he want me to say? *"Well, we can start working out. I can register us for a gym membership. That should be enough, yeah?"*

I couldn't say that out loud. There was no point anyway. I couldn't pretend I didn't understand him. It would only make the situation more awkward and tense than it already was.

"Bruce?" I whispered.

Just saying that name suddenly filled my eyes with tears. It was as if it was only then that his words sank in. The ice was melting, and my cheeks were getting wetter by the second. I hated it. I hated this feeling. I wanted nothing but to be numb again, but there was no going back. He was breaking up with me.

I wish I could say I hadn't expected it, but I had. I just wished that knowledge could have helped soothe the pain.

I watched the shocked look on his face at what I said. He was going to say I was delusional. He was going to say I was lying. The least he could do after breaking my heart was not lie to me.

"What?" He had the audacity to ask.

"Are you—are you leaving me for Bruce?" I asked, my voice breaking as the tears trailed down my cheeks.

He shifted uncomfortably, and his eyes darted to and from. He couldn't decide whether to flee or to stay and answer my questions.

I wasn't waiting for the answer, because I already knew. I knew the things that went on behind my back. He'd been cheating on me with Bruce Carlisle for the past two months. My heart broke when I found out, but I stayed, hoping we'd fix whatever was wrong with us—with *me*. I tried to become the best boyfriend I could ever be. I made time for him, and he had his way with everything.

He would cancel dinner plans at the last minute just because he didn't "feel" like it; he'd stand me up countless times because he "ran late at gym", and, when it came to making plans, his input was barely there.

I didn't argue with him about the missed calls that he never returned, or the incoherent explanations he offered to excuse his behavior. I did my best to understand him. Clearly, my passive approach hadn't worked the way I thought it would.

"What? No, Zac. I don't know where you got that," he said.

I felt a thud in my heart. Even after breaking it to me, he wasn't willing to be honest. I'd been faithful to him, and this was how he was repaying me?

He thrust his hands in his sweater pockets.

"I'm sorry, Zac," he said, turning to leave.

"I know, Chase. I know about you and him. I've known for a long time," I said, a strangled sob escaped my lips as tears started to fall on my face.

Chase turned, and his face fell. "How'd you find out?" he asked, finally admitting.

"I saw the messages. I saw you together in his room," I said.

"Zac, I never meant to hurt you. Things happened, and it…it got out of control and—"

"What is wrong with me?" I asked firmly.

"That's unfair," he said.

"Is it? You cheated on me for two months and still pretended we were okay. You lied to my face whenever I ask where you've been. You lied to my face about me being the *only* one. How is it unfair to ask you what's wrong with me? I want to know what is it with me that made you not only cheat on me but *lie to me over and over again*!" I demanded, my voice rising a few decibels.

"Zac, I'm not doing this!" he spat back, his voice rising to match mine.

I knew I shouldn't have pushed to find out, but I just needed to find out something—anything. Because truth be told, I'd been nothing but a good boyfriend. I didn't deserve to be dumped. I didn't deserve to be cheated on. I tried everything I could to make him happy.

But it wasn't just that. I *loved* him. Dating Chase was a dream come true.

I had a crush on him for a long time before I gathered the courage to ask him out. We met during our first year in college, and I spent the whole school year crushing on him. We saw each other a lot because we stayed in the same building on the same floor and started hanging out towards the end. I asked him out at the beginning of our second year, and we became a couple. We'd been dating for about a year, but all along, he'd been spending the last two months cheating on me, if not more.

"I just want to know, Chase," I said softly.

"Zac, I…," he said, a bit hesitant, before heaving a sigh. "I never loved you."

My heart stopped. Everything came crashing down yet again. I shook my head, refusing to believe what he was saying to me.

He let out a breath loudly. "I knew you liked me, and I felt sorry for you. Bruce and I, we started out way before us. I mean, I liked him, but he was unwilling to come out. I said yes to you just to spite him, but I couldn't stay away from him."

I had opened up a can of worms. Each word he said was like a knife to my heart,stabbing me over and over and over again. I couldn't believe what I was hearing. *Could someone really be that cruel?*

"I didn't mean to hurt you," he said.

"You used me!"

"This is why I didn't want to tell you," he said, starting to walk away.

"And you think that makes it all better?!"

He shook his head and walked away from me. I watched him leave as memories of our time together filled my brain. Watching him leave was all I could do. There was no hope of saving our relationship anymore.

Chase didn't love me.

He had only been pretending. He lied about everything.

Our whole relationship was a lie.

The door closed. Fresh tears made their way onto my face. I closed my eyes, as if that could stop the tears. It couldn't. Neither could it stop the pain that seared through my heart, eliminating everything in its path.

I fell to the floor as Chase's words swam around.

"I never loved you."

So, what did those *I love yous* he had uttered mean? What did our lovemaking mean to him? Had he wished it was

Bruce instead of me? Was Bruce the only person he saw when he was with me?

They say real men don't cry. I guess I'm not a real man then, because I was crying to my heart's content.

I heard some vibration and a beeping sound in the room. Judging from the sound, it came from the bed. It wasn't my phone because mine was in my pocket.

Chase had left his phone in the room, which wasn't unusual as we shared the room. It was my suggestion when we returned for the second year, and it had been convenient. Now, it was just going to be awkward and unpleasant.

I ignored his phone for a few seconds, wondering how it was going to be like staying together in one place but not together. It was going to be torture for me. He would bring Bruce over, for sure. He would try to be considerate and ask to have the room for himself to study or something, but my mind was only going to wonder if he was with Bruce.

His phone vibrated again.

I got up from the floor and followed the vibration to the bed—my bed. My mind temporarily went back to the moment he'd put the phone there. We were kissing then before he decided he was ready to break my heart.

His phone lit up. The line "Two New Messages" splashed on the screen.

An insane thought came into my head, and before I knew it, Chase's phone was in my hand. I chastised myself. I couldn't open his messages; they were private.

Even though my mind protested, I found myself clicking "Open."

Both of the messages were from Bruce. My heart sank as I read each one.

Have you told him yet? You've been in there forever.

Come to my room afterwards. I have something for you. Jackson is out. Hurry up.

I felt fresh tears graze my cheeks. Every time I calmed down, my wound would open again. It felt worse than finding out Chase was cheating on me. Back then I had hoped one day he would stop, that one day he would see that I was enough for him. I realized now, with a burning ache in my heart, that was something he was never going to see; the pain gripped me with its rawness, scorching me.

I put Chase's phone on the bed and realized something, which comforted me. If Bruce sent Chase a message that meant Chase wasn't with him at that moment. It was silly of me to think that, but I just wanted anything to lessen the pain.

I sat on my bed, wondering what on earth I was going to do. I felt lost.

My phone rang. I took it out of my pocket and looked at the Caller ID. It was my mom. I didn't feel like answering, but I didn't want to make her worry either.

I cleared my throat, erasing any trace of me crying, and answered.

"Hello?"

"Hello, honey. How are you?" she asked, her voice filled with excitement.

"I'm fine. How are you?"

"You don't sound fine," she said, her excited voice now immediately replaced with concern.

"I just have a cold," I lied.

"My poor baby, do you have medication?"

"Uh, Mom, it's just a cold. I'll be fine."

She sighed. "All right. Are you excited about spring break?"

I shrugged. "Uh…I guess."

"I know this is short notice, but I really hope you don't have any plans. I want you to meet someone," she said.

Chase and I had planned to spend spring break at his family vacation house with some of his relatives. I guess that's no longer going to happen. I hadn't yet decided on what I was going to do—we just literally broke up minutes ago!—but maybe going home wasn't a bad idea.

"Uh, I guess it's serious between you and Mark?" I asked.

She giggled. "I think so. He wants to meet you, Jessica, and Noah."

"I'll be home, Mom," I said.

"Thank you, Zachary. You don't know how much this means to me," she said.

"How does Jess feel?"

"You know your sister. She's throwing a tantrum. I don't think I'll survive it this time," she replied.

"Don't worry, I'll talk to her. She'll be fine."

The way I replied confidently when, really, I felt like breaking apart, was amazing, even to me.

"Thanks, honey. I love you, Zac," she said. She seemed a lot more at ease now.

"I love you too, Mom," I said, and she hung up.

My life was a mess, and I was assuring someone else I'd fix theirs. It was laughable how I thought I could do that, when I couldn't do it to myself. But I needed a distraction, and meeting Mark couldn't have come at a better time.

CHAPTER TWO

ZAC

I didn't possess the energy to do anything afterward, so I found myself lying on my bed. I had to remove Chase's phone from my bed, and this time, I resisted the urge to read his messages. I knew there were countless messages to and from Bruce there. It was how I found out about their deception. It was confirmed when I saw them together in Bruce's room. They never knew I knew well up until the moment Chase broke up with me.

My heart ached as I lay there alone, thinking of the moments Chase and I had shared a bed. It had been beautiful. Even after I found out he was cheating, I convinced myself it was still beautiful. If he cheated on me but still stayed, surely it meant he loved me?

I'd been a fool, and now I was paying the price. I cried again for a while, unable to fall asleep. I decided to call my sister.

It rang for a while before she answered.

"What?!"

Something told me I had caught her at a bad time. But then again, every time was a bad time. My sister was going through what Mom called 'late adolescence' phase and as a result, she was always either feeling bouts of unpredictable, temperamental behavior, or fighting with someone. I suspected a lot of it had to do with our dad's death since they were very close. I didn't expect her to be receptive to the idea of Mom dating again, and I was right—she wasn't.

"Hi, Jess," I said, injecting cheerfulness into my voice.

"Again, what?" she said, her voice laden with impatience.

"Is that how you greet your only older brother?" I asked.

"Hi, Zac. What do you want?" she asked in a voice that was too sweet to be authentic.

"I was just calling to say hello," I said.

"I'm glad you called." She suddenly changed her tune, and it was a surprise that she sounded genuinely glad I called. I soon learned why. "Can I visit you for spring break, please?" she begged.

I knew my sister enough to know she wouldn't suddenly want to visit me. Despite assuring Mom I would help her with Jess, Jess and I didn't get along, either. There was no way she just *wanted* to visit me.

"You know I live in a dorm, right?" I said. "I'm interested in why you want to visit me, though."

"Aren't you going to Chase's vacation house? Please take me with you."

My heart sank, aching at the same time. I felt a lump in my throat and coughed to stop it from leading to something else.

"I'm coming home for spring break. Anyway, aren't you supposed to be home for spring break?" I managed to say straight.

She groaned. "If it were up to me, I'd be anywhere but here."

"Mark?" I asked knowingly.

She groaned again. "I guess she's making you come home too?"

"She's not making me. I made the choice."

"Well, lucky you! You get to make your choices, and I don't. I swear, when I go off to college, I am never setting foot here again."

"You don't mean that, Jess."

"Yes, I do! Do you even know anything about the prick she wants us to meet?" she said.

"Nope, just that Mom likes him and sees a future with him."

"Pssh, she's setting herself up for a hard fall, and I won't be there to pick up the pieces."

"Jess, don't be like that. I know he's not Dad but—"

"It seems I'm the only one with sense. Since you can't save me from this impending doom, goodbye," she said and hung up before I could say anything back.

True, I may not have known Mark much but from the look of things, spring break was going to be filled with Jess's tantrums. She was already hard to deal with, but in the company of someone else she considered a threat, she was going to be worse. For my mom's sake, it was up to me to keep her in check. She could potentially scare Mark off, thwarting my mom's chance of finding happiness again.

It had been five years since our dad died. Our parents had been married for fourteen years, and their relationship was great. To Mom, Dad was her soul mate, so she was devastated when he died in a plane crash. We were all devastated.

Slowly, we started picking up the pieces and rebuilding our lives. Mom had finally found someone she liked, but Jess wasn't too happy about it. I should admit, I was skeptical at first, but I knew Mom deserved to be happy. If this Mark person made her happy, why not give her a shot at happiness?

I got up from the bed after my phone call to Jess and went to the window. Spring break wasn't the next day, but I wished it was already. There was still a week to go. In the meantime, I had to deal with my breakup with Chase while constantly seeing him.

There was a knock on the door.

My heart stopped beating. *Was Chase back?* I shook my head. Chase wouldn't knock. It was his room too. He could walk in whenever he wanted. He had ample opportunity to see me battered and bruised if he wanted. I couldn't even hide my tears from him.

Nevertheless, I fixed my hair and went to open the door.

I was enveloped in a hug as soon as a brunette beauty came into sight. I was taller than her, so the hug was a bit awkward. I didn't react much to the hug due to my surprise. When she released me, her hands stayed on my waist.

She looked up into my eyes.

"I'm sorry, Zac," she said.

Chase told her!

He had probably told every one of his friends, and I was probably the last one to find out. They had probably looked at me in pity while I smiled like the world was my oyster. I felt tears in my eyes, and I struggled to stop them from spilling.

"How are you?" she asked.

I shook my head. *How could she ask me that?* Sure, we weren't as close as she was with Chase, but she knew I loved him.

"I'm sorry. It's a stupid question. I'm really sorry. I know Chase never meant to hurt you. He loves you," she said.

I laughed. I actually laughed. It was unbelievable. *How could she say all those things?*

"Yeah, sure. I'm sure he never meant to hurt me while he was fucking around with Bruce." I was furious I couldn't mince my words.

Her mouth was slightly open in shock, but she wasn't shocked about Chase and Bruce. She was shocked that I knew. I saw it in her eyes.

I removed her hands from my waist.

11

"He…he told you?" she asked.

My heart broke all over again. I knew Claire was a friend to Chase more than she was to me, but I'd hoped her silence regarding the affair meant she didn't know. But she did and her silence actually meant she'd been keeping it from me.

I shook my head. "I found out by myself. Please leave, Claire."

"Zac, I'm sorry. Chase is my friend, and I—"

"I truly understand that he's your friend, and friends keep each other's secrets. What I don't understand is you coming here and pretending you care about me. You never did, Claire. You helped Chase use me. Now, please go."

Her face fell. I didn't care. I had had enough of people using me. I wasn't going to fall prey again. I couldn't trust any of our mutual friends anymore. That meant I was all alone. They had all chosen his side. It stung.

Claire left with her tail between her legs. To a stranger, she looked regretful, but it was all an act, just like her friendship to me was, just like Chase's love for me was.

I closed the door on Claire and walked to my bed. I had no idea what to do with myself as I sat down. Seconds later, I received a text. It was from Bruce.

Are you in your room?

Wow! The day was getting better and better. *Was he also going to tell me how sorry he was?*

I didn't reply. I wanted the day to end as quickly as it came. Spring break couldn't come soon enough. I needed to get away from my room, the building, the college, and the town as soon as possible.

For the first time in a long time, I actually longed to go home. Chase had never come to my house, so there were no memories of him there. It was going to be the best place to forget, and dealing with Jess's drama would distract me. It was only for two weeks, but it was better than nothing.

The door opened abruptly, catching me off guard. I hadn't yet composed myself to deal with Chase, thinking he'd come back later. He'd left his phone though, so I should've known it was a long shot. I also remembered that I had opened his messages. I was stupid for doing that. He would know it was me.

He walked into the room and closed the door. He walked towards me, and I looked down at my lap. I wasn't crying that time, but I couldn't expose myself to him just yet. I couldn't let him see I wasn't dealing with things well.

"Zac?" he said quietly.

I looked up slowly, hoping I wouldn't fall apart. I just needed to hold my composure; that was all. I could fall apart—just not now. I looked at the face I loved. Chase was gorgeous, and he knew it. He had a beautiful yet manly face, with few facial hair, dark brown eyes, a small nose, and dark pink lips. His brown hair was done up in a messy faux hawk, a style that suited him perfectly.

It was becoming hard to hold my façade. I was looking at the guy who had broken my heart, the guy I *still* loved.

"We need to talk about something," he said, sitting on my bed next to me.

My bed was on the left side, facing the door. Our room was big enough for both of us. It had two beds against the left and right walls and two closets near the door. We each had a study desk and chair. On the walls were pictures of us. I did that myself, and he said he liked it.

In the few seconds it took him to continue talking, I thought he was going to talk about our spring break plans which were now compromised.

"I wanted to talk about our living arrangement. After...erm... what happened between us, I don't think we can stay in the same room anymore. I spoke to the RA, and he said it is possible for us to switch rooms if we can all agree to do so. Our reason isn't exactly valid, but he's agreed to pull some strings. Anyway, Jackson is willing to switch with me if you agree to it," he said.

I couldn't stop my heart from reacting to what he was saying. It stung terribly. Jackson was Bruce's roommate. Chase wanted to move to Bruce's room. I could already imagine them sleeping in one bed every night, cuddling like he and I would do. There was no reason to sneak around anymore, no loyal boyfriend to lie to. They could spend the whole night together.

I took a long, deep breath and nodded. I couldn't say no. It would only be torture for me to watch Chase leave knowing he was going to Bruce. It would sting every time Bruce comes into our room. It would hurt even more when Chase lay only a few feet from me, and I couldn't kiss him or even touch him.

"Thanks," he said.

I wasn't doing it for him, so I said nothing.

His eyes momentarily went to the pictures on the wall. I could tell he wanted them to disappear. He looked at me.

"Tomorrow morning, we'll go to dorm admin at nine," he said.

"All right," I said quietly.

There was an awkward silence between us. I looked at his lips. I loved kissing those lips even when I knew they'd been kissing someone else's. He would kiss me like he meant it, like he wanted to, but he'd probably been imagining it was Bruce's lips.

Did he love Bruce?

That was a question I wasn't going to ask. I'd been hurt enough by my prodding.

He picked up his phone from my study desk and stood up. He couldn't even stand being in the same room as me. He started walking away.

"How many of our friends knew about you and Bruce?" I asked to his back.

I already knew the answer: it was all of them. I just wanted to see how honest he would be with me now that we weren't together. Surely, he wouldn't continue lying to me anymore. There was nothing to gain from that.

"Zac, please!" he said. There was anger in his voice. He didn't even turn.

"Chase, I just want to know. You haven't been honest to me our entire relationship. At least, have the decency to answer my questions, and truthfully," I said.

He turned. "You are only going to hurt yourself," he cautioned.

"So, you'd rather I have fake friends?" I said, my voice breaking slightly.

He looked anywhere but at me.

"Chase, all I ever did was try to be the best boyfriend. I—" I said, and he cut me off.

"Don't try and make me feel guilty!" he shouted.

That stunned me. *So even after using me and cheating on me, he wasn't feeling guilty? Was he listening to himself?*

All I wanted was for him to tell me how many of my so-called friends had stabbed me in the back. I wasn't trying to make him feel guilty. He was guilty, but I didn't want to yell and break things; it wasn't going to do me any good. I just wanted him—for once in his life—to be honest with me, to tell me the things that he never told me.

"Okay," I said slowly.

He took a deep breath and started walking away. At the door, he turned.

"Everyone knew except Livy," he said moments before walking out.

I saw the door close. I'd gotten what I wanted. He'd answered my question. It hurt to hear him admit that everyone except one person had known and kept the information from me. They'd probably been laughing behind my back. It was painful.

I thought of the words "...*except Livy*". Olivia "Livy" Wakefield was my closest friend. We became friends before Chase and I became an item. It was possible she hadn't been told because they feared she would tell me. But would she? So far, the people I expected to tell me hadn't.

I stood up from the bed and looked at the wall. I didn't want to look at each picture as I removed it from the wall, but I ended up doing just that. It broke my heart seeing Chase's fake smiles next to my genuine ones. I wanted to go back to before I even met him.

CHAPTER THREE

ZAC

Chase didn't return to the room for hours. I was sort of glad, but I missed him. I missed touching, cuddling with, and kissing him. His scent, his sense of humor—I missed it all. It was a Friday, and we all planned to go clubbing. I wasn't going anymore, obviously, so I was going to spend the whole Friday night feeling sorry for myself. I decided I would just try to sleep.

Chase came back. He went to take a shower in the dorm bathroom. Needless to say, it was awkward. He would usually dress in my presence, but I could tell he was uncomfortable then, especially with the heavy silence in the room. He wasn't even going to mourn our doomed relationship. He was going clubbing with Bruce. What did I expect? It didn't mean anything to him.

My heart ached terribly as I looked at him. He had a towel draped on his waist as he was busily looking for his clothes. I saw the dark skin I loved, the defined muscles that made my knees weak. Usually, I would distract him a bit by kissing him.

I can't do this to myself.

I stood up from my bed and left the room. Chase raised his head as I passed him. He probably gave a sigh of relief, but I didn't wait to find out.

As soon as I closed the door, a blonde-haired girl walked to me. She was on her way to my room, so she bumped me slightly.

"Good thing I caught you. Where are you off to? I need help. Maroon or blue? You don't look ready," she said, barely giving herself a chance to breathe.

It was Livy, my first college friend. We became friends when we found out we were doing the same course and liked the same things. Livy was short and petite, with blonde curly long hair, big blue-green eyes, and fair skin. Along with those physical attributes, she was a thing of beauty with her long eyelashes and small pink lips. Plus, she was possibly the bubbliest person I know who also possessed a beautiful heart.

"Maroon," I said.

I had no idea what she was talking about, but I liked the color maroon.

"Where are you going?" she asked, looking at me closely.

"Anywhere but my room," I said quietly.

"Well, you better get ready soon because I am not..." she said and stopped talking at my noncommittal response. "Zac, did something happen?"

I looked down.

"Zac?"

I started walking away. I didn't want to relive it again. Obviously, Livy didn't know. I felt a hand tugging at my arm.

"Hey! If you need to talk about anything, I'm here," she said.

I took a deep breath. "I guess you haven't heard? Chase dumped me."

I saw the look of shock on her face. "What? Why? Sorry, you don't have to tell me. How are you doing?"

Though I didn't want to relive the scenario, I found myself saying, "He doesn't love me. He never did. He lied to me."

Livy's face fell, and she closed the distance between us to hug me. "I'm so sorry, Zac."

I responded to Livy's hug. It felt genuine. My tears started spilling. It felt good just to have someone I could confide in. Keeping it all in had been eating me up inside, and I felt so alone.

When she released me from the hug, she asked, "Do you want to come to my room? Amber is going out, so it'll just be the two of us. I have ice cream."

I smiled a little at her, secretly praying to God, *Please let me still have this one friend.* I nodded, and we walked to her room. I had no idea where I was going after storming out of my room, so I was glad Livy offered.

Her room was a floor down. We eventually made it, and just as we walked in, Livy's roommate walked out.

"Hi, Zac. Bye, Zac," she said.

"Hi, Amber," I said quietly.

"What did you choose? I chose maroon, by the way, but, as always, you are the expert," she said.

I chuckled. "Maroon."

"When I said maroon, she said I had no taste. She's going to wear it just because you picked it," Amber said.

I smiled and shrugged.

"I can hear Freddie's horn all the way from the parking lot. Go, Amber," Livy said.

"All right, have fun, children. Try to do all the things I do," Amber said.

"Try to not get arrested. Go," Livy said.

Amber left. The door closed, and Livy ushered me to her bed. I took off my shoes and sat down. I was glad to be away from Chase, but I yearned for him. How stupid could a person be?

Livy went to the fridge and returned with a tub of ice cream and two spoons. She sat cross-legged on the bed next to me, putting the tub between us.

"I still choose maroon, by the way. What is it? A top?" I asked.

"It doesn't matter," she said, digging into the tub.

I grabbed my spoon. "Aren't you going to the club?"

"Not anymore. I'm staying right here with you," she said.

I scooped up some ice cream, which I loved. Livy and I were alike, in a way. We liked the same things. I liked teasing her, and she liked teasing me. In fact, I gave her the name Livy. She told me her name was Olivia, and I just called her Livy. I told everyone else her name was Livy, and she became known as Livy in town.

"You don't have to stay," I said.

"I'm not going out with the guy who hurt you, Zac," she said as we ate the ice cream.

I got teary-eyed. Just thinking about Chase was painful.

"What happened? You don't have to tell me if you don't want to," she said, her voice becoming softer.

I sighed and shrugged. "He broke up with me. He said we weren't working out."

Livy's face looked pained, but at the same time, I could tell she didn't quite understand. "But you seemed happy together. He seemed happy," she said.

"It was all an act. He never loved me or wanted to be with me. He said so himself. He got into our relationship to spite…" I trailed and let out a sigh, "He's been having an affair with Bruce," I said, the words feeling like barbed wire in my throat. It still hurt saying it out loud even though I had already known about the affair before Chase admitted it.

Livy was so shocked that she stopped eating. "Bruce Carlisle? *Our* Bruce?"

I nodded, and the tears fell.

She got off the bed to hug me from behind. She kissed me on the cheek.

"Bruce is...That bastard! I swear if I get my hands on him...How could he do this? And Chase! He fucking knew you love him, and he did that? How cruel can he be?" she said. She looked ready to murder someone.

I closed my eyes as the tears started to fall. I hated crying. But it was finally dawning on me: what Chase and I had was over. A year was not a lot, I know, but in that year, I'd given my whole heart to him, and he'd stepped on it like trash.

It's not like I forced him to date me!

"Do you want to do anything? We could—" Livy started talking but was interrupted by the door of the room opening and someone walking in.

"If you are not ready, we are leaving you!" It was Claire.

She spotted me and made an 'O' with her mouth. I felt like I had a disease, like I was the plague. I wiped away my tears furiously, angry at myself that I'd let her see them.

"I've changed my mind. I'm not going anymore," Livy said.

I looked closely at Claire. She couldn't even look at me. She looked anywhere but at me, unable to face her guilt.

"Oh...I see," she said.

She was about to back out when Avery walked in. She had her head bowed while typing something on her phone. Avery was another one of "our" friends. She was the most talkative and the least conservative. She sported bright red hair, had a flair for the dramatic, and was a beauty herself with her big eyes and pink lips she liked pouting and chewing gum with. Like now.

"You guys, Bruce and Chase are waiting! They may pretend they don't like it being alone together, but we know they do, so the sooner we interrupt their love nest, the better. Anyway, come on. Livy, what's taking you so long?"

Avery was the one person I expected to spill the secret, not because she cared about me, but because she couldn't keep her mouth shut. It was a wonder she managed. But then again, she valued Chase and Bruce's friendship. She valued their little circle, which was completed now that I wasn't in the picture.

I wondered if it had been Bruce who pressured Chase to break things off with me or if it had been "our" friends.

Avery hadn't seen me when she walked in. Her eyes had been focused on whatever she was typing.

"Livy isn't going anymore," Claire said, trying to remove Avery from the room.

"Why? It's Friday! Are you mourning something I don't know about?" Avery asked.

It was then that she raised her eyes from her phone. Her big eyes managed to get bigger when she saw me.

I summoned courage out of nowhere to say, "Hi, Avery."

"H-Hi. I didn't see you," she stammered.

I gave her a closed-lip smile. "Obviously."

"Um…we'll be going now. Come on, Claire," she said, tugging at Claire's arm.

They almost made it through the open door when Livy stopped them.

"You guys knew, didn't you?"

"What are you talking about?" Claire asked.

"You guys knew about Chase and Bruce! 'Love nest'? You guys freaking knew, and you didn't say anything!"

"It wouldn't have helped," Avery said, shrugging.

I felt like someone was just playing soccer with my heart as the ball. I forced myself to keep on a brave face despite the wrenching feeling in my chest.

"What kind of friends are you?!" Livy shouted.

"The kind who are loyal. We can't be loyal to two masters, can we?" Avery said nonchalantly.

At least, Claire had acted like she cared. Avery didn't even try. She was happy Chase had finally broken up with me.

"Well, I don't need such friends," Livy said, crossing her arms.

"Suit yourself. You always didn't fit in our circle anyway," Avery said. "Come on, Claire. I'd love to congratulate the love birds."

They walked away and didn't even bother closing the door.

Livy went to close it, and as she walked, she said, "I can't believe them. How could they? That was so low! How can someone be that fake?"

I didn't say anything even though I knew she wasn't expecting an answer. What she said and what had transpired when Avery and Claire came in the room had struck me hard. I forced myself to ignore the hurt I felt but its full impact was bearing down on me. Chase had told me who knew of the affair. It hurt when he did that, but when the people themselves revealed their betrayal proudly, it hit home. My relationship and even my friendships were a sham!

My life had managed to flip upside down all in one day.

The door closed harshly, pulling me from my thoughts and prompting me to look up at Livy. She was holding onto the door handle. I could feel her anger from where I was sitting cross-legged on the bed.

She took a deep breath and turned. Her facial expression softened, from deep frown lines and flared nostrils to a rather awkward smile.

"Sorry," she said.

"It's your door," I said lightly, forcing a smile.

She didn't acknowledge my attempt at lightening the mood, but returned to the bed, occupying her previous spot. When she had already deemed herself comfortable, she looked at me straight in the eye. Her eyes were soft but I could tell she was about to ask a hard question.

"How are you feeling?"

I sighed deeply, feeling the reality of things on me all over again. "Do you remember what happened in Hiroshima in 1945? The devastation?"

Livy and I took Psychology and had studied human behavior in post-natural/man-made disasters, so she knew the disasters I used as reference in my everyday speech. It wasn't so much like my everyday speech as it was conversations with her.

She nodded.

"I loved him, Livy. He meant the world to me. I wanted him to meet my family during summer break. I already imagined that Jess wouldn't like him—not that she likes anyone," I said and chuckled. "But Noah would. Chase would teach him how to surf because I can't. Mom would love him too. She already does."

She touched my arm and massaged it comfortingly.

"When I found out about him and Bruce, I thought I could fix whatever was wrong with us. I gave… I gave him all of me, Liv—I gave him everything. I gave him space even when I wanted to be with him all the time. I thought maybe I had become clingy, and that's why he went to Bruce. I thought he'd see that I loved him. I cried when I read the messages.

"My mind tortured me; it would play scenes of them together over and over again. I prayed that one day he would just stop. I prayed that one day I would be enough. I thought it was just temptation or lust, and that it would blow over. Livy, I…," I said and choked on my tears. "I was so stupid!"

Livy hugged me. She didn't say anything. I heard the thumping of her heart, which soothed me. When she released me, I wiped my tears.

"How could I degrade myself like that?"

"Love is not logical, Zac. You can't berate yourself like that. Anyone would have believed that he loved you. *I* believed he loved you. If anyone is stupid here, it's Chase," she said calmly.

Her words didn't make me feel any better. She didn't get it. Believing that Chase loved me wasn't the problem.

"But I stayed, Livy! *I stayed*. If he hadn't broken up with me, I'd still be with him, trying to make him happy and degrading myself even further."

"Zac, no! You are not doing this to yourself. You had a moment of weakness. You are not infallible. Yes, staying in spite of the cheating was stupid, but…that's in the past. You might not see it this way yet, but think of this as a clean slate. He's freed you," she said, and her voice lowered, "albeit probably not intentionally."

"Then why do I feel like some discarded gum?" I asked pleadingly.

"Because… because Zac, you dedicated your life to making him happy. It's only fair you feel lost. But that doesn't mean you're lost forever. You just need to learn to love yourself again, and you'll see, he'll be history," she said with a smile.

There was silence, but it was the comfortable kind. I mulled over her words then. I couldn't quite believe it just yet, but I found myself having a bit of hope. I still felt like trash, but I knew, in time, I would feel better about the situation.

"Are you…are you staying with him in the same room?" she asked, wanting to know.

I shook my head. "He's moving in with Bruce, and Jackson is moving in with me. We just need to go to the admin to finalize everything," I told her.

She nodded. "That's good. The less you see of him, the better." She bit her lip when I didn't say anything, something she did when she was contemplating something. It took her quite some time, and I was itching to know what she was thinking.

Her mouth opened. "I'm really sorry, Zac—for everything, including those treacherous idiots we called friends," she said. The sincerity in her words was palpable.

I smiled. "It's fine, Livy. You could not have foreseen any of this."

"I know, but I should have paid more attention," she said.

"You paid enough attention. Besides, it was my relationship." She gave me a sad smile. "In fact, I think you're going to make a great psychologist, and I'll make a crappy one," I said, placing my head on her shoulder.

"Don't count yourself out just yet. One day, you'll look back on your relationship with Chase and laugh about it. And hey, experience can always be an asset."

CHAPTER FOUR

ZAC

    Later that night, I returned to my room. Chase was, of course, not there. We usually stayed out really late if we went clubbing. I was kind of glad he wasn't there; it would make it less awkward for us if he found me sleeping.

    I got into bed and covered myself. I couldn't sleep right away, so I ended up thinking about home. I hadn't been home since Christmas break, so it would be good to see my mom and siblings. I didn't set any expectations upon meeting my mom's boyfriend. I just hoped he was decent, and that was all. I didn't have to like him; I wasn't the one dating him. As long as my mom liked him, I would welcome him. My mom didn't seem desperate, so surely, she wouldn't go for a lowlife, right?

    I managed to fall asleep and make it all the way to the next morning. I spent the night in bed without thinking of Chase, but when I woke up the next morning, he was the first thing on my mind.

    He wasn't a morning person, so when I woke up, I'd usually find him still asleep. He had the cutest sleeping face; he looks so innocent. His hair was usually a messy mop and his hand would touch the floor. He usually slept on his stomach, and during the times that we slept together, I would lie under him, and he'd put his arm around me.

    My eyes opened slowly, wondering if the image in my head of Chase was what I would see. I loved that image. *But I hate it.* I didn't want to see him like that. It would only remind me of how lucky I was to have him in my life, how blessed I was that I got to see him wake up every morning. That sight would be torture now that I don't have him.

I turned to my side quietly, wanting to look at Chase but not wanting him to see me. My eyes met with a made bed. There was no Chase on the bed. The bed, though a bit messy, indicated that he hadn't slept there. It was how it had been the previous night.

I felt something pierce my heart. Although I didn't want to see Chase across from me sleeping peacefully and looking like an angel, I didn't like the fact that he hadn't slept in the room. He had probably slept in Bruce's room, on Bruce's bed, in Bruce's arms.

I felt like throwing up. Chase wasn't the first person I'd had a relationship with, but our breakup stung the most. I felt tears in my eyes. It was only the second day, but it felt like the pain would never stop.

How long was I going to feel like crap?

I pushed the covers away from me and sat up, then wiped my eyes slowly. I had the urge to just go back to bed and hopefully sleep forever, but I forced myself to get out. Just as I stretched my arms, my phone vibrated and beeped. I reached under my pillow and brought it to me. It was a text from Livy.

Hey. Breakfast is on me. Tell me when you are done with the room switching thingy, and I'll come pick you up.

I smiled at my phone. I couldn't stress how good it felt having someone who wasn't against me. I wasn't an outcast and easily made friends, but the friends I'd made were already Chase's friends. They'd chosen his side, so now I was almost friendless.

I yawned and stretched my arms again. I grabbed my toiletry bag and headed to the dorm bathroom to freshen up, taking a quick shower and brushing my teeth. When I returned to the room, I dressed in a simple T-shirt, a pair of jeans and Converse sneakers. Chase was still not back.

I sat on the bed and texted Livy, telling her I would take her offer. It was a little before nine. Since Chase wasn't back, I had no idea if we were going to leave together to the dorm admin office or if he expected me to go there. I shrugged and picked up a comb.

It was while I was combing my short hair that there was a knock on the door. I went to open with the comb in my hand.

My eyes met Jackson's form. Jackson was Bruce's roommate, who was soon to be mine. I didn't know him well, and we hadn't talked much before. I met him when we all went to Bruce's room and sometimes in the corridors. I obviously did not really want him as a roommate, but he would have to do.

He was a tall and skinny guy with short hair. His light brown skin matched his light brown eyes. His eyes were friendly and warm.

"Hi," I said.

"Hi. The others are waiting for us at the office. Uh, you do know right…about…?"

I nodded.

"I'll be just a sec," I said.

I wasn't sure if I should close the door or not. I mean, this was the guy who was going to be my roommate. Closing the door kind of said, "I don't really want you to see me." But he *was* going to see me, almost every day. He could watch me sleeping if he were a creep. And he seemed to be waiting for me, so closing the door on him would be rude.

I left the door open and finished combing my hair.

I grabbed my phone and, together with Jackson, walked to the dorm admin office. There was silence between us as we walked.

A ridiculous thought wormed its way into my head. If Chase slept in Bruce's room, Jackson would know. It was, after all, his room too. Bruce would have asked him to disappear or something.

I mentally laughed at myself. What was I hoping to achieve? The answer would hurt, and I knew it. Even if they didn't sleep together in Bruce's room, they probably slept somewhere else together.

I wondered then if Jackson knew about the affair. How could he not know? They did their treachery right in his room. He knew, and he kept it from me. What did I expect? The guy wasn't my friend. Why was I expecting strangers to be honest with me?

I knew why. It felt like everyone knew. Everyone had been laughing at me behind my back. The whole thing felt like one huge conspiracy—everyone knew except me. I—his partner—was the last one to find out.

"So, you and I are going to be roommates, huh?" Jackson butted into my crazy thoughts.

I coughed. "Uh, yeah."

There was silence.

"Why'd you agree?" I asked him.

The question caught him off guard. "Hmm?"

"Why did you agree to switch? You didn't like staying with Bruce?" I asked.

He scratched his head. He could lie to me to my face. Bruce had probably begged him to switch, and he knew why.

He shrugged. "He's okay. Let's just say we don't always get along."

"Hopefully, we will," I said reluctantly.

I wasn't in the mood to have someone else in my space in the state I was in. But I didn't really have a choice. It was either Chase or Jackson, and my tormentor was the worse choice, so Jackson would have to do—a classic case of choosing the lesser evil.

"What are you doing after this?" Jackson asked suddenly. It sounded like a weird question coming from him, but I reminded myself that he was my soon-to-be roommate. Questions like that would be common.

"Going out for breakfast with Livy," I courteously replied.

We got to the foyer. Chase was standing with Bruce. They weren't very close to each other, but the sight of them together made my heart ache. What I realized next had me taking quick short breaths. Chase wasn't wearing the clothes he'd been wearing the previous night. He was wearing Bruce's clothes. I remembered the navy blue sweater with the large B printed in white and the black jeans ripped towards the bottom. Chase had slept in Bruce's room and decided to wear Bruce's clothes rather than come back to the room we shared to get his clothes. He couldn't even stand the sight of me.

I calmed myself as Jackson and I finally arrived where Bruce and Chase were. I couldn't look at either of them. I remembered that Bruce had asked me the previous day where I was. He better save what he wanted to say because I didn't want to hear it.

"Finally, you guys made it. Come on, the guy is waiting for us," Bruce said.

I thrust my hands in my jeans pocket as we walked to a room with an open window. There was a guy in the room. Chase stood next to Bruce in front of the window, and Jackson and I stood a bit back. Now that I couldn't see Bruce's eyes, I looked at him.

He looked like any other guy. Sure, he was hot and played football, but I wasn't shabby, either. Sure, he had blond hair. Well, I had blond hair too! He was muscular, yes, but I was not a walking jelly. Bruce had something I didn't, and I felt like my heart would just stop from the realization.

I just wasn't him.

I closed my eyes to stop the tears. *Gosh, I am in public! Why couldn't I control myself?*

"These are the other two guys." I heard Bruce say. He and Chase opened up space between them so the guy could see Jackson and me.

"Right. Zachary Daniel Nielsen and Jackson Milo Pritchett?" the guy asked.

I nodded, and Jackson said, "Yeah."

The guy looked at a couple of papers before saying, "Okay. So, are you all in agreement that you want to switch rooms? I'm breaking the rules here, so trust me, if you aren't sure, I will not undo it."

Bruce and Chase looked at Jackson and me. They were as sure as eggs is eggs that they wanted to room together. I wondered what would happen if their little relationship fell apart. *Were they even dating now?* Bruce wasn't out of the closet. Maybe he was planning to come out. Maybe that's why Chase had finally broken up with me because Bruce was ready for him.

"Zac?"

I didn't realize I'd zoned out until Jackson called my name. Everyone was looking at me.

"Uh..." I said, having no idea why I was suddenly the center of attention.

"Are you sure you want Mr. Pritchett as your roommate?" the guy behind the counter asked.

"Yes," I said.

"Good. You know, it's a good thing guys and girls are allocated different rooms. Otherwise, there would be more people like you here," the guy said.

I frowned. *People like us?*

Chase clenched his jaw. He didn't like what was said. It dawned on me. The guy meant people who were in a relationship and had elected to share a room together, only to break up and ask to switch rooms. *So even he knew? Oh great.* They might as well make a banner.

"I'm going to hand you guys documents to sign. Once that's done, I'll update your information on the system. Your switch will be effective by Tuesday. But that's just the technicalities. You can start moving your things today. I want to avoid murder as much as I can," the guy said and chuckled.

He passed us each some documents. I didn't even want to read it. I just wanted to sign and get out of there. We returned the signed documents to him. I was glad he was letting us move before Tuesday. It was only two days away, but I didn't want to be tortured by expecting Chase to walk into the room, knowing he was in Bruce's arms. At least, if I didn't expect him to walk in, I wouldn't think about him much.

The guy looked at each of the documents and seemed satisfied. "Okay, good. Chase and Bruce in room 566 and Zac and Jackson in room 551, correct?"

"Yep," Bruce said.

"I'm a bit confused. I thought Chase and Zac broke up, but you two seem more like the couple," the guy said, pointing at Chase and then at Bruce.

I think I froze, and my heart stopped beating for a second. Even strangers could see the romantic tension between Bruce and Chase. I felt like I had just been completely undressed by the guy's words.

Bruce moved his legs uncomfortably back and forth. Chase looked at the wall. If I didn't know about them, I would have said the guy was mad.

"So?" the guy said, waiting for something.

"Are we done?" Bruce asked. There was a bit of anger in his voice.

"Yes, you are done. But I must warn you, if something is going on between the two of you, know that you'll have to stick it out should things turn sour," the guy said. "And oh wait, switch keys, and I'll just switch the numbers."

I was the first to walk away. I wanted to walk as far away from Chase and Bruce as possible. My mind was racing with thoughts about the two of them.

What on earth could the admin guy see between them? Was there a public display of affection? Had they been touching and kissing before Jackson and I got there? Or was it subtle, like the way they looked at each other?

I found myself speed-walking to my room. I just needed some time and space alone to control my thoughts and their eventual results.

I got to my room and unlocked it, not even bothering to look behind me to see if the others were following. I collapsed on my bed. I didn't cry, but I sure as hell felt like it. I remembered Livy's offer. I would take her up on it, just not at that moment. I needed to compose myself. I almost cried in front of Chase and Bruce, and I could not give them that satisfaction.

I closed my eyes tightly as I lay on my bed face down with my legs hanging off. I heard movement outside the room before the door was swung open.

"What will you do for me?" I heard Bruce say.

"Let you do what you want," Chase's reply reached my ears.

"You already let me do what I want," Bruce said, a hint of cockiness in his voice.

Were they really having that conversation in my presence or was I dreaming? I had to be dreaming!

"Nah, I mean, I'll let you do what you've wanted to do since watching that video. We can go down later once everything is settled to buy the supplies, unless you like waiting for the chance for me to obey your every whim. You better help me," Chase said.

I'd be glad if my eardrums would just burst now.

"I happen to have handcuffs. Don't ask me why," Bruce said.

My brain was reeling by then. *Were they deliberately stabbing me repeatedly? What had I done to them?*

"Have you been naugh…?" Chase said and stopped. "Zac?!"

I turned my head. Chase and Bruce were at the door, which was now half open. It seemed they hadn't seen me during their conversation. They were too busy focusing on each other and their wildest fantasies.

I felt sick.

"Jackson said you were going out for breakfast with Livy," Chase said. He couldn't hide the surprise in his voice.

I sat up. "Yeah, I felt a little sick, so I lay down a bit. I'm better now," I said. Just hearing Bruce and him actually made me sick.

"That's good. Uh, Jackson and I agreed to move our things today. Bruce will be helping me. I hope you don't mind."

Which part did he hope I didn't mind? That he was moving out that day or that his new boyfriend was helping him do so? Oh wait, was he referring to the little snippet he gave me about his sex life with Bruce? Well, I minded—very much so!

"Uh, sure," I said instead.

"Hey. Uh, can we talk?" Bruce said, walking into the room.

"No. Livy is waiting for me," I said as I got off the bed hastily.

I bolted out of the room. *What did Bruce hope our "talk" would achieve?* What was there to talk about? He betrayed me. He was worse than those "friends" who hid it from me. He slept with my boyfriend countless times, stabbing me in the back over and over again until he reached my heart.

What words would fix that? Newsflash for him, because no one has invented them yet.

I called Livy as I walked downstairs. She sounded happy I called, agreeing to meet me on the first floor.

When I got to the first floor, I met Jackson. He was with some of his friends.

"Zac!" he called me over.

I frowned. I wasn't in the mood for people. I wanted to eat my pain away alone.

I decided I wasn't going to be rude, though. By tonight, the guy would be my roommate. It was essential to get off to a good start.

"Hey!" I said as I got to him and his friends.

"Guys, this is Zac, my new roommate. Zac, this is Kyle and Ross." Jackson did the introductions.

"Hi," I said.

I knew Kyle. He was our college football team's kicker. He was tall and well-built with short black hair and brown eyes. He wasn't in Bruce's circle, but they knew each other and talked. They were, after all, part of the same team.

I'd seen Ross a couple of times as well. I'd never really paid attention to how he looked before, but now that he was standing next to me, I noticed he was a couple of inches shorter than Kyle, with an average build. His hair was styled in a high top with a bleach blond fade, and his eyes were a warm honey brown.

The guys greeted me back.

"You are with Chase, right?" Kyle asked.

"Uh, no. We broke up," I said, trying to keep my voice emotionless.

"Oh, I'm sorry," he said.

"It's okay. It's no big deal," I said. *Yeah, right. Oh, God, why was I still hurting?*

"I'll be moving my things in once Chase moves out. I hope that's okay," Jackson said.

"It's fine," I said, giving him a smile. "I'm going out right now, but if I'm back by the time you do, holler if you need any help."

"Sure, will do. The more, the merrier."

Livy finally came down and walked towards us.

"I have to go, guys," I said to them and turned to Jackson, "See you when I get back?"

"Sure."

Livy got to me and enveloped me in a hug.

She looked at me like a loving mother. "Hey."

"Hi," I said, smiling.

"Uh, guys, this is Livy, Livy this is…" I said, but Livy interrupted.

"Kyle, Ross, Jackson, hey, guys," Livy said, pointing them out.

The guys said their greetings.

Livy grabbed my hand to usher us out of the building. I loved that her attention was on me, but I didn't want to make it obvious that I was nursing a broken heart.

"Kyle, I told you why I was switching rooms! You obviously weren't listening. What part of 'I'm switching because the two of them aren't together anymore' didn't you understand? Was it necessary for you to ask?" I heard Jackson reprimand Kyle as Livy and I walked away from them.

I doubt he had wanted me to hear. Livy heard too because she squeezed my hand as I tensed next to her.

"How did it go?" she asked.

"It went well. Jackson is moving in later today. Chase is already moving his things. It shouldn't take long since Bruce's room is only 10 doors down. He'll probably be done by the time we get back," I said. The sheer poise with which I said those words was amazing. You'd think I didn't feel like falling apart.

"Jackson is nice. I'm sure he'll make a good roommate," Livy said.

"Maybe, Livy, maybe," I said.

CHAPTER FIVE

ZAC

Livy and I walked to Jada's. Jada's was a small restaurant that wasn't shabby yet not too classy either. It wasn't far, and soon, we were there. It was situated close by to provide students good food with reasonable prices. Needless to say, it was a lifesaver for some of us who weren't that good at cooking. And since most of us are not, it was usually jammed with students.

I suppose it was the wrong place to be if I didn't want to meet my so-called friends. We all loved the restaurant, so we hung out there most of the time. When Livy and I walked in, I immediately spotted Avery at one of the tables. She was with her boyfriend Carter, and Claire's boyfriend, Sean. I knew the guys; they'd been in our circle of friends too. Avery spotted me as well, and the guys followed her eyes to look at me.

"Hey, maybe we should go somewhere else," Livy said next to me.

"It's fine, Livy," I said curtly.

"Breakfast is on me, so I don't mind going anywhere you like," she said.

"Livy, it's fine!" I said firmly.

We walked to the counter and joined a small line. I stood on the balls of my feet as we waited. My eyes moved slowly to the table we passed. They were no longer looking at me as if I was an alien. They were engrossed in some conversation and laughing.

Livy must have seen where my eyes went to because she asked, "What are you going to have?"

"Uh…" I said.

"Go easy on me," she said, smiling.

"So, I can't order the executive breakfast?" I asked, grinning.

She sighed. "There is only a week left before spring break, so you can."

"I'm kidding, Liv. I'll have pancakes," I said.

We didn't even need to check the menu; we already knew it by heart.

"That is budget-friendly. I'll have the Shape breakfast," she said.

We finally ordered our food and decided to sit at the tables outside. There weren't that many people there, and truthfully, I didn't want to be in the same room as our ex-friends. I didn't want to wonder whether it was me they're laughing about every time they laughed.

Soon, our food arrived. My pancake meal consisted of two eggs, two rashers of streaky bacon, and two pancakes served with maple syrup. Livy's Shape breakfast consisted of a fruit salad, muesli, and strawberry yogurt drizzled with honey.

I took a bite of my food.

"What are you doing for spring break?" Livy asked as she ate hers. That question was bound to be asked. Livy knew of my plans to go to Chase's vacation house for spring break.

"I'm going home," I said, giving her a small smile. "I can't exactly go to Chase's vacation house now, can I?"

Her face fell. "I'm sorry."

"Stop it, Livy. I'm fine. I'm *going* to be fine. Besides, going home isn't so bad. I love spending time with my mom, Jess, and Noah."

"Your mom must be happy," she said.

"She is. In fact, she wants us to meet Mark," I said.

"Things are serious?"

I finished chewing my bacon.

"You make us sound like a jury, but it seems like it," I said.

"Well, you kinda are a jury. If you guys don't approve, the guy will be sent packing."

"Let's hope it doesn't come to that. I want her to be happy," I said.

"How is Jess taking the news?" she asked.

"Like…Jess. She hasn't met the guy, and she already hates him," I said.

"Hopefully, he's a great guy and will win her heart."

"Her heart?" I asked.

"I don't mean it like that!" Livy said, laughing. I laughed too. "That would be awkward," she said.

A piece of my pancake was halfway towards my mouth when I spotted Sean walking towards the table Livy and I were seated at. I unintentionally frowned.

Livy looked at me with concern. She was facing me so she couldn't see Sean.

"What?" she asked.

I shook my head slightly.

She looked behind her nonetheless. Sean was close now. I was hoping he was just going to pass by, but he slowed down near us until he reached our table and stopped. Sean was good-looking, *more* good-looking than Bruce in my opinion. He had this I'm-in-a-boy-band look and the cutest smile, which had probably won Claire over. He'd fit in One Direction or Backstreet Boys.

"Hi," he said simply.

"Hi, Sean," Livy said.

I said something incoherent.

"You guys don't greet anymore?" he asked. "You passed by our table and didn't say anything. And I know you saw us."

I knew this had nothing to do with greetings. Sean was there to rub salt into an open wound. *Did he really think I would greet them after what they had done to me?*

I stayed quiet.

He gestured with his hand, saying, "I need an answer." *Would he just leave?*

"I didn't see you. Your table was masked by all the treachery surrounding you," Livy spit out.

"Whoa! Hold the claws in. What are you talking about?" Sean asked.

"Sean, don't act dumb. You know very well what I'm talking about," she said.

Sean's shoulders fell. "Okay, I do. But that doesn't mean we can't be friends anymore."

Was he listening to himself?

"Excuse me, are you crazy? If Claire was cheating on you and I knew about it and didn't tell you, would you still want to be friends with me?" Livy asked, her voice becoming louder now.

"Okay, I'm guilty as charged. But it wasn't my place to tell," Sean said.

Meanwhile, I continued cleaning my plate, pretending the conversation had nothing to do with me.

Livy shook her head in disbelief. "You are unbelievable. Like what Avery said, you can't be loyal to two masters. You've already picked your side—stick to it and leave us alone."

Sean looked reluctant to leave. He even looked slightly wounded, which was weird, to say the least.

"For the record, I'm sorry, Zac," he said before turning and walking away.

I stopped eating, surprised by his last words. He seemed sincere.

Livy twisted her lips. "Yeah, right."

"He seemed kinda genuine," I said tentatively.

"Genuine? He wouldn't know genuine if it was shoved right in front of him! He didn't mean a single word," she said.

I still had a look of doubt on my face.

"Zac, you are going through heartbreak and want to believe that those rats have hearts, but none of them do. Sean was sent here to spy on you, to see how you are doing probably by that bitch Avery!" she said.

"Why would they need to spy on me?"

"To see just how far the dagger went. Just… Look, don't fall for their pretense. I don't want you hurt again," she said.

She extended her hand to mine on the table and touched it slightly, smiling warmly.

"I'm sorry," I said.

She looked surprised. "What? You have nothing to be sorry about. I don't—"

I interrupted. "—About Sean."

"I'm not mad at you for wanting to believe him. I—"

I interrupted again. "You are mad that he too chose their side."

"I'm mad at all of them."

"Yeah, but you are mad at Sean the most," I said.

She removed her hand and looked at her plate.

"He came here. He had the nerve to—"

I interrupted calmly. "This isn't about him coming here. Livy, I know you, remember? I know Sean—"

She cut in. "Don't say it!"

"I won't, but you know," I said.

She sighed, and her shoulders fell. "I suppose him choosing the other side is for the best, no?"

"Do you think that's going to help you?" I asked.

"Yes! I hate him. He hurt you…in a way," she said.

I smiled. "If you say so."

I really hoped it would help her, but I doubted it would. Her anger told me there was still a long way to go. She wasn't just angry about my situation. She was angry at Sean the most because of something else.

"So… Mark… when are you meeting him?" she asked, changing the subject.

"I don't really know. Mom just said this spring break so it could be any day during those two weeks," I said.

"He's from out of town, right?"

I nodded.

"You've told me how Jess feels about meeting him. What about you?"

I shrugged. "I'm chill, I guess."

"Chill? He could be your stepdad in a year or two," she said.

"Livy, I'm twenty. I already make my own decisions. I doubt he'll have that much of an influence in my life," I told her.

"Yeah, but you have to think of Noah and your mom. It's up to you to make sure this man is good for both of them," she said.

I finished my serving.

"I'm not going to tell Mom what to do," I said.

"I'm just saying that you need to take this seriously," she said.

"I'll interrogate the dude. Happy?"

"You know, I'm not only talking about the bad stuff. He could turn out to be great, but…I don't know, Jess scares him away or something," she said.

"So, you want me to do what exactly?" I asked.

"If you have a good feeling, keep Jessica's claws off him, and if you have a bad feeling, give him the boot. Just stop being chill," she said.

I smiled. "Yes, Ma'am."

She smiled too. "I'm serious. Your mom's happiness and safety hang in a balance, and you, mister, are going to make sure she's happy and safe."

I didn't understand why Livy was fussing about my trip home. I was going there to stay in my room and be miserable so I don't have to see Bruce and Chase in a lip lock or hear them talk about their sex life. I had no hopes and dreams about the trip whatsoever. I wanted to be miserable. I wanted to be as passive as possible and occasionally rein in my sister's tantrums.

But I suppose going home to be miserable wasn't going to be smooth sailing. Mom would fuss over me. Luckily for me, Jess would avoid me. So really, all I had to deal with was Mom hugging me and asking if I wanted anything every two seconds, Noah wanting to play, and dealing with Mark for just a day. It wasn't daunting. I could do that.

"Anyway, how is your spring break plan looking?"

"Everything is set. I'm going to miss you," she replied with a smile. For someone who was going to miss me, she seemed awfully happy.

"I'll only be a phone call away," I said.

"Yeah, crazy expensive phone calls!"

"Okay, you have me on social media,"

"I'll text you every day."

"I'll try to reply every day," I joked with a grin.

"Oh, you better, or I'll fly to your town to beat you up."

"I'm sure South Africa isn't next door. Besides, you are going there to spend time with your dad, so make the most of it," I advised.

"Whatever, I'm still expecting swift replies," she said.

My phone vibrated and beeped in my pocket. I took it out. I had gotten a text from Chase. My heart ached as I looked at what I had named him in my phone. I'd gone out for a while without thinking or talking about him, something Livy had deliberately made sure of.

One new message from My Love

I suppose I had to change the name. I opened the text.

Hey. I didn't want to go through your closet, but can I have my black sweatshirt back? I can come to pick it up.

I slowly exhaled. I remembered the sweatshirt he was talking about. He lent it to me one night when we went out, and it started raining. I jokingly refused to give it back, going as far as putting it in my closet. He laughed at the action, telling me to "wear it when you miss me". I guess I was no longer afforded that privilege anymore, at a time when I missed him the most.

"What's up?" Livy asked.

"The other part of a breakup, returning your ex-boyfriend's things," I said, smiling so much it hurt.

"I can…" Livy started.

I shook my head. "He's coming to get them."

Livy looked at me all sad. She was displaying the sadness I felt but refused to show.

"Can I get dessert? I feel like having a huge sundae," I said excitedly.

"Yeah, you can have the biggest one they have," Livy said.

"I'll pay for mine and yours."

"I don't mind paying."

"You've already spent money on me. Besides, you've spent a lot of your savings on your ticket. I'll pay," I said.

"All right." She smiled in resignation.

CHAPTER SIX

ZAC

Shortly after finishing our dessert, Livy and I left the restaurant. We parted ways since Livy had to go to the library to do some research. She was reluctant to go, but I convinced her I would be fine by myself. I didn't like that she wanted to play chaperone, but admittedly, I was a bit uncomfortable about seeing Chase again on my own. I just couldn't see myself not breaking down and telling him I would do anything if he just gave me one last chance.

Walking back to my room, I was beginning to feel the full effects of the breakup. Chase was asking for his things back. He was asking for his sweater, the one he told me I could wear when I missed him. He was probably going to give it to Bruce. Bruce would get to know how he smelled and carry the scent with him. He would now be familiar with his slightly sweet, musky scent.

I could still remember that scent. I loved it. I loved the person who wore it. Every time we hugged, it transported me to our first kiss—Chase's lips on mine moving slowly, then gradually grazing my neck. That's when I got to really smell him—not his cologne, but him. That was when I knew I didn't just have a crush. I was falling hard and fast.

I shouldn't have remembered, but I did. I stood at my door, feeling my insides tighten uncomfortably. I couldn't bring myself to open the door, knowing there wouldn't be any trace of Chase there. The only thing remaining was his sweatshirt which he wanted back, and the pictures he hated. I knew he'd taken everything—the clock he bought when we went to the flea market, the CDs at the music store downtown, the little lamp with a wooden stand, the beer jug with his initials, the DVDs of all the movies we'd watched together, the framed picture of him and Kirby his little sister—everything was gone.

I didn't have the strength to see the proof of the dissolution of our relationship.

"Hey, there you are!" I heard someone shout.

I turned, and my eyes met Jackson. He was carrying a box and walking towards me.

"Hi. Do you need help?" I asked brightly. I couldn't let him see my struggle.

"No, I just have one box left, and Kyle and Ross are coming with it. I'm sorry about the mess in the room. Chase already moved in, and I couldn't leave my stuff outside," he said as he came to stand before me.

"No problem, man," I said as I opened the door for him.

He was right; the room was littered with boxes, suitcases, and clothes thrown on the bed. He stayed away from my side, which I appreciated. We both walked in, and he put the box on the floor.

I sat on my bed, wondering what I was going to do with my time. Livy wouldn't be out of the library for at least an hour and a half. I looked around the room. It looked and felt different. It wasn't cold because of Chase's absence, but it felt different. I just couldn't feel him in the room anymore.

I went to my closet and took out his sweater, before texting him.

I'm in my room so you can come get it.

I remembered something. I had to change his name on my phone. I found myself unable to erase the letters that had once spelled what I thought was my whole world. Why change it, though? I still loved him. Yeah, except for the first part. He wasn't mine anymore.

I had thoughts to replace it with 'cheater', 'backstabber', 'liar'…but I didn't.

I erased the name and replaced it with "Chase." There, first step done.

Kyle and Ross walked into the room carrying a box. They put it down, greeting me. I greeted them back.

"We'll be at the pitch. Meet during lunch?" Kyle asked Jackson.

"Sure," he replied.

Kyle and Ross left, closing the door. I noticed Jackson had started unpacking his things.

"Do you need help?" I asked.

"Uh, yeah, you can help with my books and stuff. Just put them neatly on the shelf," he said.

I was glad I found something to do. I started unpacking a box and setting his books up nicely on the shelf. I wasn't sure what order he wanted them to be in, but I figured he would put them in the way he wanted to some time. All he wanted was there to be fewer boxes in the room.

I looked at a textbook *Principles of Integrated Marketing Communications.*

"You study Marketing?" I asked.

He answered as he organized his new closet. "Yeah, and you study Psychology, right?"

"Uh-huh," I said.

"So, do you read minds?" he asked jokingly.

I chuckled. "I wish."

"But you know how the human mind works, right?"

"Uh, you could say that. I'm being trained to identify problematic behaviors and thought processes and basically find out how they got to that and how they can be rectified," I said.

It was my psychology-trained mind that recognized Chase's unusual patterns of behavior. It started with the moods, then the caginess, then defense mechanisms, then compensation. It was almost as if he knew I knew. He felt guilty about what he did, using "projection" as a defense mechanism to make me feel like I was the one cheating on him, not paying attention to him. When I became available to him whenever he wanted, his guilt led him to compensation.

"Do you like it?" Jackson asked.

"Yeah," I said.

"So, you want to deal with crazy people?" he asked.

I put his book on the shelf. "Oh, no, I am not going to be a psychiatrist. I'm torn between clinical psychology and educational psychology, but I don't have to make a decision soon," I said. "Do you like marketing?"

"Yeah, I hope to open my own advertising agency one day," he said.

"So, you want to be responsible for the annoying ads that come up when people are watching their favorite shows?" I joked.

"Hey, advertisements are good for people. You convince wives to leave their cheating husbands, and I convince them to have retail therapy. We do the same things."

I chuckled. I liked him already. He wasn't too bad. What he said, though, struck a chord with me. He said psychologists convince wives to leave their cheating husbands. It wasn't really what we do. We empower people to walk away from degrading situations. How could I empower someone when I've failed to empower myself? I could have confronted Chase on the cheating, but I didn't. I let him degrade me, walk all over me. I hadn't just failed myself. I had failed my profession. *What kind of psychologist was I going to be?*

"Touché," I said.

There was a knock on the door. I knew who it was.

"I'll get it," I said shortly.

I walked over to my bed and took Chase's sweater. It was the last time I was going to hold it in my hands. I felt the fabric in my hands, and for a second, I didn't wish to part with it. I walked to the door and opened it slowly.

It wasn't Chase who was standing at the door. It was Bruce. My heartbeat quickened, and my stomach tightened.

"Hi. Uh, Chase asked me to get his... sweatshirt? Says you know about it," he said.

"Here," I said swiftly, thrusting the black material in front of him, which he took slowly from me.

"Zac, can we talk?" he asked.

Didn't he realize I didn't want to talk to him? I had nothing to say to him.

"I'm kinda busy," I lied, displaying no emotion.

"This will only take a few seconds," he said.

I made a decision. He was really determined to talk to me, so it was best if I got it out of the way or he would only keep pestering me.

"I'm listening," I said.

"Can I come inside?" he asked.

"Jackson is inside, but sure," I said, shrugging. Deep down, I hoped he didn't insist on it. My bravery was all for show. I didn't want Chase's dirty laundry aired out. Jackson probably already knew, but it was best not to discuss it in front of him.

"Rather not," he said. He looked around before continuing. "I'm sorry, Zac."

"For what?" I asked, raising a brow. I wanted to hear him say it out loud. I wanted to know if he was apologizing for having an affair with my boyfriend or for me finding out.

He sighed. "I never meant for it to happen. I told him what he was doing was ridiculous, but he was so mad—"

I cut in. "After he did it, what did you do?"

"Zac, I'm sorry. I couldn't deny what I felt—"

"I am not mad that you like him or love him or whatever it is. I am mad that you still smiled to my face when you guys were fucking behind my back. You still called me your friend when you went down on him, and you didn't feel an ounce of guilt when you visited him at his house for a whole weekend and still called yourself, 'my bro'," I said. I couldn't stop. The tears were ready to spill, but I just couldn't stop. "You knew I love him. I told you that, but you still slept with him on the same bed, still kissed him, still fucked him."

"Zac, please, I am trying to make peace here. I know what happened. I was there," he said.

I shook my head as the tears spilled. "I don't know what you want from me."

I hated it. I hated crying in front of Bruce, and anyone who passed by. But control had deserted me, and I could no longer hold back. I hated myself for being so weak.

"I just want us to be civil towards each other," he said.

"Here's my civil: get the fuck away from me, and if you ever meet me anywhere, don't say a fucking word to me. I'll do the same," I said.

He shook his head. "Stop being so petty. Chase loves me, and I love him. He did you a favor by being with you. Don't be a sore loser," he said.

I was caught off guard. Wasn't the guy apologizing, like, a few seconds ago? I now knew what Livy meant, and I was glad I hadn't fallen for Bruce's trick.

I felt like grabbing Chase's sweatshirt from him and ripping it to pieces, then setting it on fire.

"I won't be a sore loser. Wish you two all the happiness possible," I said and turned, walking back into my room.

I wished Jackson wasn't in the room, but he was and almost done unpacking.

I wiped my eyes as Jackson looked up from a box. He caught my eye, and I had no doubt he'd seen the tears. It was awkward.

I sat on my bed.

"It's going to be all right, man," Jackson said.

I raised a brow. I didn't expect him to say anything.

"I was going to pretend I didn't know about the breakup, but that just makes things awkward for you. I know, so you don't have to pretend you are fine," he said.

I already knew he knew. I heard him talk to Kyle, and I'd figured long before that that he would have wanted a reason why Chase would suddenly want to move out of the room he shared with his boyfriend. I shrugged. I didn't want to talk about Chase with a stranger.

I remembered Bruce and then remembered that Jackson was Bruce's roommate. He was now my roommate. He was going to know some of my secrets, so I needed to know if I could trust him. He'd been Bruce's roommate, and from what I'd observed, they seemed to have no major problems, and they interacted on a daily basis. Maybe they weren't friends, but there was an understanding between them. He was obviously on his side. Had he known about the affair?

I knew if I asked Jackson about Chase and Bruce, and he didn't know, I would unintentionally tell him. I didn't know if Chase and Bruce were planning to go public with their relationship. Nonetheless, I felt the need to ask.

Jackson had gone back to what he was doing.

I struggled to find a way to ask the question, so I went with my first thought. "Did you know Chase and Bruce were having an affair?"

It was blunt, and it stunned him. He stopped what he was doing.

I raised a brow.

He sighed and nodded. I knew the answer, but I was hoping it was different. There was no use getting to know the guy or liking him. He was an enemy.

"You probably hate me right now, but put yourself in my shoes. I didn't condone what they were doing, but you and I barely talked. I couldn't just tell you something like that. You seemed really happy," he said.

"So, you are just like all my ex-friends," I said.

"That's not fair. I wasn't your friend. We were almost strangers," he said.

I knew what he was saying, and I understood. But I couldn't trust him. He was Bruce's acquaintance.

"Well, 'friends' is out of the question now. You are friends with Bruce," I said.

"Your friend Livy was friends with both Chase and Bruce, right? It doesn't mean she endorses everything they do. Anyway, I am not friends with Bruce. I can't stand the ego on that guy. Why do you think I agreed to switch? Bruce and I were roommates. That's it," he said. "Anyway, look. You and I are roommates now, and I'd like to start afresh."

I considered it. He was right. And I didn't want there to be any bad blood between us, but it doesn't mean I was going to serve him a platter full of my secrets, though.

"All right," I said.

"Great. I'm meeting Kyle and Ross near the football pitch. We are just going to hang. Wanna come?"

"Yeah, why not?" I said, smiling.

CHAPTER SEVEN

ZAC

Jackson turned out to be a great roommate, at least in the week we'd spent being roommates. He liked cooking, and I could barely cook, so he cooked for us. I hung out with him, Kyle, and Ross. I wasn't best buddies with them, but we had a good time together. What I liked the most about Jackson was that he sometimes left me to my own demons. There are times that I'd miss Chase, and I'd just feel like crying into my pillow. During those times, I appreciated that Jackson didn't tell me to man up. He let me cry on my own.

When I wasn't hanging with Jackson and his friends, or feeling down in my room, I hung out with Livy. She had a lot of sessions as the student psychologist for freshmen, so I didn't see much of her. We had small lunch dates and late-night study sessions. She wasn't supposed to discuss any of her cases with me after taking an oath of confidentiality, but according to her, her supervisor was clueless, so she turned to me.

I was glad when spring break was right 'round the corner—only a day away. Despite having a good roommate and feeling less lonely, I sometimes saw Chase with Bruce and the others. It felt like I was being stabbed repeatedly. I needed a time-out.

Jackson was going to Fort Lauderdale for spring break with Kyle, Ross, and some of their cousins. Livy was going to visit her dad in South Africa. I was the only one with boring plans.

* * *

It was the day before spring break officially started. Livy had left that day. Jackson and I were in our room. We were both packing for our trips—he, to his adventures. And I, to my lazy sleep-ins. We weren't talking much while we packed, but the silence was comfortable.

I had left a few clothes home, so I didn't pack much. In fact, since I planned on being stuck in the house as much as possible. I packed only a few smart-wear clothes. I wasn't going to impress anybody. The only people I planned to see was my family and, of course, Mark.

"That's a pretty small bag," Jackson commented.

"I'm going home, not to a fashion show," I said.

Jackson laughed. "Are you planning on stepping out of your house?"

"Nope," I said, simultaneously shaking my head.

"So, you insist on having a boring spring break?" he asked.

"Yep," I said.

"My offer still stands," he reminded me. He'd invited me to Fort Lauderdale.

I smiled. "Thanks, J, but I already bought my ticket. And besides, I'm really looking forward to seeing my family. It won't be so bad," I said.

"Well, you know where to find us if you change your mind," he said.

"Thanks."

I was done packing my bag, but I noticed something in my closet while I was looking for my plain t-shirts. It was a scarf—a woolen grey scarf—that didn't belong to me. I touched it lightly, and memories engulfed me.

"You love snow, right?"

"Yeah, why?"

"The first snow is gonna fall tonight. Come, you'll love it."

"I don't know. It's a bit cold outside."

He opened his closet and took out something. I didn't see what it was until he reached over and fixed it around my neck—a thick grey woolen scarf.

"There," he said. "Do you think you'll still be cold?"

I chuckled and wrapped my arms around him. "Not when I'm with you."

"Great, we are going then, right?"

I placed a light kiss on his lips. "Yes, Chase, we are going."

"I love you," he said, grinning.

"I love you too, and I'm keeping this," I said, touching the scarf.

"Baby, you can't. It is a gift from my grandma. But you can wear it whenever you like," he said.

It didn't snow for two hours, but it didn't matter to us. We sat on the roof and teased each other, kissed, and laughed. We simulated the famous scene in Titanic. And just when we were giving up, the first snow fell.

"Zac, are you okay?" I heard Jackson's voice.

"Yeah, I'm fine. Did you say something?"

"I asked if you want pizza."

"Uh, yeah, sure," I said quickly.

"Obviously, something's up. What's wrong?" he asked.

"Nothing is wrong. I was just thinking about something...uh, what time my flight leaves and what time I have to be at the airport," I said.

"Okay," he said, acknowledging my explanation but not entirely believing me.

I was still touching Chase's scarf. He said it was his grandma's gift to him. He couldn't possibly want me to have it. He probably forgot about it. I had to give it back to him. It was the right thing to do. A part of me wanted to hold on to it even if it was just to hold on to the memories, but I knew I couldn't do that. The scarf belonged to him.

"You just zoned out again," Jackson uttered abruptly.

"I'll be back," I said hurriedly.

I walked out of the room and down the corridor. I don't know what the hell gave me the courage, but I found myself at Bruce and Chase's door. It wasn't debatable. I had to return the scarf, but did I have to walk there? I could have given it to Jackson so he could return it to Chase or just texted Chase to take it himself. Either way, I was already at the door. I could turn back, or I could knock.

I found myself doing the latter.

I knocked once, twice, three times and ended up losing count. It seemed there was no one in. Oh well, I had tried.

The door swung open abruptly.

"What?!" came Bruce's irritated voice. He was only clad in his boxers, displaying his perfect, glowing toned body.

"Hi. I…uh…thought Chase would want this back," I said, showing him the scarf.

He opened the door a little bit wider.

"Baby, it's Zac," he called into the room.

My mind screamed at me for exposing myself to torture. But surprisingly, it didn't sting as bad as I thought it would. After that moment with Bruce outside my room, things had somehow gotten better. It was as if the more the people around me revealed themselves to be cruel backstabbers, the more the fairytale extinguished.

Chase grumbled something. He walked into my view a few seconds later, adjusting his boxers. I did not need to be told what had been happening before I knocked. I would probably need to wash my brain with chlorine, spray pesticides, herbicides, a sterilizer, and maybe the banned pesticide DDT to erase the images that came to mind.

"Hi," Chase said nonchalantly.

"Hi. I thought you'd want your grandma's gift back," I said.

"My what?" he asked.

"Grandma Paula's gift to you. The scarf she gave you a year ago?" I said, raising the scarf so he could see it.

Bruce looked at Chase. "Didn't Grandma Paula die like five years ago?"

"Uh, thank you, Zac," Chase said, taking the scarf from me. He looked embarrassed.

"Wait, you also lied to me about your grandma?" I asked, unable to hide the shock I felt.

He sighed. "Yes, I lied. I didn't want you to have the scarf, so I panicked."

"You could have just said no," I said.

"Maybe I could have, but you were just too clingy, and I didn't want to get into it with you. Anyway, if that's all, we'd like to—" he said before I cut in.

"That's all."

I started walking away.

"Zac, wait," Chase called out.

He walked up to catch up with me, which only took seconds.

"About spring break, I just wanted to make sure we are on the same page. You can't come to the vacation house. I'm sure you understand that," he said.

"Chase, I may have been dumb enough to believe all your lies, but I'm not *that* dumb to go where I'm clearly not wanted," I said.

"I'm sorry. I just had to make sure," he said.

I started walking away. Maybe I should have asked Jackson to give the scarf back. I knew my relationship with Chase hadn't been real; I just hadn't known the extent of his fakeness. Well, now I knew. Nothing he'd ever uttered was the truth—not the serious things, and not the casual things either.

When I got to my room, Jackson didn't ask where I'd been. Instead, he asked me what kind of pizza I wanted us to order. We ate and talked about random things. He once again invited me to join him and his friends in Florida, and once again, I declined.

When I went to bed that night, I thought about home. I was happy to go. I was also desperate. I needed to erase my relationship with Chase, and at least make coming back to college bearable. I planned to do that by drowning my sorrows in my mom's food, lazing around and caring about nothing.

When next morning dawned, Mom called me just to make sure I hadn't ditched her.

"Hey, honey, are you excited?"

I chuckled. "Yeah, Mom, I am."

"Great, at least there will be one happy soul in this house," she said.

I wouldn't exactly call myself a happy soul right now, but she didn't know about the breakup. I was going to dampen her mood too.

"I guess Jess isn't letting up?" I asked.

"She is getting more and more moody and keeps lashing out. Maybe bringing Mark over is not such a good idea," she said.

"Nonsense, Mom. Jess will come around," I said.

"I hope so. I really like Mark," she said.

"Mom, I have to shower, or I'll miss my flight," I said.

"Right. Go. Do you want me to pick you up at the airport?" she asked.

"No, I'll just take a cab," I informed her.

"You know where the spare keys are," she said. "It'll be nice to return from work to a friendly face."

"Why? Is Noah that bad too?"

"Noah is a sweetheart, but you know he doesn't talk much. He lights up when you are here, though."

"All right, Mom. I'll see you later."

"Take care," she said then hung up.

I finally showered and dressed. Jackson did so too, and we had the breakfast he cooked. His flight wasn't until later, so I left him at the dorm. A few hours later, I was on the flight home. I had a feeling of foreboding like something was going to happen. Or it may be just my wariness of planes ever since my dad died in a plane crash.

CHAPTER EIGHT

ZAC

It was a four-and-a-half-hour flight to my hometown. I was glad when the plane landed. I got my luggage and went to get a cab. Happily, about three cabs were already lined outside. I was about to get into the one in the front when a guy came out of nowhere and claimed the cab.

"Too slow," he said rudely to me.

I was taken aback. I didn't expect something like that. My town wasn't busy like New York and people weren't as rude and on the rush. Who did he think he was?

I was about to say something, but the guy was already in the cab. I didn't see much of him, just his silver short hair with black roots. It was a rare and distinctive color. I also caught sight of a rose with some initials I couldn't make out tattooed on his wrist.

The cab left its parking space, and the one behind it moved forward.

I got in and gave the driver the address. As I looked at buildings and trees we passed, my thoughts drifted towards the guy who'd stolen my cab. He seemed different, like he didn't belong in my town. There was just something about him. I chuckled to myself. *Why was I thinking about a guy I would never meet?*

The cab slowed down to a stop. I looked outside, and sure enough, I could see the white brick siding two-story house

I lived in for most of my childhood and teenage years. I paid the driver, muttered my thanks, and got out.

I walked to the front door. The house wasn't big and had battled its fair share of stormy weathers. It did look old but was still structurally intact. Mom said she'd have it repainted, but I doubted that was one of her priorities right now.

I bent down at the door to retrieve the keys from under the mat. I supposed that wasn't the safest place to put keys, but our town was relatively safe.

I unlocked and walked into the house. It smelled like…home. There was also the smell of burnt onion from that morning's breakfast. I put my bag on the couch and went to the kitchen. It was just as I remembered it, spotless and everything tucked neatly into place. My mom was a neat freak, which was one of the reasons she fought with Jess a lot since my sister was messy and couldn't be bothered with chores.

I grabbed a bottle of water from the fridge just as my phone rang from my pocket.

"Hello?" I said.

"Hello. Are you home yet?" It was Mom.

I smiled. I should have expected it. "Yeah, I just got here."

"Great. What do you want for dinner tonight?" she asked.

"Uh, anything," I said.

"You can't say 'anything', Zac. Be specific," she said.

"Uh, roasted lamb?" I said uncertainly.

"Great. I'll buy the ingredients on my way home. Do you need anything?" she asked.

"None. Thanks, Mom."

"I forgot to tell you. Did you bring your swimming things?"

"Uh…what are you talking about? I—" I said, but she interrupted.

"I'm sorry. I have another call. I'll see you later, honey," she said and hung up.

What did she mean by swimming things? We didn't have a pool, and there was no lake or beach nearby.

I shrugged and drank my water.

*   *   *

My brother is still in elementary school, so he was the first to find me at home. He takes the school bus to school, which later drops him off only a street away.

Noah is a younger version of me, physically anyway. He has the same blond hair and the same facial features—the hazel eyes, the thick eyebrows, and the pastel pink lips. He looks younger, of course, but at eleven years, he is shorter for his age.

He found me watching TV when he got home. Normally, he would stay next door with his friend, Eric, until Mom got home. However, he knew I was home.

I thought of playing hide-and-seek with him, but he walked in before I could figure out where to hide.

"Hey, bro!" I said as he walked in.

"Hey!" he said excitedly, throwing his schoolbag on the floor. Mom didn't lie; he did light up when he saw me. It felt good to be appreciated. It warmed my heart that he looked happy to see me.

"Look at you, you've grown an inch," I teased.

He furrowed his brows. "And you are still ugly," he said.

"You are my mirror image, so I guess so are you," I said.

"Whatever," he said, and then he lit up. "Do you want to play *GT Sport*?"

"Sure, why not? But take your books upstairs first. You don't want your sister to trip on them."

63

"Actually, I do. Maybe she'll bust a lip and stop talking so much."

I laughed. "Noah!" I reprimanded. I was still laughing though, so I doubt if he took me seriously.

He shrugged but still picked up his schoolbag anyway.

* * *

Jess came back while we were playing. We heard the door bang despite the loud volume of our race cars and knew instantly that Jess was back. She walked into our view from the entryway.

"Hello, bitches," she said.

I put the game on pause and looked at the young version of our mother.

Jess had straight, neck-long black hair with bangs; thin eyebrows; and the same lip color as mine, hidden under black lipstick. She also sports standout jewelry.

"Hey, Jess. How was school?" I asked brightly.

She frowned. "Like hell."

"How do you know that? Been to hell?" Noah asked.

"Shut up, you dweeb!" she said.

"It is a legitimate question," I said, chuckling.

"Well, here's a legitimate answer, fuck off!" she said and made her way towards the stairs.

I was used to Jess's moods and her vulgar mouth, so I didn't think much about it. I resumed the game, and Noah and I continued playing.

Jess came down later to make herself a sandwich. I asked for one too, and she just looked at me before giving me the finger. How do I keep her in check in Mark's presence other than locking her in the closet?

"Boo-ya! I beat you, again!" Noah said excitedly.

"Yeah, well, you spend hours on this thing," I said.

"And what do you spend your hours doing? Kissing your boyfriend?" he asked.

"Gross," Jess said as she walked past us with a plate and glass in hand.

"You could sit here with us you know," I said.

She stopped. "And why on earth would I do that? And besides, you didn't come here for me, did you?"

"I came home to see you guys, all of you."

"Yeah right, you came to meet Mark, Fuck Shmuck!" she said, walking away.

"Wow."

"She gave him a nickname, Mark Von Shmuck," Noah said.

I chuckled. "That actually doesn't sound bad."

"You don't like him, too?" he asked.

"Uh…I don't know him, so I don't have any opinion about him. Yet."

"Jess doesn't like him. She says he's probably a criminal or a con artist," he said.

"You know what? Let's play again. This time, I'm going to wipe the floor with you."

"Sure, bring it on," Noah said, rising to the challenge.

*　　*　　*

Mom came back a few hours later with bags of groceries. When I went to help her unload the car, she gave me the longest hug of my life. You'd think she hadn't seen me in over ten years. She was so happy she even shed a tear. That part worried me a bit.

"Look at you, you've lost weight!" she remarked.

"I study a lot," I said, smiling.

"Oh, you better. At least I can count on you to make something of your life," I said.

"Mom, Jess is smart," I said.

"I know she's smart. It's her attitude I'm worried about," Mom said.

"Mom, don't worry so much about her, or you'll have gray hair. She will outgrow it," I said as I picked up a few grocery bags.

We walked into the house, and I set the grocery bags on the kitchen counter. Noah came to help Mom and me unpack. Jess was nowhere in sight. Of course.

"How was your flight?" Mom asked.

"It was all right. It was delayed by thirty minutes, though," I said.

"Well, what's important is you arrived safe," she said.

My mom was anti-planes. It was understandable with what happened to Dad. She still flies, but she always got jittery about it and would rather drive long distances unless the destination is too far for her to get there by road.

We talked about college and her work until we finished unpacking the groceries. Noah and I left her to cook dinner, deciding to watch TV. Jess was still upstairs. I had no idea what she was doing in her room, but it sure seemed way more important.

*   *   *

About an hour and a half later, Mom called us out for dinner. Noah and I went to the dining room to join her. Jess was obviously not there.

"Noah, go call your sister."

"Do I have to? Dinner is kind of nice without her."

"Noah!"

"Fine," Noah said, standing up and leaving shortly.

"Smells good," I praised Mom.

"Well, you asked for it," Mom said as she sliced the leg of lamb. It looked juicy and smelled divine.

"I have the best cook for a mom," I said, grinning. I was laying the compliments a bit too thick, but Mom could use it.

"Wow, for once, the food looks edible." We heard Jess's voice.

"Jess, that's not nice," I said sternly.

"Whatever," she said nonchalantly as she took a seat. "Can we eat so I can go to my room?"

Mom gave me a look of desperation, and I shrugged. Noah sat to my right. Mom dished up for us. She said grace, and we started eating.

"So, I have something to tell you guys," she said.

"You want us to meet Mark Von Shmuck. Yeah, yeah, we've got it," Jess said.

"Jessica! You will not call him that," Mom reprimanded.

"Or what, you'll ground me? I'm being forced to meet the dude. I already feel grounded," Jess said.

"Jess, stop it!" I said.

"Why are you taking her side? She forced you to come here when you could be having a vacation with your boyfriend!" Jess said.

Mom looked at me. "Is it true? You had other plans?" she asked. I could already hear the guilt in her voice.

"I did at some point, but you didn't force me to come here," I said.

"So, you ditched your boyfriend to meet some old man? Careful, buddy, you aren't the hottest thing to walk the earth; you might just find yourself replaced." Jess's knife cut through.

She just struck a spot she didn't know existed. My thoughts drifted to Bruce and Chase, and I found my heart slightly aching.

"Zac, you should have told me. I would have—" Mom started.

"Chase and I are no longer together, so those plans went down the drain. I'm happy to be here," I said.

My mom looked shell-shocked. Finally, she reacted. "Oh, my baby, I'm so sorry. I—" she said, and I interrupted again.

"Mom, you had something to tell us," I reminded her.

Jess paused eating her food. "Wait, how come Zac gets to choose and I don't?"

"Because if it were up to you, it would be, 'never,'" mom said.

"At least there's *one* thing you know about me," Jess said.

"Gosh, Jess! One second, one freaking second. Can't you just shut up for one freaking second?!" It was Noah.

We were all surprised. Noah rarely raised his voice. He was quite possibly the softest eleven-year-old. Jess was even surprised.

"Um…well, uh…thank you, Noah. Guys, as you already know, I've decided that it is about time Mark meets you. We thought about it and figured the best way would be in a fun environment. We've decided to take a family trip to his beach house for spring break," Mom said.

"No!" Jess said.

"Jess—"

"Mom, no! I am *not* going."

"Jess, I thought that you guys would love to have fun, and you love the beach."

"Oh, I am not saying no to fun or the beach. I am saying no to staying in the same house with a psycho. For two weeks," Jess said, putting her fork down and crossing her arms.

"He is not a psycho!" Mom said.

Jess rolled her eyes. "I don't trust your judgment lately."

Mom placed her head in her hands.

I was surprised by the news. I had planned on never stepping out of the house until spring break ends. To hear Mom had already planned for us to go to Mark's beach house was not something I expected.

"Zac?" Mom said when she raised her head.

"I don't mind going. It could be fun," I said with a slight shrug. I didn't really feel like going, but I didn't want to disappoint her, either. Seeing her sad made me sad.

"Noah?" Mom said.

"Can he surf?" Noah asked.

"Uh…I don't know," Mom said.

"See? I doubt you know enough about this guy. He could be a serial killer for all we know," Jess said.

"Hey, we are going to the beach. I'm sure there'll be someone who can teach you," I told Noah.

"Then I'm game!" Noah said excitedly.

"Great. You guys can leave me here," Jess said, getting up.

"Jess!" Mom shouted as she walked away.

I stood up and touched Mom's shoulder. "I'll talk to her." Before I left, I asked, "When are we going?"

"Tomorrow," Mom said sheepishly.

It was definitely short notice, but it's not like I had other plans anyway. I walked up the stairs to Jess's room. There were so many "Do Not Enter" signs on the door you would think it was a nuclear plant or something.

I knocked.

"Go away!" came the reply.

"Jess, come on, just open up. One minute," I said.

"You know, Zac, you are like a minion," she said, describing my character in one word, or at least her perception of it.

I sighed. "Jess, come on."

The door opened abruptly. She stood there with one brow raised.

"You have to come with us," I said. *Was that the best I could do?*

"For what? You guys don't need me there."

"Think of it this way, if you don't come, Mom and Mark will have a lovely time, and soon he'll be our stepdad. But if you come, you can make sure that doesn't happen."

She narrowed her eyes. "Are you onto something?"

"Of course, I am. You don't want to miss this chance," I said. Deep down, I was cringing at what I was saying.

She smiled mischievously. "I'll pack my bag right away."

"Great, because we are leaving tomorrow."

Her eyes grew. "Tomorrow? That's too soon. I haven't said goodbye to people."

"That's what phones are for," I said as I walked away.

Mom was happy to know that I had achieved the impossible and got Jess to come. I couldn't smile fully, knowing I had planted an awful idea in Jess's mind. It was the only way I could do to get her to come, and Mom really wanted her there too. It was my job then to thwart whatever plan Jess came up with.

I took my seat and finished my plate, then helped Mom clear up the table.

"So, will it just be Mark and us?" I asked her as we set the dishes on the kitchen counter.

"No. Mark's son is coming with," she replied.

"He's divorced, then?" I asked.

"No. He's a widower."

"What else can you tell me about him? I'm not being nosy. I just don't want to be surprised." "That's all right. His name is Mark Lowe. He's a lawyer and a partner in a law firm. He has a son who's nineteen. The boy's mother died years ago. He's only been married once, but he dated after his wife's death. He lives in Corneridge, but he was born and raised in Las

Vegas," she said. "I don't think you want to know what he likes."

"That's all right. It's enough."

"Good. Now, help me with the dishes," she said.

I smiled as I handed her a few plates.

CHAPTER NINE

ZAC

The next morning, I woke up on a familiar bed in a familiar room. I had the room since we moved to the house, which was fourteen years ago. It looked like the room of a teenager, with *Avengers*-themed bedding and posters on the walls. I had many memories, with that room as the setting—including my first kiss with a guy.

When I woke up that morning, I remembered Chase. He wasn't my first boyfriend, but I envisioned that one day he would come to my house and I'd show him my bedroom. Then Mom would embarrass me by showing him my baby pictures.

I had many hopes for us. It wasn't anything like my previous relationships where I was driven by hormones and infatuation. I seriously fell for him.

I wondered if he'd already left for his family vacation house. He was going to introduce me to his cousins on that trip. Now, he was going to introduce Bruce if they didn't know him already. They probably knew him. I knew Bruce had gone to his house last Christmas break. I hadn't known what was going on between them then. They were friends, and I didn't notice anything odd.

There was a knock on my door, disrupting my thoughts of Chase and Bruce. The door opened slightly, and Mom peered in. She had slight problems with boundaries. Even at twenty years old, I was still her little boy. *Didn't she think she'd walk in on something she should never see?*

"Good morning, honey," she said apologetically.

"Morning, Mom," I said.

"I was wondering if you have everything you need for the trip. We can go down to the shops quickly after breakfast."

"Mom, I'm fine. I have everything."

She hesitated. "Oh, all right."

She still stood at the door. I raised a brow.

"I'll still go down to get some snacks for the road, want to come?" she asked.

"Uh, sure," I said.

She looked worried and nervous.

"Okay, what's up?"

"Oh, it's nothing," she said dismissively. "Just that Mark asked if we can come with his son."

"His son is here?" I asked.

"Yeah, flew in yesterday. Apparently, he models," she said.

"So, we have to leave with him? Is that why you are nervous?"

She nodded sheepishly. "I just hadn't anticipated meeting him so soon, especially without Mark there."

"Mom, relax. He'll like you, who wouldn't?"

"Your sister doesn't like me."

"Jess loves you. She's just like any teenager."

"You weren't like that," she said.

I'm special.

"She'll outgrow this phase, you'll see."

"I hope so. Anyway, come down for breakfast in 30 minutes," she said before closing the door, only to open it after a few seconds. "How are you, by the way, honey?" she said with a concerned face.

"I'm fine."

"I'm sorry about Chase. What happened?"

73

"Uh, it's a long story, Mom," I said slowly.

She nodded. "I'm here if you want to talk."

I smiled, and she closed the door. I loved my mom, but there was no way I was going to talk to her about Chase. There was nothing to talk about anyway.

Approximately 20 minutes later, I got up, made my bed, and went to freshen up and brush my teeth. I went down to the kitchen. True to her words, Mom had cooked a scrumptious breakfast. For once Jess came down without being called, and we had breakfast as a family.

After breakfast, I took a shower while Mom helped Noah pack his bag. Mom, Noah, and I went to the shops to buy snacks and brand-new swimming trunks for Noah. Jess stayed behind to say goodbye to her friends, but it's not like she would have gone with us anyway.

When we got back, I packed a couple of shorts into my bag, along with my swimming trunks. Mom said we had about an hour before leaving. The drive would be three hours long. We would arrive a little before the sunset.

When I was done packing, I joined Mom and Noah in the living room. We watched TV for a while. Mom tried to bring up Chase, but I shut her off each time.

"So Mom, Mark's son … are we picking him up somewhere?" I asked.

"Yeah, at the Samson hotel," she said. "Zac, promise me something."

"What?" I asked.

"That you won't make him feel like an outsider. You guys know each other, and he only knows his dad. I don't want him to feel lonely when his dad is not there."

"I promise. Besides, Mom, it's his beach house. I'm sure he has friends in that area," I said. "By the way, where is this beach house anyway?"

"Sapphire Beach Town," Mom said lightly. "It's about…" Mom continued talking, but I could no longer hear a single thing except for the rapid beating of my heart. It was so loud my eardrum was resonating with it.

Sapphire Beach Town is the same town where Chase's vacation house is. *This was not happening. I came here to run away from Chase, and now, I am running towards him. No! No! No!*

"...better not be like Jess." I heard a portion of Noah's comment.

"I hope so too. Three hours is a long time," Mom said. The conversation was going on without me.

"Did you say he's a model?" Noah asked Mom.

We didn't see Jess walking in until she said, "Who's a model?"

"Mark's son. He's driving with us to the beach house," Mom replied.

"Oh great! And here I was, thinking the torture wouldn't start in at least three hours," she said.

I couldn't concentrate on the conversation around me. I just learned I was a few hours away from being in the same place as my ex-boyfriend. If I were lucky, the houses would be on opposite sides of the town. *But what if they weren't? I couldn't do this. What if Bruce was there too?*

But I couldn't bail out at that moment. I told Mom I'd go. I couldn't break her heart. She was trying hard to move on with her life. She needed my support. She needed all of our support, and I was the oldest. It was my duty to keep the young ones in check, especially after I'd given my sister evil ideas.

"Or maybe he's a psycho just like his dad." I caught Jess's words. I had no idea what they were talking about now, but I knew I had to be at that beach house.

"Start loading your bags into the car. We have to leave soon," Mom instructed.

I went upstairs to get my bag, and soon, it was in the car. I tried helping Jess with hers, but she snarled at me. Obviously, chivalry didn't sit well with her. I was used to it, but I felt sorry for Mark. Maybe I should have written him a book titled, *How to Deal with Jessica Nielsen without Your Head Exploding.* The only problem was I wasn't always successful in dealing with Jess.

    I sat in front with Mom to help with the navigation. We would be relying on GPS. None of us had been where we were going, and it seemed a lot of us didn't want to be there.

    The drive to the Samson Hotel was filled with Jess's comments on how boring it was in the car. She wanted to play music, but Mom hated her kind of music. She finally took out her iPod and shut up.

    When we were near the hotel, Mom gave me her phone to call Mark's son to let him know we were near. She had called him before we left to let him know we were leaving the house.

    "Evan L," she said.

    I scrolled down to the name she mentioned, and pressed the "Call" button.

    "Hello?" he said when he answered. I noticed that his voice wasn't polite, and that he seemed irritated.

    "Hi. We just wanted to let you know that we are only five minutes away. We'll park just across the street. Black SUV," I said.

    "Okay," he said.

    "Bye," I said and hung up.

    Mom was quick to notice my frown.

    "What did he say?" she asked.

    "He said okay," I said.

    "And you are frowning because…?"

    I shook my head. "Nothing."

    We arrived at the hotel and parked across the street like I said. I got out of the car and looked at the hotel. There was no one walking our way. I figured he had to check out and stuff, so I waited. We ended up waiting for 15 minutes.

    I went to the driver side.

    "Maybe we should call him again," I said.

Mom looked skeptical. She didn't want to rush him, but we'd been waiting forever. The boy obviously thought too highly of himself. If he was held up, couldn't he let us know?

We waited two more minutes before I said, "Mom, give me the phone."

"The guy obviously doesn't want to go to his dad's house. That should raise alarm bells. Maybe his dad—" Jess said, and I interrupted.

I had spotted someone who looked like he was walking our way. He was carrying a small duffel bag hoisted on his shoulder and dressed in blue cotton shorts and a white T-shirt.

"I think that's him."

Jess lowered the window. "That can't be him. That looks like Cody Wilde," she said.

"Who's that?" Noah wanted to know. I didn't know who that was either.

The guy walked slowly. He didn't seem like he was rushing to anywhere. He also walked more and more toward our direction. It looked more and more likely that he was the guy we were waiting for.

And finally, I saw his hair clearly: short and silver with black roots, shaved on the sides.

Could it be? No, it couldn't be!

I clearly remember meeting him before.

He walked to the SUV. I was the first person he met since I was outside the car. I could see him clearly now. Light gray eyes looked at me. I saw his small, slightly pointy nose; his lips that looked gorgeous in the sun; and the piercing on his right eyebrow. This time, he didn't turn from me fast, so I saw everything. The guy was gorgeous beyond words. And he didn't just have the face; he had the body to go with it, judging from his well-built physique.

My eyes temporarily went to his left wrist. Sure enough, there was a tattoo of a pink flower with initials. I didn't get a chance to read the initials that time either because he moved his wrist.

"Hi, you must be the family I'm driving with," he said. He didn't even bother smiling.

"Uh, yeah, I'm Zac," I said.

"Evan. You look familiar."

"Yeah, you stole my cab."

"Ah...the slow guy. Hey, you hadn't paid, so technically, I didn't steal anything," he said.

We stared at each other for a few seconds. He had beautiful eyes.

"Uh, let's put your bag in the trunk. I'll do the introductions once we are settled," I said.

We put the bag with the others, and I told him he could climb in the back with Jess and Noah. We all got into the car.

"Guys, this is Evan. Evan, this is Jess, Noah, and Mom."

Mom and Noah said their greetings. Jess just stared at him.

"Jess, don't be rude," Mom said sheepishly. Of course, she'd feel responsible for Jess's behavior.

"You are Cody Wilde!" Jess finally said something to Evan, astounding all but one of us.

"Huh?" Noah voiced his confusion.

"Please call me Evan," Evan said. He seemed nonchalant.

"Yeah, sure, whatever," Jess said.

Wait. Was this guy Cody Wilde or not Cody Wilde? And who on earth was Cody Wilde?

"Umm...are we missing something here?" I asked looking from Jess to Evan, or Cody...whatever his name was!

There was a bit of silence. The car wasn't moving.

Evan sighed. "Evan Cody Lowe, son of Mark Lowe and Eva Wilde. I act and model. Cody Wilde is my stage name. Can we go now?"

There was a bit of a pause. "Of course!" Mom said. "Maybe you'd like to sit in front Evan? You can help with the navigation since you know where we are going. Technology can be deceiving sometimes."

"I'd rather not. I've never been to this boring town anyway, so I don't know how to get to the beach house from here," he mumbled.

"Oh, all right. I guess we are relying on technology. Fingers crossed it doesn't mess up," Mom said.

"I hope it does, and we end up somewhere else instead," Jess said in annoyance.

Evan laughed. "That'd be great. Then I won't be forced to do stuff I don't want to," he said, the annoyance in his voice too palpable to miss.

"All right, kids, time to go," Mom said a bit cheerfully. It was a forced cheer, I could tell; she was affected by what Evan said.

Something told me the next two weeks were going to be more than I had bargained for. There was Mark, who I haven't met yet but whom I had been told by Livy keep to an eye on. There was Jess who will drive me up the wall; mom who would be angered and hurt by Jess's antics; and Evan, the gorgeous guy with bewitching eyes and probably a monstrous ego, who didn't seem happy about the trip. There was, of course, Noah, who at that time, seemed like an angel.

"So, Jess, how do you know Evan—Cody?" Mom asked lightly as the car started moving.

"Saw him in some magazine," Jess said simply. "Thought he was some hotshot. Clearly not."

"Jess!" Mom reprimanded.

Jess shrugged. "He's here with us, *normal people*," she said.

"I'm right here! And if you haven't already noticed, I'd rather be somewhere else." Evan growled.

All I had hoped for was a quiet two-week stay at home to nurse my wounds. I didn't need this! Chase, Evan or Cody, Jess. It already seemed like too much!

Breathe, Zac, I told myself. *You are going to be just fine.*

CHAPTER TEN

ZAC

During the drive, there wasn't much talking going on in the car. Jess had her earphones on. Evan was busy on his phone. There was only silence, interrupted by the sound of the GPS lady when she'd tell the directions. It looked like it was going to be a long uncomfortable break.

I got a text from Livy asking how I was doing. I texted her back, telling her I was doing okay and how my spring break plans had suddenly changed into a two-week getaway to a beach house. I didn't tell her the beach house was situated where Chase's beach house was. She'd want to talk about it, and I still wasn't exactly sure how I felt about the whole thing.

I occasionally stole a look at Evan. The guy was handsome. I should have expected it; after all, he was a model. He also had the attitude that was—although maybe unfair—stereotypical of models. He looked very much uncomfortable. Maybe it was because he was in a car with strangers.

Three hours and a few minutes later, we arrived at the beach house which was too big to be a vacation house, if I say so myself. It was painted white on the outside and had white railings on the sides. It was just right next to the beach, standing on a rocky mountain and surrounded by lush trees. A few feet below, the ebb and flow of the waters made huge lapping sounds on the shore.

Mom parked a few feet away from the house, and I saw a man come out of the house to meet us.

"Here we are," Mom said.

"I should say 'finally', but it's not like I want to be here," Jess said as she removed her earphones.

Evan got out first. I saw him say something to his dad, and his dad shook his head. They hugged, which seemed to last for only less than a second. I doubt anyone else noticed, but there seemed to be some tension there.

We got out of the car.

"Take your bags out," Mom said. She left us to greet Mark, who was now close to the car.

They hugged, and Mark kissed her on the cheek.

"I think I'm going to lose weight while staying here," Jess informed me.

"Why is that?" I asked as we took out the bags.

"Because I'm going to want to throw up every day," she said, looking pointedly at Mom holding onto Mark, "And I probably will."

"You are so dramatic," I said.

Once the bags were on the ground, Mark came to us with Mom. He was a medium-sized man with black hair and gray eyes. He, just like his son, was very handsome, probably where Evan got his looks from. They did look a bit alike. Mark looked like he was in his late forties or early fifties.

"This is Zac, Jessica, and Noah," Mom told him, pointing us out as she held on to his arm with her other hand.

"It is such a pleasure to meet all of you," Mark said warmly, handing his hand out to shake.

I shook it, and so did Noah. Jess folded her arms and rolled her eyes.

"Jessica!" Mom scolded.

"No, no, don't force her. I understand," Mark said gently. "Anyway, I hope you'll all enjoy your time here."

"It's nice to meet you, too," I said courteously.

"Let me help you with the bags," he said, bending to pick up the bags.

"No, no, we've got them. Right, Jess?" I said.

"You are only kidding yourself if you think I'll pick up a bag that isn't mine," she said as she picked up her bag.

I picked up my bag and Mom's. Noah got his. Only Evan's bag was on the ground, and he didn't look like he was going to pick it up.

Mark sighed looking at the bag and turned. "Evan, who do you think is going to take your bag to the bedroom?"

Evan shrugged. "The person who forced me to come here."

"In that case, it'll just spend the night here," Mark said. "Come with me," he said to the rest of us.

Mom, Jess, Noah, and I followed him into the house. I saw Evan huffing before he picked up his bag and followed us.

The house was more beautiful inside than outside. It had a large living area, with big windows that let the sun's rays in. At that time, the sun was setting, so it coated the space with a beautiful orange glow. You could see the blue ocean through the windows, which created a serene atmosphere.

A woman came to greet us, wearing a maid's uniform.

"This is Rosa, my helper. She will show you where you can put your bags and assist you with everything you need," Mark said.

Evan passed us and went presumably to his room.

"Right. Come this way," Rosa said.

I handed her mom's bag then Jess, Noah, and I followed her. She showed Jess and Noah their rooms and led me to mine, which was a distance from the others. It was still part of the house, but it seemed somehow secluded from it

We came to the door, and Rosa stopped. She didn't open it like the others. Instead, she knocked.

"I'm coming!" I heard a voice come from inside. *It sounded like...Evan?*

The door opened, and Evan's head poked outside. He seemed shirtless.

"Hi, Rosa," he said brightly.

"Hi, Evan."

What were we doing at Evan's room? Evan raised a brow, probably wondering the same thing.

"Evan, Zac is going to be your roommate," Rosa said.

"What?!" Evan said.

I had the same reaction myself, only internally. Rosa just smiled apologetically.

"Why can't he sleep…somewhere else?" Evan asked.

"There are only five rooms here, and all are full. Your room is the only one with two beds," Rosa said.

"And you decided he should room with me?"

"I didn't decide. Your dad did. Besides, Evan, you look to be the same age and are both boys. What is the problem?" Rosa asked, shrugging.

"I need my privacy. I'm sure Zac does too," Evan said. They all looked at me.

"I…I don't mind which room I sleep in," I said.

"Well, Evan, you are stuck with Zac. You can take it up with your father if you don't like it," Rosa said. "I need to go. Dinner won't cook itself."

Evan groaned and opened the door wider. He walked inside, leaving me at the door. I walked in, closed the door, and placed my bag on the floor.

I didn't know why I didn't say I preferred sleeping with Noah. Evan obviously didn't want a roommate. And I couldn't understand why Mark decided it was better for me and Evan to share a room. He was obviously hoping for something.

"Welcome," Evan said, giving me a sickening sweet smile.

The room was darker than most of the house. It had a few windows which displayed a view of the mountain behind the house, making it cozy yet eerie. In the middle were a single and a double bed lying next to each other, and against the wall was a closet. There were several gym equipment in there, too, including a treadmill and a training bike.

"Why do you have two beds anyway?" I inquired.

"This wasn't a bedroom. It was a storeroom for unused things. I figured I liked it and moved here. The other bed came here from another room when my dad's girlfriend decided it was too old," he said.

"Your dad's girlfriend?" I asked.

"Yeah, you don't know?"

"Don't know what?"

"Oh, man," he said and sighed. "Your mom's not the only one."

"You are lying," I said instinctively. He had to be lying. He wouldn't give up such information easily.

He chuckled. "Okay, I'm lying. But knowing my dad, she's probably not the only one."

"Are you serious?" The question escaped me.

He just smiled. "I'm going to shower," he said. "Feel free to make space for yourself in the closet. I don't know why I'm worked up about this. It won't last."

Was this what Livy said I had to watch out for? Was there any truth in what Evan was saying or did he just want to ruffle my feathers? He obviously knew his dad more than I did, but there were reasons why he would lie.

It was all too confusing.

I focused on getting myself settled after he left, which was very hard. The closet was almost full. I had to move his things without offending him.

* * *

Later on, all of us had scrumptious dinner served by Rosa on the terrace. The air outside was beautiful and fresh. We could see the ocean and hear waves as they crashed on the rocks. Jess and Evan had to be called to the table two times. There was small talk around. So far, we had learned that Mark was a corporate lawyer, and by the looks of things, a very successful one.

"So, what do you study Zac?" Mark asked.

"Psychology," I said.

"That is interesting. What do you want to do?"

"I'm still deciding between educational and clinical psychology."

"That is nice. What about you Jess? What do you want to study?"

Jess didn't bother looking up from her plate. She was almost done with her food. She hadn't said a single word since she arrived. I knew better than to think silent rebellion was all that she was capable of.

"Jess?" Mom tried.

"What?!" Jess asked firmly.

"Mark asked you a question," Mom said calmly.

"Why don't you answer? You make all the decisions, remember?" Jess said.

"Jess…" Mom started, but Mark touched her hand.

"Let her be," he said.

Why was I scared Jess would scare him off? He seemed very patient.

"And you, Noah, what would you like to do?" he asked.

"Surfing. I'd love to be a surfer," Noah said confidently.

"Oh, you surf?"

"Not yet, I have to learn how to first. But I'm sure I'll be good once I do," he said.

"Well, you've come to the right place. There's a beach in our backyard, and Evan can surf. He can teach you," Mark said brightly.

Evan's jaw clenched. "I don't surf," he said.

"But you can," Mark reminded him.

"Didn't you hear what I said? I don't surf, and I sure as hell will not be teaching any brat," Evan said.

"Hey! I am not a brat." Noah defended himself.

"Whatever. Are we done with this get-to-know-each-other thing? I want to sleep," Evan said, standing up.

Mark sat back in his seat and looked at his son. Evan shrugged and started walking away. Jess stood up too, and soon, they both disappeared from sight.

"That went well," Mom said sarcastically.

"I'm sorry, sweetheart," Mark said, holding mom's hand.

She held his other hand. "No, I'm sorry."

They looked into each other's eyes lovingly. Okay, that was our cue to leave.

"Come on, Noah, let's go watch TV," I said, and he and I stood up.

"Ask Rosa if you need anything," Mark told us. "And don't worry, buddy, we'll get you a board and a teacher," he said to Noah.

"Thanks," Noah said, smiling.

CHAPTER ELEVEN

ZAC

Noah and I watched TV until Noah decided he was ready for sleep. I wasn't tired, but I couldn't continue watching TV all on my own. Mom went with Mark to the shore. Evan and Jess were nowhere to be seen. Jess was probably plotting on how to tear Mom and Mark apart. I couldn't think of what Evan would be doing. He was an enigma to me.

After Noah left, I stayed for a few minutes before switching off the TV and going to my temporary bedroom. Even though I hadn't seen Evan leave the house, I didn't think he was in the bedroom. I was mistaken. I opened the door hastily, forgetting the common courtesy.

"I told you it was just sex. I was explicit about that." I heard Evan say. He was on the phone, pacing around.

I stood at the door as if the slightest movement would send him into a craze, though I was sure he hadn't seen me.

"Well, I am sorry you thought otherwise. We agreed it was a casual fling!" he said into the phone.

I had no idea what the other person on the line said, but Evan replied by saying, "What do you want me to do?"

He stopped pacing, listening intently. I was about to move when he suddenly shouted, "I can't do that! My dad is holding me hostage here. I told you that."

Seconds later he said, "Are you crying? Whoa! Look, I'm sorry if you read too much into what it was. I told you I was going to be in town for two months, and that was it. I am honestly not looking for something serious right now. Sure, I'm a jerk, but at least, I told you I was one."

I decided standing there was just weird, so I walked in, hoping he wouldn't be offended.

"I'm sorry," he said with finality and hung up.

I hadn't listened to the entire conversation, but I could tell what was going on. It sounded familiar, making my heart ache.

"It *always* ends this way!" he exclaimed, looking at me. He didn't look the least bit offended that I walked in on him on the phone.

I was looking at my phone then, so I raised my head. "What are you talking about?" I feigned ignorance.

"People always fall in love with me," he said.

"That's a bit conceited, don't you think?"

"No, no. I mean…I get with a girl, purely physical relationship, just sex. But the next thing I know, she's in love with me."

It must suck to be you, I thought.

The whole thing reminded me of Chase. Maybe all Chase ever wanted was a fling. He said it so himself: he didn't love me. He just wanted someone to warm up his bed, much like Evan.

But Evan was different, wasn't he? He didn't lie or cheat. He never claimed to love the people he had sex with.

But he still left them hurt. He had no remorse.

There was silence. It was as if Evan expected me to say something back. *Did he want me to say he was irresistible and people who didn't fall madly in love with him were insane?*

I avoided his scrutiny by changing into my sleeping clothes, completely ignoring him.

"So…your dad, what happened to him?" He found something else to talk about.

"He's dead. He died a couple of years ago," I replied.

"Oh, I'm sorry," he said.

"What about your mom?" I asked.

He stayed silent for a while before curtly saying, "Dead."

Remembering what Mom told me, I felt bad about asking. Mom had mentioned that Evan's mom had died years ago.

"I'm sorry," I said. My voice came out like a whisper.

"Well, it's life. Doesn't always go the way we want it to," he said cheerfully. It didn't seem genuine. I just had the feeling that his mom's death was troubling him. "So, you're a psychologist?" he changed the subject.

"*Studying* psychology," I said with emphasis. He opened his mouth to say something, but I jumped in. "Earlier, you said something about your dad…"

He shrugged. "Your mom will see it for herself."

"Why are you telling me this?"

He shrugged again. "I've been here before—a lot more times than I care to count."

"Maybe…maybe this is different," I said. I was trying hard to cling onto something. I didn't want my mom to get hurt like I had been hurt.

"Everyone was dif—," he started but was interrupted by his cell phone ringing.

"Evan." His answer was curt.

I decided to send Livy a text message to check up on her. That was a quick act, and I ended up with nothing else to do. I didn't intend on listening to Evan's conversation, but I ended up doing that. Well, his side of the conversation anyway.

"Yeah?"

"No way! He wants me?"

"Hell yes!"

"Did you say Emilia Pjanic?"

"If I'm not available, make sure I'm available." His tone went from disbelief to excitement. But I still couldn't figure out who he was talking to and what they were talking about.

"Great. Don't worry, Rosa's food is tempting, but I'll play safe," he continued.

"I don't swim, you know that."

"Talk soon."

He hung up. On his face was the brightest smile. I thought of asking him what the call was about, but before I could get a word out, his phone returned to his ear. He was calling someone.

A few seconds later, he said emphatically into the phone. "Guess who is going to launch David Markham's new perfume?!" And with that, I had gotten my answer without asking.

"Way! I got the job. David Markham himself asked for me!"

"Yeah, it is. But that's not all. Guess who will play as my female admirer?" he continued talking into the phone.

"What?! No. She's at the bottom. I'm talking about a certain Bosnian beauty with never-ending legs."

"Yep, Miss Pjanic herself."

"It's a summer campaign, so the beginning of summer… wherever the shoot is."

"I don't know yet, but probably an outdoor shoot in the sand. I don't know the details, but I'll know soon."

"We'll talk again. Enjoy Miami." With that, the call ended.

There was silence as Evan decided he was ready to get into bed. He took off his shirt slowly. I caught a glimpse of his abs and cursed myself. Turning on my side, I closed my eyes. I couldn't allow myself to look at him, not only because I'd probably give my sexuality away, but because he…No, that was the only reason. I'd seen him half-naked before, so I already knew what to expect. And that was nothing short of man-made glory. He could very well be the reincarnation of Adonis, and I was clearly losing my mind.

"You should tell your mom to save herself before it's too late," Evan said out of the blue.

"And I should take your word because?" I said, opening my eyes.

"Because I know my dad."

"How do I know you are not just trying to sabotage him?"

"That's the thing. You won't know," he said and chuckled lightly. "Is your mom the sappy sort? She seems like the sappy sort."

"What—" I began, but he interrupted.

"I'm just wondering how she'll react. This house has seen its fair share of drama," he said cryptically.

I breathed loudly.

"Good night," Evan said abruptly, leaving me all confused.

"Good night," I said after a short silence.

I raised the duvet all the way up and covered my face. I couldn't sleep with all the confusing thoughts evoked by Evan's words, so I took out my phone and went online. I Googled pictures of funny animals before a specific thought came to mind. Evan was a model. If he was good enough for David Markham to want him, then there had to be traces of him on the web. I typed in "Cody Wilde" and waited.

I never had any interest in actors and models, so I had no idea who Cody Wilde was before meeting him. Turns out I was only one of few people who don't. Evan had his own website, a Wikipedia page with lots of details about his life and career, an Instagram with five million followers, a Twitter with a lot more—basically, a big online presence. One click of his name resulted to hundreds of pictures and articles too.

How did he get to ride with us like a normal person? Shouldn't he have an entourage?

I quickly shoved my phone under my pillow when I heard him stir. He didn't get up, though. He looked fast asleep. It was something I should have been doing, too, instead of stalking him online. I closed my eyes and willed sleep to come soon.

CHAPTER TWELVE

EVAN

"Evan." I heard my name being called. It sounded like the person was far away, or maybe I was drifting far away.

"Evan!" There it was again.

It wasn't the best way to start a morning. I hadn't gotten much sleep the past few weeks. I was looking forward to just sleeping in. I fought against bringing my sleepy mind to somewhere near being awake. I wasn't yet ready to get up, but, apparently, I had an alarm clock I knew nothing about. I opened my eyes slowly. The room was dark, which helped my eyes adjust less painfully.

"You better have a good reason for waking me up," I said sternly.

Zac was standing near my bed. He looked quite nervous.

"Uh, breakfast is ready," he said.

I frowned. "What the fuck? It's still dark," I said.

"Actually, it's almost nine," he said sheepishly.

"I'll make my own breakfast," I said and closed my eyes, irritated at being woken up.

"Your dad said he'd really appreciate it if you came down for breakfast with the family," Zac said.

I opened my eyes swiftly. "Tell him I'll make my own breakfast and eat it *alone*," I said.

I wasn't at the beach house to socialize. I didn't even want to be there. I granted Dad his wish and graced him with my presence. I didn't need him telling me what to do every five seconds.

"All right. Well, I tried," Zac said, throwing his arms in the air. He left the room shortly.

After he left, I couldn't fall asleep again. I checked the time on my phone. Zac was right, it was 9 am. The location of the room made it appear darker than most, inaccurately reflecting the time of the day.

I tossed and ended up looking at the ceiling. I had to survive two weeks. Not bad, right? I just had to steer clear of everyone; that was all. There was really no point in forming relationships when the whole thing wouldn't last. My dad played the field. He had numerous girlfriends, some of which couldn't even be older than me.

I got out of bed and changed my clothes swiftly, then freshened up and brushed my teeth. Walking into the kitchen, I found Rosa doing some inventory.

I hugged her from behind.

She smiled. "Your dad is not pleased with you."

"He'll get over it," I said curtly. "Since I missed breakfast, can I have breakfast?"

"You have hands," she said, closing the pantry.

"But Rosa..." I said, and she interrupted.

"What? Your model hands can't do anything?"

"Ouch, you didn't have to go that far. I'll do it myself," I said with a pout.

She gave me a sly smile and walked out of the kitchen.

Rosa was the only woman in my dad's life that was constant. She had been there since I was a few months old. She was brought in to help take care of me and ultimately ended up taking care of everyone. She had a lovely soul, and we got along well. She was the only person in that house I looked forward to spending time with. But knowing her, she'd be busy most of the time.

I started making a breakfast of oats and yogurt.

"Do you have anything else besides orange juice?" I heard a voice coming from the door. "Oh, I thought you were Rosa."

"Check the fridge," I replied, turning to see Zac standing by the door.

He walked past me to the fridge. He grabbed the door handle but didn't open it. Instead, he turned to me.

"Um…Evan…your dad wanted to know if you'd like to go with us to town in a few minutes," he said. He seemed quite uncertain.

"No," I said, delving into my oats.

"Oh…it could be fun," he said. "Everyone is going."

I looked up. "That sounds perfect."

"Excuse me?" he said, fully turning on his heels to face me.

"I am looking forward to having you all gone," I said with a mock smile.

"Oh…are we in your spotlight, Mr. Irresistible?"

"More like my space," I said with a grin.

"I think I've figured out why you want to break our parents up," he said accusingly.

I put down my spoon. "And why is that?"

"You are used to having all the attention on you. Now that daddy's looking somewhere else, it bothers you," he replied confidently.

I laughed. "I couldn't be bothered where he looks."

"That's what you say," he said with the same confident manner. "Your actions speak otherwise."

"You are the cynical sort, aren't you?" I said with a smile on my face.

"Wait, what?"

"You'd rather believe that I'm trying to sabotage our parents than believe I told you the truth out of the goodness of my heart. I have a heart, you know," I said with the same playful smile on my face. The conversation was amusing to me.

"You may have a heart, but you have no proof, and I'm not cynical. I'm a realist," he said, finally taking out grape juice from the fridge.

"Ahh...a romantic," I said.

"How did you get that from this conversation?" He couldn't hide his confusion.

"You look like one," I replied, picking up my spoon.

He stared at me with a frown.

"You don't believe me because that would mean the end of a fairy tale." I theorized.

"I don't believe you because you have no proof, and you likely have ulterior motives," he said, pouring the juice into a glass. "So, are you planning on doing something while we're gone?"

"Absolutely nothing," I replied, continuing to eat.

"So, you're staying to do absolutely nothing?"

"Absolutely," I said. I wasn't lying.

"Okay. In that case, I hope you enjoy," he said, leaving the kitchen with his glass.

"Oh, I will," I said to his back.

* * *

ZAC

Evan was intriguing, from a purely psychological perspective. He smiled and laughed while trying to defend his viewpoint of our parents' relationship. He didn't seem to think much of what he was saying and the repercussions it would have. Mom was the sappy sort like he'd assumed, and if things didn't work out with Mark, she'd be hurt.

His stance of treating the whole thing as a joke gave me an idea of the kind of person he was. He didn't seem to take things seriously. If Mom got wind of what Evan was saying, she'd be worried and cautious even without proof. It would surely put a dent on her and Mark's relationship.

My thoughts unceremoniously drifted to Chase. I found myself thinking about the good times we had together and his famous words, "I never loved you." I found myself breaking just a little bit as I wondered where he was, what he was doing. I had an insane desire to call him, to hear his voice, and to hear him take back all the hurtful things he'd said. My heart ached when I realized just how much I still loved him and how much it still hurt. I was away from college from where our relationship had been concentrated, but it didn't seem to help.

I wondered then what part of Sapphire Beach Town he lived at. How far was he?

* * *

After breakfast, I retreated to the room I shared with Evan. He wasn't there. I took a shower and dressed for our town visit. I finished early, so I called Livy to chat. When I hung up, I had nothing else to do. I found myself logging back in Facebook. I hadn't been on Facebook in a while. It had lost its popularity with me. I skimmed through my News Feed before spotting something that made my heart ache.

Because of my inactivity on Facebook, I hadn't the thought to unfriend Chase. I just never bothered, and at that moment, I wished I already did. Chase had updated his relationship status to *"In a relationship with Bruce Carlisle"*. Both their profile pictures displayed the two of them in a loving embrace.

Chase had never done that with me. He was an active user throughout our relationship but said he wouldn't update his relationship status because it was no one's business. It was no one's business when he dated me, but it was everyone's business when he dated Bruce because Bruce was one to be flaunted to the world, and I was not.

My weak heart ached. I suddenly wanted to toss my phone against the wall. It wasn't so much that their relationship was sickening. It was knowing I had degraded myself by staying when I should have left.

I unfriended Chase and Bruce and everyone else I'd called a friend except Livy.

"Zac!" someone shouted.

I didn't want to walk out just yet. I had no doubt I looked sad, and if my mom saw that, I would never hear the end of it.

Noah walked into the room.

"Mom and Mark are ready to go if you are," he informed me. He didn't seem to notice the sadness on my face and if he did, he didn't say anything about it.

I gave him a small smile and stood up from the bed. "I'm ready."

"Great!" he said, turning back towards the door. "I can't wait to get my own board! I'm gonna train every day until I get it right."

I chuckled half-heartedly as I followed him out. "I'm sure you'll be great," I told him quietly, to which he gave me a grateful smile.

* * *

When we walked to the terrace, we found Mark talking to Evan. It was more like arguing rather than talking.

"I didn't volunteer to come here! So, don't tell me what to do. I just don't feel like going," Evan was saying.

"I would if you stopped acting like a six-year-old!" Mark said.

"I'm not going, that's it," Evan said walking back into the house.

I also didn't feel like going anymore. I was in a foul mood and was just going to spoil everyone's mood. I wanted to sulk like I'd planned. I also didn't fancy meeting Chase. *What if he was in town too?*

"Hey. Uh, guys. I don't think I'll be able to go with you today. I have a headache that doesn't seem to let up," I lied.

"Oh, baby…" Mom and her fussiness began. "Is it bad?" she said, coming to hold my head like that would soothe my nonexistent pain.

"No," I said, wincing a bit. I felt bad about lying, but I knew the truth would only derail the whole trip because Mom would cancel it.

"Maybe I could sta—" she said, and I interrupted.

"Mom! I'm old enough to stay on my own. It's just a headache," I said. "I'll sleep it off."

"Do you want me to stay with you?" Noah said. My family knew how to go above and beyond.

I chuckled. "Go, buddy. You need to choose your board, remember?"

He nodded and ran to Mark's Jeep Wrangler.

"Rosa, can you get Zac some painkillers?" Mark said.

Rosa was already in the car.

"No, I'll get them myself. Just tell me where they are," I said.

"Kitchen, first top door on the right, or in cabinet underneath the basin in the guest bathroom," Mark told me.

"Got it," I said.

"It's a shame you can't go with us, but you can go some other time. Maybe Evan can show you around," he said.

I smiled. Behind that smile, I was hoping that his hope of Evan coming around wasn't misplaced. He refused to come to the table, or when he was there, he was anything but pleasant. He'd said it himself: he'd rather not be there. He would rather be in Paris, modeling some clothes.

"If you get hungry, you know where the kitchen is," Mark said as he descended the last stairs and walked to the car.

I watched him get in, and the engine roared to life.

CHAPTER THIRTEEN

EVAN

After my rather amusing argument with my dad, I walked to the other side of the house, walking out of the doors. I was greeted by the terrace and the mountain overlooking my bedroom. I stood there and just looked at the mountain, which cast a shadow over the house and terrace. I used to love standing there and just looking at the view. This was where I hid. My dad never knew where I went, and he didn't search. It never worried him, though, because in the end, I would always return. We had the beach house since I was two years old so I knew every corner of it. We came here a lot before Mom died and shortly after that. But as I grew, it became a place I didn't want to see.

I looked at the tattoo on my hand. E. F, the initials read. Eva Francis Lowe. My thoughts were suddenly bombarded with incomplete memories that frustrated me to no end. I didn't want to think about it.

"Hey." I heard a voice. I was glad for the interruption even though I was surprised.

I turned just in time to see Zac join me on the terrace.

"It looks peaceful out here," he said.

"It looks like your kind of place," I said with a smirk.

"It doesn't look like a photoshoot set, so I'm shocked to find you here," Zac said with a little smile on his face.

I chuckled. "I thought everyone left."

"Everyone left except me. I have a headache. I just wanted to let you know in case you heard something, and you thought it was a robber or something."

"How'd you find me here?" I asked.

"Followed the stench of a saboteur-wannabe," he said, smiling.

"Must not be potent enough because you've come to the wrong place."

"Oh, it's potent enough. So, what are you up to? Thinking of other ways to ruin their relationship?"

"I'll indulge you. You say what I want is my dad's attention. Yet I'm here, and he's in town," I said.

"You're doing what most brats do when they don't get their way. You're sulking," Zac countered.

"And you're annoying."

"That's a good counterargument." Zac found it necessary to be sarcastic.

"Aren't you supposed to be sleeping your headache off or something?"

He put his hands up in surrender. "Okay, okay. I get the message. I will now leave you to your *sulking*."

* * *

ZAC

I watched TV for what felt like hours. I needed a distraction. Only, I wasn't finding it where I sought it. Thoughts about Chase and Bruce drifted in and out of my consciousness, and flipping through each channel after five seconds wasn't helping.

I was playing with the remote absentmindedly when Evan walked past the living room, back to the room.

"What are you doing?" he asked suspiciously.

"What does it look like I'm doing?" I raised a brow.

"I'm gonna sit by the deck."

"Thought you didn't want company."

"I don't," he said with his nose in the air.

"And yet you're telling me where you're going."

"Just informing you," he said with an almost inaudible "hmph."

I smiled mockingly. "Okay."

He left the room, and I chuckled to myself before switching off the TV and following him outside.

"Can I join you or are you still sulking?" I asked when I got there. Evan was perched on a deck chair, eyes closed.

"Can you keep your mouth shut?"

"I can do that," I said, chuckling slightly.

I selected a deck chair a few feet away from him and leaned back on it, closing my eyes. My eyes weren't even closed for two seconds when Evan's phone rang. I opened my eyes in surprise.

"Evan," he answered curtly.

He didn't say anything for a while, but he was tapping on the chair.

"Okay" was the only word he said, and his phone left his ear. He groaned afterward.

"Bad news?" I risked asking.

There was a bit of silence. "Not really," he finally replied.

"You don't sound or look happy," I said, letting him know my observation.

"Well done, Mr. Psychologist. You are very observant," he said. "Stop fishing." He genuinely looked irritated this time.

"Sorry, my bad," I said.

There was silence between us. I hated it. Silence opened up room for thoughts about Chase which will only torture me. I needed a distraction.

"Do you like modeling?" I questioned Evan, deliberately ignoring the fact that he didn't want to talk.

"Yeah." His answer was abrupt.

"You seem to be really big in the industry."

"Did you Google me?" There was an amused twinkle in his eyes.

"No," I said as if it was the most obvious thing. "Jess knows you, so I just assumed you are."

He seemed to believe me because he didn't prod. Instead, he said, "I like acting. I get to be someone else. I like modeling too. I just hate the hours. There are some good things and some bad things. For instance, I get to be the brand ambassador for David Markham's perfume, which is great. My manager just told me I have to walk for Marc Yaris in Milan because one of the models dropped out. That's in two weeks. The day I 'stole' your cab I had just literally flown in from New York Fashion Week. Dad brought me here to play nice-nice. I already get that a lot from my manager. I don't need it from everyone else! I rarely get to do what *I* wanna do!"

I didn't say anything for a while, surprised by his outburst at the end.

"Look I know having other people in your space isn't great, but Mom is a wonderful person. She—"

"You don't get it!" he said, but he too was interrupted this time by the sound of the car as it drove onto the driveway.

Evan pushed his head back into his seat. I heard a muffled groan.

I stood up and looked out at the car that had just stopped in front of the house. It was the Jeep Wrangler, blue and grey with a tough exterior.

I walked to the guardrails as Noah got out of the car. He looked so excited as he walked with a spring in his step. I realized as he walked to the back that he had gotten what he wanted: a surfboard. I instantly remembered that Chase could surf. I told Chase that Noah wanted to surf, and he'd said he'd teach him when he came to meet the family. That was early on in our relationship, and the words had been spoken lightly, but

I had faith that someday that would come true. I fell fast and hard for Chase, which only ended up biting me in the ass.

I watched as Mark and Noah unfastened Noah's new board, but my attention suddenly shifted to Evan.

"Can you surf?" I asked him.

I saw his jaw tighten. "No." His words were barely audible.

"Why does your dad insist you can surf?"

"Because the idiot doesn't know me," he said angrily and stood up, walking into the house without another word.

That was odd. Could a father not be so in tune with his son that he did not know what his son could and couldn't do?

Mom and Rosa got out of the car. They were carrying grocery bags and went to put them in the kitchen. Noah was still standing at the car, admiring his board. Mark joined me on the deck.

"How's your headache?" he asked with interest.

"All gone," I said.

We stood against the guardrail for a few minutes in silence.

"Can I ask you a question?" I asked.

"Sure."

"Can Evan surf?"

He sighed. "Yes, since he was six."

"Six? He must have been a gifted boy," I said.

"Yeah. We got him a trainer. It was easy for him. It sort of came naturally, I guess. I'd never seen a kid control a board like that."

I nodded and continued looking at Noah.

"He used to love it," Mark said. "Lately, he doesn't, I guess."

"Do you think that's why he's insisting he can't?" I said.

"He's just being a brat!" Mark spewed the words out. "He thinks now that he's famous, he's above everyone. He hangs out with these cool, famous people, and suddenly, he doesn't even want to spend time with his own father."

I didn't know what to say. I always thought my family's presence was the root of Evan's discomfort, but now, I wasn't too sure. Things with his father weren't rosy either.

I looked at the sight of Noah walking to the shed to put his board away before I excused myself to go to my room. When I got to the room, Evan was on the treadmill. He was half-naked, and his glorious body was glistening with sweat.

I stood at the door for a few seconds. Chase had a good body. Bruce's was good too. But Evan's was great. At least, I had a great view. I smiled to myself and ended up chuckling at my thoughts. Bruce had Chase. Evan was such an impossible target; it didn't even make sense thinking about it. Still, that didn't stop me from noticing how attractive he was.

I didn't even see him remove his earpods, and next, he was saying, "Could you please stop staring? I may be used to attention, but you are creeping me out."

I died, and no, I didn't go to heaven. I went to hell where the devil was roasting me in a never-ending fire. Well, that would explain why my cheeks turned red, and the temperature felt like it increased by a million degrees Fahrenheit!

"Sorry, my mind was somewhere else," I said, walking in and closing the door.

He raised a brow, silently asking for details.

"I've always wanted to work out. I just never got time to do it," I said. I wasn't lying. I thought about working out when I found out Chase was cheating. I never got around to doing it, not that it would have mattered.

"You should. It has health benefits. And you already have a good body. Wouldn't take much to turn that into a female magnet," he said, slowing down to a stop.

I prefer male, but thank you, I said in my head.

He said something that sounded like "shower" and walked out of the room.

Without the distraction, my thoughts unceremoniously went to Chase and Bruce.

Bruce had a six pack he liked flaunting. Maybe it was that which attracted Chase. Because it couldn't have been the foul mouth or his rudeness. It had to be something physical.

I was a nice person. I was considerate and kind. I wasn't Mother Theresa, of course, but I *cared* about people. And I wasn't boring; I can have fun too, and my self-esteem was okay. It was okay, right?

I was at a stage where I doubted myself. People build you up just to tear you down. Before Chase, I was okay, and now, I was crumbling like a house of cards. I had made Chase my life without even noticing. He had become the reference for everything. It had to stop. I would not allow myself to think in Chase terms. I would not allow him to dictate my life even when he wasn't in it. Chase had to go.

My phone rang from the bed. I pounced on it. Livy was calling.

"Hi, Olivia," I said with cheer in my voice. I wondered if she could tell it was forced.

"Hey! I know we talked earlier, but how are you?"

"I'm pretty much the same as earlier," I replied.

"Do…do you still think about him?"

I sighed.

"Part of healing is talking about things that hurt you," she said, reminding me of psychological babble.

"There's nothing to talk about," I said, making sure to keep my tone expressionless.

"Tell me about your roomie then," she said.

"Why?"

"Just tell me. Do you guys get along?"

"He's fine."

"Is he hot?"

"What?" I couldn't resist asking. I hadn't told Livy much about Evan except that Mark had a son, and he was at the beach house with us. I also told her we were sharing a room.

"Is he hot?" she repeated, enunciating every word.

"He's okay," I begrudgingly replied.

"A six?" she said.

"Nine," I said without thinking.

"He sounds like a gem. Take a picture."

"I'm not doing that. Besides, you have a crush on someone else," I reminded her.

"Can we not talk about that douchebag and just talk about your stepbrother?" Livy said.

"He's not my stepbrother!"

"Mark has made you guys meet. It's serious," she said.

"Well, my 'stepbrother' is a brat. He's very famous too. Cody Wilde—look him up." I shared.

"Just a sec," Livy said. I heard her gasp. "Oh my god, he's truly a gem."

"And an A-class brat." I repeated.

"You didn't tell me he was famous. He has millions of followers. He's in a movie!" Livy was squealing like a fangirl. "Do you think your stepdad would mind if I show up at the house?"

I chuckled.

She chuckled too, but then she became serious. "Seriously though, Zac, how're you feeling?"

"About Evan?"

"Who's Evan?"

"Cody...Cody is Evan," I clarified.

"Oh, no. About Chase. About being in the same place as him?"

I shrugged as if she could see me. "I don't know."

"Do you think about him?" she asked.

I sighed. "Yeah. No. I mean, I think about how he trashed my heart and how I stayed knowing he was cheating. I don't know if I actually miss him."

"I hope you forgive yourself one day," she said.

"I hope so too, Livy."

At that moment, Evan walked in. He had only a towel wrapped around his lower half. His hair was wet, and tiny drops were trickling from the ends to his perfect torso, making him even more glorious.

"Nothing like a workout and a shower to refresh someone," he said as he ran a hand through his wet hair.

"Is that Cody? Even his voice is sexy!" Livy squealed, snapping me out of checking Evan out. "Sorry, we were talking about you."

"We were done talking about me. I'll be fine," I said into the phone.

Evan thought I was talking to him because he turned to me with a confused face. I showed him my phone.

"How're you?" I asked Livy.

"Still okay since the last time. We went to the beach. We're going to Table Mountain tomorrow."

"That's pretty cool. Enjoy!" I said.

"Thanks. I have to go, though. Speak soon and say hi," she said hastily.

"I'm not doing that. Bye, Livy." I hung up.

When I looked up from my phone, my eyes caught a beautiful view. Evan was standing by the closet in his briefs only, looking in. I could only see his back and butt, but that was already sublime.

He started dressing, wearing blue checked shorts. He didn't wear a T-shirt just yet, deciding to dry his hair first.

My trip home was certainly more than I had hoped, planned or even packed for.

CHAPTER FOURTEEN

ZAC

The next morning, Evan showed up to have breakfast on the terrace, bringing a non-disclosure agreement with him. Evan's people had drawn it up for us to sign. We were to say nothing about certain aspects of his life, online or offline. We couldn't post any status about him or any pictures with him in them. I thought he'd gone overboard, but I signed on the dotted line anyway. I didn't fancy his life.

Mark was not happy with the contract, and they had a very passionate argument about it. Mark must have lost because Evan did not withdraw the document. It was not a good start to the day, and I hoped it would change as the day progressed. It didn't. Mom cornered me to "talk". Mark and Noah excused themselves to look at Noah's board after breakfast. Jess and Evan had excused themselves as well.

Rosa cleared the table, leaving Mom and me at the table.

"This place is beautiful and serene, isn't it?" Mom commented.

"Yeah, it's nice."

"Jess seems less of a monster today."

I nodded.

"How're you?" she asked out of the blue.

"I'm fine," I said quickly, wondering why she asked.

The mystery was soon revealed. "How are you taking the breakup?"

Mom went past caring. She took on the role of mom and dad and maybe took it too far. I knew she was bound to prod about the breakup. I just didn't know she would do it that morning.

"Fine," I said. It wasn't the truth but it wasn't a lie, either. I was certainly doing better than the first few days.

"You know you can talk to me, right?" Mom said softly.

I just smiled, acknowledging her offer.

"Baby, what happened? Things were great. He even invited you to his vacation house."

"Things just didn't work out, Mom."

"'Things just didn't work out'," she reiterated.

"In this case, *they* did," I said.

"Zac, what happened? I know you loved him, and maybe you still do. Maybe you can still fix whatever happened," she said.

"Mom," I said, sighing.

"Zac, I know you didn't have a headache yesterday. You stayed because of Chase. You think I can't see it, but I can. And I see you aren't happy."

"Of course, I'm not happy. He broke my heart!" I said, a little louder than I had intended. I sighed, regretting my tone.

"W-what...?" Mom was confused.

"He...he cheated on me," I said, my voice coming out strained. If I had been trying to hide my feelings, I certainly gave them away with that one sentence.

It opened up wounds. I was not by any shot over Chase, but I was somewhere along the path. I didn't want to think of him—to relapse or yearn for those moments I knew would never happen again. I didn't want to feel hopeless.

"Oh God, I'm sorry, baby," Mom said helplessly.

I chuckled humorlessly. "Remember Bruce?"

"The quarterback? Yes," she said quickly.

"Turns out they'd been having an affair."

I saw mom's eyes widen. "I thought he was your friend!"

"He was, at least he pretended to be."

"What a terrible friend! He does not deserve you. And shame on Chase. He doesn't deserve you, either," she said. "And baby, you'll find that one special guy who won't dream of cheating on you."

"Maybe, but I'm not looking," I said.

"Don't give up hope. There's someone out there for you." I shrugged.

"What did Chase say?" She caught me off guard.

"Hmm?" I said.

"When you found out he cheated? When you broke up with him," she said.

I felt like she'd slapped me with those words. She thought I broke up with him. I didn't. Even after finding out he was cheating, I didn't break up with him. I was pathetic like that. I was willing to be second best as long as it meant I had a tiny bit of Chase. Who else on earth does that? If Chase hadn't broken up with me, we'd still be together, and he'd still be cheating on me.

When I found out about him and Bruce, I'd decided it was best to change myself instead of confronting him about it. I'd been willing to forgive him for cheating, and he didn't even apologize first. I was a fool. I deserved to be cheated on.

I couldn't let my mom know that I had degraded myself to that point. It was embarrassing. My mom held me in high regard, and I couldn't just taint that.

"He said he was sorry," I lied.

"Damn right he should be! To cheat on you and not only that, but to do it with your friend…it's unacceptable!" Mom said. "Are you still friends with Bruce?"

"No," I replied.

I wish Mark and Noah would return now. It was hard lying to my mom.

"Do you think you could ever forgive Chase?"

I nodded.

"Get back with him?"

"Absolutely not! Mom, can we not talk about this?"

She nodded.

"Do you like it here?"

"You are asking like we are moving here," I said, my eyes narrowed.

"Well, we aren't. But we might have some vacations here," she said sheepishly.

I smiled. "I like it."

"And Evan?"

My ears stood up. "What about Evan?"

"How is he?" she asked.

"He's okay," I replied, wondering if she heard something.

"He doesn't seem to talk much."

"Well, he's not thrilled to be here. He said it himself."

"He must hate me," she remarked. It pained me to hear my mom say such words. She was a wonderful person, and the brat was making her feel like she wasn't.

I breathed audibly. "He just needs to get used to the presence of other people in his dad's life. It has nothing to do with you."

"Has he said anything to you?"

"Like what?"

"How he feels about me," she said.

"No," I replied, simultaneously shaking my head. I wasn't lying. Evan hadn't told me how he felt about mom.

Just a few minutes later, Evan walked onto the terrace. He was looking at his phone, typing something.

"Hey, Evan," Mom said brightly.

Evan didn't look up from his phone. Instead, he raised his hand in a little insignificant wave towards my mom. I didn't know what to make of it. Mom didn't either because she looked at me sheepishly. I knew Evan could be rude, but I didn't think he'd be *that* rude.

"Would it hurt you to…?" I began with my usual tone which was replaced by anger, when Evan put his hand up, signaling me to stop.

"Hey, guys! A lot of you have been asking me where I am. So, I am on a tiny weeny break from…*everything*. I decided to hit the coast. It's nothing fancy actually. I'm just…laying low a bit, soaking up some sun and relaxing. I'm actually quite…" Evan started talking into his phone.

I stopped listening, very much aware that he was taking a video of himself. Of course, he was the kind who walked with his phone in the air. I bet not updating his followers on his whereabouts had been eating him up inside.

"No…she's not with me," he said. "Okay, that's it, guys. I will see you some other time."

He lowered his phone, and he turned to me. "You were saying?"

"You didn't have to be rude," I said firmly.

He feigned confusion. "What?"

"Would it have killed you to remove your eyes from your phone and greet my mom properly?"

"If you didn't notice, I was in the middle of something," he replied.

"What I noticed was you being a brat. Wouldn't have taken you much to turn and properly say 'Hi'?"

"Zac, let it go. It's fine. Evan was obviously busy," Mom said hastily. "I'm going to check up on Jess." She stood up and left the terrace.

"You heard your mom. Let it go," Evan said to me.

"You don't have to disrespect her!" I said and stood up, walking away from Evan.

115

* * *

Evan and I stayed out of each other's way after our little argument. He ignored my mom altogether. I thought about why I had been so angry. The incident wasn't that big to garner such anger. I was angry because Mom was getting the raw end of the deal, much like I had. Mom was nice, and Evan was being bratty towards her. I'd been nice to Chase and Bruce, and all they'd done was stab me in the back. It seemed like nice people never win.

Two days passed at the beach house with no incidents. Everyone was just ignoring everyone. Jess was on the phone to her friends back home most of the time. I caught a whiff of the conversation at one time, and she mostly talked about how she hated Mark but had no idea how to break him and Mom apart. Noah had started his surfing lessons. I hadn't seen him yet, but Mark told me he was doing great.

I hadn't interacted with Evan until the day Evan asked for his dad's car to go into town. There were apparently no Jelly Babies in the house, and he was addicted to them. It was a pretty lousy excuse, so I watched him closely. It must not have been enough because his dad decided to throw me into the car with him.

"Only two options, you take Zac with you or you walk," Mark said to Evan. He was sitting in the living area, and Evan was standing.

"Why?" Evan asked with visible irritation.

"Because I don't trust you," Mark said blatantly.

"What the fuck? What do you think I'll do? Drive off a cliff?" Evan said.

"Exactly. You take Zac with you, or you walk. You have less chance of falling off a cliff if you walk, so either choice is good for me," Mark said.

116

"Since you are adamant I should have a chaperone, I'll take Jess," Evan said. He and Jess got along because they were both brats.

"No. You can take Jess *and* Zac," Mark said.

"Zac doesn't even want to go. Right, Zac?" Evan asked, turning to me.

I was sitting on one of the couches, playing with my phone. I raised my head.

"I'd like to," I said slowly, knowing fully Evan wasn't waiting for that kind of answer.

I wanted to take my answer back the moment I said it. I didn't want to go out of the house. I did not fancy being in the car with Evan. I'd probably end up killing him.

Mark looked at Evan triumphantly, silently asking him what his choice was going to be.

"Fine," Evan groaned. "Zac, would you like to hold my hand while I pick out Jelly Babies?" he asked with a mock smile.

Mark chuckled.

Evan went to get the keys, only for Mark to throw them to me. I caught them hastily.

"Don't let him drive," he instructed.

Both Evan and I opened our mouths in surprise.

"Wait, you want Zac to drive?" Evan asked. You couldn't miss the disbelief and irritation in his voice.

"I believe that is why he has the keys," Mark said.

Evan groaned and marched himself to the car. I stood up with uncertainty.

"Don't let him manipulate you," Mark said.

"Sure," I said.

I didn't get why Mark insisted I babysit his son. Evan did need some babysitting, but why did I have to be the babysitter? The guy was an enigma to me, and babysitting him was not something I wanted to do. But admittedly, it would be nice to get out of the house even if it was with Mark's bratty, rude son.

I found Evan waiting impatiently inside the Jeep, and I got into the car in silence.

CHAPTER FIFTEEN

ZAC

"I'm not in the mood to talk, so don't try to initiate any sort of conversation. Got it?"

Those were the first words Evan said to me after I got into the car. He was definitely in a sour mood.

"Sure," I said, shrugging and wondering why I had set myself up for the torture. I could have said no.

I started the car, and the engine roared to life. Soon, we were on the small path that led to the main road. The air rushing around us was amazing. I hadn't known how marvelous it would feel to drive with the sea breeze blowing in my face or I would have asked for the car a long time ago. I enjoyed having the air in my face and hair. It didn't matter that my companion was sulking.

Finally, we got to the main road.

"Can you not drive like an old lady?" Evan asked.

"If you haven't realized, there are twisting curves ahead," I said nonchalantly.

"So? You are way below the speed limit," he said.

"I don't mind. But if you do, you can walk," I said.

"That sounds like a good idea. I can go and get the Jelly Babies faster by walking than with you driving," he mumbled.

"Should I pull over then?" I asked giving him a sickening smile.

"Yes, and move from the driver side," he said.

"Not a fat chance," I said.

I did increase the speed, though, and noticed him nod in approval. We were still going under the speed limit so I could easily maneuver the curves. In the distance, I could see there were a lot of them on a cliff that overlooked the beach.

The beach was beautiful. Only two people were walking along the shores. Mark obviously had the best location. He practically had that side of the beach to himself and his family, and there rarely were people there.

"How come you've never gone down to the beach?" Evan asked.

"I thought you weren't in the mood for talking," I said.

"I'm not, but I find that quite fascinating about you," he said, giving me a smile that didn't even attempt to appear genuine.

I shrugged. "I haven't had the chance."

"Busy sucking up to my dad?"

I chuckled. "Something like that."

He looked me over for a few seconds. I was paying attention to the road, but I could see him in my periphery.

"I can see why he likes you," he said.

"What?" I said, taking a curve. From then onwards, it was straight road ahead.

"Well, you drive like an old lady," Evan said, shrugging.

I stole a look at him. "He likes me because I drive responsibly?"

"Yeah, exactly. You are responsible, focused—all those boring things," he said.

"Oh. And what are you?"

"Fun," he said confidently.

"Being responsible does not equate to boring."

"Yes, it does." He disagreed. "You look like you have a stick up your ass, no offense."

120

"Just because you say 'no offense' doesn't mean what you say is not offensive. And I'll have you know, I know how to have fun while being responsible."

"Of course, you do," Evan said. He didn't sound like he believed me. *Why did I have a feeling he was setting me up to do something dangerous in the name of fun?*

He fiddled with the car radio until he found a radio station he liked. They were playing a song I had never heard—modern but tinged with 80s aesthetics. It was a nice song, which I found myself moving along my head to.

Evan was doing the same, and as our eyes collided with the vision of us moving our heads in the tune of the song, we smiled. His smile was subtler than mine, but I knew he did. It was a strange scenario, but it didn't feel awkward at all.

I focused on the road, wondering what the guy next to me was thinking. I didn't get to make some guesses since the remaining journey was short, and soon we arrived in town.

It was a nice town. The streets were quiet, and the air was mesmerizingly fresh. It was nothing like the cities. It was serene with a small number of people moving about its streets and spacious with large pavements for walkers and small restaurants for the food enthusiasts. I spotted a few beach bars as we delved more into town. I spotted more buildings too, many of them old and weathered. They fit in well with the lazy and relaxed vibe of the town.

"So where am I going?" I asked my companion.

"There's a convenience store just at the corner, carries all small stuff. Unless you want something major, then we'll have to go to the grocery store two blocks away," he replied.

"Convenience store, it is," I said, smiling.

I drove further and managed to get parking just outside the store. Evan and I got out. I stretched my legs, and soon we were walking into the store. I didn't intend on buying anything, so I felt like a chaperone.

Evan picked up his Jelly Babies. He picked out about five packets. Some people spotted him, and he spent some time talking to them and taking pictures. They weren't rowdy, though. I felt awkward just standing there, so I walked outside to wait for him.

"So, what's with the Jelly Babies?" I asked when he walked to me. I'd seen about five packets in his closet.

He shrugged. "I just like them."

"More like addicted."

"Let me guess, you are busy diagnosing me in your head."

I chuckled. "Do you think psychologists walk around diagnosing people?"

"Don't they?"

"Of course not," I said, playing with my fingers.

"Oh, but I bet you've already diagnosed me."

I narrowed my eyes. "Do you think there's something wrong with you?"

"I'm perfect," he said, flashing that lovely smile he possessed. Sure, that was the most egotistical thing I'd ever heard, but I couldn't help but smile with him.

"Anosognosia is a symptom of many psychiatric conditions," I said jokingly.

"Ano...what the hell is that?" he asked, looking at me all baffled.

"Lack of insight," I said.

"So, what you are saying is I am unaware of a mental condition I have?"

"Exactly," I said chuckling slightly.

"Hit me with a diagnosis."

"Based on your addiction to Jelly Babies?"

He shrugged. "I don't know what you want to base it on, but you say I lack insight, so hit me with what you've got," he said.

"Narcissistic personality disorder, substance abuse disorder, separation anxiety disorder…" I jokingly said.

He chuckled sweetly.

"You are going to be terrible," he remarked.

"Well, for a diagnosis I would have to take a proper case—know what you do, what others say about you."

"Well, I can tell you right now. I don't have any of those things you mentioned."

"Sure," I said, smirking.

There was a bit of a silence before I said, "Maybe we should get going before someone else spots you?"

"Does it bother you?" he asked accusingly.

"What? No. I just thought maybe it bothers you," I said quickly.

"This is a quiet beach town, and I've actually lived here for a while. I don't get all that much attention."

"Oh. We should probably get going still. Your dad…"

"You should really learn to stop being uptight," he interrupted.

"Responsible," I corrected.

Evan was right about me being uptight, and I knew it. I planned on spending the whole spring break being miserable. A part of me still wanted that.

"I thought we should explore the town. I can—"

"No. We got what we came here for. We're going home," I said.

"Damn, you're really boring," he said. He somehow hoped those words would change my mind, but I just looked at him. "Okay. We can go. Can I at least drive?"

I shook my head.

"You get to relax. You get to just sit and be driven around by Cody Wilde."

"I don't even know who Cody Wilde is," I teased.

"What do you want? An autograph? A picture?"

I chuckled. "I want to go back to the beach house."

"I agreed to that, didn't I? I'll drive like an old lady."

I shook my head. "Your dad said—" I said, but he interrupted.

"My dad doesn't have to know. We'll change seats when we are close to the house," he said.

"Your dad must have a good reason for not letting you drive."

"He doesn't! He just wants to spite me for this morning. Why on earth would I intentionally drive off a cliff with myself in the car?" he said.

He had a point, but I doubted Mark thought he'd do it intentionally.

"Pretty please," he said out of the blue. He kind of looked cute begging me. My resolve was getting thinner with every second that passed.

I sighed and handed him the keys slowly, hoping I wouldn't regret that decision.

"Promise you'll be careful and give me control before we get home. I don't want to get into trouble."

"I promise. I'll give you the car. I'll help you kiss daddy's ass."

I gave him a stern look.

He put his hands in the air. "Sorry! What do they call it nowadays?" he said, chuckling.

"Hey!" I warned.

"Sorry, sorry, sorry," he said, but he was still chuckling.

I shouldn't have gotten so sidetracked, especially because I trusted him with something that wasn't mine, but I found myself mesmerized by his pearly whites. No one could have teeth that white without a visit to a cosmetic dentist. Either way, he had perfect teeth and a gorgeous smile. It didn't help that the sun was shining on him.

He unlocked the car and got in. I followed soon. He started the car and turned the radio on. It was the same radio station we had listened to on our way to town, and they were playing the same modern song with some of the musical elements characteristic of the 80s mixed in.

We drove for a while listening to the music. It was relaxing. We didn't say a word to each other, and it was comfortable. He was driving at a reasonable speed and hadn't swayed once or applied the brakes harshly which was a good sign. What could go wrong?

"Can I take a detour?" he asked suddenly.

"No," I replied.

"Thought you'd say that," he said as we neared a curve. Instead of following the road to the curve, he turned left to a dirt road I hadn't even known existed.

"Evan, what did you promise me?" I asked loudly.

He shrugged. "Promises are meant to be broken. I want to show you something."

Seriously, what could go wrong?

"Whatever you want to show me better be good," I said.

We drove on the dirt road for a few minutes. I could see white sands far up ahead. I could smell the ocean. He was taking me to the beach. Before we got to the beach, he made a bumpy turn, and the car seemed to be going downhill. I could still smell the ocean, but I could smell the earth more. We came upon a small hill that hid the beach from our eyes, making the place darker. I couldn't see the beach anymore, but I could still smell the ocean.

"Where...where are we going?" I asked uncertainly.

"We are here," he said, giving me a mischievous grin. "Relax, I'm not kidnapping you. Though, that could serve a purpose."

"Hey!" I said sternly.

"Would it kill you to relax?"

The car came to a stop. We were at the entrance of what looked like a cave. Evan got out. I stayed put in my seat.

"You brought me here?" I asked.

He shook his head. "I took the detour for my benefit, not yours. So, I brought *myself* here. You just happened to be with me."

"Okay, what are you doing here?" I asked.

"Exploring," he said and started walking. "Are you going to get out of the car or stay there?" he said as he stopped and turned back to me.

"I'm not sure this is safe."

"City kids."

Did he—the model—just call me a city kid?

I got out of the car and followed him to the entrance of whatever the hell was standing in front of us. I caught up with him just at the entrance. The area smelled like earth, salt, and something peaceful. We walked into the cave. It was a large spacious area surrounded by rock walls. It wasn't exactly a proper cave. It had large and small openings on the sides, giving us a view of the clear ocean. It also had an opening at the top as well. All in all, the place was beautiful and serene. In the middle, rocks seemed to grow out of the ground in various sizes. Evan walked further to an opening, and I just stood mesmerized at what I saw. The rocks growing in the middle had crystal-like substances on their ends. Light shone through them, making them even more beautiful. I went to touch some.

"I wouldn't do that if I were you. Legend says one touch of those sapphires and the cave will completely seal in all directions," came a voice out of nowhere.

Evan was at one of the openings, leaning on the wall. He wasn't looking at me when he said those words.

I chuckled. "I suppose you don't fancy being stuck here with me? I know how to make fire and stuff."

He looked at me and smiled, hands in his shorts pockets.

"I don't fancy being stuck anywhere with anyone."

I touched the rocks. They felt like…rocks. I didn't know what I expected them to feel like.

"What's this place?" I asked.

"It was once one of several sapphire mines."

"It's quite nice," I commented.

I walked to where he was standing. It was like the window of the cave. Unlike the main opening which was at sea level and covered with sand, the opening Evan was at was a bit elevated. If you stood there and looked down, you could see greenish-blue water.

Evan wasn't quite at the edge.

"Wow. The water is pristine," I remarked in awe.

Evan didn't say anything. He seemed to be thinking about something. His back was rigid. He was looking ahead but didn't seem to be seeing anything. It looked like he was having an absence seizure. Okay, maybe I'm exaggerating, but there was something strange about the way he was looking out into the ocean.

"Aren't we trespassing or something?" I asked.

"Does it look like anyone is trying to keep us out of here?" It was a statement more than a question.

"How come you know about it?"

"I told you I grew up here. I discovered it on...some random day," he replied. He wasn't looking at me.

A crazy thought came to mind, inspired by our conversation earlier on our way to town.

"I dare you to jump into the ocean," I said clearly.

"What?" he said, looking at me as if I was insane.

"I dare you to jump into the ocean," I repeated without faltering.

"You're crazy," he remarked.

"You said I don't know how to have fun. I…"

"That doesn't even make sense, you dummy. It would if you were the one jumping in, not me," he said.

"Well, I'll jump in after you do," I said, looking down into the water. The drop wasn't scary.

He shook his head.

"The model is scared he'll get his hair wet?"

"I am not jumping in there," he said with finality.

"So much for 'fun' guy," I said.

"Whatever."

"What are you so scared of?"

"Nothing," he said through gritted teeth. "We should go."

"We just got here," I said.

"And I'm saying we should go," he repeated firmly.

"Such a little baby," I teased.

"Fuck!" he swore. "Can't you just fucking let it go?"

"No need to be so uptight," I said.

"Can we freaking just go?!" he yelled. The amount of agitation in his voice shocked me. While he'd looked expressionless for the most time he stood there, on his face was displayed something akin to anger now. His sculpted eyebrows met in a frown and his jaw looked taut.

"All right, all right. Geez," I said and followed him out of the cave.

I couldn't tell what had just happened. Evan was fun, and suddenly, he was yelling at me. I couldn't tell why he was so pissed. Sure, I called him a baby, but I was only teasing. His reaction was just too much.

When we got to the car, he passed me the keys, indicating that I should drive. I thought about his reaction as I started the engine, and we proceeded to leave the cave. I just couldn't put two and two together. I had to ask.

"What was that all about?"

"You should learn to let things go," he quietly informed me.

"You tell me I'm uptight, and then you almost go all Godzilla on me," I reminded him.

"Zac, shut up!" was the only thing he said.

We didn't talk after that. I occasionally looked at him. He seemed better than earlier, but every now and then, when he thought of something he didn't like, I couldn't miss the frown lines. When we got home, he totally changed. The easygoing guy was replaced by the egotistic model. He said a few rude words to Mom and fought with Mark again.

    I couldn't diagnose him. And without a diagnosis, I didn't know what sort of treatment to try. I wanted to find common ground for Mom's sake, establish some sort of relationship. I wanted to understand him. Instead of focusing on Jess, Evan was taking up my time. I was now taking an interest in him that had nothing to do with Mom. *Was I making him my pet project?* It was a way some people dealt with loss, and in this case, a breakup. Studying somebody else, solving somebody else…solving the case. He was the distraction.

CHAPTER SIXTEEN

ZAC

"Evan, I will not ask you again. Did you touch my phone?!" Mark's voice bellowed from the terrace. He'd been on the terrace with Evan for the last five minutes. They'd been talking in hushed tones, but now, Mark was visibly angry.

I was inside the house in the living area. The sun was just setting, so it wasn't yet dark outside. There was an orange tinge on the horizon. In a few minutes, it would be dark.

"I didn't touch your freaking phone!" Evan shouted.

I wasn't the only one who was listening to the conversation. We were all in the living area, and the door was open. Besides, the way they were shouting made it seem like they wanted us to hear them.

"Only you would have the guts to touch it!" Mark said. "If not, then who?"

"How the hell am I supposed to know? Do I look like your personal assistant?" Evan said.

"I know it was you. When the hell will you grow up?" Mark shouted.

"*I* need to grow up? Oh, wow. Maybe I will. When you start becoming a decent father!" Evan spat.

I saw the worried look on Mom's face. She couldn't stand it any longer that Evan and Mark were fighting. She started standing up.

"Mom, sit!" I ordered.

"But…" She started, but I cut in.

"It's their fight, let them solve it," I told her.

She sat down hesitantly. I knew it was hard for her to do that, but she needed to learn to let people deal with things their own way. I included.

"…father you don't even deserve! I've tolerated your childish behavior more than any father would." I caught the end of Mark's words.

"Really? You have the nerve to stand here and tell me you've been a decent father?" Evan said. "Maybe that bitch of yours was right; I am so worthless I don't even deserve a decent father."

That was heavy.

"Typical Evan, blaming everyone else but yourself," Mark said. He seemed unfazed by Evan's words.

"I don't have time for this shit!" Evan shouted.

"Of course, you don't. The only thing you know is run away!" Mark said.

"Maybe I wouldn't run if there was nothing to run away from!" Evan said. His voice sounded broken.

He must have stormed off because Mark shouted. "Evan! Get the hell away from my car."

Seconds later, I heard the sound of a car speeding off. Mark stormed into the house.

Mom walked to him. "Shouldn't you follow him?" she asked quickly.

"Why should I?" Mark asked curtly.

"Mark, he's not thinking straight," Mom begged.

"He just wants attention."

"Either way, he could hurt himself, or something could happen."

Mark threw his hands in the air. "Where the hell am I supposed to go looking for him? He could be anywhere. He could be wherever he settled for a week or so. He never sits still."

"I...I think I know where he went," I said uncertainly.

"Where?" Rosa asked.

"It's quite hard to describe. I could go...look for him?" I suggested to Mark.

"Is it far?" Mom asked with concern.

"No, but I'm going to need a car."

"Noah, get your brother my car keys," Mom said urgently.

"You people are just wasting your time. I know my son. This is typical of him. He always runs away when things don't go his way," Mark said.

Noah looked at Mom after Mark's words. "Go!" she shouted.

"He wants attention, and you are just giving it to him," Mark retorted.

"Maybe I am not the best parent..." Mom said and looked at Jess for a few seconds before looking at Mark and continuing, "...but I can recognize a broken voice."

"He's an actor for goodness' sake!" Mark said, unfazed.

Noah returned and handed me the keys.

"Go!" Mom said. "If you find him, call us."

I don't know why I volunteered, but I found myself walking outside to Mom's car. Maybe I was taking this babysitting project thing way too far. Mark was probably right. Maybe Evan wanted attention.

But I'd heard the broken voice too.

Besides, if Evan wanted attention, he certainly wanted Mark's, not mine. Me being the one looking for him would certainly not lead to him achieving his agenda.

I got into the car and raced to the place I thought he would be at. I initially meant to drive to town, but I remembered the place he'd taken me to the previous day. I didn't know why I hoped he'd be there, but it was the only other place I could think of.

I kept my eyes peeled for the turn he took the other day. When I couldn't see it, I thought I'd passed it. But then I saw a dirt road come out of nowhere on the left side. I made the turn hastily and prayed it was the right road. I drove on for a few minutes. The SUV was vibrating uncontrollably. I made a bumpy turn, and the road seemed to become steep. I was definitely on the right road.

I saw the Jeep Wrangler before I got to the entrance of the cave. I parked the SUV and got out. Evan wasn't in the car.

I made my way to the entrance and just stood there. It was almost dark, and inside the cave, it looked even darker. I swallowed a lump. *What could possibly be hiding in the cave besides the boy who'd run away from his dad?*

I walked in. I spotted a figure at one of the windows, where Evan had been standing just the previous day. I swallowed another lump and walked to it. It occurred to me that someone could have hijacked Evan and drove to the cave. It was a preposterous thought.

Evan spotted movement. He was standing at the edge like he'd been intending to jump. It was quite strange that he only noticed my presence then. *Wouldn't he have heard the car pull up outside?*

He turned to me, and I watched as his face displayed recognition and then anger.

"What the fuck are you doing here?!" he shouted.

"Just wanted to see if you were okay."

"Like the fuck you care, you suck ass."

"What are you doing here?" I asked.

"You people are just bloody impossible! You won't get the fuck out of my life, and when I try to distance myself, you follow me," he shouted. He was really angry.

"Look, I can go. I just wanted to make sure you are okay."

"Go! Go back to your fucking perfect new family. But trust me, it won't last," he yelled.

"You need to stop acting like a brat. You don't want a stepmom, I get it!" I yelled back.

"You fucking get nothing!" "Then enlighten me!"

"I am sick and tired of you! Can't you just freaking leave me alone?!"

"You fucking need to grow up, you asshole!" I yelled. I was getting angry too. Evan was saying a lot without saying anything. It was frustrating. I turned to leave.

"I need to grow up? You need to fucking open your eyes and grow a pair!"

His words had me turning towards him. "What the fuck?"

"You're such a wimp. A suck ass. No wondered Chase lied and cheated on you!"

I couldn't fathom what I was hearing. Evan knew about Chase. I didn't care how at that moment. Evan was using Chase to hurt me in an argument that had nothing to do with him. I snapped.

I don't know how I did it, but I found my hands around his throat. I was raging with fury. He'd awoken something in me I never knew existed. It was all the pent-up anger I had suppressed after I found out Chase was cheating on me. The sheer amount of it was scary even to me.

"Don't you fucking dare bring my relationship into this. You know nothing about it!" I said.

"I know enough. He cheated on you, yet you stayed. He cheated on you with your friend. Brent…Bry…Bruce!" he said with a smile. "You have the guts to call me a brat, and yet, people trample all over you."

"At least I'm not selfish," I spat.

"Yeah, you're just a spineless doormat," he said. "How about you stop telling me how to live my life and focus on your trashy one?"

My anger was bubbling.

"Get your freaking hands off me!" he yelled.

He struggled to remove my hands from him, pushing and shoving. I tightened them. I was never the violent type, but I couldn't help but want to shove him away from me hard. That's what I did. I didn't count on there being nothing but air behind him and didn't foresee him falling through the cave window into the water below. But that's just what happened.

I stood in shock at what I had just done. I had just thrown Mark's son into the ocean. Shock turned into mirth. I couldn't help but chuckle.

I—the so-called wimp—had done that!

I looked down into the water after I heard a splash. What I saw brought shock back to the forefront. Evan wasn't swimming or floating. He was *struggling* against the water. He went down and then came up again. A few seconds later, he went down again, fighting with the water.

What the...?

The bastard couldn't swim!

Either he didn't know how to, or he hit something that hurt him. Panic rushed through me. I didn't think about what to do or how to do it. I didn't think of how angry I felt. I took off my t-shirt and laid it down on the cave floor along with my phone and dived through the window into the ocean. Sure, he wasn't Evan's biggest fan at the moment, but Mark would never forgive me if I killed his son. I would never forgive myself.

CHAPTER SEVENTEEN

ZAC

The water was cold. I felt it initially, but adrenaline kicked in. I swam to where Evan was, ignoring the way my wet pants clung to me. My heart was beating faster. I had to save him, come hell or high water. He wasn't my favorite person, but he didn't deserve to die.

The moment I got to him, he extended his hands to my arm and clung to me like I was a life raft. His weight and the water were heavy on me, pulling me down.

"Evan! Stop moving," I ordered.

He didn't seem like he was going to. I moved my legs to trap his under the water. That seemed to slow him down a bit. I took that moment to try and position myself around him. He wouldn't let my arm go. If I had some thoughts that he might have been pretending to drown, those thoughts were erased.

"Evan, give me two seconds," I said loudly.

He started struggling even more. His struggles led to him loosening his grip. I took the moment to swim behind him and grabbed him by the waist. The first thing I noticed was that his body was trembling next to me, although the water wasn't that cold. *Why was he shaking so badly?*

The second thing I noticed was that we weren't in deep waters at all. It was not that far from the shore, yet Evan had been struggling like he was in the middle of the ocean. There were no strong waves. It was a calm night.

I tightened my grip around him and began swimming to shore. I wasn't the best swimmer, and sidestrokes were not my forte, but I managed to swim with Evan out of the water. It was a test of endurance, and I was exhausted by the time we got to shore, even though it wasn't that far. Evan had been clinging to me, weighing me down.

When we got to shore, I stood up and helped him up. He didn't loosen his grip on me, and his trembling didn't stop. He closed his eyes, and I helped him walk into the cave. My feet picked up sand as we walked, but it was the least of my worries. I had to make sure Evan was fine and assure him he was safe.

The cave was dry and shielded us from the night air which had gotten colder because of how wet we were. I walked Evan to the eroded cave wall, going to the step-like areas which could be used as seats. I sat him down and looked him over. I couldn't see any cuts or blood.

I ran to where I left my t-shirt and phone. I picked them up and removed some of the dirt that had settled on my shirt.

I walked to where Evan was sitting. He was still trembling. I thought of taking him home but decided against it at that moment. I'd have to explain how he nearly drowned.

I sat next to him. He was looking at his shoes, which were covered in sand.

"Are you okay? Did you hit something?" I asked.

He surprised me by shaking his head.

"Are you sure you're not hurt?"

He nodded. Okay, we weren't at the "words" stage yet.

"My t-shirt is dry. It's not much, but maybe you could wear it," I said.

He didn't say anything. I stayed quiet too. The cave was silent. I thought about the situation as we sat there. There was just something odd about it. Things didn't make sense. The way Evan was acting didn't make sense. Sure, nearly drowning was scary, but Evan's reaction was that of a little boy. He looked deathly scared.

I turned to ask him if I should take him home just as he turned to me and offered his hand for me to place my t-shirt in. I obliged, slightly relieved that he was actually doing something other than tremble and stare at his feet.

I watched him take off his t-shirt slowly, and saw his body glistening with water in the moonlight. Without his t-shirt on, I could see just how much he was trembling. I watched him as he wrung his hair to get some of the water out and put on my t-shirt. It instantly got wet in some parts, but it was better than his totally soaked shirt.

I looked at my naked abdomen. I was starting to feel cold. Since Evan wasn't saying anything, I decided to do something. He said he wasn't hurt, which meant he'd been capable of swimming himself out of the water. So, why hadn't he?

I went onto the internet with my phone and looked up any reference of Cody Wilde and swimming. There was nothing. His phobias only listed spiders and insects. There was nothing about water. There was also nothing about him not being able to swim. Interestingly, surfing wasn't there either.

I turned to him. "Do you want to go home?" I asked softly.

He shook his head.

I acknowledged his answer. Seconds passed by before I noticed something. He was trembling even more. It didn't make sense. It wasn't *that* cold. I couldn't offer him a jacket or make his clothes dry instantly. There was, of course, the shelter of the car and the heater, but at the moment I didn't think of it.

Instead, I thought of how I was stupid to throw Evan into the water. He seemed wholly traumatized by the situation.

I hadn't forgotten the things he'd said, but even that couldn't stop the guilt racking me.

"I'm sorry," I whispered.

That certainly didn't stop him from trembling. I instinctively put an arm around his shoulders. He didn't react. I put my other arm on the same shoulder, effectively pulling him towards my chest. The one around his back lowered until it was around his waist. His head lay against my chest. He didn't resist at any point. If my body heat didn't do the trick, I didn't know what would.

I knew the position was slightly awkward, but I hoped he didn't reject it. It was the only thing I could do to stop him from shivering.

I held him for a few seconds, feeling him tremble against me. My right arm lowered from his shoulder to his abdomen. Instantly, I felt a drop of water on my hand. And then I realized something. Evan wasn't just trembling because he felt cold, he was crying.

I wrapped my arms around him a little tighter than before, hoping to transfer as much body heat as possible. His wet hair on my bare chest was a little uncomfortable, but I ignored it.

"I'm sorry," I whispered again. "I didn't know. If I knew, I wouldn't have pushed you."

Again, he didn't say anything.

"I really am sorry," I said.

I didn't feel I had the full story, but I felt guilty as hell. Evan was in distress, and it was my fault. He didn't look like the Evan I shoved a few minutes ago. He looked vulnerable, beaten, and bruised.

I didn't know if it was my words, but his trembling was lessening.

I noticed that my t-shirt on him had pulled up a little bit on his abdomen, showing his bellybutton. I moved my hand to move it so it could cover him, but when I touched his abdomen, he put his hand over mine, stopping my movements.

"I just wanted to move the shirt down," I explained.

He moved his hand slowly as if he was unsure whether to trust me or not. I pulled his t-shirt down and put my hand over it. I could feel his abdomen move up and down as he breathed.

"Take deep breaths, and breathe slowly," I advised.

He listened to my advice. His abdomen was no longer moving rapidly. He seemed calmer. We sat like that for a while. He was no longer trembling and possibly no longer crying. I couldn't see his eyes, but he was calm. There was no reason for him to still be in my arms, but I still held on to him. It was comfortable, and admittedly, it felt good in the cold night air.

Evan coughed.

"Can I ask you something?" I started. "Your dad says you can surf, but how can you surf if you don't know how to swim?"

Silence.

Maybe it wasn't the right time to ask him. Nearly drowning was already too much to deal with.

"Would you believe me if I said my dad doesn't know anything about me?" He finally said something, his words intruding into my thoughts. He seemed to be amused.

"I don't know," I said. "I did ask him. He seemed certain you could surf since you were six."

"Is that why you pushed me into the water?" he asked. His tone hadn't changed. That was good.

"Again, I'm really sorry about that. It wasn't my intention." I apologized. "I mean, I pushed you because you were a jackass. I didn't think you'd actually fall into the ocean."

"So, you expected me to hit the wall instead?" he said calmly.

I sighed. "At that moment, I really didn't care what happened to you."

I should have removed him from me by then, but I didn't. He didn't move, either. The position was just naturally comfortable.

"I guess you're not a wimp after all," he said. He didn't seem angry anymore.

"Back to my question," I said. "How can you surf and not be able to swim?"

There was silence. We could hear the waves crashing against rocks. Evan was no longer trembling, but he wasn't saying anything either.

"I can swim," he said finally. "At least, I know how to."

"What the hell do you mean by that? Did you fake drowning?" I asked. I was ready to toss him into the water again.

"No," he said and took a labored breath. "I'm…I…I'm deathly scared of water. I panicked."

"I'm confused. You can swim, but you are deathly scared of water?" I asked.

There was a strained silence. I heard a sob before he said, "When I was nine, I nearly drowned. Um…it wasn't…it was…I wasn't alone."

CHAPTER EIGHTEEN

ZAC

I instinctively held him tighter. I could feel the pain in his voice. That incident hadn't been just a black spot in his life. It had been very significant. His fear of water showed that. It could be seen as irrational to some, but he clearly hadn't moved on from it.

"Was your mom with you?" I asked cautiously.

He shook his head. "My mom was already dead."

"Your dad then?" I asked.

"My stepmother," he replied curtly. His tone was just dead.

"What happened?" I asked.

"She was the first woman my dad dated after mom died. It was just months after. He thought I needed someone to take care of me, so he dumped me with her. But she wasn't up to the task. She only signed up to be the trophy girlfriend, not take care of a bratty nine-year-old. So, she tried to get rid of me," he said.

I think my heart stopped beating for a few seconds. My eyes widened.

"You mean she tried to drown you?" I asked.

Evan didn't say anything. His increased breathing, though, said a lot.

"Ev—"

"Dad didn't believe me. Everyone said I wasn't properly dealing with losing my mom, so Dad sent me away. Just like that," he said. His voice sounded so strained. I didn't want to remind him, but I was curious.

"Where did he send you?" I asked.

"Where all the undisciplined lying brats go—boarding school. I was nine then. He visited—with her. I stopped hoping he would come alone, so I started refusing to see him when he did," he said.

"That must have been awful," I said.

"Not many people get to have dinner with a person who tried murdering them. I had breakfast, lunch, and dinner," he said. His tone was of jest, but I knew he wasn't in good spirits. His body was tense. "My dad doesn't even know I freeze in water. He never noticed. He never even noticed that I stopped surfing after the incident. He knows nothing about me."

My heart clenched. Evan was egotistical and rude, but deep inside, Evan was a scared little boy whose childhood had been stolen from him. It pained me to hear the pain in his voice, to feel the tension in his muscles. I couldn't see his face, but I knew I would buckle if I did.

I was a psychologist in training. One of my modules included patient counseling. I had done patient counseling practicals with real cases. I'd heard stories of grief and other sad stories. One of the things I was taught was not to care too much. Today, I was pushing my education aside for Evan.

I had started caring for him. A part of me wanted to get him away from his misery.

"Yesterday, when we were here…" I said and trailed.

He took a deep breath. "This place was like a sanctuary for me. I used to come here to get away from my stepmother. I would sit by the window and just look at the ocean. One day, she followed me. That was the day she tried to drown me. She found me here and dragged me into the water. She knew people didn't come here. She put my head down into the water a couple of times…but then, she stopped. I don't know if she heard something or her conscience hit her, but she left me in the water and drove off." He sniffed. "I hadn't been here until yesterday. I thought…I thought I'd feel that serenity I once felt, but the moment I saw the water, I just remembered swallowing water and struggling for air."

"It must have been awful," I remarked. "And I teased you…" I said regretfully.

He sniffed and moved slightly. "What's my diagnosis?" he asked suddenly. He looked up at me.

I shook my head.

"PTSD, isn't it?" he said.

"Evan, I don't want to diagnose you," I said.

He chuckled humorlessly. "You know you do. That's why you are here, listening. That's what you guys do. You sit there and listen so you can have a diagnosis. The diagnosis is what's important, isn't it? You need to have a name so you can shove me into a category. I was diagnosed with prolonged grief disorder, also known as PGD. What's your diagnosis, Mr. Psychologist?"

"I don't want to diagnose you," I repeated. "It's obvious what happened haunts you. You need to talk to someone—"

"My dad never calls to ask me how I'm doing. He only calls to tell me where he wants me to be who he wants me to be. Do you know what happened with Stepmother Number Two? She slapped me in front of him. He only told me to suck it up and stop disrespecting her."

He quickly jumped from the nearly drowning trauma to issues with his father as if the trauma was irrelevant. He was definitely not over it.

"Mom is…" I said, deciding to go with his pace and not drag him back.

"This is not about your mom! I keep telling you. You don't get it. It's about *him*! It's about all the torture he put me through but still expecting me to smile. I don't want to be here because it taints every good memory I have of being here—when Mom was alive, when Dad wasn't just...*a person* in my life," he said. "I'm sure your mom is a wonderful person, but *he doesn't deserve her.*"

"Maybe you should tell him—" I said, but Evan interrupted.

"You heard our earlier conversation, didn't you? We don't get along, and we'll never get along. When Mom died, our bond broke. He saw me as the brat he was *forced* to raise," he said. "Oh God, I can't believe I told you all this." His tone was one of regret.

"Your secret is safe with me. I signed a non-disclosure agreement, remember?" I said with a chuckle but turned serious when he just looked at me. "Evan, I won't tell anyone and not just because you might sue me for money I don't have. I wouldn't do that to you, or anyone else. I'm not like that. I know it took a lot for you to tell me all these things."

He looked down and moved out of the embrace. I even forgot I still had my arm around him.

"You're a good guy, Zac. I'm sorry too."

I looked at him expectantly.

"You want me to say it all out?" he said. "Geez. I'm sorry I've been crappy around your family. I took out my anger on my dad on you guys. I'm sorry about all the things I said involving Chase. I don't—"

"Stop. Don't tell me you don't think I'm weak. I am. I stayed in a relationship without even confronting Chase about his cheating and hoped everything would just go away."

"You loved him."

"Still makes me weak."

"Okay, I've never felt like you had or been in that situation, but I really think you're strong. You...," he said and sighed, "I do think it was weak of you to stay, but it's pretty much strong of you to not take it out on everyone. You still want your mom to be happy, and you're not going psycho over Chase and Bruce. You're stronger than you think."

I felt my heart swell up hearing Evan's words. His words got to me and dispelled my self-doubts and self-condemnation. He'd seen my strength when I hadn't.

"Thanks," I said.

"For what?"

"I don't know," I said and shrugged. "For your words."

He smiled a little. "I still think you're boring."

"Do you want to end up in the ocean again?" I said with a smile.

He chuckled. "That was pretty cool actually. I'll give you that."

"You could have died!" I reminded him. *What was wrong with him?*

"You did traumatize me, but…that anger was so liberating, wasn't it?"

"Oh, so now you're a Samaritan," I mocked.

He just chuckled.

"How do you even know about Chase and Bruce?"

"Heard you talking to your mom and while you were on the phone with your friend," he explained.

"You don't have manners." "Shh, this moment has proven it was necessary."

"What was the fight between you and your dad about?" I found myself asking.

He moved his body slightly away from me and rubbed his face with his hands. "I went through his phone."

"Why?" I couldn't help but ask.

"To find the proof you so want," he said.

"And?"

"None so far. I'll find it eventually," he said.

"Maybe he's not cheating, Evan. You're the cynical one," I said.

"He's cheating," he said confidently.

"Could it be that you just don't want him to be with a wonderful person because you feel he doesn't deserve to be happy?" I said cautiously.

"Think what you want, Zac," he said, standing up. He didn't sound offended, just resolute.

There was silence in the cave before someone chose that moment to call me, filling the cave with the sound of my ringtone. I removed my phone from my pocket.

"Mom" was splashed on the screen.

I answered hastily, "Hello?"

"Zac, thank God! I've been worried sick. Have you found him?"

"Uh, yeah. I'm sorry, I should have called."

"How is he? Is he okay?" Mom asked, concerned.

I looked at Evan. He was standing far from me.

"Yeah, he's fine," I said.

"Are you guys on your way home?"

"Uh, yeah," I lied. *Shouldn't the absence of the sound of cars tell her something?*

"Good," she said. "We'll be waiting."

"I don't think that's a good idea," I said quickly.

From the corner of my eye, I saw Evan take off my t-shirt. He put it where he was sitting and started walking away.

"Mom, I have to go," I said quickly and hung up before she had the chance to say anything.

I picked up my T-shirt and ran after Evan. I caught him at the entrance of the cave, near where the cars were parked.

"Were you planning on leaving without telling me?" I asked.

"It's not like I can escape you. We share a room."

I rolled my eyes.

"Did you tell him where we are?"

"No," I replied.

"Wanna do something crazy?"

I raised a brow. "Like what?"

"Like run away," he said.

"Are you…serious?"

"Yeah. I feel trapped here. Don't you feel trapped?"

"Not…really. My mom would—"

"God, I have to kidnap you," he interrupted with slight irritation. "Okay, let's go to the beach."

"Now?"

"Yes, now. I'd rather not go home now. Are you in or out?"

"In, I guess. I'm already wet anyway," I said.

He shook his head. "That would sound really dirty if you were a girl."

I chuckled at how he'd jumped to the meaning as I followed him to the cars. I watched him get into the Jeep. I put on my T-shirt and was instantly engulfed by a mixture of his scent and mine. Admittedly, my t-shirt smelled better than before. It was a really nice scent.

I got into the SUV and started the journey to the beach, following closely behind the Jeep.

As I drove, I thought of the moments in the manmade cave. It started off terrible but ended on a good note. I almost killed Evan. Seeing him flailing in the water scared the hell out of me. It was definitely not something to be repeated, but I had learned a lot about him. He was suffering from a post-traumatic stress disorder and hated his dad, which led him to be a jackass. It was no excuse, but I understood.

Thinking about what he said about my reaction to Chase's cheating made me smile all alone in the SUV. I still felt shitty, but Evan's words had soothed the self-hate.

CHAPTER NINETEEN

ZAC

Evan didn't drive to the beach where Noah practiced his surfing at. He didn't go to the private beach we had access to. He drove to the beach next to town. For a quiet town, the beach seemed lively. It was about 7 pm. The night sky was dark. Evan parked the Jeep, and I parked the SUV next to it. I still wasn't so sure about being there, especially after I'd told my mom we were on our way back to the house.

"Looks like there's a bonfire down there!" Evan said excitedly. "Let's go crash a party!"

"Uh...I don't think—" I started, but he interrupted.

"Zac, don't think."

"Not thinking led me to almost killing you."

"I'm alive, aren't I?" he said. "I promise I won't take revenge and throw you inside the bonfire."

"I guess we can stay for a few minutes," I said.

Evan led the way to the bonfire. He seemed to know the beach very well. We walked down a poorly lit boardwalk before going down some steps, passing by some people who were eating and drinking, or leaning against the small bar next to the pier, or making out, like the couple huddled in the dark. When we were close, I saw about ten people surrounding the bonfire, chatting loudly. All in all, there were about twenty people there. In the background, music was playing. The sound of rapid staccato percussive beats and handclaps filled the air along with synthetic riffs and preppy vocals.

I wasn't wearing beach footwear, but my boots were actually perfect for the beach. There was no sand sticking to my toes as we walked on the sand towards the bonfire. I could see ocean waves disappearing on the shore, bringing with them a cold breeze.

Evan made sure to greet everyone we passed. He just looked at home even though he knew no one there.

"Do you want a beer?" he asked abruptly.

"Uh…yeah sure," I said. "Actually, no!"

"Uh…what's your answer?"

"I don't want beer, and you shouldn't have any either. You'll be driving."

Evan face-palmed himself. "Have you ever done *anything* you weren't supposed to do?"

"Probably!" I said and stuck my nose in the air. "I know driving under the influence is a celebrity craze, but you could go to jail or *die,* you idiot!"

He laughed, but then bit his lip. "And you care because…?"

"Because…because…" I mumbled. He'd caught me off guard with his question.

"Because…?" Evan milked the situation.

"…Because I am human. I value life."

"That's a lousy answer," he said, shaking his head.

"Do you think your fans would cry if you died?" I wanted to know.

"I hope so!" he replied.

"Do you think they know you?"

"Well…" he said and trailed off.

"Psychology has taught me that we don't only mourn for people we know or love. Sometimes we just have to share a moment with people to be sad when they leave. It doesn't even have to be personal. We... You and I shared something. I'd be affected if you died," I explained.

He smiled. "Okay, I won't break your heart. Juice?"

I chuckled. "My heart? Whoa! It does not have to go that far."

He faked relief. "Thank God! I have enough people falling for me already."

I rolled my eyes.

"So...juice?"

"Yeah, that's fine."

He smiled at me. "Let loose, make some friends. I'll be back," he said encouragingly and left my side.

I wasn't comfortable not having him there anymore. I felt a little out of place. I awkwardly said hi to a girl who passed me. My phone rang in my pocket.

"Hi, Mom," I said with trepidation.

"Zac, where are you? I'm worried sick."

"Mom, I'm fine. I'm sorry. We had to make a stop on our way back because Evan was hungry," I lied.

"Oh. But you guys are okay, right?"

"Yeah. We'll be home soon," I said.

"Okay," Mom said and reluctantly hung up.

I looked at my phone for a few seconds before looking up. Evan was still not back. What I saw, though, had my heart skipping a beat. I had anticipated it sometime earlier when we got to Sapphire Beach Town, but it died down. Well, now it was here, in the flesh and my heart is now beating like crazy.

Chase and Bruce were standing in front of me. They seemed to have been standing there for some time. While I was awash with guilt, staring into space, they'd snuck up on me. I noticed that Bruce's arm was around Chase's waist. I couldn't tell how I felt about that, but my heart wasn't aching.

"Hi, Zac, didn't think I'd see you here," Bruce said, in a tone that suggested I wasn't worthy of the place.

I smiled. "It's a small world."

"What are you doing here?" Chase joined in on the conversation.

"Pretty much the same thing as you are," I said.

He looked at Bruce and bit his lip seductively. He turned to me. "Nah, I don't think so."

I didn't know what to say to that. I wished the ground would swallow me whole. Would it be a crime if I tossed Chase into the ocean, too?

"So, what are you *really* doing here? Thought I told you not to follow me like a whining puppy," Chase said.

"What the fuck? Do you seriously think I came here for you? Get over yourself," I said. I couldn't believe his nerve. *Did he really think my self-esteem was that low?*

"So, let me guess...You saw my Facebook post about where I'd be and thought you'd—" Chase said but was interrupted. It wasn't by Bruce, and it certainly wasn't by me.

"Hey, babe." Evan shocked the hell out of me. "I got your juice. Oh, you've made friends," he continued.

I was stunned. I turned to look at him, and he winked. He was a few feet away from us. His face was a bit hidden, but I knew that voice.

"Uh..." I began.

"That's pretty cool but, hey guys, can I borrow him for a while? I'd really love some...*attention*," Evan continued, drawling his words out at the end.

If I was shocked at what he said earlier, I didn't know how I felt after those words. I looked at Chase and Bruce and they were just as shocked as me.

What was Evan up to?

"Um... yeah, I gotta go. I'd be lying if I said it was nice bumping into you guys," I said confidently.

I walked over to where Evan was standing, and he locked his hand with mine, surprising me yet again. He handed me a bottle of juice and pulled me slightly. When we had gained some distance away from Chase and Bruce, he leaned in and whispered, "Go with it."

Go with what?

"What are you doing?" I couldn't help but ask.

"Pretending to be your boyfriend, duh," he whispered.

He put his arms around my waist. My breath got in my throat for a few seconds. It had been a while since I had someone's arms around my waist. I was very much aware of every inch where Evan's arms touched my body. It was on my clothing, but the pressure was very much noticeable. I couldn't say that I did not like the feeling.

"Why?" I got myself together enough to ask.

"Because your ex-boyfriend and ex-friend are jackasses," he said.

"But I don't...How did you even know what they look like?"

"I didn't. I heard them talking to you. I put two and two together."

"I suppose that makes sense. Still, what are you...?"

"Shh. Did you see the shock on their faces? That was priceless," he said with a chuckle.

His chuckle was infectious. I chuckled too. I couldn't say I didn't enjoy the shock on their faces. Evan's words had deflated their gigantic egos, and I got this feeling of immense pleasure of seeing them deflated and shrunken like balloons that had flown into the fire. The pettiness I had suppressed was rearing its head.

"Their jaws *were* on the floor." I chuckled.

"Did you know they'd be here?"

"What? No! You're the one who su—" I said, and Evan cut in.

"No, I mean this town," he said.

"Yeah. I knew Chase was going to come up here for spring break, well, before spring break. I was gonna come with him. But then he dumped me, and he's here with Bruce. I wasn't even supposed to be here," I told him.

"We could still run away," he said. There was mirth in his voice.

"I'm not giving my mom a heart attack," I said and finally opened my juice.

Evan's arms left my waist, and he too opened his juice. I immediately missed the contact. It had been comfortable, *too* comfortable. It may be all fake, but the contact had been very real, and the feelings, too.

I took a sip of my juice. Evan stared at me weirdly. He had a funny look on his face. It made me uncomfortable, and I raised a brow.

"Can you dance?" he asked.

"Nope," I said clearly. "Can *you?*"

"Anyone can dance, and so can you," he said.

"No. Anyone can *move*. Dancing is a different story."]

He snorted. "That's a load of shit. Show me what you can do."

"Not in a million years."

A couple walked past us. I watched them for a bit. I was suddenly reminded of something.

"You need to—" Evan was saying, but I interrupted him.

"Evan we can't pretend we're dating."

"Why not?" He genuinely seemed not to know why we couldn't.

"Have you forgotten? You're famous!" I reminded him.

"Oh, yeah…that part," he said. It seemed he had really not factored that in. "Your exes didn't see my face, and no one here has spotted me. It's only for tonight."

I chuckled. "It's gonna blow up in our faces. Someone is bound to notice you. And Chase and Bruce will know it's fake, and I'll…I'll never hear the end of it."

"Okay, we might have to ditch this party too early," he said and chuckled.

I laughed, really laughed. "You're an idiot, and you aren't even drunk."

"Let's go...*boyfriend*," he said, extending his hand. I took it.

We walked quickly to our parked cars. Evan tried hard to hide his face, which only made me laugh.

"Race you home!" he said when we got to the cars.

"Well, that's not fair. Your car accelerates to sixty miles per hour in less than seven seconds." I declined the challenge by pointing out the flaws.

"Chicken," he said before he got into the Jeep.

CHAPTER TWENTY

EVAN

I told him.

I had never told anyone. I kept it all to myself.

For years, it had been my secret, my burden to bear. I tucked it away and almost forgotten it was a part of me. It was a weakness, and Cody Wilde never shows any weakness.

I was a public figure. People I didn't know knew my name, and strangers followed me around. Things I said and did made tabloid news and, sometimes, national news. Being in the public eye meant any display of weakness would not only taint but leave an irremovable stain on my reputation. It will be in people's minds and lips and it'd take forever for them to forget. I'd be lucky if they will.

More than that, I was a brand. My public relations team made sure I was presented to the public as a strong, likable guy with no daddy issues and a charming matinee idol who's a little loose with the ladies and a little too confident from the rest of the aspiring performers. They molded me into that person, and I had been only too happy to bend to their whims.

The image I presented benefitted me. I was on the run from my past. I needed to hide my childhood traumas from everyone, including myself. What better way to hide one's self than to be someone else?

In the modeling industry, everyone is busy and highly competitive. There was no time to think about the father who couldn't care less about my well-being, and the grief I never processed. I changed clothes in the blink of an eye. I changed "girlfriends" like underwear. I flew all over the world in a few days, and met a lot of influential people.

My job allowed me to build a wall. It allowed me to be arrogant and a jerk, which kept everyone at arm's length. And it works because arrogance is just one of the things people don't like. It pushed people away, just enough for me not to get attached, open myself up and get hurt. Arrogance worked pretty well indeed. I got away with it because of my fame, because I was people's definition of sinfully handsome. I had people who wanted me in their beds—people who didn't try to have an emotional connection with me and only wanted me for my body. Those who wanted more, I pushed them away.

I lived in a world of lust and desires. Love didn't exist. I was a few steps away from being mechanical, and ever since the day I had made a promise to myself to leave my life behind, it had never bothered me. The one person I had truly loved was taken away from me at an age where I still see monsters under the bed. I was thrown into the wild, but I survived. And I would continue surviving as long as I showed no weakness.

People believe that being famous is detrimental to one's personal life. They think it opens the world into your whole life. It isn't true if you are strategic about who you present to them. People don't realize they are fed an image. People know what I wanted them to know. They think what I wanted them to think, and they never realized it was only a charade and they were puppets.

It was my world—the world I lived in, the world Cody Wilde thrived in.

Earlier with Zac, I tripped. The moment my body hit the ocean, all the memories I'd suppressed came flooding back to me. Everything was too vivid it felt like it had just happened the previous day.

I remembered the day my dad had told me my mother was gone. My mother had terminal cancer. She'd decided to spend the rest of the days at home. I had come home from school and immediately ran to Mom's room only to find the bed made. I knew she was already sick, but my immediate thought was that they'd taken her back to the hospital. That they had discovered a cure, and she was there getting cured. She was going to be all right.

But she wasn't going to be all right. She was gone. My father had broken the news to me in the coldest voice. He screamed the words out, causing a chill to run down my spine. He didn't hold me; he didn't tell me it was going to be okay. Instead, he turned away from me as if I disgusted him.

I ran. I ran until I could hear my heart in my ears. It had rained the previous day. My feet got stuck in the mud. I disentangled myself and ran until the cave appeared before me. I took cautious steps inside. It was warmer than the outside in some parts. I spent hours there crying, fantasizing. In the days and months following my mom's passing, it became a place of refuge. I couldn't cry in front of my father.

But then everything changed again. My father moved on from my mom just months after he buried her. His new girlfriend didn't like me. The feeling was mutual. Only, I didn't try to kill her.

Telling Zac all those things was a result of the comfort he provided when I was at my most vulnerable. I felt safe. I felt connected to him to tell him things I had never told anyone. It was a moment of weakness, and yet, it didn't feel like that. A part of me felt relieved while another part felt guarded.

I had told Zac my innermost secret. People wouldn't immediately believe him without proof, but the mere existence of the news in the media would unsettle me enough to make me act of out character, opposite to the script.

Somehow, someway, with no logical reasoning, I trusted him. He knew betrayal. He knew what it felt like. He was nursing a broken heart.

Speaking of his broken heart, I couldn't pinpoint exactly what it was that made me defend his honor in the face of his ex's insinuation. It just felt like the right thing to do, and I had just done it. And maybe, I got a thrill out of teasing him.

Did I just say that? Never mind saying it, but did I actually get some sort of satisfaction out of teasing him?

* * *

My thoughts occupied my brain for most of my journey home. It was like the silence in the car had opened up the floodgates. I avoided thinking of everything when I suggested going to the beach. It was an escape plan. It had worked—temporarily.

When I turned onto the driveway, I wasn't ready to face my dad. Truthfully, I didn't want to face him at all. He was going to give me hell for taking his car and going through his phone. And he wasn't going to listen to anything I'll say.

He never listened, and I didn't really talk either. We were just that kind of family.

After parking, I waited in the car for Zac so we would walk in together. He would take the spotlight off me, and I could walk to my room unscathed.

I watched as the SUV parked next to me. I got out and waited for Zac to get out. When he caught me waiting for him, he smiled.

"I think you are taking this fake boyfriend thing a little too far." He chuckled.

I extended my hand to him. "You'll never know who followed us home."

"Seriously?" He rolled his eyes.

I took my hand away. "Okay, I'll tell you my true motives. I want to use you as a shield," I said.

His shoulders dropped. "Another person who wants to use me," he said quietly.

"No. Shit! I—I..." I stammered.

He chuckled. "Shut up. I'll shield you, Evan. After everything you went through—" he said, but I cut in.

"About that, can we never talk about it? It happened, and I already got over it."

He shook his head slightly. "I don't think..."

I put my hand up, halting him. "You are not my shrink. I didn't ask for advice," I said firmly. "Now, come on, I wanna get out of these wet clothes."

He looked like he wanted to say something but decided against it. I started walking, and he followed suit. When we walked into the house, everyone was in the living room. Dad looked bored, and Zac's mom looked at us expectantly. Rosa looked relieved. I couldn't decipher what Jess's look meant. Noah wasn't even paying attention to us.

"There you guys are! I was worried sick," Zac's mom said.

"We are okay, Mom," Zac said softly though dismissively.

"Are you guys wet?! Are you okay?"

"Uh, yeah, we..." Zac began. I walked out of everyone's view towards my bedroom, leaving Zac to lie. I hoped he lied.

I noticed that my dad didn't do or say anything. I felt...hurt. Most of the times that we fight I didn't expect him to care, but that day, I really wished he did. I was still vulnerable even though I was no longer in the cave. I hated it.

When I got to my room, I stripped out of my wet clothes and took a shower. I stayed in the water longer than necessary. The water was warm, and the sound of it splashing on the floor was peaceful. I didn't think much.

When I went back from out the shower, Zac wasn't in the room. I settled on putting on my body lotion while listening to some music through my headphones. I was in danger of thinking. I needed a distraction.

The door opened abruptly. Zac walked in with his back to me. When he turned, he jumped back slightly. I pulled my earphones out of my ears.

"Sorry! I should have knocked," he said quickly.

"You've never seen a naked guy before?" I asked, rolling my eyes.

"I...I didn't expect you to be naked," he said.

"Could you please close the door? There's a draft...and for obvious reasons," I said.

"Oh right, sorry!" he said and closed the door. "I'm really sorry."

"It's fine," I said and applied body lotion to my toes. "Were they grilling you this whole time?"

"Um...uh...yeah," he said. He seemed uncomfortable.

I grabbed my towel from the bed and wrapped it around my lower half to put him out of his misery. I was done applying body lotion anyway. I saw his face light up in relief. No one had ever reacted like that to my body. Most guys didn't care, and girls looked at me with eyes that said "Take Me Now." Zac looked very much flustered.

"What did you say?" I asked, looking for clothes in my closet.

"Before I say anything, I must tell you I was under immense pressure," he said.

I turned to him. Tilting my head down, I said, "From your mom?"

"Yes," he said as if it was the most obvious thing. "My mom may look soft, but she can pack enough heat to make a man melt."

My heart skipped a beat. "Did you tell them?" The question escaped my lips.

"No, no! I just meant…don't laugh at my lie," he said.

"Okay, what did you say?"

"I told them I found you at some beach party. You were drinking and already soaked, and then you pulled me in. I convinced you to leave, and we stopped at some shady restaurant to eat. You didn't say anything about why you ran off, and we didn't talk about anything relevant," he said.

"Shady restaurant? Shady restaurant?" I said.

"Look at me!" he said, pointing to his chest. "What restaurant would let me in dressed like this?"

"You got a point," I said. "Well done. I didn't know you could even lie."

"What? Everybody lies. Some just do it more than others," he said.

Now that he'd drawn my attention to his clothes, I was wondering why he wasn't taking them off. They couldn't be comfortable at that point.

"You…" I said and shrugged, finally taking out a t-shirt and jogging pants. "You struck me as the forever honest guy."

"You've made so many assumptions about me. But yeah, I believe honesty is crucial in every relationship, regardless of the relationship. I don't like lying to my mother, much as I don't like lying to anyone. But I do lie when I deem it necessary."

He was remarkably still standing in the same place.

"You still believe in honesty even after you got the raw end of the deal?" I said. It was more of a statement than a question.

"I believe in it more. If Chase had been honest with me, he'd have saved me a lot of heartache."

I put on my pants and shirt while he was talking. "I'm sorry I made you lie," I said.

"What? No man, I understand why you wouldn't want people to know—" he said, and I cut in.

"No, I mean, the fake boyfriend thing," I clarified.

"Well, technically, we didn't say anything," he said, chuckling only slightly, but then he looked serious. "Why did you do it? And don't say why not."

"I've always wanted to pretend to be another guy's boyfriend. It's on my to-do list," I replied evasively and realized I used the wrong words. "I don't mean I wanna do you."

"I did not think that at all," he said with a grin.

"Good. Cause you know, I'm straight," I said. Why was I still talking?

"Nice to know," he said.

"I don't have anything against gay people. I just…you know, I…actually respect you. I'm just not…" I stammered, butchering myself in front of Zac.

"Don't you have people who tell you what to say? Cause I think you need them right now," he said with an amused smile.

I rolled my eyes. "Aren't you cold?"

"Uh, yeah. I'll get out of these." Instead of stripping in front of me, he left the room.

I took a deep breath after the door closed. I couldn't wrap my head around what had happened. Cool, calm, and collected Cody Wilde had mysteriously disappeared. I stammered. Zac had made me stammer without making me vulnerable first.

The situation was amusing, but it was also intriguing. I was too relaxed around Zac. It seemed I didn't feel the need to put up a front—to be Cody Wilde.

CHAPTER TWENTY-ONE

ZAC

"It's so fucking early for... Oh God, are you crying?"

I'd been sleeping peacefully until the sound of Evan's voice entered my sleepy mind and shook me awake. The arousal wasn't quite potent. My body wasn't ready to wake up. My mind wasn't either. I felt the pits of sleep dragging me towards them until...

"Look, I'm sorry. I can't apologize any more than I can leave right now. There's nothing I can do."

My sleep was shattered. I opened my eyes to the scene taking place in Evan's bedroom. I had no idea what time it was, but it was a bit dark. It looked more like early morning than nighttime. Evan was lying on his bed next to me, with his phone to his ear. I didn't miss the frown lines on his face.

"Carrie, you are not making sense right now," he said, frustration audible in every syllable. "Fuck," he said quietly, as if to himself.

"The problem is I don't want a relationship!" he yelled in a low tone. "I do not want to be attached to anybody. I think relationships are crap. I don't want any of the controlling and pain."

He put his free hand up as if he couldn't believe what he was hearing. "I don't...I don't love you. I'm sorry. I... Carrie, I'm not that kind of guy. You'll find a guy who loves you and wants to be with you. But I'm not him."

"No, no! There's nothing wrong with you. I just don't get into relationships, period," he explained.

There was a bit of silence. I assumed the person on the other side was talking. It didn't feel right listening in on the conversation, but I couldn't close my ears. I couldn't go back to sleep either.

"Talking in person isn't going to change my mind," Evan said firmly. "I can't leave anyway. I need this break."

There was a slight pause, and then he said, "Okay, we'll talk when I get back."

He put the phone on the side of the bed and groaned.

"...and I thought you and I were in a relationship." I surprised even myself by saying. My voice was light. I turned to my side and faced Evan, who seemed to not have been aware I was awake.

"Oh, of course we are! I only do fake relationships," he said. I saw a little smile. "Why are you even awake?"

"Uh...*you*?" I said with a "duh" hidden in the word.

"Sorry about that. Carrie was having one of her moments," he said.

"I figured," I said. "Sorry I listened. It was quite hard not to. You were yelling."

He sighed. "She just won't get it through her head," he said desperately.

I crossed my arms. "Why don't you get into relationships anyway?" I was curious to know.

"It's pretty simple. Look at you," he said.

I raised a brow that he probably couldn't see. "Me?"

"Yeah. Chase lied to you and cheated on you."

"Not everyone is like Chase."

"Everyone is like Chase. They only look out for themselves. They only look out for their own happiness."

"That's *partly* true. Yeah, we get into relationships to be happy, which is selfish, but the other person's happiness also matters. Healthy relationships are built on the needs of the people involved being fulfilled."

"Then, tell me. Are all relationships healthy?" he asked. "Do all people really sacrifice in the name of a happy relationship? Because I know *I* don't want to make sacrifices."

I stayed quiet for a bit. He was right, but he was missing the bigger picture.

"You can make sacrifices and still be happy," I said.

"But I don't want to make sacrifices."

"Then you don't want the connection, the comfort, the knowledge that someone is in your corner who will fight for you, love you, and support you."

He chuckled humorlessly. "I get all that from my management and my fans," he countered.

"Maybe Cody Wilde does. I'm not sure about Evan," I said.

He turned his whole body to face me, planting his feet on the floor and moving his body into a sitting position. Something in that move told me he wasn't happy with what I just said.

"Cody Wilde and Evan is the same person!" he said through gritted teeth.

"Maybe," was all I said. I wasn't going back on my statement, but I didn't feel like arguing with him. He knew himself better than I do, obviously.

"I don't know what you think you've seen, but I can assure you, I am not one of those celebrities who portray a life they wish they were living. Just because I have a…blemish in my past doesn't mean my life is fake."

I nodded, acknowledging his words.

"How are you so pro-relationships after a breakup?" he asked. I thought my silence had brought an end to the conversation, but it hadn't.

"Because I believe not everyone is like Chase," I said with a slight shrug.

"You are so naïve." He threw the words out. "Is this what they teach you in psychology?"

"I thought you said it was a strength," I said with a teasing whine.

"You not taking out your anger on everyone is a strength. You still believing in fairy tales is naivety," he said.

"My parents were happy," I told him. "My grandparents were too."

"How are you certain they weren't just putting up a happy front?"

"They weren't," I countered lamely.

"My dad cheated on my mother. She still smiled and told me everything was going to be fine. He cheated on her while she was dying. She *loved* him. She died loving him, and he spat on her grave. Relationships are stupid," he said with much conviction. "Good night, Zac."

I watched him get back into bed. His head hit his pillow, and he closed his eyes tightly. I watched his chest rise and fall rapidly. When my eyes returned to his eyes, he was blinking repeatedly. I couldn't help but think he was trying not to cry.

I felt really terrible. I just didn't know what for.

"Good night, Evan," I said quietly. It wasn't even night time. It was dawn.

*   *   *

I thought Evan would be in a sour mood in the morning. He wasn't. He was cheery and spoke nicely to my mom. And for the first time, he even had a little conversation with Noah. The heaviness of our conversation and his deep words was gone. It was like it had never happened.

He was used to it—pushing things to the back like they didn't matter. I concluded he had to be if he was as successful as he was in the industry he was in. He knew how to smile and how to laugh on cue. He'd only been in one major movie, but I bet he also knew how to cry on cue. He knew what to say and what not to say. He was good at pretending.

He spent the morning talking to his fans on Instagram. He made stupid faces and laughed at his phone. Mark didn't show up for breakfast, said he had some work to do. It must be the reason why Evan did. He ate his food without complaining, and teased and kissed Rosa on the cheek.

We hadn't talked at all that morning until he said, "Want to take a walk?"

It was a little after eleven. The sun was shining brightly outside. It was hot but not too hot. It erred on the side of warm, but a cool breeze was blowing. It was perfect beach weather.

I'd gone to my room after breakfast to call Livy. Conversations with Livy had to be private for obvious reasons. She brought up Chase, and apparently, everyone's ears stood up whenever his name was mentioned.

She did bring up Chase again. I thought of telling her I'd seen Chase the previous night just as Evan opened the door and peered in. It was all too well. Telling Livy about the previous night would bring up Evan pretending to be my boyfriend. The little fangirl in her wouldn't be able to keep quiet.

"Huh?" I said to his question. I'd heard it. I wasn't sure it was addressed to me.

"Do you want to go for a walk?" he said slowly, too slowly.

"You don't have to ask like I'm retarded. I wasn't sure you were asking me," I said, putting a hand over my phone's speaker.

"Do you see anyone else in here?" he said, cocking his head to the side.

I rolled my eyes. "Just a sec," I said to Evan and removed my hand off my phone. "Hey, Liv—" I began, and Livy interrupted.

"Is that Cody? His voice is melodious," she said. I imagined she was closing her eyes when she said it.

I chuckled before saying, "It's not. I gotta go. I promise I'll call later."

"I'll probably be sleeping. Have fun. Tell him I said hi."

"I won't. Bye," I said and hung up.

"I'm ready to go when you are."

"No, you're not," he said after looking me over.

I looked at myself too, absentmindedly pulling on my t-shirt. "What's wrong with me?"

"Well, for one, you are naïve and responsible. But if you're referring to now, you don't look like you are at a beach town."

I looked down at my pants. I was wearing jeans and Timberland boots. My white t-shirt hung loosely on my torso.

"I look fine," I said.

"You look fine if you were going to the woods, but you're in a beach. Don't you have shorts?"

"I'm sure no one will care what I'm wearing." I pointed out.

"I do. I don't want you fainting on me."

"And I thought my sister was dramatic." I shook my head. "I planned a spring break of sulking sessions and zero fun, so I don't have any shorts."

"I thought you believed in relationships. How will you get a guy stuck in your room and wearing all that on a beautiful sunny day?"

I scrunched my face. "Me believing in relationships doesn't mean I'm looking. I'm not jumping on the first available guy."

"Not dressed like that, you won't," he said.

"What do you even know? You are straight."

He opened his mouth and closed it. I smiled triumphantly, thinking he'd given up, but he hadn't. He walked to the closet and picked out a pair of burgundy cotton shorts. He threw them to me. I caught them only slightly, barely managing to hold on to them.

"Try these."

"Won't fit in these," I said, holding the shorts by the waist.

"Sure, your butt is bigger and rounder, but you'll fit," he said. He wasn't looking at me when he said those words. *Had he at one time stared at my butt?*

I was glad his eyes had been somewhere else. The increase in temperature I felt told me my cheeks had turned at least slightly crimson. I was instantly reminded of the time I walked in on him naked. It was only the previous night, but the image was still fresh in my mind.

Evan was a well-built specimen, and he fine-tuned himself quite nicely. I was sure his exercising had some impact on his physique. He was taller than me, which was important for the kind of modeling he did. He was slightly muscled, with a mouth-watering six pack and arms that looked like they could lift anything. The dips and bulges transitioned smoothly, giving out effortless and beautiful curves.

But that hadn't been the only thing I'd seen. I tried hard to not look further, which only frustrated me. I felt too exposed like he'd deliberately been naked to see my reaction. The relief I felt when he covered himself up was immense.

"Are you gonna put those on or stare at them? I have other colors and fits if those aren't your type," he said, bringing me back to the present.

He'd reminded me of one more thing I'd discovered the previous night. I couldn't undress in front of him. I could undress in front of Jackson just fine, but Evan was a whole different person. I didn't know why. I chucked it to the fact that Evan was definitely way hotter than Jackson, and I was just average.

"No thanks," I said, extending the shorts to him. I did want to wear them. I just didn't want to do it in front of him.

"Okay, fine, suit yourself. If you faint, you're on your own," he said, taking the shorts from me. He put them in the closet. "We should get going before it gets too hot."

"Yeah," I said.

I followed him out the room. He didn't want to tell anyone we were going out, but I told my mom anyway. She asked us to take Jess with, but Jess declined. I was happy she did, which surprised me. Sure, she was unpleasant to deal with, but that wasn't the sole reason.

"So where are we going?" I asked Evan as we stepped off his dad's property.

"Nowhere in particular," he said with a smile. "We're exploring."

"Don't tell me you want to run away again."

"I want burgers."

"You want to go to town on foot?"

He put his arms around me and spun me in the direction opposite the path that led to the tarred road. "We're not going into town. Come on!"

He left my side and started walking. Remind me why I had agreed to this?

CHAPTER TWENTY-TWO

ZAC

I ran a bit to catch up with Evan after deciding he probably knew what he was doing. He'd gotten off the main path, following a foot trail I had never seen. The trail ran parallel to the beach house, towards a thick forest. Because it was on a cliff, the path rose a little high, requiring me to take a few deep breaths as we walked. We walked further from the house. Here, the path was surrounded by tall light green trees and some shrubs. The whole area was shaded, providing a small breeze of cool air.

"Evan, wait, do you know where we're going?"

"Come on!" was the only thing he saw fit to say.

I stopped, looking around. We were surrounded by tall and short trees, most of which I had never seen. Light entered the place in only a few parts, so it was a bit darker. I could still see Mark's house through a clearing. The ground was dry but contained a few twigs and creeping roots. The place was peaceful, eerily peaceful.

"This place looks dangerous," I said.

Evan stopped walking and turned to me. We were probably three feet apart at that point.

"I know CPR," he said with an amused twinkle in his eye. "Come on."

"You think CPR will save me from a snake bite?" I said.

"And I thought I was the dramatic one. There are no snakes here, and if there were, do you think standing there like a statue would stop them from biting you?"

I huffed.

"Walk! I'm hungry," Evan said.

I groaned but walked up to catch up with him. I followed behind him. We seemed to be walking around the beach house. Then all of a sudden, we were going downhill, albeit not steeply. We walked downhill for a while until we got to a clearing. The path had led us to a drop-off point that was studded by boulders all the way to the ground. It was about ten feet high.

The ground led to the beach. I could see powdery white sand down below and hear the water crashing against rocks and the sound of people happily chattering.

Evan balanced himself on a boulder and lowered his body.

"Whoa! We're actually going down?"

"Yes," Evan replied clearly.

I shook my head. "No."

Evan lowered himself one step at a time, taking care to position his feet firmly on the boulders. He made it seem so easy. At the bottom one, he jumped to the ground.

"So, you're not coming down?" he shouted.

"I can't!"

"Why not?"

I took a deep breath. "I'm uneasy with heights."

"It's not that high!" he shouted.

"I don't care! These things look slippery!"

"The key is to not think about it," he said.

"No," I said simply.

"Zac, you need to let go! Do something crazy."

I crossed my arms. I didn't need to do something crazy. My life was fine the way it was. I knew how to have fun, and it didn't involve falling twenty feet to my death. Excuse me, I wasn't sure it was just ten feet. I could be wrong.

He shrugged. "Okay, well, you stay. I'm gonna get burgers." He started walking.

I groaned. A part of me felt I was a coward, but the most frustrating part felt I was letting an experience that could potentially be a memorable walk away from me. I groaned one more time and lowered myself slowly to the ground. Gladly, my boots provided a lot of traction on the boulders. My journey to the ground was smoother than I'd expected it to be even though my heart was frantic to escape from my rib cage.

I caught up to Evan.

He smiled when he saw me. "I knew you could do it."

"Are we going up the same way?" I asked.

"Pretty much, unless you want to go around that huge mountain," he said, pointing to a mountain behind us. It was the mountain outside his bedroom window.

There was a bit of silence as we walked along the shore. We spotted a few people in the water and some on the shore, chatting and eating. Some were sunbathing.

"I can't believe I let you make me do this." I groaned.

"Cheer up. I'll buy you a burger," he said. He still had that amused twinkle from earlier.

"I didn't know models eat burgers."

He shrugged. "I cheat. The kind of burger I'm talking about would make even vegans cheat."

I chuckled and kicked some of the sand as I walked.

"For someone whose body is an asset, you sure do some dangerous stuff," I mused.

"I live. You should too," he said moments before I was hit by flying sand.

I was stunned for a bit, wondering where the sand had come from. Then I saw it. Evan had collected some sand while I was talking, hitting me on the chest with it. He ran away from me afterward. I kneeled down quickly, collecting some sand in my hand. I chased Evan and managed to get a little bit of sand on him. The sand fight continued for some time.

"This is just not fair!" Evan complained. "My body is my asset, and you're just aiming to ruin it. Do you want me to become poor?" he said theatrically.

"You started it!" I defended myself.

"You weren't supposed to retaliate."

"Really? Is that how models play this game?"

He laughed. I did too. I emptied my hand of the sand I had collected. And so did he. We continued walking. Evan started walking fast when we spotted a fast food cart. It was a little off the beach, next to where the sand started.

I caught up with him at the cart. He was already having a conversation with the big-bellied man behind it. They seemed to know each other.

"You haven't been here in a while," the man was saying.

"Yeah. Work's been keeping me busy," Evan replied. "But now I said, 'No way, I'm not going to Colombia. I'm going to Sapphire Beach Town for Grant's burgers.'"

The man, who I presumed was Grant, laughed, his belly rumbling along with it. "Ever the charmer," he said. "The usual?"

"Yeah. Make it two and two juices," Evan replied. "We'll come back for them."

* * *

We walked around for a bit. Evan pointed out a few cafés to me as we walked. Surrounding the beach was what I called a beach village. There were cafés and small shops. Evan told me it was a small neighborhood. We walked along cobblestone pavements until Evan decided he was too hungry to walk. We then went back to Grant, who had our burgers ready. He'd wrapped them in a paper wrapper. Evan took a bite of his burger before we even found a place to sit. He looked like he'd just tasted heaven.

We found a secluded spot to sit. It was on the hill we'd come on, but it was slightly elevated above the sand-covered shore. There were a few large rocks there, and lush trees surrounded us. It would be the perfect picnic setting, except there may be a few snakes roaming around.

I finally took a bite of my burger, and it... was glorious.

It was a beef burger with the usual lettuce, tomatoes, cheese, and pickles, but it tasted like something I'd never tasted before. It could have been the sauce or the beef patty, but something in there—like a secret formula—or maybe just the right combination of the ingredients made it perfect. I could eat that burger every day for the rest of my life.

Evan finished his first. He drank his juice while I munched on my burger. Even though I didn't want the taste to end, I finished my burger too and washed it down with some juice.

"Verdict?" Evan said.

"Heaven wrapped in paper," I said.

He smiled. "I'm always right."

"Well..." I dragged the word, showing that I was inclined to disagree.

"Hey!" he warned with a chuckle, but then his face became serious.

"Uh, what's up?"

"Your exes are here."

I looked around quickly. Sure enough, Chase and Bruce were at the beach. They looked like they had spotted us because they were walking towards us.

"Will you quit saying exes? I didn't date both of them," I said. "Ugh, I'm not in the mood to see them."

"Saying 'ex-boyfriend and former friend' takes too long," Evan said.

Chase and Bruce were not just walking in our direction, they were walking *to* us. And right now, they were getting nearer and nearer.

"Fuck," I swore under my breath.

"I'm willing to pretend we're dating again," Evan said with what I concluded was an unintentional flirty smile.

"You're Cody Wilde!" I whispered through gritted teeth.

"Oh shit," Evan said. "You can just pretend your boyfriend went to get a drink or something. I'll back you."

"No. That'll just blow up in my face. This is screwed up. I'll just tell the truth," I whispered.

"And tell them what? That you pretended to have a boyfriend last night? What do you think are they going to think?" Evan said, his tone suggesting it was going to be an epic fail.

"It wasn't me! It was you. It's entirely *your* fault! You're the one…" I whispered vehemently.

I don't know how it happened. I would be lying if I said I saw it coming, but I didn't, not even for a nanosecond. One moment I was talking, and the next, I wasn't. I couldn't talk anymore. Something was preventing me, something that felt a lot like lips—human lips.

Specifically, Evan's lips.

His lips were on *my* lips. Shock was flowing through me, freezing not only my body but my mind. I couldn't comprehend what was happening. I felt a little tug of my lower lip. That distracted me, allowing Evan to capture my lower lip in his mouth. I felt the warmth of his mouth immediately.

Along with that, I felt a lot more than I thought a kiss would elicit. My body melted at Evan's kiss. I found myself latching onto his lip; I was consciously returning the kiss. Our lips moved slowly at first. Evan took charge, and I followed diligently, naturally. He kissed and licked my lip, biting slowly and gently. His lips hovered over mine, fanning them with his sweet breath. I felt his hand on my neck.

I found myself dissolving in his embrace, sinking into the charged air between us. I felt dizzy, the satisfying type of dizziness. There was peace yet I felt a fire burning. I didn't want to get away from it even though it threatened to burn me alive.

I felt his hand move from my neck to my abdomen. When it went underneath my t-shirt, I moaned silently, capturing Evan's lips instantly. My body was becoming too warm and my breathing too fast. The kiss was becoming feverish. Evan's hand didn't venture anywhere besides my bare abdomen, but it sure felt like he was touching me all over.

When he bit and dragged my lip, I wanted to push myself more into his embrace. The air around us was too heavy with my desire. It was pulling me into his arms.

But suddenly, everything stopped. Evan's lips were no longer on mine. His hand was no longer on my abdomen. He had pulled back. The move was too sudden I felt like I was about to fall.

I steadied myself. And then, everything came crashing onto me. Evan had kissed me. The kiss hadn't been with some random person. It was with Evan, the famous actor and model known as Cody Wilde. I enjoyed it, immensely so. It was memorable, too memorable.

That wasn't the only thing that came back to me. Last I looked, Chase and Bruce were on their way to us. They were only a few feet away from us. I looked in the direction immediately. Chase and Bruce were nowhere to be seen.

"Are they gone?" Evan asked. It was the first words said between us after our kiss. Evan was looking at the path Chase and Bruce had taken towards us.

"Yeah," I replied.

"Phew. At least they do get a hint," he said, no longer hiding his face.

"Am I missing something?" I asked. I was genuinely confused.

"I saved you from embarrassing yourself. Now, we should go before your exes return," he said casually and stood up.

I was still pretty much confused and possibly dazed from the kiss, but I stood up too. I couldn't understand the situation, and it was frustrating.

Evan kissed me. Unlike our fake relationship, it didn't feel fake. It felt like something written in magic but all too real all the same.

But Evan was an actor.

"Come on!" he said firmly before leading the way down the slight elevation.

I followed behind him with a million questions clouding my mind. With the way I couldn't focus, climbing the hill was going to be a tougher challenge.

CHAPTER TWENTY-THREE

EVAN

I wondered what my public relations team would say to me at that moment. I wondered what my manager would say. Would she be proud? Would she pace around the room, her heels making annoying sounds as she walked? Would she look down her nose at me?

I was not to be left to my own devices, she once told me. I was reckless. I didn't think. I had people who thought for me. They were hired to *know* what should be said and say it on my behalf. My manager said they were a necessity. If I did things myself, my career would end before it began.

Maybe she was right.

I kissed Zac. As his *exes* advanced towards us, I thought for a second about what I was going to do. It made sense, and so I did it. I advanced toward him, not giving him a second to react. Our lips met. He froze.

He was the first person I kissed whose lips didn't move for a considerable amount of time. I shocked him. It was an unusual situation. For a second, I didn't know what to do but decided I had to go forward. Backward wasn't an option. The vultures that were his exes were very close to breathing down our necks.

See, I panicked. Zac's words had hit me in the core. I was the one who made his exes believe he had a boyfriend. I couldn't let him tell them it was an elaborate lie. My solution was to kiss him. It served the purpose of deterring his exes from getting to us. If they saw us in a passionate lip lock, they wouldn't move any closer, if they even had any courtesy, that is.

Kissing him would also allow me to hide my face from them. There was a chance it could fail, which made it reckless. My manager would have a field day with me.

Thankfully, it worked. Only, it had done more than just work. The kiss was…different. It pulled me into a web I hadn't known existed. I forgot it was only meant to be a fake kiss, but it didn't feel like it. It felt warm, serene. My body *and* my mind felt at peace. It was indelible, too indelible.

It went beyond what I had intended. I couldn't get my mind off it. For most of the day, it was all I could think about. I avoided Zac as much as I could. It didn't help. It was like he was imprinted on my mind.

The kiss admittedly *scared* me. I got lost in it, something I'd always taken caution against. I knew it was possible to just lose myself, but I'd never allowed myself to…*until Zac.*

Not only had I let my guard down, but it had also been with a guy. As far as I knew, I was straight. I never explored anything contrary to that. I was attracted to females and had never really thought about a guy in an intimate way.

The idea of kissing a guy wasn't that strange. I was an actor. I had kissed lips I didn't intend on getting frisky with, and I intend on kissing a lot more lips I didn't get frisky with. It was part of the job. Enjoying the kiss said a lot more than I could admit at that moment.

There was something, or there was nothing. I didn't know which one it was. If there was something, I didn't know what it was.

There was no one I could talk to. I had friends. Correction: Cody Wilde had friends. The relationships were anything but personal. They claimed to be personal, but a lot of things were off-limits. I couldn't complain, though. I'd built the walls.

*   *   *

The thoughts in my head reached a boiling point. I couldn't look at Zac without wondering if there was something there. I needed a distraction, something that would stop me from thinking so much.

It was night time. I waited 'till everyone was asleep. I'd gone to bed earlier, so I was in my room under the covers. I didn't need permission to go out, but I needed a car. My dad would throw a fit, and I'd end up throwing him in the ocean. So I guess it was best for both of us if I snuck out.

I got out of bed and opened my closet, taking a jacket out. I took out a pair of jeans and t-shirt along with a sweatshirt. I was putting the items on when I heard the object of the chaos in my head stir.

"What are you doing?" he asked sleepily.

"Nothing. Sleep."

"Doesn't look like nothing."

"Okay, I'm going out," I told him.

"So late?"

"Midnight is not late," I replied, putting my shoes on.

"*Where* are you going?"

"I'm not running away. I just need some fresh air."

I focused on putting my sweatshirt on. When I put my jacket on, I realized the room was quiet. I thought Zac had gone back to sleep. I turned, but he wasn't in bed anymore. He was standing next to it.

"I can go with you," he offered.

I shook my head. "No. I want to be alone."

"I can be your chauffeur."

I thought about it. I had only one reason to go out. I wanted to get drunk, drown all the inhibitions and thoughts in my head. Driving while drunk was obviously not a good idea. I could get a cab, but I wasn't just anybody. People would take advantage of my celebrity status and do some stupid things. Having Zac there would be beneficial...

...Except he was the very person I was trying to get away from.

"Okay, but I need you to promise me something," I said. This could potentially end well or be a complete disaster.

"Our parents won't know about it," he said, joining me by the closet to get his clothes.

"That's not what I wanted to say, but I do want that too." He turned to me. "What's up?"

"Don't...Don't...," I said, putting emphasis on the word. "...tell me what to do. If I do something you think is stupid, let me do it."

"How stupid?"

"Anything except killing myself," I said.

"What if—"

"No, Zac. No. Nothing. I don't want to hear a word coming out of your mouth."

He chuckled. "Okay, I'll let you be stupid."

"Good. Hurry up before my old man wakes up," I said and left my room to get the Jeep's keys. My dad had about two more cars at the beach house, but the Jeep's keys were more accessible. I would have personally preferred the Mercedes, but the Jeep would have to do.

I opened the car and waited for Zac. I had half a mind to leave him. If I got too drunk, I'd just find a hotel...provided I won't get too drunk to find my way. But I couldn't guarantee that. My manager would have a field day for sure.

* * *

Zac took about two minutes to get to the car. I was slightly annoyed he made me wait. I was usually the one who made people wait. It was in my job description.

"What were you doing? Putting on makeup?" I asked as soon as he stepped into the car.

He batted his eyelashes at me. "Do my eyelashes look pretty?"

I just stared at him, showing my annoyance.

"You're the one who wears makeup. I don't," he said as if it was the smartest thing. "I was waking up everybody, so I can tell them what you're trying to do."

"I will gut you like a fish," I warned.

"Just drive."

I turned the key in the ignition, and the car roared to life.

"Your dad can probably hear the engine."

"I know. I don't care if he knows after the fact," I said, pulling out of the driveway. "It's the before I was worried about."

We joined the path that led to the main road, and soon, we were on the main road.

"Why didn't you just hire a car instead of stealing?" Zac asked.

"It's not stealing. It's borrowing. And to answer your question, I don't have a license."

The alarmed look on Zac's face upon hearing my words was too funny for me not to laugh. I chuckled heartily.

"You mean you can't drive?!" he said.

"I get so much pleasure scaring the hell out of you," I said. After laughing once more, I said, "I have a license, and I am very much capable of driving. I just like stealing my dad's car. The yelling the next day is always priceless."

"You know, maybe, you should talk to him instead of provoking him. You…"

"Stop talking," I said lightly though with finality.

"I'm just…"

"Zac, I am not afraid of pushing you out of the car and leaving you here," I said. "I told you I never want to talk about my dad again. There's nothing to fix."

Zac stayed quiet but not for long. "You provoke him because something inside you is hoping he'll bring up the past. You can't directly talk to him about it because that leaves you vulnerable."

I gritted my teeth. I wanted to lash out, scream at Zac. But that would be giving him what he wanted. He wanted to break me open like he'd done the other day. He was provoking me, doing the same thing I did to my dad.

"When you get your Psychology degree, burn it. They obviously don't teach you the right things," I said calmly.

I turned on the radio, increasing the volume to maximum to stop him from talking. Thankfully, he didn't try to compete with the radio. He didn't say anything until we got to town. I knew the club I wanted to go to so I headed there.

"So, this is where we're going?" he asked, pointing to the building in front of us. We were at the parking lot.

"Yes," I said with a smile. "Live a little, Mr. Shrink...or you can just wait for me in the car."

He rolled his eyes. I got out, and he did too.

The club was rowdy. I knew that very well. I would. It was the hottest club in town. I'd been there a couple of nights—nights like these when I couldn't get stuff out of my mind. Neither Zac nor I were old enough to get in, but no one was watching. It was just a small community club. Everyone was allowed.

The first thing I did was go to the bar and order a couple of shots. Zac seemed shocked by my behavior, but he didn't say anything. He seemed to have taken heed of my warning.

I danced on the dance floor while drinking. The club was too crowded, so no one was paying attention to me—no one except Zac. He bought some gin and tonic but was sipping it slowly. Every now and then, his eyes swooped on me.

The atmosphere was exhilarating. I got lost in the music, trying hard to avoid looking at Zac. Bodies around me were moving to and fro. People shouted over the music. I drank and drank and then I drank some more. I couldn't keep count of how much I was drinking or even identify what I was drinking.

I could remember Zac's lips on mine. I could remember knowing I needed to stop kissing him but not wanting to. The kiss was only meant to be fleeting, not searing.

I bought vodka and some tequila shots. Zac tried to stop me, but I disappeared into the crowd. The music was louder. I could feel my thoughts fall away. My inhibitions were lowering. My body was faltering slightly. It felt good.

And then, Zac looked so good. He had baby blond hair with platinum micro-highlights, hair that seemed to absorb all the flashing lights in the club as they kissed it. He styled it into a casual short tousled haircut, which was perfect for his oval head, and framed his perfectly sculpted face.

He had all the right contours and an exquisite bone structure, not too sharp, and not too soft either. Adorning his face were a pair of mesmerizing hazelnut brown eyes guarded by long thick eyelashes, a pair of thick eyebrows, a slightly narrow nose, and pale pink lips. His facial hair was slight, just a little above his upper lip and along his jaw. He was shorter than me but was of average built—not tough, not soft—with lightly tanned skin. He wasn't the most handsome man to walk the earth, but he followed closely behind.

His eyes were looking at me. His enchanting eyes were looking at me. I found myself drawn to him as if they were pulling me.

"You should dance," I whispered in his ear.

He shook his head.

"No guy is going to notice you sitting at the bar like an old hag," I said. It was hard to say the words out loud.

"I don't want to be noticed," he shouted over the music. "You shouldn't either."

"I live on publicity!"

"You're drunk," he told me. "We should go."

"You owe me a dance."

"I don't owe you anything."

"Come on, dance with me." I didn't know why I was pushing.

I pulled Zac to his feet. He only indulged me a few minutes of swaying his body left and right before he said, "Okay, we gotta go."

"Why?" I whined.

"Because Jackass and Asshole are here," he said.

"Who?"

"My exes," he whispered harshly in my ear.

"Oh, them, I'm not afraid of them," I said. I was starting to slur. "I'm gonna go right up to them and tell them they're ruining my fun." I tried to move but realized I couldn't. Zac was holding onto me.

"No, you're drunk. You'll make a fool of yourself and sabotage your career. We're going home."

"No! I need to give them a piece of my mind. They need to know they can't fucking mess with people, fucking jerks. They are assholes. You...you're..."

"You'll only embarrass yourself," Zac reasoned.

"I told you not to tell me what to do," I said defiantly.

"Shut up," Zac ordered firmly. I was stunned into silence by the firmness in his voice. He put his arm around me and pulled me towards the door. I didn't feel like it, but I walked.

When we were outside the club, I faltered slightly. Cold air rushed past me. It wasn't enough to sober me up. Zac still had his arm around my waist. The streets outside the club were deserted. It looked like it was just us outside.

"You are such high maintenance," Zac was saying. "Are you always an idiot or is it just with me?" Despite his words, he didn't seem angry.

I put my finger on his lips. "Shh."

He removed my finger from his lips but didn't let go of it. "I just stopped you from making a fool of yourself. You owe me your whole career."

I stopped walking, forcing him to stop too. "Thank you, Mr. Shrink," I said in a mocking tone.

Our eyes locked. He still had his arm around my waist. His eyes were just so beautiful. His lips looked so delectable. I closed the distance between our lips before I could stop myself. I couldn't have been able to stop myself. I was too far gone. My inhibitions were nonexistent.

Zac didn't freeze like the last time. He kissed me back fully, holding nothing back. He gave as much as he took. Our kiss was too quick and a bit sloppy. It felt like it was all we had wanted to do the whole night. I reveled in it. I loved the taste of gin and tonic in Zac's mouth.

My eyes were closed, but I didn't fail to notice the appearance of a brighter light than what had already been there. It came too quickly, and in a flash, it was gone. My lips left Zac's. I opened my eyes. A flash had just gone off, and I hoped it wasn't what I thought it was. My heart skipped a beat.

Chase and Bruce were standing a few feet from Zac and me. Chase had his phone in the air. I didn't need physical evidence to know they'd just taken a picture of us, *kissing*.

Zac looked like he'd just seen a ghost.

Chase took another picture.

"What the fuck man? Geez!" I yelled.

"Cody Wilde, who would have thought? Do your fans know you're gay or is that some deep dirty secret?" Bruce opened his mouth.

"I want you to delete those pictures!" I said firmly. I took a step forward, but Zac stopped me.

"No," Chase said simply. "So, Zac, how much is he *paying for it?*"

I didn't see Zac move. Maybe it was because I was intoxicated because he just moved too fast for my eyes to follow. The next thing I saw was him raising his fist. Chase's reaction time was just as slow as mine. He didn't anticipate the fist that landed on his jaw. His immediate reaction was to retaliate, but Bruce pulled him back.

"What the fuck?!" he yelled while massaging his fist. It sure looked like the punch stung.

"I should have done that a long time ago. You can get me arrested for all I care. That felt *really* good," Zac said clearly.

I actually felt really proud.

"Come on. Let's get you home." His words to me were authoritative, leaving no room for negotiation.

I followed him to the car.

"Keys," he said firmly when we got to the car.

He unlocked the car, and we got in, with him in the driver seat. He placed his head on the steering wheel and sighed.

"I'm sorry." I barely heard him say.

"For punching your ex-boyfriend?"

"No," he said and raised his head. "You're drunk, and you don't get it right now, but Chase and Bruce are evil. The pictures they took are going to make the tabloid. I'm sorry."

I sighed. "Let's just go home."

Zac nodded. I noticed he was avoiding my eyes. The engine roared to life, and the car started moving. I fell back on my seat. A storm was coming, too fast for my liking. I had no control over it. My thoughts were all over the place. I wasn't ready for my confusion to be thrown into the spotlight.

I wasn't ready.

CHAPTER TWENTY-FOUR

ZAC

I'd reckoned I wouldn't get much sleep after bumping into Chase and Bruce. Our encounter had been too dramatic, explosive. I'd done something I never thought I'd do. I punched Chase. The anger had built up until it erased all the hurt. I'd gone from yearning for Chase to wanting to confront him for what he'd done to me, with no love and no tears this time.

Punching him felt good. I knew violence was never the answer, but I felt so liberated. Chase was becoming more and more like a speck in my life.

The same couldn't be said for Evan. I found him more and more interesting, but it wasn't his stance on relationships that had me thinking about him at four in the morning. He kissed me again. Correction, *we* kissed.

The first time, he took the first step. I hadn't had much time to think about the impact of the kiss or why he kissed me in the first place. The second time was a lot different.

We both took steps towards each other, and our lips met with much intensity. While the first kiss had been soft, this one was passionate from the get-go. Our eyes only met for less than a second before our lips were glued to each other. We were like the polar opposites of a magnet, drawn to each other by invisible forces.

At least, it was like that on my side, and that scared me. I admittedly found Evan intriguing, but not so much to actually kiss him. At least, I thought it hadn't gotten that far. Yet, at the moment I had my arm around his waist, unbeknownst to me, kissing him had been my greatest desire. That kiss too was memorable, and I wanted it to continue forever and ever. It could have been the taste of vodka in his mouth or the charged air between us, but I felt contented yet I found myself wanting more than I was getting.

Was there something or was it just a human reaction?

I was almost certain there was nothing on Evan's side. He was drunk, and he is straight, he told me himself. There couldn't be anything.

While I reckoned I wouldn't get much sleep, I actually slept for three hours after Evan and I returned. We got to the house a little after 1 am and went straight to bed. I was up for about an hour before the sound of Evan's phone ringing broke the silence in the room and my unanswered questions. By then, it was 5 am.

Evan was lying on his bed. He didn't look awake, let alone alive. I was surprised when I heard him groan and try to smother his phone with a pillow. That dwarfed the sound a bit, but I could still hear it. That went on for a few minutes. Evan's phone was ringing nonstop. He repeated the same thing he'd tried the first time. He was very close to wrapping his phone with the pillow.

I looked around the room. It was quite dark. The sun hadn't risen yet.

"For fuck's sake!" Evan groaned, forcing me to look at him again.

He took his ringing phone from underneath the pillow and pressed it furiously. I thought he would answer the call, but he actually ended it. He stuffed his phone under the pillow again.

"Maybe you should answer it," I said quietly.

He raised his head like he had no clue who said the words. "It's too early in the morning. I have a hangover," he said.

"Switch it off then?"

"Way ahead of you. Why are you even awake?" he asked groggily.

"Your phone...I'm a very light sleeper," I lied.

He sighed and banged his head on the pillow. I thought he was going to say something, but he didn't. Instead, he turned on his side and pulled his duvet over his head. I assumed he was sleeping.

There was silence until the sounds of *Desire* by *Years and Years* filled the room. Evan turned sharply and pulled the duvet down. He pulled out his phone and looked at it. I couldn't see his facial expression, but I bet it was one of bewilderment.

"Mine," I said quickly. Evan's reaction amused me. Our ringtones weren't even distinctly similar, yet he assumed his phone was the one ringing.

I took my phone from the nightstand. Livy was calling. I wasn't sure I should answer given Evan's mood. I did anyway.

"Make it quick," I said into the phone.

"You... secret keeper!" Livy said with emphasis as if it was a bad thing. "You kissed Cody Wilde! There's a picture of you...You guys...You...Zac, how come I didn't know about this?" she yelled in my ear. I winced a bit.

I knew Chase and Bruce wouldn't keep the pictures to themselves. They were exposing Evan to get to me, dragging his name in the process. It had to be about me, or maybe I was just assuming? Chase and Bruce had no interest in Cody Wilde until they saw me with him...Or maybe they did. What did I know? They clearly lied to me about a lot of things.

I knew it was only a matter of time before things blew up. I had been expecting it ever since the club incident. I was naturally a light sleeper, but that night my sleep had been light because the adrenaline was coursing through me, leaving me restless. That and the thoughts about the kiss.

I didn't have answers to the questions I knew would follow. I just hoped the story wouldn't be big. Maybe it would be fleeting, and no one would be interested. Maybe not everyone was interested, but the news had gotten to Livy, and she was very much interested.

"I don't know what to say to you," I admitted to Livy. There was a lot I hadn't told her.

"Then tell me everything!"

"He was drunk," I said the words hastily.

I didn't miss the groan Evan gave at my words.

"So, he was drunk and kissed you?"

"Pretty much," I said. I wasn't lying. Evan had been drunk when he kissed me. I had been sober, but she hadn't asked that.

"Drunk enough to punch someone too?"

"What do you mean? I'm the one who punched Chase," I said.

"Punched Chase? What are you on about?"

I was confused. "I'm...what are *you* on about?" I asked her.

"The article... it said Cody Wilde punched the person who took the picture," Livy clarified.

I could not believe what I was hearing. "What the fuck? That's clearly a lie. How could Chase stoop so low? I'm the one who punched him, not Evan."

"Whoa, whoa, wait, how does Chase fit into this?"

"He took the pictures. Of course, the bastard leaked them anonymously. That coward" I said, the anger evident in my voice.

Chase had outdone himself. It was one thing to leak the pictures, but to blatantly lie? He couldn't stand the thought *I* had punched him, or was he just out to ruin Evan's reputation?

I refused to believe he had something against Evan. It was me he was after. He wanted Evan to hate me.

As if hearing my thoughts, Evan groaned again.

"So, you've actually been in the same place as those treacherous bastards? Why didn't you tell me?"

"Yeah, unfortunately. Look, Livy, now's not a good time to talk. I know it's late in South Africa, but here, it's really early. I'll call you later."

"You better."

I hung up before she could say anything.

"I'm sorry, Evan," I said quietly. "I forgot I'm not in this room alone."

"I'm that forgettable? Ouch," he said playfully. I hadn't expected that with how he'd been groaning like a sick dog. I was thinking of what to say when he said, "So after I punched Chase, did I gut Bruce like a fish?"

"Not that I know of, but I can very well see how that would have been perfect," I replied. "Can't believe Chase did that. I'm so sorry."

"Am I trending?" he asked casually.

I was stunned. "Uh...I don't know. Do you...*want* to trend?"

"Every celebrity wants to trend," he simply replied.

"Oh...I thought this is bad. I thought you wouldn't want—" I said, but he cut in softly.

"Oh, it *is* bad. I wasn't done. I was going to say we want to trend—but with good things, not bad things."

"I'm sorry I—" I said, but he cut in again.

"I need to sleep, so if you could keep you and yours quiet, that'd be great."

"Mine?" I asked, with a cocked brow he couldn't possibly see.

"Your phone." he clarified. "Good night."

* * *

The sun rose around 7:30 am. I hadn't been able to sleep since the call with Livy, so I watched as light wormed its way into the room, lighting up everything in it, including a sleeping Evan. The light wasn't strong enough so I couldn't see everything in detail, but I saw enough.

Evan was curled on the bed. Although he'd covered his head earlier, the duvet was now pushed back. I could see his face and his body down to his waist. He was sleeping on his tummy, with his head facing away from me. His hair was messy. His grey sleeping tank top revealed his toned arms. He looked peaceful.

I was anything but peaceful. I looked at Evan for a bit, wondering how big the story of us kissing was. I decided I was ready to know. Maybe it wasn't a big deal, and Livy just *made* it a big deal because she knew me.

I was wrong. Cody Wilde was trending. There were messages of support and messages of outrage. The article which originally published the picture described Cody/Evan as a closeted gay who'd been caught in a passionate kiss with his lover or a prostitute by the name of Zac Nielsen. The picture was Cody Wilde's outing. The public was in a frenzy.

While some posts were supportive, no one questioned the veracity of the outing. Homophobic people came out in numbers. Some people were so happy they were inviting Evan to gay pride. It was a bit comical, but I didn't know how Evan would take it.

I was much more worried about Evan than I was about myself. The public wasn't much concerned about me. Only the people who actually knew me would find it necessary to question my involvement. That Chase had described me as a prostitute made me laugh. He couldn't stand the idea of someone like Cody Wilde taking an intimate interest in me. Of course, it wasn't like that, but Chase didn't need to know that.

I stalked the internet for a while, well over an hour. The news of someone's supposed sexual orientation was breaking the internet. It was a strange world we lived in.

I was still scrolling through Twitter when Evan stirred. He turned to his side, and his eyes opened.

"This is why I didn't want a roommate. Could you please switch off the light?"

"What light?" I said with a slight grin. Either he was still drunk, or he had a massive hangover.

"That li...oh crap." He groaned. "What time is it?"

"Nine thirteen."

He sat up, planting his feet on the ground. There was silence between us as he ran his hand through his hair. He looked like someone who'd been on a battlefield. His eyes looked tired.

I was about to ask him if he needed something like a painkiller when there was a knock on our door.

"Zac and Evan, breakfast is ready!" Noah shouted.

"Coming!" I yelled back. I had no intentions of showing up for breakfast. I heard Noah's footsteps as he left.

"Shouldn't you be out there for breakfast like the good boy you are?" Evan asked, taking notice of the fact that I was still in bed.

"Don't feel like it."

"I've only spent a couple of days with your mom, but I'm sure that'll make her worry," he said.

He was, to an extent, right. When I didn't go with the family to town, Mom thought Chase had something to do with it. She pestered me about it. She'd think the same thing if I didn't show up for breakfast.

I groaned and got out of bed.

"What about you?" I asked Evan.

"Wouldn't be the first or the last time. I gotta call my manager and fix my shit."

"Good luck," I said, walking out of the room to the bathroom.

CHAPTER TWENTY-FIVE

ZAC

Breakfast was on the terrace again. It was a lovely sunny morning. The food was scrumptious, but the mood at the table was anything but. Mark only greeted me and kept looking at me like he wasn't pleased. He probably knew Evan and I had stolen the Jeep. He was waiting for me to confess. Jess had her phone at the table. That got her in trouble with Mom. They threw a couple of curtailed snaps at each other.

I was playing with my fork around my almost empty plate when Jess caught my attention. Her mouth had opened in a wide "O" before she said, "Oh my god. Zac…You…Oh shit, tell me you didn't just do *that*!"

"Jessica, watch your mouth," Mom warned.

"You should probably tell Zac to watch where he sticks his tongue. Can't believe you and Evan… It explains all those mysterious disappearances…"

I wished the ground would swallow me. I was anticipating too much on my ex-friends' commentary about Evan and me that I'd forgotten about my family. I was screwed.

"Jess, um, could you not…" I said quietly, indicating for her to shut up.

Of course, the brat wouldn't.

"Hey, Mom, did you know Zac and Evan have been swapping saliva behind our backs?" Jess said.

Mom was confused. "What are you talking about?"

"This!" Jess replied and shoved her phone in Mom's face. Mom took it slowly. I had half a mind to grab it and throw it in the forest.

Mom's eyes grew wider as she looked at the phone. She looked at me and stared.

"He was drunk," I spit the words out. "We were both intoxicated."

"What's happening?" Mark asked.

"Evan is gay, and he and Zac are in a relationship," Jess replied with a huge smile.

I narrowed my eyes dangerously at her, and she just shrugged, giving me a fake smile.

"Is that true? Marianne, give me the phone," Mark said. Mom reluctantly handed him Jess's phone.

"Evan is gay?" he asked no one in particular.

"Oh, goodie, we're discussing me!" Evan's voice entered the scene. I hadn't seen him walk onto the terrace. "What did I miss?" he asked cheerfully.

"You and I need to talk, right now!" Mark ordered.

"You mean you want to yell at me?" Evan said with a shrug.

"My study, *now*!" Mark barked while standing up.

Evan pushed air outside forcefully and followed Mark into the house.

"So, who's the bottom?" Jess had the audacity to ask.

"I will fucking beat your ass up right now. I'm not mom," I warned.

"You would beat me? You're too soft: a mommy's boy."

I took a deep breath.

"Jess, go show your brother where the box of sweets we bought is," Mom said quickly.

"It's in the pantry. Why do I need to show him?"

"Just go!" Mom yelled. Jess reluctantly stood up. Noah took the hint too because he stood up. They left the terrace.

Mom and I were the only people left at the table.

"So..." Mom began.

I sighed. "He was drunk, I was drunk. We just kissed, there's nothing to it," I said.

"Jess said—" she said, and I cut in.

"Jess is like whoever published that article, they don't have a fucking clue what they're talking about," I said.

"Language," Mom warned. Her face softened. "So, there are no feelings?"

"No, Mom. It was a one-time thing. I have zero feelings for Evan."

"Are you sure?"

"Why wouldn't I be?"

"I know you. You fall hard for people. You love the idea of relationships. You don't just kiss people randomly. You guys have been hanging out a lot," she said.

"Mom, I'm twenty!"

"And?" She looked convincingly confused.

"There are things I don't tell you."

"Oh."

"Look, Mom, Evan and I, there's nothing between us. He was upset and drank too much, and I drank too. We kissed for two seconds. He's not even gay," I said softly.

"I wouldn't be upset if you two were...you know. I want you to be happy," she said.

I smiled and held her hand.

"Now, please don't beat up your sister. I know she's insufferable, but she's still your little sister," she said.

"I'm not capable of beating up anyone," I said with a smile, the previous day's incident lurking at the back of my mind. "I'm gonna go shower."

"Okay," Mom said.

* * *

When I went to the room I shared with Evan, I walked into a sight I was not expecting. Evan was in the room, pulling out clothes from the closet. An open duffel bag lay on the bed.

"What's going on?" I asked uncertainly.

"I'm leaving," Evan uttered the words I didn't know I'd dread hearing.

"What happened? Did he do something?" My voice came out strained.

"I need to clear the air, set the record straight about that... that whole thing," he said. He wasn't looking at me. The way he was avoiding me was suspicious.

"I-I suppose that's the right thing to do," I said. "Do you have a flight booked?"

"I'll figure that out," he said, stuffing clothes into his bag. He didn't even bother folding them.

One time, he looked up, and I caught his eyes. They were red. I knew he was hung over, but his eyes hadn't looked like that before.

"How'd your talk with your dad go?" Curiosity got to me, and I asked.

"He yelled, and I yelled back." His voice was monotonous.

"Was he mad about the car?"

He stopped packing and looked at me.

"I would rather pack in peace," he said firmly.

I swallowed thickly. "Right. I will get out of your hair."

I was on my way out of the room when Evan stopped me with his words.

"What did your parents say?"

"Parents?" I asked, curious at his use of the plural form.

"When you told them you are gay," he said.

I was surprised by the question. I thought he wanted to know my mom's reaction to our kiss because he'd walked in while we were discussing it. It was now clear why he'd said "parents".

I deliberately coughed, wondering why he was interested in my coming out. "Uh…I told my mom first. She just smiled and told me it didn't matter. I wasn't that close with my dad, so I didn't know how to tell him. I wasn't scared he'd reject me. We just never talked about girls or boys, so I didn't know where to start. Mom told him. He was okay, didn't treat me any differently. He gave me tips in junior year on how to approach my crush, which I didn't follow," I said and finished with a laugh as the memories flooded my brain.

Evan nodded and didn't say anything.

"Why do you ask?" I was curious.

He shrugged. I thought he would say something, but he didn't. *Could he have possibly told his dad he was gay?* It would explain the sudden interest. Knowing him, he might've only done it to provoke his dad.

When he didn't say anything for what could have been a minute, I decided to leave him be and went into the shower.

* * *

I took a quick shower. It was not like I had anywhere to be, but I found myself doing everything quickly. I didn't want to miss out on something. I had a hunch it had something to do with Evan and him leaving.

I walked into the room wondering if he'd already left, preparing to be disappointed if he had. We weren't the best of friends, but I was going to miss him. My memories at the town mostly included Evan. We had some stimulating conversations too.

Evan was still in the room. He was on his way out when I opened the door, hitting him with it. I opened it too fast, afraid of what I'd find in there, or what I would *not* find.

"Ouch," he whined.

I walked in and closed the door. "I'm so sorry," I apologized profusely.

"This is gonna leave a bruise!" he complained.

"I'm sorry. I didn't know you were here. I thought you were already gone," I said.

He massaged his forehead. "I suppose it lends credibility to Chase's story. I punched him, and he punched me back." His tone was casual. At least, he wasn't angry.

"Or you could say he punched you, and you punched him," I said with a chuckle.

"That would work. Society sympathizes with victims, especially the ones who stand up for themselves," he said thoughtfully.

"There you go!" I said with a smile. "It's a pity most victims are *not* victims."

He laughed at my thinly veiled shade. "So why are you on a rampage? First Chase, now me. And I heard you want to beat up your sister."

I ran my hand along my neck. "Those were all words. My conscience would not let me beat her up."

"Your conscience let you beat up your ex," he said.

"I didn't *beat* him up, I just…punched him. He called me a prostitute. He deserved it."

Evan surprised me by smiling. "That was cool," he said with emphasis.

"You find odd things cool."

"You're living," he simply said.

"Is your definition of living punching people and pushing some into the ocean?"

"When you suppress anger, it consumes you," he said. "I gotta go. I'll see you in my next life." He walked to the door and opened it.

"Evan, wait!" I stopped him. He said something that didn't make sense to me. I had a strong belief he was suppressing his own anger. *If he knew it wasn't good, why was he doing it?*

He peeked into the room. "Yeah?"

I looked down a bit and then at him. I was nervous about saying what I wanted to say, given his previous reactions on the subject. "When...when you're ready to talk about...everything you've been suppressing, I'm here."

He took a few steps toward me. His bag dropped to the floor. Our bodies were too close I could feel his heat, or maybe my temperature had risen significantly.

"There's nothing to talk about," he said quietly. His breath fanned my lips. His lips were appetizing.

"Think about it," I said softly.

Our eyes met. His were still showing signs of fatigue. They were still slightly red. They were gentle too like he was tired of fighting.

"I'm not one of your case studies," he whispered.

"I know," I said curtly. "You're a pain in..." I said but was interrupted by something I hadn't expected.

Evan had inched his lips towards mine, halting my breathing. The distance became only centimeters, and bit by bit, it became unnoticeable. I closed the tiny gap between us. Our lips touched. Evan sandwiched my lower lip between his lips and moistened it with his tongue.

He pulled his head slightly back, breaking the short kiss. My eyes opened. I opened my mouth to say something even though I had no idea what to say. Evan cut into my unsaid words by pushing me backward, still holding onto me until we were both in the room. Using his free hand, he pushed the door with enough power to close it.

I had no idea what he had in mind, but my sanity was already questionable at that moment.

This time, it was me who initiated the kiss, pulling him towards me and positioning my lips on his. He welcomed me, parting his lips so we could kiss properly. We kissed slowly, feeling every movement. His lips tasted great, driving my desire to hold onto my insanity for just a little bit longer.

Our kiss deepened and quickened. Reasons why it shouldn't be happening were forgotten. I was getting lost, and I didn't care. I wasn't thinking. Nothing mattered.

Except…

Evan's forehead was still painful from me hitting him with the door earlier. When my hand touched him there, the spell was broken. He winced and pulled his head back.

"I'm sorry," I said quietly.

"I should get going. My cab's gonna be here in five," he said simply. "Bye, Zac."

He grabbed his bag and disappeared out the door before I could say anything. I was stunned. I just stood there, looking at the door he'd just left. I wanted to stop him. I wanted to tell him not to go.

But I didn't do or say anything.

CHAPTER TWENTY-SIX

EVAN

There were times when I thought maybe Dad and I could fix our relationship. We were both older and wiser. I wasn't young anymore; I didn't need much of his attention. I didn't need his money, either. I was independent. My job didn't just bring the fame; it brought lots of money in too. I made six figures from a single photo shoot. I was too expensive even if I had to say so myself, but whoever wanted me had to shell out the big bucks. And there were quite a lot of people who wanted me.

My father didn't need to hold my hand. I could manage on my own. I didn't need him, but at times, I wanted him, especially at times when I saw my best friend Clive Norton with his dad. As a fashion photographer, Roman Norton was a busy man, but he always made time for his son. They talked on the phone, they laughed, and they went on vacations together. Clive spoke highly of his dad. They have conversations I couldn't with my dad. Those times, I envied him.

It only lasted for a few minutes, though—the envy. There was no point to it. My dad and I were not like that and will never be like that. Our bond had been severed the day my mother died. Besides his obvious failure as a dad, my dad made it very hard for me to like him. He was older, yes, but not wiser. He didn't even try to understand me.

Our relationship had been broken for a long time, but when he called me "filth", it severed the last thread. The conversation played itself over and over in my head as I sat on the plane that was taking me back "home".

"What the fuck are you doing?" he yelled at me as soon as the door was closed. It had evidently been taking a lot for him not to start yelling before we reached his study.

His study still looked much like the last time I'd seen it. It was full of and smelled like law books. The books were stacked to the ceiling. A desk sat in the middle with two chairs opposite each other. I immediately felt a chill the moment I walked into the room. It reminded me of the years before, back when I was a kid. It was the room I got reprimanded in. Sometimes, he lost his cool before we got there. Not today. There were important people in the house.

"What do you mean?" I asked. I was genuinely not sure what he was talking about.

"The kiss, dammit!"

"Why are you suddenly interested in my life?" I shrugged.

"Listen here, you little punk. If you think you are going to ruin my life and I'm going to let you, think again!" he warned with emphasis on the last two words.

I opened my mouth and closed it. "God, you are more self-centered than I thought. How is me kissing Zac ruining your life?"

"You are playing some little game, and you think you can get away with it. I know you're not gay. What is it? Do you want more fame?"

I couldn't believe what I was hearing. "You know nothing about my life to tell me what I am and what I'm not!"

"I know enough to know you are a brat. You want to ruin my relationship with Marianne. What will society think if you are dating your stepbrother? You want to make sure Marianne and I never get married," he said.

I shook my head in disbelief. "Not everything I do is about you. Has it occurred to you that I may genuinely like Zac?"

"*No son of mine is filth!*"

I balled my hand into a fist. My belief had already been suspended, but now, it felt as though I was imagining the conversation.

"*Did you just call me filth?!*"

"*You heard me. Gay people are filth. I have tolerated the things you do, but I draw my line on that. Don't come in here with the nonsense you celebrities get up. I don't want that bullshit in my house.*"

I laughed humorlessly and momentarily sat down on a chair and just looked at him. He was a formidable man. Air of authority oozed out of him. "*You have gone far and beyond what I thought you were capable of,*" *I finally said.*

He crossed his arms. "*I want you out of my house by the end of the day,*" *he said slowly but firmly.*

I was stunned. "*You yelled at me to come here…*" *I said, and he cut in.*

"*Marianne has proof you exist, and she thinks you're a brat. You've served your purpose. When she asks why you left, I'll just tell her you couldn't stand being with normal people any longer.*"

I stood up. "*Don't forget to tell her you think her son is filth.*"

He shook his head with a wide smile. "*It's not relevant. He's not my son.*"

"*Well, you know what? I wish I wasn't, either,*" *I said and left the office, banging the door. The first teardrops escaped my eyes.*

I'd spent a few short breaks with my dad after I left home, suppressing my trauma and building enough walls no one had attempted to scale. I honored his invites mostly for Rosa's sake; she and I got along well. She was a lovely soul stuck with an evil man. Of all those visits, my dad and I only yelled at each other. And in all of our fights, I had left unscathed. Until now.

I unintentionally opened myself up. I hadn't done it. Zac had. I let him do it. He'd been nice, too nice. He had a counterargument for everything. He made me want to face my past, but not anymore.

He was the reason I felt rejected.

*   *   *

Zac took over my thoughts for the rest of the flight. I surprisingly missed him. We hadn't spent an eternity together, but those few moments had been more action-filled than a movie. Somehow, I'd gotten lost in those moments.

There was not much time to think when I finally got to my apartment in New York. It was about 5 pm. Clive was there. We shared an apartment for two years. I earned enough money to afford my own penthouse, but I'd learned solitude was a breeding ground for unwanted thoughts. Sometimes, I needed a distraction, and Clive provided that.

He was a food blogger who spent three quarters of his life prowling restaurants and eating. With how much he eats, it was a surprise he was as skinny as he was. The rest of his life was spent on clubs (with me), fashion shows, girls, and yearly trips with his dad to some remote part of the world.

I was glad Clive was home, but only for two seconds. He, along with a million other people, had heard about my supposed sexual orientation, and he couldn't wait to hear it from me.

"I was drunk," I said as I dragged my bag to my room. I was going to close the door, but Clive followed me to my room.

"You were drunk and you kissed a guy," he said as if he thought I thought he was talking about something else.

"At that point, I could have kissed a cactus."

"Who is he?"

"You sound like my mother," I scowled, taking my jacket off. "He's an acquaintance I made, who out of the goodness of his heart, tried to help my drunken ass. I kissed him, embarrassing him."

"So, he's not a prostitute?"

"I don't know," I lied. "If he is, I didn't sleep with him."

"So...you're not gay?"

I let my father believe I was gay. I'd done so to provoke him. His homophobia was shocking, but it also surprisingly *hurt*. I wasn't as certain about my sexual orientation as I thought I was.

I had kissed Zac more than once. The first time, I'd made a decision. The subsequent times, I'd been drawn to him by forces unbeknownst to me. It was as if now that I knew how he tasted, I wanted more. It wasn't just the taste. It was...everything.

Clive raised a brow when I didn't answer. I could tell him the truth, or I could lie. The truth was... I didn't know the answer. That would feel like saying I *was* gay. Clive wouldn't judge me, though; I knew he was accepting. He had a few gay friends. But...we didn't have that kind of friendship. The confusion in my head was best kept *in* my head.

"I'm not gay," I said quietly.

"Okay. Do you wanna go clubbing? There's this new club at—" he said enthusiastically, but I cut in.

"Not tonight. I have a meeting with Jennifer tomorrow, and I'd rather not be hung over.". Jennifer was my manager, and I wasn't looking forward to the meeting.

"Right. She called this morning. She wasn't pleased," he told me.

I groaned. "I'm surprised she's not banging down my door."

"She'll probably be calmer by tomorrow. Good luck," Clive said and finally left my room.

I took off my shoes and threw myself on the bed. I wasn't ready to meet with Jennifer or anyone. I needed time to think about what had really happened in Sapphire Town. Without anyone to bounce my thoughts on, it was going to take time. I didn't have that luxury. The world I lived in didn't afford me with such.

Maybe it was for the best. The madness had gone on long enough. It was time to return to my world—Cody Wilde's world.

It was where I belonged, where Cody *and* Evan belonged. After all, they were the same person.

* * *

The next day, I woke up earlier than I normally would. I was anticipating the meeting with my manager. She was going to give me hell for getting drunk in public, and, of course, kissing a guy. It wasn't a secret I was loose with the ladies and had been caught lip locking with one or two famous people, but a guy was a first. The world was shocked.

That morning while I lay restless on my bed, I learned I was already a slash fiction sensation. The books about me were endless. Some scenes were cringe-worthy, and some made me laugh. People were arguing if I was more suited to Cullen McCarthy, my co-star in my recent movie, or Blake Willow, a fellow model. There was already a picture of me gazing lovingly into Cullen's eyes.

I was scrolling through my Twitter feed when my phone rang. I didn't look at the Caller ID before I pressed "Answer."

"Hey, baby," a cringe-worthy squeal greeted me.

I anticipated a call from my manager that I hadn't thought anyone else would be calling except her. It clearly wasn't Jennifer on the phone.

"Hi, Carrie," I replied.

"I've been trying to get hold of you all day since yesterday."

"Yesterday was a...busy day for me," I said with a scowl she couldn't see.

"We have to talk," she said. "The picture of you—"

I cut in. "Now's not a good time. Jennifer is here so I gotta go," I lied.

I hung up before she could say anything else. It was clear she was going to say something. She, like Clive and everyone who thought they knew me, wanted to know what the kiss was all about. Translation: they wanted to know my sexual orientation.

After Carrie's call, I got out of bed and showered. I had yogurt, oats, and fruit for breakfast. Clive wasn't awake. I doubted he'd be awake until at least the afternoon. I'd heard him get into the apartment at about three in the morning. I assumed he was in his room nursing a massive hangover.

There was a knock on the main door by 11 am. Jennifer had decided to move our meeting up without telling me, maybe to catch me in the act. I don't know. She probably hoped to find me in bed with a male prostitute.

I opened the door to be greeted by the scowl on her face. She was a woman in her early forties with long blond hair and a penchant for heavy makeup. But even the foundation with the highest coverage can't hide the sternness of her face. Jennifer oversaw everything I did, from the modeling to the acting. She negotiated my deals, created, and maintained my image. I had another agent who got me auditions, and she ran everything with Jen.

My relationship with Jen was okay. She knew I was loose, liked parties, and tended to be reckless. She let me be, but when it came down to it, she *told* me what to do. Sometimes, she actually scared me, like when she wouldn't take a fair deal until her demands were met, and at the end of the day, they usually were.

"Hi, Evan," she said clearly.

"Hi, Jen," I said casually. "You're early."

"I'm never early," she said and walked past me into the apartment.

The place we're living in was a two-bedroom apartment with a large living room, an open space kitchen, two bathrooms, and a balcony which overlooked the city of New York.

Jen took a seat on the two-man couch facing the TV.

"Do you want something to drink?"

"No thanks. You should sit down," she replied.

I sat down uncertainly.

"Are you gay?" Her question was clear, unfaltering. I couldn't pretend I hadn't heard it.

"No," I replied quickly, as if by reflex.

"Bisexual then?"

"No. I'm straight," I replied. I knew I could be lying, but at that moment, I didn't know otherwise. I was in a foggy territory.

"So...what happened?"

"I was drunk," I said slowly. "We were having fun, and I got carried away."

"Is he a prostitute?"

"No, no. He...I met him at the club. He was just trying to help me." I was piling lie after lie.

"How do you get drunk at a club when you're not even old enough to drink?" she asked sternly.

I sighed. "It was stupid of me. I...I..." I stammered. "I wasn't thinking."

"Your problem is you don't think. On top of that, you punched a guy. Do you think David Markham wants to be associated with such recklessness?"

I didn't say anything. Instead, I looked down at the ground in shame.

"Hopefully, we can still salvage this situation," she said. "Here's what's gonna happen. I've booked you a spot at *A Night with Carroll dos Santos*. There are two ways we can spin this, and I've mulled this over with the public relations team."

I indicated that I was listening.

"You can either apologize for being a stupid, thoughtless teenager and put the gay story to rest, which may or may not pacify David Markham, or you can change your story altogether," she said.

I raised a brow.

"Here's my version of what happened. You met Zac earlier in Sapphire Beach Town, and you struck some sort of friendship. He called you that night, drunk and wasted. You knew you shouldn't go to the club, but you couldn't leave him there knowing he could hurt himself. Your good heart wouldn't let you. So, you rushed to the club and coaxed him into leaving. You never tasted a drop of alcohol. He kissed you drunkenly, and that was when the picture was taken. He was the one who punched the guy who took the picture. You were only trying to do a good deed and got caught in the crossfire," she explained.

I was shocked.

"Jen, that's...that's devious!"

"I would use 'clever'."

"I can't do that. I can't lie like that," I said.

"Of course, you can lie like that. You're a good actor."

"No...you know what I mean!"

She rubbed her hands together before locking them. "Why can't you lie like that?" she asked slowly.

I opened my mouth, but the words wouldn't come out. I already said Zac was some random acquaintance I made. I couldn't tell her he was more than that.

"I did some digging on Zac Nielsen. He just came out of a relationship, and he's gay. Doesn't seem odd that he'd be drunk, probably drinking the pain away. My version doesn't seem so far-fetched," she said, totally ignoring me.

"I'll take the first option," I said quietly.

"No, you'll take option two. It makes you a Samaritan. Victims always win," she said forcefully. "I'm not letting you blow up a chance to endorse a brand as huge as David Markham's *Eclipse*."

"I cannot lie!" I emphasized.

"You've lied before. You can do it again," she said casually.

"I've lied about myself, what I eat, where I am, but I don't lie about other people!"

"Now's a good time to start. Veronica has a list of things you are to say. I don't believe in speeches. Act natural and make sure you include all those things. We'll have a practice interview two hours before the show." She concluded and stood up.

"The show is at eight o' clock. You are in at eight-fifteen. You have to be there at least thirty minutes before. Veronica will take you there. I'll be with you before you go up. And Evan, if you think of sabotaging yourself, think of why Cody Wilde is so big."

She then got up, leaving me to my thoughts. I couldn't believe what had happened. I knew she wouldn't be pleased with me. I did anticipate that she'd want me to tweak the details, but I didn't expect her to blatantly want me to put all the blame on Zac.

I couldn't do it, yet a part of me felt I had to.

* * *

Veronica arrived a few hours after Jennifer left. She was my publicist. She gave me the list of things I had to mention, "prompts" as she called them. We did the two practice interviews. She reprimanded me on my hesitancy, calling it a weakness. Normally, when I did television interviews, my PR team required a list of questions to be sent before the interview. They chose which questions they were comfortable with and prepared me for them. If a question was deemed too personal, it was struck off.

I was a protected person. Journalists were predators, I was warned. They wanted drama, a story, something juicy to feed the hungry masses. It was in my interest not to give them that. But Jennifer never trusted me not to, so a list of questions accompanied interview requests.

This time, it wasn't the case. Carroll dos Santos was free to ask me anything. The interview was meant to be free and open. Veronica told me I didn't have to answer everything, but it was important I "set the record straight" about the kiss incident. Never at one moment did she ask me to be myself.

A stylist chose my outfit for my interview, and then Veronica drove me to the studio. She gave me last-minute instructions as I sat down to have my makeup retouched. Jennifer told me to not look so gloomy. Carroll dos Santos looked excited to see me. It occurred to me that I would rather just be home curled on the couch, watching cartoons and eating Jelly Babies.

The producer cued me in. I put on my mask and smiled.

The audience clapped as I made my way on to the set. Carroll was seated on a couch in the middle. She stood up as she saw me and extended her hand. I shook it and took a seat on the couch near her. Not once did my smile wane.

The clapping died down.

"Cody Wilde, welcome to the show," she said beaming at me.

"Thank you, Carroll."

"Thank you for taking time off your busy schedule to indulge us, nosy people," she said, and the audience laughed. I bet there was some sign somewhere pleading with the audience to laugh regardless of whether they thought Carroll was funny or not.

"It's a pleasure," I replied.

"Now, of course, you didn't just come to the show to sit on that couch and be pretty, am I right? Then again, you do sit on some couches and look pretty…and make a million bucks."

I chuckled a bit. "I did come to the show with a purpose."

"Would you like to tell the audience what that is?"

"I know some of you may already know, but I've been making the rounds on Twitter lately," I said.

"Twitter rounds?" Carroll said, shaking her head. "Boy, you were trending yesterday and are still trending. You're no longer on the number one spot, but you're still up there."

The audience laughed.

"Okay, I'm trending," I said and chuckled, but my face grew serious. "I want to set the record straight. I owe it to my fans and everyone to explain what happened."

"For some of you who don't know, a few pictures have been doing the rounds on the internet. In one of them, Cody Wilde is seen kissing a *guy*, who has been identified as Zac Nielsen outside a club in Sapphire Beach Town. The second picture shows the two of them separate with their faces *clearly* visible. An article published by *ZMT* alleges that after the pictures were taken, Cody assaulted the man responsible, punching him in the face. Zac Nielsen is alleged to be a prostitute, by the way, so the article says," Carroll informed the audience and her viewers.

Hearing the story all over again was annoying.

"So, Cody, what really happened?" she asked. "Are you homosexual? The world wants to know."

I took a deep breath I hoped was inconspicuous. I couldn't see Jennifer, but I could hear her words in my head. I could see Zac's face. I could remember kissing him.

My mouth opened.

CHAPTER TWENTY-SEVEN

ZAC

Evan hadn't just left his fans confused. He left me confused. He bolted before I had a chance to figure out what was going on between us. I knew we would part ways eventually, but I hadn't expected him to leave so soon. His sudden departure caught me by surprise, and more so, his final act before he left.

He kissed me again. *We* kissed, but his reaction was more appalling than mine. The kiss wasn't fleeting. Neither of the kisses was fleeting. I didn't know why he kissed me, the first, second, or third time. I hadn't had a chance to ask him.

I thought I knew why *I* kissed him. We hadn't gotten off on the right foot, but we'd shared some personal stories. We connected. He didn't feel like a stranger to me. That wasn't the only reason I kissed him and let him kiss me, though. There was an unspoken physical attraction between us. He was a well-built specimen, and the carnal desire in me reacted to that.

That was the reason...right?

Evan left me with more questions than answers, and so, when I saw he was going to give an interview on *A Night with Carroll dos Santos,* I knew I had to watch the show. I'd been scrolling through social media when I saw the announcement. Evan and I hadn't talked ever since he left, so it was a chance to hear him speak.

Everyone but Jess and I had gone into town to have dinner. I had the chance to watch the show live instead of waiting for the YouTube uploads, which I presumed would come up only after the show ended. Jess was somewhere in the house when eight o'clock finally hit.

I watched the show on television in the living area. Carroll interviewed a celebrity and had a game before Evan was scheduled to come up. At 8:17, she was met with applause from the audience as she introduced Cody Wilde as her second guest.

The moment I saw him, I felt my intestines tie themselves into a knot. I was nervous, and I didn't know why. Jess must have heard the announcement because she chose that exact moment to join me in the living room.

"Oh cool, I'm just in time," she said, taking a seat away from me. "This will be interesting."

I wanted to glare at her but decided not to give her the satisfaction. I focused on the TV instead.

"For some of you who don't know, a few pictures have been doing the rounds on the internet. In one of them, Cody Wilde is seen kissing a *guy*, who has been identified as Zac Nielsen outside a club in Sapphire Beach Town. The second picture shows the two of them separate with their faces *clearly* visible. An article published by *ZMT* alleges that after the pictures were taken, Cody assaulted the man responsible, punching him in the face. Zac Nielsen is alleged to be a prostitute, by the way, so the article says," Carroll said the words that made the knot in my intestines tighter.

Jess struggled to contain her laugh, sounding like she was choking. "So, you've been selling it, huh? And Mom thinks I'm the rotten apple."

I grabbed a cushion and threw it her way, which she managed to duck. "Shut up!" I ordered.

"...really happened?" I heard Carroll's words. "Are you homosexual? The world wants to know."

"I am *not* homosexual. Things are not as they appear," Evan said clearly. I had no time to react to what he'd said. Carroll started talking.

"What do you mean? Please explain," she said.

Evan rubbed his hands together. "I met Zac in Sapphire Beach Town through some family members. We talked a bit. The night the picture was taken, he called me. He was at the club; he was upset. He sounded really wasted. He broke up with his boyfriend, and he was distraught. We're not close, but I felt sorry for him. I couldn't…I couldn't just hang up and leave him there, so I went to the club to get him. I got him out. He was so drunk…I don't think he knew what he was doing. He kissed me. I was stunned…and all of a sudden, flashes were going off. Everything happened so fast."

"Oh," was all Carroll said.

"What the fuck?!" was what I said. I couldn't believe my ears. Evan had turned the whole thing around.

"And the punch? Is he a prostitute? You haven't answered all the questions, Cody."

"When I finally reacted and got him to stop kissing me, he realized someone had taken a picture. He got mad. Next thing I knew, a punch had flown. I managed to stop him and get him out of there. I didn't punch anybody. As for him being a prostitute, I don't know. I don't know him that well," Evan said.

He was too convincing. If I didn't know the story, I would have believed him. Only one thing he'd said in that story was true.

"Oooh, *you* punched someone? Maybe I was wrong about you." Jess got my attention.

"Shut up!" I yelled.

"I don't know if it's just me, but you looked like you were returning the kiss in that picture," Carroll said slowly but clearly.

"It looks like it, but I wasn't," Evan simply said.

"So, there are no feelings? No attraction?" Carroll delved deeper.

"There's *nothing*. The only thing I felt in that moment was shock," Evan replied.

Was he really acting like I sexually assaulted him?

"Damn brother!" Jess exclaimed, followed by slow clapping.

I stood up. Jess thought I was going to walk over to her, so she cowered. I walked past her. I had no idea where I was going. I just needed to walk far enough to dwarf Evan's voice.

I ended up walking to the terrace outside Evan's bedroom. I was instantly greeted by the memories of standing against the rails with a sulking Evan. We hadn't talked much, but it was one of our earliest interactions. I now knew more of him than I did that day.

One of those things was that he was an opportunistic coward. He spun the story about the night we kissed to save his career. He intentionally excluded the important details: he was the drunken one, and I was the one who tried to stop him from embarrassing himself.

I was initially angry about what he had done. But the more I thought about it, I understood why he'd done it. Getting drunk at a club he wasn't even supposed to be in and allegedly punching a guy was bad publicity. It was going to damage his brand. I wasn't that attuned to celebrity lives and gossip, but I'd heard about some young celebrities doing outrageous things that tainted their image.

Some had whole articles written about their scandals.

I was okay with taking the blame only if he'd asked me to do it. I was a nobody. People would eventually forget. But of course, he hadn't asked me. He just painted me out to be a drunken, heartbroken guy who punched people and kissed him without consent. *And how dare he say I was distraught about Chase?*

As if Chase didn't already have a huge ego! He was going to have a field day with just that one comment.

Evan deserved my anger, but I was just mildly upset about the twist. I wished he'd asked me.

As I stood on the terrace, Evan's twist on the story wasn't the only thing on my mind. He clearly said he felt nothing for me. Those words stung. I didn't expect him to love me. I would have been surprised if he did. I thought the kisses weren't just…an experience. I thought there was something—attraction, intrigue, fascination, temptation, curiosity. Something that drew him to me—just *me*.

Well, he did feel something—shock!

It was all too well. I had gotten a little lost, but I could pull myself back. The damage could be reversed. Evan was out of my life; at least he'd be for a long time. It was about time I got my real life back. It wasn't too long before I had to go back to college.

* * *

A few days passed at the beach house. Jess provoked me every chance she got, but I could deal with her. Her jokes were light, not malicious. The incident with Evan seemed to have brought us a bit closer. We sat together and had small conversations, which always ended with her taunting me.

While Jess chose my company, I had a sense Mark was avoiding me. He barely said a word to me. He just seemed standoffish, in a way I couldn't put my finger on.

Livy called me to discuss Evan's interview. I declined the offer. I already closed the chapter on Evan; I didn't need to discuss him. He just felt like a holiday fling you never talk about. Of course, I had no idea what holiday flings felt like, but I considered Evan as one. He was better kept in the past. It would be easy to forget about him, as long as I didn't go into any social media *ever*.

It was a bad idea to go somewhere we'd gone together, but I found myself doing just that. I was bored with being in the house; I felt like a caged animal. I enticed Noah to go with me, with the promise of a mouthwatering burger.

I would get out of the house, have a heavenly made burger, and bond with my little brother all in one go. It was hitting three birds with one stone.

It was possible it was four birds, but I wasn't going to acknowledge that.

Noah—as timid as he was—was quite an adventurer. He loved the idea of going to a neighborhood through what he called a secret passage. Not at any time did he seem scared when the trees surrounded us and he could no longer see the house. He exclaimed how cool the path was.

He reminded me of Evan.

I hoped he was as excited when we got to the end of the path and had to lower ourselves down. I hoped he could at least do it because the closer we got to the beach, the more I wanted to be there.

We got to the end. I was leading the way, so I stopped and looked down.

"We have to go down there," I told him.

"Okay," he said simply and bent to tie his Converse sneakers.

That was so easy. He made me feel like a little baby. I was glad he wasn't there with Evan and me that other day because Evan would have laughed his ass off at my reluctance. I took a breath and lowered my legs onto the boulders. My heart still beat faster even though I was doing it for the second time.

I managed to lower myself onto the ground. I watched as Noah did the same, readying myself to catch him if he ever slipped. Marianne would not be pleased if I killed her son.

Noah got to the ground safely. He exclaimed how beautiful and secluded the beach was as we walked on the sand toward the burger place. Grant recognized me from the last time I was there. I bought two burgers and paid.

"So, we've never gotten a chance to talk. How's school?" I asked Noah as we munched on our burgers while walking.

"It's okay," he said and shrugged.

"Just okay? No crushes? Fights?"

"Well, now that you ask…there's this girl," he said.

"You like her?"

"Ew, no. I want to punch her. She's such a bitch," he said.

I cringed at his last word but excused it. "Did she say something to you?"

"She's been spreading rumors about me. She says I'm a momma's boy," he replied.

From the corner of my eye, I saw the place where Evan had surprised me by kissing me. It was deserted at that time. That fleeting moment started a chain reaction. I remembered the kiss, the way he tasted.

If I wanted to close the chapter, then why was I entertaining the memories?

I could have gone somewhere else.

"Well, you know, buddy, people are gonna say a lot of things about you. You don't have to stoop to their level," I finally said.

"But she says my mom bathes me!"

I put my arm around his shoulders. "Even so, punching her isn't going to solve this. You'll get into trouble, or she'll escalate. You'll retaliate, and it'll be an endless cycle."

He stopped walking and looked up at my face. "*You* punched Chase."

"That's different," I said.

"How?" he asked.

"Chase…" I began and abruptly stopped.

The sudden subject of our conversation was suddenly standing a few feet from us. Chase was with Bruce, and they were heading towards us. The scene was too familiar. *Was this like some kind of do-over?*

"Zac?" Noah enquired, wondering why I had stopped talking.

"It's just different," I said hastily, coaxing him to walk.

He didn't walk fast enough, and soon enough, Chase and Bruce were already upon us.

Bruce looked at my arm that hung around Noah's shoulders. "Already found yourself another victim? Looks too young, don't you think?"

Noah looked at me, no doubt wondering what was going on.

"Could you just leave us alone?" I said. I had no energy to deal with them.

"Aww, we'd love to. Just…smile," Chase said and pulled out his phone to take a picture of me. "This will look very good for Zac The Prostitute's Facebook page. You already have one thousand followers. They especially love the *naked* pictures of you."

For a second, my heart stopped, and my hearing went out. I couldn't hear anything. I felt my brain go back in time, pull out files, put them back then turn pages and cross-reference. *Had I ever sent Chase a nude picture of me? Had he taken them without my knowledge?*

"The pictures are fake!" was all I could say.

"Of course, they are…but, they don't need to know that," Chase said.

"What the fuck do you want from me, Chase?"

"Nothing. I *never* wanted anything from you. I feel nothing. And apparently, neither does Cody Wilde," he said and laughed. Bruce joined him.

"Does it hurt?" Bruce asked.

"You wanted the fame when you kissed him, didn't you? I made you famous, *honey*. It's a pity even he doesn't want you. Oh well, I can't give you that," Chase said.

"Leave my brother alone, you fucking bullies!" Noah surprised all of us.

"Oh, the little Nielsen talks. I always thought you were mute," Chase said.

Noah escaped my embrace. I didn't even see him move. Next thing I knew, Chase had burger sauce all over his face. Noah had thrown his half-eaten burger at Chase, hitting him right in the face. The patty and buns had trailed down to the ground, but the sauces and pickles were still there.

"You fucki..." Chase threatened while advancing towards Noah.

I blocked his way. "If you fucking touch my brother, I will make sure the next red sauce dripping down your face is actual blood. You can mess with me all you want, but no one messes with my brother," I warned firmly. "Maybe you think it's a weakness when I don't stoop down to your level, but maybe you need to ask yourself why *you're* so *obsessed* with me. For someone who doesn't want anything from me, you sure as hell are in my business. Bruce, maybe you need to bend him over a kitchen table every now and then, it's clear he needs some...*attention*."

"What the—" Chase said, but I cut him off.

"Nuh-uh," I said, shaking my head with cool calmness. "*You* need to let go of *me*."

"You're the one who stayed even after I cheated on you. You're the sappy puppy I used! You begged me to stay with you."

I smiled. "That's the past, *honey*. Who's busy creating fake profiles of me and commenting on *my* life?"

"You—"

"Chase, live *your* life. I don't know if the spark between you two is no longer there now that you're not sneaking around, and frankly, I don't give a damn. I don't want to be a part of your lives. Stay out of mine." I concluded firmly.

I turned to Noah who was standing a bit away from me, ready to defend himself.

"Hey buddy, want another burger?"

He nodded but looked menacingly at Chase. I walked over and put my arm around his shoulders, dragging him away.

"Thank you," I whispered.

"I didn't do anything," he said.

"You gave me the spark I needed to deal with Chase once and for all. It was cool, the way you stood up for me."

"Sometimes, big brothers need help too," he said with a chuckle. "But you were cool too."

"You think?"

"Yeah. You left them speechless, and you didn't have to hit them."

I smiled. I felt really good about the incident. I'd taken my power back. I hadn't just said words to Chase, I believed them. He stepped on spots that hurt, but I realized I didn't have to take crap from him. He was nothing but a bully. His pleasure was tormenting me, but he only gets it because I let him.

I turned the tables on him in ways I still marveled at. It occurred to me while we were talking that even though he'd broken up with me, he was very much still in my life through his own doing. He was the one who couldn't let go.

"I'm gonna ask Poppy what she wants from me," Noah said, pulling my attention away from my thoughts.

"Is that the girl spreading the rumors?" I asked.

"Yeah. I'm not gonna stoop to her level," he replied.

I ruffled his hair. "Tell me how it goes, and no more swearing."

"Sure, but I can't promise you the latter," he said with a chuckle.

* * *

Noah and I had our burgers and returned to the house toward the evening. While I was happy about the day's turnout, there was something else that was bothering me. Mark's attitude towards me hadn't changed. He didn't say a word to me unless I spoke to him. I brought the issue up with my mother.

We were seated on the front terrace. Everyone else was in the house. Mark was in his study, catching up on some work.

"Mom...does Mark ever talk about me?" I surprised Mom. I'd mulled over how to ask the question, and it was the best I'd come up with.

"Uh...what do you mean?"

"Like, does he ever mention me?" I said.

"Well...he has on several times, mostly talking about your attitude towards school and your goals and how I've raised a fine young man," she said with a smile.

"Is that...recently?"

"Uh no. Why are you asking?"

"I...I don't know. I think he's standoffish towards me lately," I said.

Mom looked at me sternly. "Well, you *did* steal his car."

"Evan stole his car!" I corrected.

"You were with Evan. You both snuck out. He's obviously not pleased," she said.

"I thought there might be something else," I said. Maybe he saw the Facebook page Chase and Bruce created.

"Well, Zac, you haven't apologized, not once."

"I suppose I should," I said.

"You should," Mom agreed.

"I'll do it right now," I said, standing up.

Mom said something about Mark being busy with stuff about his work, but I was already in the house. I figured I'd apologize really quickly so I wouldn't bother him too much. In fact, if he were eager to get back to work, he'd forgive me quicker. It was a good strategy.

I walked over to the door of his home office. I was about to knock when I heard him talking. I didn't mean to listen, but I heard some of the things he said. A few sentences, in particular, stayed with me. He seemed to be on the phone.

"....pushing for a settlement, which they will obviously grant quickly."

There was a significant pause. I couldn't hear him properly now.

"She'll say yes...weak, pathetic...there's no way she'll say no...access money...before she knows it..." There was a pause. "...trusts me. My son isn't the only one who can act."

"...brats. I hate... the last one is a nightmare. I've got to go. Work is..."

I couldn't hear the last word Mark said. I waited for a bit outside the door. He didn't continue talking, so I assumed he'd ended the call.

I wasn't sure what I'd heard, but it sounded suspicious. It didn't feel right talking to Mark after that. He'd know I'd been outside and if whatever he'd been talking about wasn't legal, I'd be a witness. I didn't want to be a part of it. I walked away from the door, deciding I'd apologize some other time, if ever.

Something about what I'd heard wasn't right. I just couldn't say for sure because they were in snippets, but it sounded like Mark was planning on swindling money from someone. *Who was he talking about, though?*

My immediate thought was my mom, but Mom didn't have money. We weren't poor, but we definitely did not have *that* kind of money lying around. It was possible we did, and I just didn't know, but ever since my dad died, mom has told me everything.

It was also possible that Mark was talking about a case involving one of his clients. I was blowing things out of proportion. Just because Evan hated him didn't mean the man was all bad. Right?

CHAPTER TWENTY-EIGHT

EVAN

It was true when they said material things couldn't fill an emotional hole. It didn't matter how many things I bought. He just wouldn't leave my mind—him and the guilt.

I screwed Zac over. I panicked. I didn't exactly have a squeaky clean image, but I knew adding more scandals to it would put my contract with David Markham in jeopardy. Without jobs, I'd soon be forgotten. Cody Wilde was a necessity. I couldn't let him slide into oblivion.

Once I started, I couldn't stop. Everything came effortlessly. Veronica had done her job well, and Jennifer was proud. The story hadn't dissipated yet, but, at least, it was calmer. I was still trending, but it was now more about my interview than the story, especially after several websites published articles about the interview.

When the PR stunts died down, I descended into manic shopping—buying shirts, suits, shoes, and watches in all brand names. I bought t-shirts, pants, bracelets, and rings I had no intention of ever wearing. I just needed a distraction. Most importantly, I needed to fill the void I was feeling.

I missed Zac. Everything felt so mundane, routine. There was no spark. I missed the freedom to do whatever I wanted. I missed the company. All my conversations felt flat. Zac occupied my mind for hours on end. No one had ever done something like that, at least no one who wasn't a fictional character. I'd left *something* behind in Sapphire Beach Town. I just didn't know what. It was certainly not the whole person, was it?

I didn't understand how I could miss someone I'd only shared a couple of days and memories with. I didn't understand how I could miss someone, period. I never let people get close to me, and I absolutely forbade myself from getting close to people. I believed that only professional relationships were beneficial. There were contracts, with repercussions if breached. Personal relationships weren't like that.

There was the risk of leaving with a broken heart and shattered dignity. Just ask Zac.

Even though I'd gone to the beach house with the same walls that surrounded me all the time, Zac had gotten too close. Instead of cutting all ties, I wanted to call him. I wanted to apologize for how I'd portrayed him to the media, for the lies I'd told. The guilt was eating at me. I felt as though I'd betrayed his trust, even though we didn't have such a relationship.

It felt like he was haunting me.

* * *

I smiled when the cashier rung the item I had brought with me to the front. She recognized me because her customary smile grew wilder. She stopped folding the sweatshirt I handed her.

I was on one of my crazy shopping sprees. I already bought an expensive watch that day when I noticed a fancy sportswear shop by the corner of the street I'd bought the watch in. I perused through the shop until I found something I liked. It was a fitting blue cotton sweatshirt. It was the only thing I bought that I genuinely liked.

"Cody Wilde, I didn't know you do your own shopping," she said.

"Sometimes, I do," I said with a quiet chuckle.

"It must be my lucky day."

"If you consider it luck to meet me, then it must be…Marissa," I said, tilting my head slightly to read her name tag.

"You know, instead of looking for an excuse to look at my boobs, you could just ask."

My eyes widened. "No, no, I was just—"

She cut me off with a chuckle. "I'm just kidding. I like the sweatshirt. It'll look good on you," she said as she resumed folding the sweatshirt.

"I'll take your expert advice," I said, to which she nodded.

I handed her a credit card. She didn't even look at it, which was perfect for me because it wasn't even mine. Apparently, with a face and fame like mine, I could commit fraud easily.

She handed me the card back, and I signed for my purchases. She shot me a flirty smile when she gave me my bag with the sweatshirt in it. I courteously smiled and walked out. I didn't feel like combing through the streets of New York anymore, so I got into my car and drove back to the apartment.

I went straight to my room when I got there, instructing Clive not to bother me.

My room was a mess. I bought too many things I didn't bother unpacking. Shopping bags littered the floor and the bed. I made enough space for myself on the bed and sprawled on it. I felt tired, but I hadn't done much that day. It was only midday.

I pulled out my phone from my pocket. I was itching to hear Zac's voice. It seemed to be the only way I could get him out of my mind. He needed to know how sorry I was and why I had left so suddenly.

My finger was hovering on the "Call" button when I heard a knock on the main door. It had to be for Clive because

I wasn't expecting anyone. I heard Clive open the door. He said a few words to someone before the door to my room flew open.

"You *are* here!" A girl shrieked.

Carrie was standing in front of me. She was a fellow model. She was tall and beautiful with long blonde hair and prominent cheeks. We met in Johannesburg at Mercedes-Benz Fashion Week. We talked a bit. We had sex at the back of a car twice. I explicitly told her before the act that I didn't want a relationship. A few months later, we bumped into each other at New York Fashion Week, and she professed her love to me after stalking me for a while.

I ran. Apparently, I could run, but I could not hide. Carrie had found me, and I had a feeling she wasn't letting go this time. I had to get rid of her, once and for all.

"Uh, hi," I said.

"Hi baby, I missed you so much. Give me a kiss," she said.

Before I could say or do anything, she swooped on me and placed her lips on mine. It was only a peck, but I couldn't let things go further.

"Didn't Clive tell you I was sleeping? I'm really tired," I said desperately.

"He did, but I just had to see you," she said. "We can cuddle. I am a very good cuddler."

"Uh..." I said, but she pushed me just a little to make a spot for herself so she could sit.

"How was the break? And your dad?" she asked.

"It was fine. He's fine," I replied with a shrug.

"Looks like someone went shopping. Oh my goodness, you shop like a girl. What did you buy?" she asked excitedly, giving herself permission to ransack through my purchases. "Oooh, this watch is nice."

She had pulled out my watch and was trying it on. She had quite a small wrist, so it was too loose on her. She smiled while wiggling her wrist, watching the watch move.

"It's really nice to see you. I thought you had found another model. I missed you," she said to me.

"Well, you can be assured, I haven't found another model," I said. "We need to talk," I told her, moving into a sitting position.

She started taking off her dress seductively. "I don't want to ruin it by sleeping on it," she explained, probably when she realized I was frowning. "We can talk while cuddling."

"Carrie, this is serious. I'd really prefer it if you—" I started, but I was interrupted by my phone ringing. I accepted without bothering to check the Caller ID, annoyed at the interruption.

"Cody Wilde," I said curtly.

"You have some nerve," the person on the other side barked.

I chuckled tauntingly. "What did I do now?" I said, recognizing the voice as my father's.

"You stole my credit card. That's what you did!" he said.

I played daft. "I...stole your card?"

"You're the only person with the guts to do something like that. And no one that I know is in New York right now!"

"Oh, so because I'm in New York and I have guts, I stole your card? You're a crappy lawyer," I said.

"I will not hesitate to get you arrested, Evan!"

My heart skipped a beat. I hadn't thought my plan through. Quite frankly, I hadn't thought of anything. The card had been on his desk the day he'd called me filth. I just grabbed it on my way out. I didn't know what I wanted to do with it until I started my shopping spree. I had enough money to pay for all the things I bought, but why use my money when I could use his? He owed me.

"Go ahead. Reveal your true colors," I said quietly.

"I am done with you!"

"You had been done a long time ago. You think you can make up for—" I said, but stopped myself. I was about to reveal secrets in front of Carrie.

"Cat got your tongue?" he taunted me.

"Don't fucking call me again! Do whatever you want to do!"

"Very well, from now on, you are dead to me!"

"I've been dead to you for a long time! You think inviting me to your 'family' get-together so I can put up a happy family front for your benefit makes up for all the times you deserted me? You were and are still a crappy father! Your freaking girlfriend tried to kill me, and what did you do? You beat me up for telling you the truth. You sent me away. You visited once in five months! You fucking cheated on my mom while she was on her deathbed, in front of me! So when exactly did I matter to you? Marianne doesn't deserve a *jackass* like you!"

I had lost all restraint. All the anger inside of me was just spilling out. I'd suppressed everything for so long. My anger was explosive.

Dad had scolded me before. He'd used more or less the same words. They were his go-to words. He hated that I had chosen modeling over college. He hated that I "paraded myself for money", comparing me to a prostitute. He cut me off financially. He tried to dictate my life. He probably just hated me, period. I had never exploded like that, and there was more.

"I grew up without you! You were never there. I raised myself. I'm sorry you don't like the person I have become. Actually, I'm not sorry. You don't freaking desert me and then come back years later to tell me how to live my life. Sure your money was there, but you fucking weren't. You call me a brat. Has it ever occurred to you that all I wanted was for you to love me? You left me alone to take care of Mom when she couldn't do anything for herself. *You deserve to rot in hell.*"

I broke down. For the second time in a long time, I found tears rolling down my cheeks. I hadn't cried in years. That was until the night Zac pushed me into the ocean. And now. Only then did I realize just how much of my armor was missing. It was almost all of it. I was bare.

There was a short silence after my breakdown before Dad started talking. "Evan, you have no idea what you're saying! You—"

I cut him off.

"Should I have yelled louder while you were beating me? Would that have made you stop and listen to me? And yet you told me to shut up. Do you know I freeze in large amounts of water? Do you know what the tattoo on my wrist is covering?"

"Evan, you—" he said, and I cut in again.

"Save it."

I hung up and dried my cheeks. Carrie was fiddling with her phone, but I'm pretty much sure it was just an act to cover the fact that she'd been listening in on the conversation. She moved the phone suspiciously behind her when she realized I was looking at it.

"Um…" I started, trying to get rid of the awkward air.

She surprised me by hugging me. She had taken off her dress earlier, so I could feel the perkiness of her breasts against my chest since she wasn't wearing a bra.

"I'm sorry," she whispered.

I put my arms around her and whispered back, "Make me forget."

She pulled out of the hug and cupped my cheek with her hand. "My pleasure."

I gave her a weary smile. I didn't know why I thought sex would help, and I didn't have the energy to question myself. Despite the repercussions of that act and the ache I suddenly felt for a different set of arms, I gave in. I needed the distraction. I felt too bare I could fall apart.

It wasn't as smooth sailing as I thought it would be. Despite the feverish kissing and touching, I couldn't get my mind in the right zone. Even Carrie with her perky breasts and small hips just couldn't get me excited enough.

I thought of Zac. He'd call me an idiot at that moment. Even when Carrie was swaying her hips against me sensually, I thought of Zac.

The thought of him still haunted me.

CHAPTER TWENTY-NINE

ZAC

Spring break ended a few days after Evan left. I think it ended the day he left. He didn't just leave me upset and confused. He left Mom feeling guilty for something she didn't do. She blamed herself for his sudden departure even when I reminded her that before he left, he'd been trending on social media. He had to go fix that.

I stayed out of Mark's way. I never got round to apologizing. I realized it didn't matter. If he was still angry about the car and Evan and me sneaking out, then he would just have to tell me about it. Anyway, maybe whenever we meet again, he would be in a better mood, or at least not be standoffish towards me.

When we left the beach house, I stayed the night at our house before leaving for college the next day. I wasn't looking forward to Livy asking me about Evan. She was a sucker for happy endings, but this was real life. There wasn't going to be a happy ending to this story. There wasn't even going to be an ending at all. Whatever fire sparked on that beautiful beach house was extinguished already. Evan was in New York, and he seemed happy, from his Instagram posts anyway.

I got to my dorm room at night, having elected to take a late flight so I could spend some more time with my family. I specifically wanted to spend more time with Mom without Mark there. I got a sense that maybe not everything was all right in Romanceville, but she assured me she was happy and content. She couldn't stop singing Mark's praises.

When I got to my room, Jackson was already there. He was unpacking his bag while listening to music on his phone.

"Hey!" he said, the moment I walked in. He seemed excited to see me.

"Hi," I said, walking in and closing the door. Putting my bag on the floor, I said, "Did you just get back?"

"No. Ross and Kyle dragged me away before I could unpack," he replied. His facial expression had been fairly bland when he said those words, but then he had a big grin on his face.

"I don't take it you're just happy to see me. What's up?" I said.

"I'm happy to see you," he said casually. "Seems like you didn't have the boring spring break you planned on, after all."

I groaned. "I guess you heard too."

"I didn't just hear, I saw too," he said enthusiastically.

I nodded. "It really is not as big as you think it is."

He walked past me to put a pair of jeans in his closet, but before he could do that, he turned to me. "You kissed a celebrity. It's big."

"There's nothing special about him; he's a doofus," I said, finally sitting down on my bed and taking off my shoes.

"Well, either way, I'm glad you didn't sit around moaning about Chase," he informed me.

I chuckled. "You don't even know half of what I did."

"Okay, that's true. But I *hope* you didn't sit around moaning about that jackass," he said, finally turning to put his jeans away.

"We are calling him a jackass now?" I said.

Jackson and I had never really talked about Chase, other than acknowledging that Jackson knew about the affair. He'd let me cry on my own when I needed to.

"I've always thought he was a jackass, a very proud arrogant one, too. I always wondered what you saw in him," he said, walking over to his bag on the bed.

I stayed quiet for a bit. I knew Chase was arrogant, but he'd been nice to me. When I developed a crush on him, it was mostly because he was hot. Before I knew it, I fell in love with him.

"Me too," I said in reply to Jackson's words.

"Seriously though, what else did you get up to besides making out with celebrities?"

"Singular form, gosh! And we didn't *make out*. It was something that resembled a kiss," I corrected.

"Yeah, yeah…and, answer me this: did he or did he not kiss you back? Because to me, it looks like he was all for that kiss," he said.

I chuckled. "I was drunk, I can't recall anything."

But in truth, I could remember that kiss very well.

Still.

"Tell me about Fort Lauderdale," I said quickly before Jackson thought of a follow-up question.

* * *

Jackson didn't interrogate me on my very public kiss with Evan, but I knew Livy would. There were inconsistencies with the stories. For one, I told Livy Evan was drunk. Evan told the world I was drunk. Someone had lied. It was a matter Livy would feel the need to discuss, and I wasn't up for it. While Jackson saw the whole thing as me having fun, Livy saw it differently. She was a psychologist-in-training. She knew there was more than what met the eye, and she was right.

We met outside our dorm's main door the morning classes resumed. She was excited to see me. I was somewhat excited to see her, even though she was going to ask the hard questions. She didn't do it then though. I asked about her trip to South Africa as we walked onto campus. I may have asked to prevent her from talking about Evan, but I was genuinely interested in her trip. She awed me with talks about her safari adventures, her shopping, and the interesting sights she'd laid eyes on. Of course, there were pictures.

That talk was enough to fill the time to get us into campus. Soon enough, we arrived in the building where our classes were held. Unfortunately, it was also the same building Chase and his friends were in. The corridor wasn't busy. We were walking from opposite directions which only meant we were going to pass each other. Before spring break, I would have opted for taking unnecessary turns just to avoid them, but not anymore.

"You should really see the tiny cell Nelson Mandela was jailed in. Robben Island was so—" Livy was saying then abruptly stopped when she spotted Chase and his friends who were literally in front of us. She'd been too absorbed by her stories to notice them.

"Look who we have here!" Avery was the first to speak. She sported bright pink hair this time which my eyes were very much irritated by.

"Hi, Barbie," Livy said with a fake smile.

"You see, that's a compliment because Barbie is hot, like me," Avery said.

Livy rolled her eyes.

"I know I don't have to ask about your spring break. How was *the rejection*?" Avery asked, looking at me. "You traumatized the poor guy."

She laughed, so did her boyfriend, and Claire.

I was unfazed by what was happening in front of me. I really couldn't be bothered to take their insults or laughter to heart.

"Let's go, guys," Chase said quietly.

"No, wait. I'm having fun. Za—" Avery started talking, but Chase interrupted her harshly.

"I said let's go!"

Chase started walking. Bruce followed suit, and soon enough, all of them walked away from us.

Livy turned towards their disappearing backs with a look of confusion. "What just happened? Shouldn't Chase be taunting you the most? You punched him!"

"I did it twice," I said, grabbing her hand so we could continue walking. We had little time before class started.

"You punched him twice?" she said, shock evident on her face and in her voice.

I chuckled. "The second one was figurative."

"Tell me!" she instructed.

*   *   *

Although Livy did not bring Evan up during our walk to class, I knew it was only a matter of time before she did. We stopped talking when we entered class. I'd already explained to her my encounter with Chase. I thought we were done talking for at least an hour, but she had other ideas.

"Zac," she whispered loudly, enough to get my attention. We were in class, sitting at the back of the auditorium. We usually sat in front, but we arrived a little late that morning.

"I have one pen," I said.

"I don't want your chewed-up pen, I have mine," she mocked. "You've ignored my text message for too long."

"What text message?" I asked.

"The one asking you about Evan," she replied. She'd sent me a text message the previous day after attempts to get me to talk about Evan. Attempts I thwarted.

"There's nothing to talk about," I said.

"Then tell me what really happened!" she whispered vehemently.

"He told you and the world what happened. I have nothing to add," I said and shrugged. "Can we not talk now? I'm trying to get my money's worth," I said.

"He's literally reading off his slides. About Evan—" she said, and I cut her off.

"There's nothing to talk about. He was drunk...I was drunk...someone between us was drunk. We kissed. Chase took a pic and called me a prostitute. I punched him. That's the whole story," I said with finality.

But Livy wasn't done. "He said you were distraught over Chase and kissed him. You wouldn't do something like that. And I think Chase doesn't affect you anymore."

I sighed.

I didn't realize that the class had turned dead quiet. Everyone turned to look at me, as if they were seeing me for the first time.

"Is there something you want to share?" the lecturer asked me.

"No."

The lecturer resumed talking.

"Livy, you probably think there's more to this Cody Wilde thing, but there isn't," I said softly. I hoped that closed that chapter. Only I couldn't count on that the moment the lecturer paused talking. My words had garnered the attention of the class. Again.

My eyes widened. Once again, everyone was looking at me. And this time, even their ears were tuned to me.

"Thank you, Zac, for reminding us what's important because clearly what I'm saying isn't. Class, if you don't already know, Zac kissed Cody Wilde," the lecturer said. *He knew too?*

Everyone turned to look at me again. *Seriously? Did they really need to look at me?* It wasn't like it was my first time in the class. I'd talked to three-quarters of the class before.

I placed my head on the desk slowly. *Damn you, Livy!*

243

"So…since you clearly think we need to know, was there more to the kiss?" the lecturer said.

I raised my head. "I would rather not answer. It's personal," I said.

"You brought your personal life into my class and had the audacity to talk about it while I was lecturing. It is no longer personal. Quite frankly, it was never personal."

"Prof. Winslow, it's my fault Zac started talking, and I'm sorry. He's sorry too. Can you please continue with the lecture?" Livy said.

* * *

"I am so sorry for that embarrassing moment back there," Livy said as we walked out of class. The lecturer had taken her plea and stopped talking about me, but the moment remained. Some people were still looking at me.

"I'm not talking to you," I said, toying with her.

"I'm sorry, Zac. I was selfish. I'm sorry," she said softly.

I shook my head.

"I'll buy you coffee."

I rolled my eyes.

"And muffins. Cappuccino muffins, your favorite," she said.

I smiled. "I'm still mad, but I can't say no to that."

She put her hand around my waist. "Can we talk about Cody Wilde now? You know it's not okay to push things to the background," she said sweetly.

She knew there was more. She didn't know what it was. I did, and it was something I had pushed into the background. I didn't want to talk about it because there was no point. I snapped.

"For fuck's sake, Livy, just stop! Stop putting so much pressure on me. You don't see me reminding you that you have a crush on Sean! It's been a whole year, and you still don't want to talk about it. You've pushed that to the background, yet you have the nerve to keep telling me about Cody Wilde. Guess what, you are a freaking coward like me. So, stop trying to make me do what you can't do!"

Livy was shocked. Maybe even beyond that. She just gave me a wide-eyed stare.

"Oh gosh, Livy, I'm…" I said. I was so shocked myself I couldn't finish.

We were in the middle of a hallway. And I had just shouted. People stared. And one person stood out from among them. Who wouldn't? With that pink hair, she was sure to pop out from the crowd. And right now, Avery was boring holes into Livy's head with her eyes, like she could rip her head off at that moment.

"You are such a tramp!" she finally said what she had been thinking.

"Don't you fucking say that!" I retorted.

"Why not? She is. Sean is Claire's, so stay the hell away from him!" she said to Livy and started walking away.

She wasn't the only one. Livy did the same.

"Livy, wait! Liv!" I shouted behind her.

She didn't turn around, just kept speed-walking. I wanted so badly to follow her, but decided to give her space to calm down. Hopefully, she would eventually.

CHAPTER THIRTY

ZAC

Livy sat as far away from me as she possibly could in the last classes that we had. I didn't want to prod, so I didn't try to be close to her. It was better not talking in class, as we had not so long ago realized. I would visit her later in her room. We'd have privacy, and I could possibly grovel at her feet.

Livy was my best friend, the only real friend I had. She stuck with me after our friends had deserted us. No, they deserted *me*. She'd chosen my side and stuck with me on my worst post-breakup moments. And she was the only one I could have a real conversation with it.

Well, maybe, Evan was an option.

I hated thinking about Evan. The silence between us was stretching, and that came with the realization that whatever moments we had were fleeting. They hadn't so much as made an imprint on Evan's life. He was back where he belonged, and so was I.

I had lunch on my own that day. I hung out with Jackson and Kyle for the evening; Ross had gone home for some family emergency. At night, I decided to talk to Livy. I hoped her roommate wasn't in when I knocked on the door. I knocked a couple of times before I was asked for my identity. It was odd, but I figured I was probably on the list of people she didn't want to see, so she was making sure it wasn't me.

"Zac," I said.

A few seconds later, the door opened. Maybe I wasn't on the list.

Livy was a sight. Her blonde hair was all messy, and she was wearing a onesie with Uggs. It wasn't even that cold. But besides the mess she'd obviously intentionally created of herself, she still looked beautiful.

"Hi," I said sheepishly.

"What do you want?" she asked.

"I'm sorry, Livy. I didn't mean to shout or call you a coward. I was just upset," I said and sighed. "You're right, there's something." It was the first time I had said that out loud.

She opened the door wider and walked into the room. I followed her and closed the door. She sat cross-legged on her bed, and I sat on a chair next to her.

"I'm still mad. But, do you want to talk about it?" she asked.

I took a deep breath. "That kiss…the—the one Chase took a picture of, it wasn't the first one."

"It wasn't?" she said. You could spot her excitement a mile away.

"It wasn't even the last," I admitted.

"So, he drunkenly kissed you more than once? Or were you the drunk one?"

"The first time was at this secluded beach. We were just eating burgers, and we spotted Chase and Bruce. Evan just…kissed me. Wait, no, the day before that we went to the beach, and he pretended to be my boyfriend. That was after…God, there's a lot I didn't tell you," I said.

"You could…tell me. I could give you perspective," she said with a smile.

I smiled and proceeded to tell her the story, leaving out the reason Evan was upset. For the story to make sense, I told her something had happened. She didn't push to know what, respecting his privacy.

When I was done, she looked at me. "Can you honestly say there's nothing?"

"I don't know."

"Do you want to know why he kissed you?"

"Hell yeah!"

"There's your answer," she said.

"You're not making sense."

"It's fairly simple. If any of the kisses meant nothing to you, it wouldn't matter why he kissed you. For you, it would be a closed chapter. You want to know because you're hoping for something."

I pursed my lips.

"Are you angry that he twisted the story?" she asked.

Before I could answer, her phone rang. She took it from under her pillow, pressed "Ignore" and put it back.

"Not important?" I asked.

"No. You were saying…?" she said quickly.

"I was upset initially. Now, I don't know. I understand why he did—" I said, and her phone rang again.

She did the same thing as last time, only this time she went further and actually switched it off.

"It seems important," I said, referring to the phone call.

"It's not." She shrugged. "Maybe you should talk to Cody. At least, close the chapter properly."

"Absolutely not! I'm making a big deal out of nothing, and he's probably going to laugh in my face," I said. I couldn't believe she would even suggest it.

"I didn't mean you should tell Cody you like him. Just…talk to him about random things and just see what happens."

"First things first, I don't like him. Secondly, stop calling him Cody. I feel like we're talking about two different people," I said.

"Oh, but I'm not on a personal name basis with him. You are," she said with a wink.

"I don't think that matters," I said with a chuckle.

There was a knock on the door. Livy didn't show signs of moving. In fact, she looked alarmed by the sound.

"Aren't you going to get the door?" I asked.

"No. I'm talking to you."

I stood up. "Liv, this…," I said, pointing between us, "…is not an emergency. We can talk whenever even in class if you are up for embarrassing me again."

She laughed. When she realized I was walking towards the door, though, she gave me a look of horror.

"Don't!" she shouted.

It was too late. I had already opened the door. I realized why she looked so alarmed when I saw who was standing there. Sean, who I had told the world Livy was crushing on, was standing there. Livy must have known he was coming, which could only mean he had contacted her. He was the person whose phone calls she was ignoring. He knew! Of course, he knew about the incident. Avery was a blabbermouth.

"Hi," I said slowly.

"Hey. Is Liv in there?" he asked, going straight to the point.

"Uh…" I said.

"Don't lie. You and Amber aren't friends, so you can't be in there with her," he said. "Can you tell Liv that I need to see her?"

"Uh, sure. Just a sec," I said and closed the door.

"I'm really sorry. What I did was moronic," I said as I turned to Liv, who was lying like a star on her bed.

"Is he gone?" she asked wearily.

"He wants to see you."

"Tell him I don't want to see him," she said.

"Livy."

"Zac, I can't see him. I'm not going out there to embarrass myself. He's going to tell me he's happy with Claire, and of course, he should be. She likes him, she's good for him," she said.

"She didn't write the letter that won his heart. You did."

"It wasn't the letter that got them together," she said.

"It was the letter." I disagreed. "Claire stole that letter and made it seem as if it was her own. I bet Claire doesn't even know Sean secretly draws or wrinkles his nose when he's thinking," I said.

"You make me sound like a creep."

"Liv, go out there and tell him you hate his guts. Just talk to him! What about closing the chapter properly?" I used her words against her.

"I was referring to you!"

Sean knocked again.

"Livy, we are no different. You've spent forever crushing on him. Yes, he's Claire's boyfriend, and she very much used underhanded tactics to get him. That doesn't even matter. He could be your one true love. You have this chance. Go out there and ruin it. At least, you have done something instead of wondering how things could be. Maybe that ginger guy downstairs is your true love, but you'll never see it until you close this chapter," I said.

"You think?" she said. "The ginger guy does look cute."

I pulled her to her feet and fixed her hair, tucking it behind her ear.

"You can come…" I said, and Sean knocked again. "You can come to my room later. Jackson is with Kyle and won't be back any time soon, so I heard."

She gave me a small smile and walked to the door. I followed behind her and passed her by the door after she opened it.

"Hi," Sean said to her.

"Hi," she said.

"Can we talk? In private?"

"I'll see you guys!" I said.

I think both of them were no longer aware that I was even there.

I made my way towards my room, hoping Livy and Sean both said what was really in their hearts. Livy's crush on Sean dated eons, at least the first day she saw him. Claire swooped in and declared him hers. Livy shoved her feelings to the back, but now push had come to shove.

* * *

Sean and Livy talked for way too long. At least that's what I thought they were doing the entire time I was lying on my bed and listening to music. I had played my playlist twice. *How much did they need to say?*

While I was waiting, I got a call from my mother. She had two things to tell me, both of which were shocking.

"Honey, I have something to tell you," she said after the usual greetings.

I moved slightly on the bed, adjusting my position. "Yeah?"

"So, remember after your dad's plane crash, the National Transportation and Safety Board started an investigation into the cause?"

"Yeah?" I said again, wondering where she was going with it.

"Well, they released the report, and the airline was found to have been negligent on maintenance issues."

"Oh…so what's gonna happen?"

"I didn't want to tell you this before, but we're suing the airline. They want to settle out of court. Mark is handling the settlement. He's quite good. He's getting us more than the airline initially wanted to pay," she explained.

"How much is more?"

"A million dollars," she said. "Your brother and sister don't know yet, so I'd rather you didn't tell them. Once the money is here, we'll discuss what to do with it as a family. Maybe we can create a foundation in your dad's memory..."

I was no longer listening. My family was about to be million-dollar rich. Mark was handling the settlement, the same Mark whose conversations a few days prior had given me chills. I could still remember the things I heard. I dismissed them because mom had no money he could swindle out of her. Mom was about to have money he knew everything about. Something was fishy.

"Oh honey...the other thing," she said quickly. I could hear the excitement in her voice. "Mark proposed! He wants to marry me."

What?

"Uh...Mom, I..." I said, and she cut in.

"I said yes! I'm so happy. He's such a wonderful guy. He's even representing our family free-of-charge," she said.

Of course, he was doing it free of charge. He knew he'd have access to the money.

"Mom, I don't think Mark is who you think he is," I said.

Her excitement deflated like a balloon. "Zac, don't be like this."

"There's something off about him. He's—"

"Don't!" she said sternly. "He warned me that Evan would feed you lies. Don't you see that he's just trying to not have a stepmother? He doesn't want us in his life."

"Evan has nothing to do with this. I don't think Mark is representing us out of sheer good will. There's something in it for him. He...I heard him—"

She cut in. "I expected this from Jess, not you! Why can't any of you just be happy for me?"

"Mom, you know I love you. I would never sabotage you. Mark is—"

She cut in again. "Save it." She hung up.

I tried calling her. She just let it ring until it went to voicemail. I hated being the bearer of bad news, but I knew I wasn't wrong. Mark was up to something.

* * *

I didn't think about Mark or the million dollars for long. Livy was done talking to Sean. There was a knock on my door just as I gave up calling my mom.

"Livy?" I shouted. I was too lazy to get off the bed.

"Yeah. I don't care if you are naked, I'm coming in," she said.

She was still her crazy self, which was a good sign.

"Lucky for you, I'm dressed," I said while she was opening the door.

I sat up. She walked in like she was hiding from someone or something.

"Phew. I need a bodyguard," she said swiftly.

"Why do you need a bodyguard? Did you kill Sean?"

"Umm…kind of. The first two letters are correct, the rest aren't."

My eyes widened. "I bet you didn't kick him. You bad girl. You kissed him!"

She grinned and blushed.

"So why do you need a bodyguard?" I asked.

"Because when Claire and Avery see me, they will likely decapitate me and hang my head on the dorm door."

"Such drama. Tell me everything," I said.

"I recorded us."

"Even better!"

"Gosh, no, I didn't! Guess I'm not the only nosy one."

"Whatever. Tell me. And thank me with coffee and muffins tomorrow before class," I said.

She sat on the bed next to me.

"We talked," she said.

"Of course, you talked. I didn't think you did anything else besides talking, which you did. Can you be more specific?"

She laughed. "Uh...he likes me, too. Since the day we got stuck together on the bleachers when you ditched me to go stalk your crush, he said. It was a nice night. He spent it explaining football, and I spent it psychoanalyzing him. I told you about that night. He said he didn't have the guts to tell me and didn't think I liked him, too. He was ready now, and apparently, he wasn't going to leave until I talked to him. I told him how I felt—maybe not everything I've told you—but close enough. I told him about the letter Claire stole," she said.

I smiled genuinely. "So, what now?"

"Now, I need a bodyguard," she said.

"Livy, that is not what I meant."

"He broke up with Claire," she said.

"When?"

"About three days ago. I didn't believe him at first, but he showed me the texts."

"So, you are a couple now?"

She nodded slowly like she wasn't quite sure.

"What's up?" I asked softly.

"I feel bad."

"For Claire?"

"Yes. And how can I even be sure he genuinely likes me? It could be a trap. Like Chase. Maybe he didn't even break up with Claire. Maybe they are all in on it. Zac, why am I so gullible?"

It's heartbreaking when you see yourself in someone else. I had experienced what she was talking about. I couldn't tell her if she was being played for a fool or not. Sadly, that was love. You could never be a hundred percent sure.

It was possible that Sean had set out to embarrass her. It was also possible that he genuinely liked her. How do you know which one it is?

"Take the plunge," I said out of the blue.

"What?"

"Be with him, Liv. There is no way of knowing. Love is about making mistakes and getting up again. How many people can say they have married their first loves and lived happily ever after? How many people can say it's guaranteed that the person they are with right now is the only person they'll be with for the rest of their lives? Sure, they might say it, but who's to say it will happen that way? I don't know if Sean is the right guy for you or if he's playing you, or if he genuinely wants to be with you. Fall in love and get your heart broken, just as long as you love again. Let go of your fears and just love," I said.

It felt like a mouthful, and it was. I didn't even know where the words had come from. Something opened my eyes.

"What about Claire?" she asked.

"What about her?"

"If Sean genuinely wants to be with me, I will be stealing him away from her. Even if they broke up, maybe she did love him."

"Love is never wrong, Livy. Love is beautiful and strange. We sometimes fall for the unlikely people. Maybe eighty percent of people out there will believe you are a 'home wrecker,' but why should it matter? You fell in love. You didn't even want to tell him. Chase cheated on me. I wasn't mad that he loved Bruce. I was mad he cheated and lied to me. Love is only wrong when it makes people cheat. Claire will be hurt. She will feel like killing you. But she has no right," I said.

She smiled slightly. "You aren't mad that he's the same guy who didn't tell you about Chase and Bruce?"

I sighed. "I can live with that. Sean is a great guy even with his faults."

She surprised me by hugging me. I hugged her back.

"I won't push you, but it's your turn to talk to that one person you can't stop thinking about," she said while we were hugging.

I let go of her gently. "I never said I can't stop thinking about him," I said.

She shook her head lovingly at me. She got a text and looked lovingly at her phone. I could swear she was blushing. She was glowing too. It was a beautiful sight to watch.

"While you are texting your boyfriend, tell him if he plans on hurting you. I hope he has health insurance," I said.

She didn't even look up.

"Gosh, Livy, is this how it's going to be? Because I am ready to get rid of him already," I joked.

"Sorry," she said sheepishly.

"You are beautiful."

She looked up. "Uh...thanks?"

"I don't mean...I mean that you glow when you're happy."

"I have a boyfriend," she said, giving me a serious look.

We burst out laughing.

"Thanks, Zac."

I smiled. If only I could find the courage to deal with my situation. Not just ignore it, but actually face it.

CHAPTER THIRTY-ONE

EVAN

Two weeks passed since I got back from Dad's beach house. Two weeks of silence between us. It wasn't unusual; we went months without talking. But the silence after my meltdown was a bit deafening. I guess I expected him to do something. But, no, he did nothing.

I berated myself for letting it get that far. I was never supposed to reveal just how much he hurt me, not to him and not to myself. The past was better buried in the past. He'd proven that by not calling me even once after I unloaded a load of shit on him. He brushed it all aside like I'd said nothing.

He hadn't taken action against me for stealing and using his credit card, either. It was as if I didn't exist. It was good. All ties had been severed. I symbolically cut up his credit card. The shopping spree had gotten me more than what I needed, but it wasn't worth it. I couldn't keep provoking the man. I was fine.

My life was silent too. The spotlight had dimmed down and I was no longer the talk of the town. It was a good thing for David Markham. After my recklessness, he considered replacing me, but Jennifer managed to talk him out of it. He suggested meeting up in person, just the two of us. He was particular about the kind of people he asks to represent his brands. The lunch date had gone well, but I hadn't put pen to paper yet.

I had a feeling I passed the test, so I wasn't worried. I was, however, worried about something I planned to do.

After the night Carrie had spent at my apartment, she'd taken it upon herself to visit me every day. She was even thinking of publicizing our relationship. I had to put an end to it.

I invited her to talk—in public, of course. I figured she wouldn't go crazy on me in public. She was, after all, a fellow model. Her reputation mattered too.

I got to the restaurant and waited for her. I could have sworn I said one o'clock, but she was running late. I considered standing up and leaving, but I forced myself to be patient. I had to talk to Carrie. I had to set things straight, once and for all.

I spotted her as she walked in and beckoned her over. She kissed me on the cheek before sitting down.

"I'm sorry I'm late, honeybun. I couldn't find anything to wear. I needed to go shopping," I said.

"It's okay. I haven't been waiting long," I informed her. I lied. Ten minutes was too long in my world. I could have told her that, but it was crucial to start on a good note.

"Are we celebrating your deal?" she asked.

"Uh, how do you know about that?" I asked. Everything was hush-hush at that moment. Contracts hadn't been signed. Even the media hadn't gotten wind of the story.

"I heard you talking on the phone. You thought I was sleeping. I didn't mean to listen, honeybun," she said.

"Did you tell anyone about this?"

"No. I'm sure Emilia Pjanic can't wait to start shooting," she said. She sounded disgusted.

"Did you hear me mention her on the phone too?"

"No. You were talking with Clive about her and the shoot, and her legs," she said contemptuously.

"Oh. Anyway, we aren't celebrating the deal. The contract hasn't been signed yet."

"When are you signing?"

"In about a week," I said. "I wanted to talk to you about something."

She smiled.

"Carrie, you are a nice girl, but this...I can't do this anymore."

"Are you breaking up with me?" she asked softly.

I nodded. "Yes. I don't want to be in a relationship right now. I never wanted to be in a relationship," I said gently. I left out the part where I didn't even know we were in a relationship.

"But Evan, I love you."

About a month prior I would have pointed out that she knew the terms of our "association" and just stood up and left. I couldn't stand up and leave her there with teary-eyed. I was hurting her even though it had never been my intention.

"I'm sorry, Carrie."

"Please give me a chance. I'll do whatever you want," she cried.

"I can't. I'm sorry."

"It's because of Emilia, isn't it? I heard you talking with Clive. You want to..." she said and realized she had raised her voice. "You want to get with her," she said, lowering her voice.

"Emilia has nothing to do with this."

"You are gay then?" She snorted.

"I'm sorry. I never meant to lead you on if I did," I told her softly. "Please don't *ever* show up at my apartment again." My tone was stern. I'd told her numerous times there was nothing between us, but she never listened. I hated being stern, but I had to be. She had to get it this time.

"Cody..." she said gently.

"I have to go now. I hope to see you around," I said and stood up, praying she didn't make a scene.

She didn't, which was a relief. She just sat there and watched me leave.

She didn't attempt to contact me that day, and I went to bed in peace. The next morning, I woke up to my phone ringing and someone banging on my bedroom door. I certainly did not wake up in peace. I ignored both the phone call and the knock on the door.

"Evan, I know you are in there. Would you open up?" Clive shouted from outside my bedroom door.

"Why are you up so early and what do you want with me?" I asked.

"Have you read the news this morning?"

My phone started ringing again. I ignored it and focused on Clive.

"Obviously not. I was sleeping, which you obviously don't think is important. What do you want?"

"You are in…everywhere," he said.

"Yeah, I'm a supermodel. Can you be precise?" I said, showing my annoyance in my voice.

"Your story—about your dad abusing you."

A story about what?!

Zac!

Zac was retaliating. He was angry about what I'd said and was taking revenge. *Didn't he realize that was the worst thing he could use against me?* Only he knew about it. He'd gone straight for the jugular.

My phone rang again. I finally looked at the Caller ID. It was Jennifer. I didn't have to guess why I was being called so early in the morning. I sat up and went to unlock the door.

"Clive, what are you talking about?" I asked as soon as Clive came into view.

"This," he said, handing me his tablet.

I read what was on the screen quietly. It was an article about the blow-up I had with my dad. It contained all the things I'd said. The journalist speculated that I was abused as a child, citing it as the reason why I never talked about my family life.

"How many…" I said.

"Too many to count. I got a lot of hits just on Google. Local, international…it's *everywhere*. You are…you are trending on Twitter, again," he said. "There's also a…there's a recording."

Suddenly, things didn't make sense. Zac couldn't have been behind the article. I remembered the day I had the blow-up with my dad. I remembered the moment like it was the previous day.

I said one word. "Carrie."

"She leaked it?" he asked.

"Yes," I replied. There was only one person who'd have a recording. "She has a motive. How could I have been so dumb?"

"But Evan, if he abused you, isn't it better…" Clive started.

"I don't want it out there! I just…Fuck!" I shouted. I wanted to bang my head against something. I wanted to yell. I wanted to scream. This was not happening. I'd managed to keep that part of my life a secret. Now, it was out there. Everyone knew. Everyone had their own opinion. They all "knew" what I should have done. They're probably debating it amongst themselves now.

Everything I had built had crumbled. Everyone would see Cody Wilde was a farce, something created to evade my past.

They *knew*.

"I want to disappear."

"If you could do that, that would be great because you have a lot of people camping outside the building for you, and I don't think they are fans," he said. "And your fans are with you one hundred percent. They empathize with you."

"I don't want empathy! I want the whole thing to be erased from their memories! Can you do that?"

Clive gave me a sheepish look.

"This is a disaster!" I yelled.

"What will you do?"

What could I do? I couldn't just disappear although I really wanted to. I was a celebrity. Wherever I went, people would recognize me. There wasn't anywhere I could hide. Actually…there was. If I played my cards right, I could hide out for a while.

"Disappear," I replied to Clive's question.

"To where? Unless you are thinking of the Amazon jungle, 'cause this story is everywhere."

"Somewhere I can curl up and hide, and it's definitely not here," I said. "Give me a sec."

I reached for my phone. Truthfully, I wasn't sure what I was doing. It could potentially blow up in my face. It *was* going to blow up in my face. It was reckless, but wasn't everything I did reckless?

I scrolled down to a contact I'd saved only a few weeks prior. I pressed 'Call' and waited a few seconds before the person picked up. I hadn't heard that voice in so long. It felt like ages.

"Hello?" he said. He seemed uncertain who he was talking to or maybe he knew and was still mad at me.

"Hi, it's Evan," I said.

He coughed.

"I need a place to stay," I told him.

"What?"

"I need…I can explain when I get there. I just need a few days," I explained. Sort of.

"I live at a dorm," he enunciated.

"I know. It'll do. It's precisely where they wouldn't expect me to be," I said.

"Who are '*they*'? Evan, are you okay? Are you sure you know who you're talking to?"

"I'm fine, Zac. So, what do you say? Can I visit?"

"It's a dorm, there are rules. You seem to forget this a lot, and I always have to remind you, you're *famous*. There's no way you can show up here and not cause a scene," he said.

"Leave that to me," I said hastily.

"The last time I left things to you, you twisted the story and painted me out to be some predator!"

Ouch! He still remembered.

"Zac, I'm sorry about that. It got out of control. I'll explain when I get there."

He sighed. "Dorm room," he reminded me. "I have a roommate. I share a kitchen with a bunch of other people. The only thing that's private is my bathroom, and even that isn't really private, I share with my roommate. I have one bed."

"I can deal with that," I said. I was definitely being reckless.

"How do you plan on getting into a dorm unnoticed? You're *Cody Wilde*. I don't wanna be caught up in your life. Last time I helped you, I got burned."

It was my turn to sigh. "You're right, I was a jerk. The truth is I need to get away from being Cody Wilde. I promise I won't get you in any trouble or bring attention on you."

"Why do you even need this?!"

"I can't explain right now. It'll only be for a few days."

"I suppose I could…" he said and took a deep breath. "I have no idea why I'm doing this, but okay, you can come. But I swear if you say anymore lies about me, Chase won't be the only one to have the unfortunate luck of meeting my fist. I don't care that you're famous."

I suppressed a laugh. "I'm in New York so I can be there in about two hours if I can get a flight or…" I said and turned to Clive. "You can drive me, buddy."

Clive just looked at me like I was crazy.

"Text me the address," I said to Zac and hung up.

"Did you just call the prostitute?" Clive finally said something.

"He's not a prostitute," I snapped. "I need you to drive me somewhere."

He shook his head. "You're crazy."

"I agree. But for once I'm doing what I want to do. Clive, I need this," I said moments before I got a text from Zac with the address.

Clive bit his finger. "Okay, let's say I agree to this. How can we pull it off? If you didn't hear me before, there are people camping outside for you."

"We have an underground parking lot, Clive. I'll be in the trunk until we're a considerable amount of miles away, and then I'll be in disguise," I said.

"What? If you want to kill yourself, I won't assist you!"

"Okay, I'll be in the backseat," I said, opening my closet and picking out a few clothes. "We need to leave before Jennifer gets here."

"I am so going to regret this," he said. "Are you going to say anything to your manager or the agency at all?"

"No, and you aren't either," I replied while packing my bag.

"I don't get why you want to leave. You could stay here until it dies down," he said.

"I already feel like an animal in the zoo," I said.

"And you think going to this Zac person would help? Who is he anyway?"

"The lesser you know, the better," I said, zipping up my bag. I hoisted it on my shoulder.

"Uh...you haven't showered or brushed your teeth. You just woke up," he reminded me.

"Oh right," I said, putting my bag down. I was prepared to walk out.

I took a quick shower and freshened, donning jogging pants and a T-shirt. I looked fairly decent if I say so myself. I had no makeup on, which made me feel bare. Clive and I set out towards Zac's college.

I didn't know what to expect, but I knew what I needed. I hoped Zac was up to it. I had done a lot of wrong things, and I hoped he didn't dwell on them. I didn't know how it would be seeing him again. I couldn't think about it long, or else, I wouldn't go. I was hoping not to see him in a long time, and yet he'd been the first person I thought of in my time of need.

I was rationally reckless...at least, I thought I was.

CHAPTER THIRTY-TWO

ZAC

When I got the call from Evan, I was shocked. I was shocked more at his request. Evan was famous and probably knew a lot of people. *Why did he need to stay with me?*

I had been thinking about him the last few weeks, especially every time I saw Livy and Sean together. They were officially a couple now, and they just looked beautiful. Livy had decided to take the plunge, and I was happy for her. But it also reminded me of what I wasn't able to do. I'd given her one of the best advice I had ever given to anyone (I think), but I couldn't follow my own advice.

Evan and I were complicated. I wasn't even sure what I felt for Evan. Maybe I was just reading too much into what happened between us. Maybe the connection had just been from my side only. Besides, the guy was straight— something that he felt compelled to remind me.

Two weeks had passed. I thought he had forgotten about me. To get a call from him was unexpected. I got butterflies when I realized he was on the other end of the line. They weren't pure butterflies, though; I was just nervous about what he wanted.

We'd parted on a somewhat okay note until he lied about me. I couldn't forget that he'd lied, but I also couldn't forget that we'd kissed passionately. I had a chance to set the record straight, and close the chapter. Seeing him again could actually be good for me.

But...it wasn't that simple.

Evan wasn't just any guy. He was famous. He attracted attention wherever he went. His presence could throw me into the spotlight once again. The first time hadn't been so bad, but I liked my boring not-worthy-of-Instagram life. Evan could be doing some follow-up story to accuse me of misconduct once again. Maybe the first had gotten him more deals and fame, and he just had to do it again.

I didn't know why, but I chose to trust him.

I still didn't know how he planned to get into my room unnoticed, but I shoved that thought to the back of my mind and prepared to receive him. The first thing I had to do was get rid of my roommate. It wasn't simple, and I had no idea how to go about it.

I'd gotten Evan's call while I was in my room. Jackson had gone out to breakfast with Kyle. I'd declined the invite because I was just too sleepy. It was a Saturday morning, and I hadn't felt the need to go anywhere.

I waited for about thirty minutes for Jackson to come back so I could ask him to leave. When he got back, I still hadn't figured out how to ask him, so I went with the first thing that came to mind when he walked in.

Fortunately, Kyle wasn't with him.

"Hey, can I ask a favor?" I said nervously.

He put his phone on the desk in front of him and started taking off his sweatshirt. "Yeah?"

"I...umm...I need the room to myself for a couple of days," I said. It sounded stupid, and I hated it.

Jackson stopped what he was doing and looked at me. With a brow raised, he said, "Why?"

"Uh..." I trailed. It was so hard to say the words. "I met a guy."

"So…you want to…" Jackson said, unwilling to continue.

I nodded without looking at him. If I were someone else and was presented with such a scene, I would laugh. It was too comedic. But I wasn't someone else. I felt a heap of embarrassment on top of me.

Jackson crossed his arms. "How long is a couple of days?"

He didn't seem pissed, and I was relieved. I was practically kicking him out of his room, which he *paid* for. He was probably used to it because Chase and Bruce did their shenanigans in his room when he was sharing with Bruce, but I didn't want to be like Bruce. Still, I felt like a jerk.

I had no idea how long Evan intended on staying so I just guessed at random numbers. "Two or three days."

"And where do you suppose I'll be staying in those three days?"

"I could pay for a hotel room," I replied. The things Evan made me do!

Jackson chuckled. "While I'm glad you're moving on, I'm not happy about this. But…I'm willing to give you space. You don't have to pay for a hotel room. I'll room with Kyle for a while. Ross is still not back, so he won't mind."

"Thanks."

"I can't believe you offered to pay for a hotel room! You're too good for your own good."

"I *am* kicking you out of your own room. It was only fair I pay for your accommodation," I said sheepishly.

"Just be willing to return the favor," he said. "Anyway, who is this guy you're kicking me out for?"

I chuckled. "You've never met or heard of him. Speaking of him, please make sure you take everything you need with you. If you forget something, text me, and I'll bring it to you."

He looked at me for a while and then smiled. "Are you keeping him a secret? Secrets have a way of coming out, you know."

He was right. Of course, he was right. I was only digging my own grave.

"Just...pack everything," I said.

"When is he coming?"

"He should be here in about an hour or so," I said with a sheepish grin.

"Are you serious?"

"Yes. I'm sorry, it's short notice. It's an emergency," I said.

He put his hands on his waist. "An emergency? Seriously? You know what, I'm just gonna pack my stuff and leave," he said, chuckling.

"I have another favor to ask."

"What else could you possibly want?"

"Can I have your pass card? It's just much easier if he doesn't have to sign in at the front desk. I know he can get his own pass, I just...it's complicated. I'll return it to you, I promise."

He delved into his pocket and took out a card. "Only because I trust you," he said, handing the card to me. "I hope this doesn't come to bite me in the ass or you for that matter."

"It won't," I said quietly. I *hoped* it won't.

*   *   *

We talked while he packed. He called Ross, who had no problems with him using his bed. That reminded me that although I had solved the roommate issue, there was still the issue of *where* Evan was going to sleep. My room had two beds, one of which wasn't mine. I wasn't about to ask Jackson if I could use his bed even though I could change the sheets. He'd have more questions that I won't be able to answer.

Only my bed was available for use. One bed, two guys. I didn't see how that would work. I did, however, have a portable camping futon called a Shiatsu Massage mat for a camping trip I had yet to take. Evan could sleep on that. I wasn't giving up my bed. I didn't care if he thought his spine would break or something.

My phone vibrated just as Jackson finished packing his food supplies.

"Hey, I'm outside," the text read.

The butterflies in my stomach then ran rampant. Evan was outside my dorm. He was there, in the flesh. It felt like a long time since I'd seen him. In a few minutes, I would be seeing him again.

I couldn't do this.

"Are you done?" I asked Jackson.

"Yeah. Is that him? Why do you look like you've seen a ghost?"

Because I was about to.

I nodded.

"Okay, I'm gone. Have fun and stay away from my bed," he said, grabbing his bags.

I chuckled to ease my nervousness.

I walked with Jackson outside my room. Just as I opened the door, we were met with the view of Livy clutching her tablet.

"Where are you going?" she enquired, looking at Jackson.

I shook my head slightly. Livy couldn't know that Evan was going to be my temporary roommate, not right then anyway.

"Study session with Kyle," Jackson replied. "Don't look at my snacks like that. I *need* them."

Livy smiled and nodded. Jackson left the two of us standing there.

"I can't talk right now. I have to be somewhere," I said, remembering that Evan was waiting for me.

"I thought you'd want to see this. It's about Cody," she said urgently.

"What do you mean?"

"Look at this," she said and handed me her tablet. I only saw the headline on her screen before she said, "That's some really deep stuff."

My mouth hung open. Evan's past had been dragged to the present. There were allegations of abuse and affairs. It was more or less the same things he'd told me, but from what I've known, it was something he didn't want anyone to know. He couldn't even discuss it for more than five minutes. There was a whole article about it.

Was this why he was outside my dorm?

"There's a recording of his outburst. It's so heartbreaking," Livy said.

"I have to go. Seriously. I'll talk to you later. Don't come to my room, I'll come to yours," I said quickly.

I didn't stay for a second to see Livy's confusion. She had definitely expected a reaction from me, and not getting one had left her confused.

I ran outside the dorm. I couldn't figure out where Evan was until I got a text from him.

"Parking B, black car."

He must have seen me walk out. I noticed the car and walked towards it. *Thank God, the parking lot was pretty much deserted.* He got out as I approached.

For a few seconds, my heart stopped. I took in his form. He was really there in the flesh, wearing jogging pants and a sweatshirt with a cap and a pair of sunglasses. He wasn't really in disguise, but I suppose the hood, cap, and sunglasses helped hide his face a bit. He was standing in front of me. I could touch him if I wanted to. I didn't want to, but I could. I could also punch him for lying to the world about me. It would serve him right.

"Hi." My voice came out too soft for my liking.

"Hey."

"How'd you get here? Um...who's...?" I said, indicating the car.

"My friend drove. His name is Clive. He's in the car," he said.

I looked at the driver's window. It was closed, but the person inside was pretty much looking back at me, craning his head.

"He's umm..." I said and trailed.

"Clive, cut it out!" Evan barked after looking at the window, too. "Can we go now? The longer I stay here, the more I run the risk of someone recognizing me," he said to me.

"Yeah, sure," I said and started walking.

CHAPTER THIRTY-THREE

ZAC

It was surreal that Cody Wilde was in my room, him with his million followers who'd bend over backward for him. That person was in my room. I was his refuge. It didn't make sense. *He could be anywhere, but why my room?*

After his phone call, I just focused on making sure things were ready for his arrival. At that moment, it didn't feel real. Now it was real. He was in my room, my *locked* room.

We got to the room without any hassles. Evan kept his head low, and I didn't walk like I was harboring a fugitive celebrity. We hadn't bumped into anyone I knew or anyone who felt the need to talk to me. Evan pretended he lived at the dorm, using Jackson's card to get in. When we did meet people, none of them paid much attention to us.

Now we were in my room. What now?

"You can put your bag on the floor. I'll make space for you in my closet. You can sit on the chair or the bed, the one you're standing next to," I said quietly, realizing the silence between us had stretched quite a bit. My words weren't conversation starter material, but they were something.

He removed his hood, cap, and glasses. For a second, I was stunned by how beautiful he was. I wasn't supposed to be reacting to it like it was the first time I'd seen him, but I was. Gods, goddesses, demigods, titans—Evan was gorgeous beyond words. He still had those beautiful gray eyes. Few freckles I'd never noticed before dusted the bridge of his nose and the top of his cheeks. His lips made me yearn to just grab him by the waist and part them.

Did I just…? Was I yearning to grab him by the waist and kiss that traitor?

"I know, I know. I look different without makeup," he said, smiling.

More like *gorgeouser*, if there ever was such a word.

I needed to do something, or I'd act all stupid. I went to the closet and moved a few things around. *Why was I seeing Evan in a different light?* I knew he was good-looking, and I'd acknowledged that, but why was I suddenly reacting to it?

"Zac, come here," he called out. He'd taken a seat on my bed.

"I'm not done yet," I said. I needed to touch something, and it would really be great for both of us if that something wasn't him.

"Just come here," he said.

I stopped rearranging my clothes and grabbed a chair, so I could sit next to him.

"I owe it to you to, at least, explain why I'm here," he said. "After what I've done to you, it's only fair I explain things."

I nodded and listened intently.

He exhaled loudly. "During one heated conversation with Dad, I said some…things in the presence of someone. When she got mad at me, she released the contents of that conversation to the media and they, in turn, published everything. They all want to hear my side of the story, but I'm not in the mood to say anything to anyone. So like the coward that I am, I'm hiding," he said.

"You're running away, I get it. But why *here*?"

He took a deep breath and drummed his fingers on his thigh. "You're the only person who knows the other side of

Cody Wilde. I mean now, everyone knows…but you knew before them. I feel much more comfortable with you."

I stood up and went to the closet.

"So, you just want to use me again," I said while rearranging my clothes, repeating the same motion. I couldn't look at Evan in the eye.

"It's not like that!" he said hastily. "I'm a jackass, I know. What I did was wrong. I panicked. Cody Wilde is… I didn't want to break. I couldn't afford to. I worked so hard to be Cody Wilde. That was just one crack, and it was gonna get worse and…Zac, I'm sorry. I didn't mean to hurt you," he pleaded.

"Now you're here. You're gonna go back after a few days and possibly lie about where you've been, and life will go back to normal, right?"

"It's not like that! I don't know. I don't know what I'm gonna do. I don't know what I want."

He sounded genuinely distressed. Maybe I was being too hard on him. The world just learned about his past—a past that was obviously still hurting him. He didn't need me giving him hell about the lies he'd told. Maybe he would really leave after and pretend I hadn't helped him, but it didn't have to matter. I could do something without expecting something in return.

I turned to him to ask if he wanted to talk about the vulnerability he felt. What I hadn't realized was that he'd stood up from the bed. I had been preoccupied with my thoughts I hadn't seen him walk to me, and now he was close. Too close.

I coughed. "Uh…do y-you want to talk…about your dad?" I said, trying not to stutter and failing miserably.

He shook his head. "Not now."

"We could…" I said and stopped talking. Evan's lips were too close to mine. My breath got caught in my throat.

I felt his hand move tantalizingly to my waist, pulling up my T-shirt a little bit. I loved the sensations his hand evoked. His eyes were full of desire, touching a soft spot in me. He didn't say anything. I didn't either. We just looked at each other.

Did I really find him that attractive I went mute?

This couldn't be happening again. How did I think I could be with him in a room alone after everything that had happened between us? Maybe it was nothing for him, but it sure as hell was something for me.

I had much more to lose.

"Evan, this…we can't…you ca—n't…" I stumbled over my words.

His hands started moving around my back as if I hadn't said anything to him. I moved a few centimeters towards him. I felt like I was being pulled by his aura. We didn't break eye contact even when our lips moved slowly towards each other. He parted his, allowing me to nibble on his lower lip as soon as our lips made contact.

I hadn't known just how much I missed his lips. The moment my lips met his, I was transported to the first time we kissed, the time I had probably given something of mine away. His lips on mine were sweet—captivating and encouraging me to explore the mysteries ahead. I was melting in the most wonderful way. I was losing all control. My brain had shut down. I couldn't remember why I shouldn't be kissing him.

I felt his hands on my back, with no barrier, driving me crazy.

We kissed at a tantalizingly slow pace. I felt and tasted everything. I loved all of it. My hands moved towards his abdomen, sure enough, that wouldn't be the act that broke the spell. I raised his t-shirt just a little bit and placed my hand there. I felt him bite my lip slightly at that moment, goading me on. I raised his t-shirt further and put both my hands underneath it, moving my fingers in a teasing manner.

He moved closer to me. I wanted him closer to me. I wanted him so close, even though there was literally no more space between us. Our kiss gained pace. We kissed faster and faster. We were breathing faster too. He pulled back and hid his head in my neck, kissing and licking me there. My hands went onto his back. With every kiss or bite, I grabbed him tighter.

This was further than we'd ever gone. It was too much. I couldn't do it.

I pulled back rapidly, the move almost giving me whiplash. Evan just looked at me, his hands still around me. I put my hand on his arms and pushed them down gently. They fell to his sides with ease.

I took the few steps towards the door, and soon, I was outside my room, leaving Evan in the middle of it. When the door closed, I took a deep breath.

A few minutes in and I'd already failed the test.

But how could I not when Evan was just so…evil? Somehow, he knew the effect he had on me. He knew I wouldn't be able to resist. I was doing it again. I did it with Chase, and now I was doing it with Evan.

Chase didn't love me, but I still fell hook, line, and sinker. Evan professed to the whole world that he was as straight as a ruler, but I still fell for his charms. I wasn't in love with him, but it might as well be the same thing.

He was going to use me and leave. *Hooray, Zac, you've learned from your mistakes!*

* * *

I couldn't just stand outside my door. Evan was unlikely to open the door to look for me, but standing there looking lost wasn't helping me, either. I needed to talk to someone. It wasn't really what I wanted, but I needed it. Someone had to tell me I was an idiot.

There was only one person I trusted. Fortunately, Livy was in her room. She welcomed me heartily, thinking I was honoring my word. I'd said I'd join her in her room to discuss Evan. Well, I *was* there to discuss Evan.

"Liv, tell me what to do," I begged her the moment I closed the door.

"About what?"

"About Evan!" I almost yelled.

"Are you...talking about the story?"

"No! I'm talking about him... him coming here and kissing me."

"Whoa, slow down! Cody...is *here*? Are you sure it wasn't a dream?" she said. She was sitting on her bed cross-legged with a magazine at her feet.

"Evan is in my room! Stop calling him Cody!" I yelled quietly.

"Okay, sheesh," she said. "So, he's in your room, and he kissed you?"

"Yes! I kissed him back...like all the other times," I said. "Tell me what to do."

"Talk to him," she said encouragingly.

"There's no point in that whatsoever."

"How do you know that?"

"Because he doesn't do relationships. He's incapable of love. He's notorious for one-night stands," I said. "He's obviously physically attracted to me. Otherwise, why is he kissing me every chance he gets?"

"I still think—" Livy started, but I cut in.

"I am obviously physically attracted to him. The attraction is mutual," I said. "But...what should I do? Tell me to kick him out right now, and I'll do it," I said desperately.

Livy shook her head. "I can't do that. *You* have to decide what you want to do."

"Livy, just tell me! I'll do anything you say."

My frustration had reached a boiling point. I hadn't realized just how deep the situation was. I was literally asking Livy to make a decision for me. I was readying myself to follow through whatever she decided. I couldn't decide, and it wasn't just because either decision was scary.

"Forgive yourself first," she said softly.

"What?"

"You may be over Chase, but you haven't forgiven yourself for staying. You don't want to make a decision because you're afraid of making one." Livy had figured out my turmoil. "You think that if you don't make the decision, you can't blame yourself if it doesn't work out. That's why you want me to tell you what to do. But Zac, I can't."

"If I kick him out, he leaves. Then I'll never hear from him again. But if I let him stay, he'll use me and degrade me...," I said, mulling over my options aloud.

Livy was right. The last time I made a big decision, I decided to be someone's doormat. I couldn't be trusted with making a decision. I was obviously terrible.

"You could talk to him before you make a decision and find out why he kisses you." Livy suggested.

"I told you. He's physically attracted to me," I said. "You know what, I've made my decision."

"Which is?"

"To have fun," I said with a smile. "Thanks for being my sounding board."

I walked towards the door.

"Wait. Is Cod...Evan *really* here?"

"Nope. As far as I know, he's in New York," I said and walked out.

* * *

It was a long journey to my room, but it felt too short for my liking. I left Livy's room with a purpose, a solution. I didn't want to lose my guts before I got there. It was a risky solution, and the risks were more than one. Some were scarier than others. It was a decision I'd taken, and I was sticking to it, so long as I got there before my confidence deserted me.

I stood outside my room and took a deep breath. I placed my hand on the handle and turned. The door didn't budge. Evan had locked himself in. Come to think of it, he did say he needed to hide. He didn't actually need me to be in the room for him to hide. But what if he refused to let me in?

I knocked on the door forcefully.

"It's Zac," I said.

I heard movement in the room, but Evan didn't unlock.

"Get your ass to this door and unlock it."

"What's my mom's name?" A question came from the room. He was asking me a security question. *Was I supposed to know this?*

"Uh…" I said.

"No…that's not her name. Don't think my grandparents ever considered that one."

"Cody Wilde…Evan Cody Lowe…" I muttered underneath my breath. "Eva Wilde!" I said triumphantly.

I heard the key turn. I turned the handle and pushed the door open. When I was inside, I closed and locked it.

"That was impressive," Evan said. He'd gone back to my bed. I realized he was lying on it. Of course, he'd do whatever he wanted, including getting his hair moisturizer all over my bed.

"Huh?" I said.

"I didn't expect you to know it. I was just toying with you," he said, sitting up. "How do you know it?"

"You mentioned it," I said. "I—" I started, but he interrupted.

"We should—" he said, but I cut into his words, too.

"Shh, I'm talking," I said, stunning him. "Don't interrupt me again."

He stared at me. "O…kay."

"Good. I've realized that whenever we're alone, you can't keep your horm...your *straight* hormones in control. You obviously want some of me. I won't lie, I think that...," I said and pointed at him, "...is good-looking. I don't think you have the body of a god, though. I think it's something to work with. On that note, I have a problem with you kissing me like some random floozy."

He opened his mouth.

"I've thought about this. If you want to keep kissing me, we have to talk. Actually, we don't have to. You just have to listen. You can only do so on my terms. I know you don't get into relationships and are incapable of love. You can relax. I don't expect that from you. I want a...physical thing. No emotions. You don't talk about me, and I don't talk about you. I use you, you use me. I'm sure you're familiar with this."

"I..."

"I think you're an idiot and a coward and a selfish son of a bitch, but I can tolerate you. I also respect your privacy, obviously giving you more than you deserve. What I want from you is to respect mine. It's pretty simple. You get me, I get you." I finished with a smile that was in danger of wavering.

He crossed his arms and looked at me for a bit. For someone who'd been keen to interrupt me, he was now surprisingly quiet. *Did he just want to talk when I talked?*

"Okay," he said quietly.

Did he just...? I was a bit stunned. I'd expected him to agree, refusing to think otherwise, but I was still shocked he'd agreed.

He stood up and walked to me.

"Should we seal our deal with a kiss?" he said, biting his lip.

It was me who kissed him this time. It gave me the illusion of control I did not have. It was a dangerous game I was playing, but the thrill of it was exciting. I got to have Evan

281

for a while. I got to have my lips quiver at the thought of kissing him.

I was playing with fire, and I was going to get burnt. I knew that, and I still gave in. I only live once, might as well sneak around with a gorgeous model. Love would come when it will. For now, I was having fun…on my terms.

CHAPTER THIRTY-FOUR

EVAN

Zac's lips tasted better than before. It was almost like they tasted better every time I kissed him. I hadn't known I yearned to kiss him, so when I finally did, I gave it all I had. The movement of his lips on mine was breathtaking. He was giving as much as he was taking from me, if not more.

The desire for him was much stronger than I thought it could ever be. Kissing him was eliciting things in me I thought I could never feel. I wanted him to experience them—the pleasure I got when he placed his hands on my waist or when he sucked on my lower lip.

It seemed like he was. The moans that escaped him were evident of that. They were so raw yet so soft. They drove me crazy.

The pace of our kiss increased. We kissed fiercely, passionately. It almost felt like we were making up for all the time we'd been apart. I buried my head in his neck, and he pulled on my hair. I was getting lost in the kiss, and the result was pure bliss. For once, I wasn't guarded. I didn't think about where to stop or how to. Zac was wearing a cotton t-shirt, and when I pulled it off him, he had no objections. He took off my sweatshirt and t-shirt, and soon our bare chests were pressed against each other. We continued kissing almost insanely. The pleasure was mounting, and so was the pressure against my underwear.

I pulled my head back and grabbed Zac by the hand, pulling him to the bed. Within seconds he was on top of me, straddling me. He bent to kiss me on the abdomen and worked his way up until he was at my lips. I grabbed his lower lip and dragged. He was hovering over me, so I pulled him down onto me by the waist. He wrapped his hands around me, tracing whatever lines he made up on my skin. I'd felt his hands on me before, but there was just something different this time. My skin was hot. His hands were hotter. Every time he moved his fingers, every fiber of my being throbbed for him.

Heat seared on the spot where he was sitting on me. I could feel him growing above me as well, and that drove all my senses crazy. I claimed his lips, kissing with intention. It was an effort to stop myself from slightly pressing up against him, but I pretty much did that anyway.

It was hard to keep myself steady by now. I wanted to move. I put my hands on his sides, grabbing tightly. I held him too tight for him move, so he looked at me. Before he knew it, I had flipped him over, my leg digging in between his thighs.

"How do you do that?" he said.

I usually minded talking during intimate moments, but with Zac, it was different. It felt good knowing not just his carnal desire was interacting with me. "I told you, train, and maybe you'll be able to flip me over. I can help you," he said.

"I might take you up—" he said and stopped abruptly. It could be because I'd taken him by surprise by placing my hand on his crotch.

"You might what?" I asked with a smirk.

"That sounded wrong. I didn't mean take you up like...*you*. I meant, take you up on that offer," he stammered, turning red in the process. "I mean we could...but..."

I smiled and bent to give him a short, sweet kiss. "Tell me when you want me to stop," I whispered in his ear.

* * *

Zac never told me when he wanted to stop. I didn't know if that meant he never wanted to stop or if he was trying to prove something, but I took it upon myself to stop before things went too far. He'd practically given me a license to do whatever I wanted, but I wanted to be certain it was what he wanted.

I never really cared what the other person wanted in the past, but Zac was different. Zac made me feel things no other person has made in my life.

I admittedly wanted to have sex with him. It was really hard not to, but I found a way not to let it get past oral sex. I had to start slow, and prove him wrong. Zac was giving me some kind of test. I knew it.

I hadn't known Zac long enough, but I knew the guy believed in love. He was the sappy sort, the one to have sentiments. I couldn't believe, for a second, that he genuinely wanted to have a physical thing with me. It was a test. He thought if he gave me what he thought I wanted, I would leave.

What he didn't factor in was he hadn't given me what I wanted. He'd only given me fragments. I evidently wanted to be intimate with him, but it wasn't all I wanted. I wanted more.

I had never wanted more. I had forbidden myself to even think of more. I never got close to people, and they never got close to me. It was something I'd lived by, and it had worked for a long time. It wasn't working anymore. I was vulnerable, and surprisingly, I didn't find that abhorrent.

I didn't know what I wanted with Zac. All I knew was I wasn't about to have sex with him and leave. I felt safe with him. Comfortable. Maybe I was selfish. Of course, I was being selfish. I was being like Carrie, sticking around even though it was clear nothing could ever happen.

Before Zac got back to the room and told me about his proposal, I'd also been thinking we couldn't go on without addressing the elephant in the room. I was ready to tell him my true state of mind, but his proposal halted that train. His proposal wasn't what I had in mind, but it wasn't ludicrous. I would still have a part of him, and maybe over time, he'd realize I wasn't after sex. Okay, I was, but it wasn't all there was to it.

When I told the world I wasn't gay, I hadn't been entirely honest, but it had seemed logical at that time. I hadn't known how far the thing with Zac went. Now, there were no two ways about it. I may not have been gay, but I was definitely sexually attracted to a guy. We hadn't spent an hour in each other's presence, and I already kissed him.

I was thinking maybe I wanted to kiss him every day.

* * *

"What do you want for lunch?" Zac asked me while putting his pants on. He literally sprang off the bed the moment I reached my climax, having reached his a minute sooner.

He grabbed the box of tissues on his desk and proceeded to wipe off the white stuff on his chest.

He looked up slightly. "I asked you a question." Even then, he wasn't looking at me.

"You could come back to bed," I said.

"You want *me* for lunch? Actually, don't answer that."

I chuckled. "I'm not hungry. *Please* come back to bed."

"Why?"

"Because I want to talk to you," I said, patting the space next to me.

He put his t-shirt on. "And you can't talk while I'm standing here because…?"

"Would it kill you to indulge me?"

"Possibly."

I got up from the bed and walked over to him. Wrapping my arms around him, I smiled, "I can't talk when you're so far away from me."

He rolled his eyes. "If you want sex, just say so."

"I actually really just want to talk," I said truthfully. I did want to do more than talk, but sex wasn't on my mind.

"Okay, I'll indulge you. But just this once."

I took the moment to give him a short kiss and pull him to the bed. He lay on the bed a considerable distance away from me that a single bed could afford him, but I moved closer anyway. I couldn't tell him, but I could show him I wanted more than what he offered.

"So, what's bothering you? Except the fact that you're a looney," he said.

"It doesn't bother me that I'm crazy. What bothers me is...I don't know," I said. I'd taken a decision to talk about my dad and my life, but it wasn't easy.

"Evan..." Zac said and trailed.

"Earlier you asked me if I wanted to talk about my dad. Are you...willing to listen?"

"Of course," he replied with an assuring smile. "I don't know why I have to lie down while listening, but yeah."

I put my hand on his shirt-covered abdomen and caressed it. "You were right. I provoked him because I thought he'd bring it up, ask for forgiveness, something."

"Evan, what really happened? Was everything I read true?" he asked softly.

I sighed. "When Mom wasn't sick, we were okay. We weren't close, but he never hit me. When she got sick, it was like he changed. He cheated on her, not even hiding it from me. He fired Rosa and left us alone. I had to take care of her. I had to cook or we'd starve. It was okay when she was in the hospital, but when the doctors said there was nothing else they could do...," I stopped and let out a sigh, "They shouldn't have let him take her home. The way he disrespected her, I wouldn't be surprised if he killed her."

Zac put his hand on mine, stopping my movements on his abdomen. He massaged it gently.

I took a deep breath. "He moved on two months after she died with one of the women he'd been having an affair with. She didn't like me, so she got me into trouble with him. He hit me and let her hit me. But of course, that wasn't enough. She decided to get rid of me, but she didn't. He dated someone else and then someone else and then some eighteen-year-old. I grew up, and I left."

Zac's hand left mine to caress my cheek. "And you made up Cody Wilde."

"Cody Wilde is an escape, yeah. He's separate from Evan. He wasn't abused or neglected as a kid. But now, everyone knows."

"Why is having such a past such a bad thing? You got out of there. You made a name for yourself," he said gently.

"I don't want to be labeled," I admitted. "Cody Wilde isn't entirely a farce. I'm still an idiotic, reckless jerk."

He grinned. "That's true. But I think you can be both Cody Wilde and Evan. You don't have to choose. I know this is not about people liking you or not, it's about you hiding your past because it still hurts. But if you face it, you can just be one person."

That moment, it felt like every situation that had ever hurt me burrowed its way into my consciousness. I found tears flowing down my cheeks. I immediately wanted to close up, to pretend it didn't hurt anymore. *Why did I insist on talking?*

"You know it doesn't—" I started, but Zac interrupted gently.

"When my dad passed away, Jess pretended she was fine. She became someone else—someone disrespectful, someone who didn't have to face the fact that she'd lost someone who meant the world to her. She wears black, has tattoos, but it doesn't make her happy. The rationale is, even though it doesn't make her happy, it doesn't make her sad as well. But then, what's the point? Evan, you can't hide. The only way to be free and not have to look who's watching is to accept it, deal with it, and move on."

"How do I accept that millions of people out there love me and one person doesn't even give me the time of day?"

He toweled my cheek with his hand. "By accepting yourself," he said.

"I..."

"You're proud of Cody Wilde, but you shun Evan because Evan is the little boy you think you left behind, the one that's still scared. You do provoke your dad, but it's not about him. You don't try to get away from him; you try to get away from yourself. You think if he did apologize, you'd finally be free of Evan, but you won't."

I stayed quiet for a while. He was right. I hated that I cared. I cared enough to hide my whole past so no one could make me cry again over how weak I was. I didn't carry a torch for my dad, but I did wish he'd loved me enough, so I didn't have to hate myself for being so weak. I didn't really wish he'd love me even though I'd told him that. I didn't need his love. I thought if I had it, then Evan would just disappear. Maybe my "weakness" wasn't really a weakness.

Maybe I could accept that the scared little boy who spilled the food he was trying to cook was me. He was Cody Wilde, and that was okay. My fans would be willing to accept me. It was me who couldn't accept myself. I was obviously not happy. Why not try something else?

"You really think I could accept myself?" I said quietly.

"Of course, you can. I can tell you that Evan is someone I'd love. It's someone you can love, too," he said.

I felt a lump in my throat. For the first time, I felt butterflies fluttering in my tummy. My heart was beating too fast but not uncomfortably. I think I was happy. Or maybe it was something else. I don't know.

I put my hand on Zac's cheek and turned to my side. Lowering my head towards his lips, I said, "Remember that time I said you should burn your psychology degree? I changed my mind."

I caught a bit of a smile before our lips met. We kissed leisurely. The kiss felt so peaceful yet so intriguing. We weren't rushing anywhere. I wanted to do something stupid.

I pulled back. "You know, Zac, I think I'm f…"

I didn't finish. Zac's cell phone rang. The sound powered through my ears and the haze in my brain. It made what I was about to say clear, and the contents shocked me.

Zac reached for his phone on the desk. I thought he was going to answer, but he ended the call and switched his phone off.

"Come here," he said, wrapping his hands around my neck. "If we make this quick enough, maybe I won't die of hunger."

He'd spoken. There was no time for words. He made that clear by pulling me to him and kissing me before I could process what he even said. Our kiss got hungrier in no time. I forgot what I'd wanted to say. At least, I put it at the back of my mind.

Zac had beckoned, and I couldn't say no to Zac.

CHAPTER THIRTY-FIVE

ZAC

I never thought I'd wake up in someone's embrace so soon after Chase. Even if I did, I never thought that person would be Evan Lowe, also known as Cody Wilde.

It was Sunday morning. I couldn't tell what time it was, but it looked like the sun had been up for a while. My room was bright, illuminated by the sun's rays. I was lying in bed, having opened my eyes a few seconds prior. I lay motionless, shocked by what my eyes were seeing.

Evan was lying on the bed next to me. That wasn't the shocking part. He'd chosen to sleep on my bed after I offered him a futon the previous night. I didn't like the idea, but when the kisses came, my objections were silenced. We made out for a while and eventually fell asleep.

Evan was lying on his tummy with his head facing away from me. He had his arm around my abdomen, locking me in place. The sight made a part of me ache. It was such an intimate position; it gave the illusion that we were more than we really were. But Evan couldn't know where his hand was, much like the previous night when we ended up in a spooning position, and he put his hand around my waist.

He'd been fast asleep then, and he was fast asleep now. For all I knew, that was how he naturally slept. My presence on that bed had nothing to do with it.

But maybe it did.

Evan said he felt comfortable with me. He came to me when he couldn't stand the public's eyes boring into his past. We talked about his situation. He seemed much at ease after we talked about the reason Cody Wilde existed. I wasn't certain he wasn't going to change his mind to accept himself and bolt, but I was happy knowing I'd given him some perspective. He seemed willing, and I was happy with that.

That moment had given *me* some perspective. I couldn't have a physical relationship with Evan. I cared about him. I truly wanted him to love himself again because despite his past, his cowardice, and his jackass behavior, I believed there was something to love.

I can tell you that Evan is someone I'd love, I'd said that.

Evan wasn't someone I *would* love. Evan was someone I loved.

I loved him. As unbelievable as it was, I'd fallen for him. Somewhere in the conversations in the kitchen, the drowning incident, the moments he pretended to be my boyfriend, the walks in the forest, and the kisses, he crept into my heart.

But of course, the heart was irrational.

Evan was incapable of love. He didn't get into relationships. He'd told me twice that he didn't want to make sacrifices nor did he want to compromise. He put himself first, and he'd always do that.

It wasn't his fault that I was a fool. Twice I'd betrayed myself. I'd not only fallen for him but decided to have a physical relationship with him. I couldn't do it. I hadn't known then that I loved him, but I should have known that "something" I felt wouldn't survive a physical relationship. It was torture knowing that no matter how comfortable he got with me, he'd never be mine.

It didn't help that he was interacting with me in a way I deemed belonged in a relationship. We made out but never got to the sex part. We talked, he cried in front of me, and we slept on the same bed with his arms wandering on my body but not sexually. He made fun of my cooking skills after I'd cooked for him and told me stories about some of his crazy photo shoots. We cuddled, maybe unintentionally, but we still cuddled!

It was a recipe for disaster. There was nothing to it, and clinging on to it would just leave me heartbroken, much like my relationship with Chase.

But why was smiling at the view of Evan sleeping so bloody irresistible?

I had to get out of that room. I moved my body slightly to try and get out of the cage Evan's hand had put me in. I could swear my move had been inconspicuous, but I felt Evan's arm tighten around me.

Was this some sort of reflex?

I tried moving again, this time a little more forcefully, so I could run before he actually woke up. I didn't get to; Evan was just too bloody strong. I huffed frustratingly.

"Morning." Evan's sleepy voice entered my ears. He turned his head to face me. Even then, his arm did not move.

I gave him a closed-lip smile. "Could you move your arm?"

"Where are you off to so early in the morning?" He wanted to know.

Running away from you! I haven't figured out yet where I'm going, but wherever I end up is okay as long as it's not here!

"I need to go grocery shopping. And it's not early," I said instead. I didn't exactly lie. I was running low on supplies. I didn't filter in housing a celebrity fugitive the last time I went grocery shopping.

He moved his arm slightly, but not off me.

"Stay a bit," he said.

"Do you want to starve?"

His hand moved up to my face. "Two minutes," he said.

My shoulders relaxed. I liked the feel of his hand on my jaw. "The sooner I go, the better." I forced myself to say.

"But then I'll be lonely," he whimpered.

My heartstrings were tugged at his words and the sight before me. I thought I actually felt my heart physically move. Evan was gorgeous. Early morning barefaced Evan was cute. His eyes were brighter, his hair messier and his freckles more visible. He seemed vulnerable too, and the softness of his voice would melt any heart.

With mine, it wouldn't have the same effect. My heart was just too far gone already.

"Okay. Two minutes max," I said.

He responded by leaving soft kisses from my cheek to my neck. When he emerged from my neck, he said, "You look different in the morning."

"You haven't earned the privilege to make fun of my just-woke-up face," I warned.

"How do I do that?" he asked brightly. He seemed so interested.

Love me! Love me and throw in some amazing sex, and you can tease me all you want.

"It's an inborn thing," I replied.

"That doesn't sound fair," he whined. "And for the record, I was going to say you look…"

"No!"

"C…"

"Evan, shut up!" I said sternly, putting my finger on his lips.

He tried to remove my finger, and we ended up play-wrestling. Of course, he won, managing to pin me on the bed with his weight. He was straddling me with his hands, pinning mine on the bed.

I understood why I was comfortable, but why was he comfortable play wrestling with me with morning breath, bed hair, and sleepy eyes? To be fair, he woke up in pretty good shape and didn't stink, but shouldn't he have run to the bathroom to put on concealer the moment he woke up? Wasn't that what celebrities did? They couldn't possibly wake up the way they made us believe they did. And why was Evan comfortable with *me*? I wasn't a gem in the morning.

"You look very cute in the morning," he said.

That was my line!

"Your two minutes are up. I gotta go," I said, trying to loosen his grip on my hands.

He let me go. "Next time I'll let you win."

Next time?

"I *let you* win. You know…model…your body is your asset? Yeah, I'm not evil," I said, trying to pull myself up. Evan still had his butt on my crotch. Yeah, I wasn't good at curl ups.

I planted my hands on the bed and pushed my body up, right into Evan's upper body, then he put his arms around me.

"Are you always this grumpy in the morning?" he teased.

Only when I make stupid decisions and end up with models on my bed, who blur the lines between a physical and a normal relationship… Those words were never said out loud, of course.

Instead, I said sternly, "Get off me."

"Okay," he said brightly and got off me, which was definitely unexpected. It was also unexpected that he'd run to the bathroom, but he did just that, closing the door behind him.

I sighed and fell back on my bed.

Evan was going to be an enormous problem. He did things I liked. I had to pretend I didn't like them.

I was about to get off the bed when my phone rang. It was from an unknown number. I had a hunch it was the same person who'd called the previous day. I hadn't answered the call, deciding making out with Evan and digging my own grave was much more important.

"Hello?" I said lazily after accepting the call.

295

"Hi. Am I speaking to Zac Nielsen?" someone inquired at the other end of the line. It sounded like a man.

"Uh...who am I speaking to?"

"You're speaking to Matthew Cole from *ZMT*. I just want to ask you a few questions about that night with Cody Wilde. In fact, I'm offering you a platform to tell the world your side of the story about that night," he said.

I hadn't been following the story after Evan's interview with Cecilia dos Santos, but I thought it had died down. Evan had clarified the situation, so what was there to talk about? Shouldn't they have been focusing on the dad story instead of the kiss? It was old news!

"I have nothing to say," I said confidently.

"Are you sure?" the man asked. "We're willing to pay you a good sum of money."

I chuckled. "There's nothing to say because the version Cody Wilde told the world is the real version."

"Is that so? So, when you leaked the recording of his conversation with his dad, it wasn't revenge?"

"I didn't leak anything because I couldn't have possibly recorded anything. You have your sources very wrong. Now, if you'll excuse me, I gotta go," I said and hung up.

"Who was that?" Evan's voice caught me by surprise. He was standing at the bathroom door, leaning on the frame.

"Some guy from *ZMT*," I mumbled.

"These people are vicious. They never let things go. I'm so sorry," he said, walking up to me. "I'm sorry I dragged you into this." He sat on the bed and looked up at me. "You okay?"

The concern on his face was heartwarming. He hadn't rushed to ask me what else I'd said.

"I'm fine. I can handle people. I've dealt with Chase and Bruce, and they were like vultures on a stale carcass," I said.

"The carcass being you? You're so *fresh* though," he said with a wink.

Was he flirting with me? What had I done for him to torture me like that?

I got out of bed silently, deciding not to indulge him. If we talked, I probably wouldn't leave that room, ever. I needed a break from him. I didn't want it, but the need was more important.

I stepped into the bathroom and closed the door.

* * *

I took Livy shopping with me. I needed to stick to my routines so she wouldn't suspect I was harboring a fugitive. I saw Livy almost every day. She would start getting suspicious if I disappeared, so I had to make sure I didn't. I didn't want her knocking on my door. She probably wouldn't be suspicious if she didn't see me for a day or two, but I couldn't be sure.

I bought some basic food, like pasta and frozen vegetables and ramen noodles. If Evan teased me on my very basic cooking skills again, he'd eat ramen for breakfast, lunch, and dinner. I'd made him breakfast that morning, and even if I had to say so myself, the eggs were overdone. To be fair, I'd been thinking about why I had agreed to share a room with him.

Livy pushed my trolley, occasionally adding something she thought I should buy. We strolled into the confectionery aisle because Livy wanted chocolate. I wasn't a fan of sweet stuff. I couldn't eat half a bar of chocolate of any kind before wanting to wash my mouth. Livy always said it was a shame; chocolate was heaven-sent, she said. For the few minutes, I could stand it; it wasn't so bad.

"Don't look at my chocolate with those eyes. You know, it's very offensive. Just by not liking chocolate, you are the world's least loved person right now," Livy said while she decided which brand of chocolate she was going to make me pay for.

"Thankfully, I don't care," I said.

She gave me a short, closed-lip smile.

While she was choosing, my eyes wandered around the aisle. I caught sight of something my eyes found riveting. It was something aimed at kids. It wasn't so riveting for me, yet the adult in my room couldn't get enough of it. I spotted a packet of Jelly Babies.

I walked over and took three packets. He hadn't brought any supplies, so he was probably in his addiction withdrawal. Withdrawal couldn't be nice.

"Look at you!" Livy said slowly. "Are we eating sweets things now?"

"I could try…something," I stammered.

"You have three packets of sweets," she uttered her observation. "Chocolate is much more…"

"Shut up," I said, putting the packets in the trolley and pushing my way out of the aisle.

* * *

We took a cab back to the dorm with our purchases. Livy insisted on walking me to my room to share the weight of the shopping bags. I couldn't find an excuse to say no, so we walked there.

"I wanted to tell you something, by the way. It's some rumor I heard," Livy said as we stepped out of the elevator.

"Yeah?"

"It's about…Chase and Bruce," she whispered.

"Are they unintentionally bald? That'd make me happy," I joked.

Livy laughed. "I can actually picture that. That'd make my day too. But sadly, they aren't."

"I doubt I'm interested in what they are."

She shrugged. "You might be over him, but you're still petty. Pettiness is life!"

"Okay, okay. I'm only interested if they're bald or have tumbled down some stairs. Oh wait, is Bruce impotent?"

Livy laughed, almost dropping my bag. "Actually, rumor has it he has such an appetite, he's been spreading the joy."

"No way! He's cheating on Chase? Is the cheater being cheated on?"

"It's just a rumor, but apparently he is. Most interesting is he's doing it with a girl," she replied.

"That would definitely be interesting. Anyway, here we are," I said, realizing we had gotten to my door.

"My arms are killing me. Unlock the door," Livy said impatiently.

I had no idea what to do. I loved my best friend and was grateful for her help, but I wished she could just disappear. Her heart was in the right place, but I needed my space...or rather, Evan needed my space.

"Liv...um, I'd rather be alone right now," I said, hoping I didn't offend her.

She smiled. "No problem. Just open the door so I can place this inside, and I'll leave."

"Um...okay. I'll open the door, but please leave after, okay?" I said clearly, much louder than I needed for Livy to hear.

I fidgeted, tapping on the door with my fingers. I was trying to get the message to Evan, and I really hoped he got it because I had run out of things to say. I put my key in the slot and turned, pushing the door only slightly, and peeked in. Livy pushed past me. I loved the girl, but boundaries were elusive to her.

I followed behind her. The absence of gasps told me Evan wasn't in the room. He wasn't. Well, he was, but he wasn't visible.

Livy placed the bag she was carrying on my desk. I did so, too, with the bags I was carrying.

She took her chocolate before smiling and saying, "I'll see you tomorrow."

I smiled back. My smile was of relief. She walked out and closed the door. I locked it and just stood looking at it. *What was I doing?*

"This is fun." Evan's voice startled me. His arms wormed their way around my waist behind me.

I didn't turn immediately. "Your definition of fun is stupid."

"It was dangerous, but you got away with it," he whispered seductively. "Hear that heartbeat?"

"Where were you even?" I said, finally turning, only to find myself too close to him. I was already close to him, granted, but now I was facing him.

"Bathroom," he replied.

I put my hands on his arms and pushed them down so I could get out of the embrace. I walked over to my shopping bags.

"You caught on too fast," I commented.

"Experience," he said, walking to the bed.

Of course, he had experience! Did I think his clients in his physical relationship business only included single people? "Committed" people were the perfect candidates. They were already committed and only wanted fun with him though their commitment was very much questionable.

"I've been clubbing since…I don't know, ever since I can recall. I've needed to get out of places quickly before I got myself and the owners in trouble," he explained.

Had he seen how unhappy I was with his answer? Even so, why did he explain? He didn't owe me anything…other than the money I spent on him and retribution for the humiliation and the heart attack I almost had because of him!

He did owe me…and Jackson too!

"What did you buy?" he asked, ransacking through my shopping bags before I could stop him. He pulled out the packets of Jelly Babies. "Is this for me?" There was a huge smile on his face.

I'd wanted that. I could lie and say I just bought them because they looked cute, but truthfully, I bought them for that moment I'd see his whole face light up. There was a sparkle in his eyes. His smile was just beautiful. I'd be happy if I made him that happy to see me.

"Yeah," I replied to his question quietly.

He placed his arms around me, pulling me in for a hug. This was different from all the times he'd hugged me. Then, he was seeking intimacy. Now, he just seemed happy.

"You're the best!" he squealed. "I can't believe you remembered."

I only smiled. The grave I'd been digging was ready for me to throw myself in. I didn't even need a coffin. That'd be too dignified.

* * *

Later on, we had pizza for lunch and another pizza for dinner. I wasn't in the mood to cook, and Evan couldn't go to the kitchen. He did, however, promise me a three-course meal in the future, promoting his superior cooking skills. I doubted he'd ever do that, but I nodded anyway.

I didn't spare a thought about what Livy had told me about Chase and Bruce; I had bigger fish to fry. Mark was the name of the fish. Evan's unexpected visit had shifted my focus, but that evening, he was all I could think about. I still hadn't managed to convince my mom there was something off with him.

I feared I was running out of time. It was possible I was being paranoid.

Evan was sitting on my bed cross-legged. He'd been on his phone, but now he was telling me about some Carrie girl who'd recorded him. I was sitting on a chair next to him, only half-listening. Not only was I thinking about Mark, but I also wasn't keen on hearing about a girl Evan had slept with, even more so about her unrequited love for him.

"If I knew she was—" he said. I'd finally "heard" enough, so I interrupted.

"Your dad—" I started, and *he* interrupted me. It has become our dynamic.

"I don't need to talk about him, don't worry. I don't care that he doesn't—"

You may have guessed it, I interrupted him.

"No, no! This is not about you," I said, and he made a theatrical-shocked face, followed by a smile. *How could I not love him when he was so foolishly cute?*

"What's it about?"

"My mom," I replied.

"He's cheating on her," he said with certainty.

"No, no…shut up!"

He made a motion of zipping his lips.

"Is it possible your dad is a con artist?"

He just stared at me.

"Evan?"

He made a motion of zipping his lips repeatedly. I grabbed Jackson's pillow and hit him with it.

"I take orders very well," he said with a shrug and chuckle. "But to answer your question, no. He's rich and successful. What he is is an unfaithful man."

"What if he got his money illegally?" I said.

"That's possible. Why are you asking?"

I told him my suspicions, including the conversation I'd heard outside Mark's office and the conversation with my mom.

He took the news in before he said, "Do you really believe that?"

I nodded.

He nodded too. "I can't honestly say. I've never caught him or heard him do something shady for money, but I support you on this. He's definitely not a model parent, so not being a model citizen isn't so farfetched."

"I just wish I knew what to do!" I let my frustration be known.

"Well, how would you feel about going to Sapphire Town?" he said enthusiastically.

"What?"

"Sitting here is not doing anything. Let's go to Sapphire Town. I'll pretend I'm the prodigal son who just wants to be close to his dad and get a confession," he said. "...or we can just go *digging* for evidence."

"That doesn't sound like a good idea. He'll never let any of us close," I said.

"A lot of reviewers on *Rotten Tomatoes* believe I'm a good actor," he whined.

"I'm sure your acting is fine. Your dad is not dumb," I said.

"That's true, but you heard him, didn't you? He slipped. He can slip again, and we'll be there to catch him in the act."

"I can't leave. I have classes. Besides, we can't leave together. You can't leave," I said.

"Are you holding me hostage?"

"You know what I mean!"

"The only thing I hate about Sapphire Beach Town is your exes. They won't be there. I love the place, and the people treat me like an ordinary person. We just have to worry about getting there, but once we're there, we're scot-free. And then, we'll get your mom free of the shackles my dad has put on her. You can skip classes for two days or so," he said.

"What an influence you are!" I remarked. "We can't accomplish that in two days."

"I said 'or so.' Didn't you hear me?" he said.

I rolled my eyes. "This plan of yours is idiotic and is going to fail."

"You used present continuous. I like that," he said. "When are we leaving?"

"Never." I scowled at him.

"Tomorrow, it is," he said. "I'll look up separate flights."

I sighed, and my shoulders fell. "Fine."

"I hate seeing you so stressed. Come here. I'll give you a massage you'll never forget," he said, beckoning to me. I was too weak to resist.

"You're the reason I'm so stressed." I couldn't resist taking a jab at him as I sat in front of him, with my back facing him. That statement didn't dissuade him from the massage he had offered me.

"Evan Lowe and Mark Lowe are two separate people. Thank God, I'm in your sweet dreams, and he's in your nightmares," he said.

He wasn't wrong, not about his statement and not about his massage. Within seconds, I was putty in his hands. He knew how much pressure to apply and where. He was only massaging my shoulders, but I felt the effect all over my body.

"Shh," I silenced him.

I couldn't see his face, but I had a feeling he smirked. I relaxed against him, feeling at peace. Evan's idea wasn't foolproof and only had a slight chance of working, but I was looking forward to going on a mission with him. We could save my mom from a con artist and maybe kindle something in Sapphire Beach Town.

It was false hope, but a guy could dream.

CHAPTER THIRTY-SIX

EVAN

Zac thought we'd done the impossible. He couldn't believe we could leave his dorm, get onto a flight to Sapphire Beach Town and get into a hotel room unrecognized. Honestly, I didn't think we could either, but we did. At least I thought we did. So far, I hadn't popped up on social media so it was safe to assume success.

I hadn't gotten entirely unrecognized. The flight attendants definitely recognized me, but they didn't bother me. They seemed not to bother about my life, either, so that was a relief. I got to Sapphire Beach Town before Zac so I checked into a hotel. It was about midday. Zac wouldn't be there until the evening.

I missed him already. Taking separate flights had been a good idea for obvious reasons, but as I lay on my hotel bed, it felt like the worst idea. I didn't know where he was or what he was doing. I couldn't wait to have him there.

I already longed to kiss him and tell him how cute he was. Our mission to Sapphire Beach Town wasn't just for his mom's benefit. It had sounded like a good idea to confront my dad, spy on him or trick him, but where he was was icing on the cake.

It was in Sapphire Beach Town that I'd had my worst years. When Mom was alive, we lived in the city. But in our beach house, we had fun vacations. We visited it at least six times a year. I met some of the locals and established childhood friendships. When Mom got sick, we moved to the beach house permanently. Dad said it was Mom's wish that she preferred to be at the beach house. As I grew, I saw it as an isolation tactic. Dad could leave us alone, and no one would know. The torturous years began. They didn't end even after I left because I hated myself. That place was where it all began.

It was also the place I made memories with Zac. I could still remember the day he pushed me into the ocean. It had echoed the day my stepmother tried to drown me. But then he'd done something different. He comforted me, holding me in his arms. He made me feel safe even when I was vulnerable.

How could I forget the night we met his exes, the walk in the quiet neighborhoods, the burgers at the beach, and of course the kiss that stunned the world? All of those things made me smile. Sapphire Beach Town was bittersweet. But the sweet part didn't have to be a mere memory.

Zac didn't have to be a memory.

I loved being with him. He was intriguing. He was strong and strong-willed. I took joy in making him smile. I loved cuddling and just talking with him. I missed him and we'd only been separated for a few hours.

I had committed the ultimate betrayal. I was in love.

It was too much to wrap my head around. Many people had set out to make me fall in love with them. They sought my presence and catered to my every whim. They tried to get close. They never succeeded. Zac, on the other hand, had to be convinced to let me room with him for a while. He called me an idiot, a jackass, and a lunatic.

Apparently, that was the recipe for a love potion.

Falling in love was too unsettling. It was the forbidden, the only other thing I had absolutely banned from myself from doing. I'd seen how it destroyed my mother. She could have died in peace, but she died in pain. Something beautiful that had turned into poison.

Zac got his heart broken because of love.

Zac seemed fine. He still believed in love and relationships. If a person could bounce back like that, surely love wasn't as rotten as I thought?

But is it worth it, though?

* * *

Zac arrived in Sapphire Beach Town in the evening. We'd booked separate hotel rooms down the hallway from each other. I would have preferred sharing a room, but that would be a dead giveaway of our relationship. After we'd both claimed there was nothing between us, I could imagine the damning headline: *Cody Wilde escapes to hotel room with male prostitute Zac Nielsen for another tryst.* Some people still believed Zac was a prostitute, thanks to his ex boyfriend.

One more thing I couldn't deal with: vindictive exes. Although, I didn't need to be in a relationship to have vindictive exes. Look at Carrie. She'd gotten revenge on me for ending a relationship that never existed.

I showed up at Zac's door precisely a minute after he'd told me he'd checked in. I had to confirm to myself it was him and not some imposter. Okay, I missed him and my hormones were a bit too hyped to see him.

I knocked on the door while facing the ground. The door opened jerkily.

"Hi handsome," I said, teasing Zac the moment I saw his face.

"Hi dimwit," he said with an evil grin and opened the door wider. He walked towards the bed.

"How was your flight?" I asked after walking in and closing the door.

Zac's hotel room was simple with a double bed in the middle surrounded by two nightstands, a desk and chair by the corner, a closet and a wall-mounted TV. The door next to the

TV led to a small bathroom. My room was a replica of his, including the warm lighting that created a soulful ambience.

"Fine. I'm hungry," he replied.

I walked over to him and made him stand up, wrapping my arms around him.

"I missed you," I said.

"I miss food," he said in a bored monotone.

I leaned over so my lips were close to his ears. "I can feed you."

I felt his hands slide up my waist to my back, pulling up my t-shirt as they went.

"Do you always get what you want?" he drawled.

"Pretty much," I replied.

He shook his head. "Not today." He pulled out of my embrace. "We have to talk about our plan. You…"

I pulled him to me by the hand and he crashed against me. "We can talk later," I said, bringing my hand up to caress his arm until I got to the jaw. I turned his face towards me, aligning his lips with me. He parted them immediately.

We started off slow, despite the frenzy my hormones were in. Our lips moved together in unison. Within minutes, we'd escalated. There was more passion in the kiss, more fire. I brought my hand to his face, trailing my thumb along his lower lip. I felt him moan again. For a second, I stopped moving. That had been one of the sexiest things I had ever experienced. He seemed to be enjoying the kiss just as much as I was.

We then moved to the bed. I turned my body to the side and snuck my leg between his. I felt his hand underneath my t-shirt on my back, scorching me with its presence. I rested my knee against his crotch, simultaneously moving my head so I could kiss his neck. His hand moved to the front and his fingers traced my six-pack. His movements were slow and seductive.

The room was getting hot and the kisses steamier. I moved my lips skillfully onto his neck, kissing, biting, licking and sucking. That seemed to have much of an effect on him because he was releasing moan after moan, each more strained than the last.

Each sound drove me on, and it made me want him even more. He was enjoying what I was doing, and I was enjoying it, too. I was getting hot, my breath coming in quick rasps and my heart pumping blood faster.

I moved my lips back to his. I couldn't stand the separation. I parted his lips gently, but couldn't contain myself. I snuck my tongue in, found his and danced to our own tune. The kiss was getting more erotic with every second that passed.

I moaned into it, surprising myself. My hand went to grab Zac's waist. I had to hold him to stop myself from moving on top of him.

"Evan," he said. His voice was heavy, his breath sultry.

"Hm?" I said.

"Since *I* can't flip you over, I have to ask you, so…" he said and I chuckled.

"I'm quite glad you can't flip me over," I said. But I did as he wanted.

Before I knew it, he was sitting on my crotch, straddling me. I looked up into his face. He looked so seductively gorgeous.

He placed his hands on my t-shirt and I helped him take it off. We took off his t-shirt, too. He had this glint in his eye. He looked at me like I was the sexiest thing he had ever seen. Many people looked at me like that, but it wasn't quite the same with Zac. I loved him.

He bent down to kiss me and I welcomed him. The kiss wasn't long. He'd barely touched me when he decided he wanted to kiss something else—my body. I was a bit not pleased about being teased, but I forgot all about that when Zac's lips met my chest. He hovered over my skin, fanning me with his hot breath. I had never wanted someone's lips on my skin that bad.

I closed my eyes in anticipation. Zac finally decided he'd teased me enough. He kissed my skin erotically, lingering in some areas. My eyes were closed so I couldn't see what his target was before his lips landed on me.

He kissed a nipple, put it between his lips and licked slightly. I brought my hand to his back without realizing it, pulling him into me. I also didn't realize I released a moan until I felt him stop.

He got to my happy trail. He kissed around and down it. I bucked up my hips.

There was a moment's hesitation before I felt his hands on my pants, and then he was unbuttoning them. I froze for a few seconds, anticipating the pleasure his actions would evoke. The sound of the zipper going down was louder than normal. Seconds later my pants were no longer on me.

I don't know if Zac forgot that he was hungry, but it was as if he was bewitched. He took his time with me, giving me so much pleasure I didn't know what to do with it. He kissed, he licked, and he drove me to the depths of pleasure. He knew just what to do and how to do it. He knew when to be serious and when to play around, when to be fast and when to be slow. It wasn't the first time. I didn't want it to be the last.

I vowed to give him the same pleasure. I don't know if I really did, but his moans when I touched him and the way he gripped the sheets told me I was doing something right. Everything was slower than I was used to, but that made it more memorable. I was aware of every touch, like when his lips grazed mine while his hand snuck lower, encircling me and moving. I was aware of the moment he wasn't kissing me, when his eyes looked so lustful, and of course when they glazed over. I heard the sound he made when he hit his peak.

It was glorious.

I took a deep breath and threw myself on the bed, pulling him into my arms. His breathing wasn't back to normal. I could feel the air of him panting on my neck.

We hadn't gone past oral sex again, but it felt more intimate than the last time. He'd listened to my needs and I'd listened to his. I'd taken my time learning him, doing things just the way he liked.

It hadn't been just physical.

I trailed my fingers up and down his arm. I couldn't imagine ever parting ways. I was in too deep and it was blissful. He needed to know that. I was irrevocably in love with him.

"I…" I said but his voice upstaged mine.

"We should talk about your dad and the plan," he said.

"We could talk about him tomorrow," I said dismissively.

"No! We have to do it now. I can't stay here forever. I'm missing out on my classes. So, what have you thought of since you've been here?"

You!

"Not much really, I… Can we get some food first?"

He got up from the bed. "You're very much useless, but yes."

* * *

It was a chilly night. I didn't fancy going out on a night like this, but Zac could convince me to do stupid things. He was good for my soul, but I'm not gonna tell him that yet.

Because of Zac's persuasion, I found myself driving on the cliff that led to my father's house. If it was up to me, I would be in bed with him eating Jelly Babies. But there I was, driving into the lion's den with my bag in the trunk.

Zac thought I needed to apologize to my dad for exposing him for the horrible parent that he was. I needed to do it, just not that night.

I rounded the last curve towards my dad's house, hoping he was there. I knew from Rosa that he was still in Sapphire Beach Town, but I hadn't been in contact with her that day. If he wasn't there, I would have driven all the way there for nothing.

I drove into the driveway. I noticed there was another car there besides my dad's Mercedes-Benz. I got out of the car and pulled my bag out of the trunk. Every molecule of my body protested when I knocked on the door. The last time I'd been at that house, I'd been thrown out.

Rosa opened the door.

"Evan?!" She was shocked. It was ten at night and the prodigal son had returned, sneaking at night like the embarrassed, homeless idiot he was. Only, I wasn't any of those things. Well, maybe just one of them.

"Hi," I said with my head bowed. "Is Dad here?"

"Um..." she said and paused. "Uh yeah. You look..." she said and left her sentence hanging. She took my bag from me. "I'm sorry but your dad said you aren't welcome here. I told you he doesn't want you here."

"I need to talk to him," I said, walking into the house.

"He's hosting an important guest. You can talk to him tomorrow morning. Come back tomorrow."

"I'd rather talk to him now. Where's he?" I said. By now, I had walked into the living room.

"Like I said, he's busy," she said. She let out a breath and brushed my cheek with her hand. "I'm sorry he hurt you."

She had no doubt heard about my outburst. Dad had no doubt heard it too. I had some explaining to do.

I took her hand on my cheek and held it. "I'm fine Rosa," I said with a smile. "If you could kindly tell me where Dad is..."

"If I say he's sleeping, will you stop asking?" she said.

"No," I said and walked away from her.

I checked the rooms but Dad was nowhere to be found. When I walked towards his room, I heard people laughing. It sounded like it was a female. I took out my phone and put my headphones on. I opened the door hastily, hoping to catch him in the act. I had to only take a picture of him in bed with some woman and send it to Zac. Zac's mom would leave him, and he wouldn't get the opportunity to con her. This was easier than I thought it would be.

Only, there was no one in the room. Baffled, I walked to its center. It was then that I realized the laughing people were on the terrace outside Dad's room. It was still fishy enough. I walked over to the glass door.

Dad had a dinner table outside his terrace. He was sitting across a redheaded woman. They seemed to just be talking. The scene didn't exactly scream "I'm cheating on you" although that was exactly what was happening. It would take much more than a picture of Dad sitting with some woman to convince Zac's mom.

I knocked on the door, getting my dad's attention. He stood up immediately.

"What the hell are you doing here?" he barked at me as soon as he closed the door he'd walked in through.

Okay Evan, show time!

"I-I..." I stammered and let out a breath. "I'm so sorry," I cried.

"Damn right you should be! You dragged my name through mud."

"Dad I'm so sorry I just...I was an idiot, I'm an idiot," I said.

"You're not my son!" he barked.

"Dad please...please forgive me. I'm so sorry, for everything."

"You are an ungrateful son of a bitch! I gave you everything!" he yelled.

"I know. I thought I was better than you, I thought...My life has fallen apart. I need you," I said. I could cry on cue, but crying in front of my father was hard. I'd sworn it was a privilege I'd never afford him, but desperate times called.

I bawled my eyes out. I went down on my knees. "Dad, please..."

He crossed his arms. "Get up!"

I had the urge to punch him in the guts while I got up. I couldn't believe I was doing this. I was ready to bail on the plan. I was saying things I swore I'd never say to my father. I didn't mean them, but I was saying them. The idea was to have him believe them, but I didn't want him to believe them. It was too much.

"Are you gay?"

"Absolutely not. I said that because I wanted to provoke you," I said. The first part was a lie, but the second definitely wasn't.

"Okay Evan, I'm willing to give you a chance."

"Thank you," I said, jumping into his arms for a hug. It was like hugging a streetlight at night—cold and hard. "Is it okay if I stay a few days? We could do some father-son things," I asked, wiping my cheeks.

"You can stay, but I have company," he said. "I'll give you a key tomorrow."

My apology wasn't real, but damn, did he just pass up an opportunity to spend time with me for some woman? Remind me never to think of fixing things with him for real.

"I can ask Rosa..." I said and he interrupted.

"She doesn't live here anymore. She only comes in to clean and cook. She does absolutely nothing beyond that. I'll give you a key tomorrow. Now, I have to go," he said.

I pointed towards the terrace with my thumb. "Is that your..." I said and trailed, realizing his stone-faced expression. "Relax, from here the view is spectacular. I never liked Marianne, anyway. She's so...stiff."

"It's not what you think."

"Really? Cause if she's available, I'd like to try my luck. She's hot."

"Stay away from her!" he warned.

"Okay, geez. I was just saying...You know...I'm single," I said with a chuckle.

"She's off limits."

Goddammit! Why wasn't he saying what I wanted him to say?

"Dad come on, stop protecting her. I'm a changed guy," I said.

"You can't have her because she's mine! Now go away," he said and turned away from me.

I waved at him even though he could no longer see me. I walked out of the room, pulling out my phone as I walked. I'd gotten a confession...somewhat. Zac's mom wasn't going to believe it was Mark on the recording. The plan wasn't accomplished, though. The whole point of me apologizing was to get access to the house. Phase one was complete. Now I just had to find some information.

I went to get my bag from Rosa and retreated to my room. It held beautiful memories, which greeted me the moment I walked in. I could remember kissing Zac there, and giving him shorts just so I could look at his round butt. Who could forget the moment he walked in on me naked and tried hard not to look?

"I'm in," I said to him, the moment he answered his phone when I called.

"Either your dad is gullible or you're an amazing actor," he said.

"I'm an amazing actor."

"He's gullible."

"He's not gullible. He doesn't trust me," I said.

"That sounds dangerous."

"It's not. I don't think he thinks I'm up to something, though. He just thinks I'm up to my old tricks of provoking him, or that I just came back to steal another credit card."

"*Another?*"

"Long story. What're you wearing?" I teased him.

I felt his scowl even though I couldn't see it.

"*Clothes*! What do you mean 'another' credit card?"

"Take them off," I drawled.

"I'm going to hang up," he threatened.

"Are you in your underwear yet?"

He groaned. "What was I thinking trusting a child to do this?" He sounded like he was talking to himself.

"You sound stressed, hon. You know I don't like it when you're stressed. Lie down," I said. "Listen to my voice, okay? I never sing for anyone so consider yourself lucky."

He said the quietest "okay" I wasn't even sure I'd heard it. I started singing. The best song I could come up with was *Strings* by *Shawn Mendes* in a slow tempo. I definitely didn't sing it better than Shawn Mendes, but I did pretty well if I say so myself.

I wanted all the strings attached. With Zac.

"Zac," I whispered.

He didn't say anything.

"Zac!" I said more forcefully.

"Good night Evan," he whispered sleepily.

I sighed. "Good night Zac."

CHAPTER THIRTY-SEVEN

ZAC

When the sun dawned on the next day, I was up, staring at the ceiling. There was nothing particularly interesting on the ceiling, though; it was just a plain white ceiling. It wasn't it that caught my attention. No, I was just thinking.

Evan was perfect. He was flawed too, but he was still perfect. It sounds like an oxymoron, but he was perfect for me. He was a jerk, but he was also the sweetest person. He calmed nerves I didn't even know I possessed and sang me to sleep. He knew just how to tease me. He was making it hard for me to say no to his whims.

I wasn't only awake thinking about how sweet he was though. I had sent him to the lion's den. I was worried about him. Mark was his dad but given his track record with him, I wouldn't put it past him to hurt Evan. If Mark was really the con artist we suspected he was, then he was dangerous. Put in a corner, we couldn't tell what he'd do. After Evan inadvertently hung his dirty laundry for the world to see, Mark had a score to settle.

But of course, Evan wasn't worried. From the first time I met him, I knew he didn't take things seriously. He was too chill even in situations that required utmost caution. Going to Mark's house had been his idea, and the idea had been sound when he explained it that I immediately pushed for him to go to Mark's house.

Now I wasn't so sure. Mark was the same man who abused Evan. Evan was older but Mark looked stronger. The beach house was a considerable distance from the town. If things went wrong, there wouldn't be anyone near there who can help in at least a considerable amount of time.

Evan could be in danger.

The idea shocked me enough to push my covers down and grab my phone from the nightstand. I needed to know that Evan was fine. I scrolled to his contact and pressed "Call".

"Morning Gummy bear," he answered sleepily.

Gummy bear. Seriously.

"Uh…hi. It's Zac, in case you haven't noticed."

"I know," he drawled. "It's a bit too early. Miss me?"

His sleepy voice was deeper and raspier than usual. It sounded quite sexy. How was that possible? When I wake up, I sound like an alien only just starting to learn English on the phone. But when Evan does, he sounds alluring. What sorcery was that?

For a second, I forgot why I had even called him, having been so mesmerized by his voice. I could wake up to that voice every day.

"I wouldn't miss you even if I tried," I said, remembering that he'd asked me a question. "I was just…uh…seeing if you are okay."

If I didn't sound like I missed him before, I sounded like I just did after my last words.

I heard him shift before he said, "I'm fifty percent fine."

I cocked a brow, forgetting that he couldn't see me. "I'm gonna hang up now," I said, deciding it was best if I didn't indulge him. He seemed fine, and that was all that mattered.

"Aren't you going to ask why just fifty?" he said.

"No. It doesn't matter to me."

"Oh. Way to ruin my morning, cupcake."

I groaned. "You aren't a hundred percent because you didn't wake up in New York on your Egyptian cotton sheets."

"Hmm...nope," he said. "Try again."

I rolled my eyes. "Silk sheets?"

He chuckled. "I didn't wake up next to you."

"Thank God," I said dramatically.

"You're breaking my heart," he whined.

My heart ached. He knew I loved him. Why else would he be so sweet if he didn't? He knew and he was using fake affection to torture me.

"Zac?" he said when I didn't say anything.

"Here! Your words stunned me. How does a nonexistent heart break?" I said.

"You'd be surprised by the things you don't know about me," he said. "Can I video call you?"

"No!"

"Why not?"

"Because we have nothing else to talk about. I'm gonna shower now."

"Before you go, wanna meet up for breakfast?"

"Are you insane?"

"Maybe. I'll be at the hotel in about two hours. We can order in. Dad isn't going to leave the house before then. Don't worry, I'll find out his plans for the day before I leave."

It wasn't a terrible idea. I did want to see Evan and it would give us an opportunity to discuss the plan again. I wasn't comfortable with him being at that house, so seeing him in the flesh would be good for me. For however long we spent together, I'd know he was safe.

"Okay," I conceded.

"Wear something sexy," he whispered.

"Fuck you."

He chuckled. "See you in two hours."

* * *

I couldn't tell if Evan had been joking when he told me to wear something sexy, so after I took a shower, I lingered at my open closet, wondering what I could wear. Too bad, since I didn't have any clothes I deemed sexy. I was a jeans and t-shirt kind of guy, with some occasional shorts and chinos. I wore t-shirts that had funny slogans on them. I adored my hoodies and couldn't get enough of my boots. I didn't even know what kind of clothing was deemed "sexy" for men.

I settled for a pair of brown chinos and a cream white flimsy t-shirt that had buttons. I didn't deem the look sexy, which was all too well. I wasn't about to indulge Evan's whims. He'd want to make out first thing, but we had a pressing issue. I still wasn't sure we should proceed with the plan. Evan could get hurt, and I wasn't about to have that on my conscience.

I took too much time in the shower and getting dressed it wasn't long before there was a knock on the door. Evan was there. He looked happy to see me. He was no doubt anticipating the moment he'd undress me. *Why had I agreed to this physical relationship again?*

"Hi Gummy bear," he said sweetly.

I shook my head and walked away from the door. He walked in and closed it.

"I'm happy to see you too."

"I…" I began to say but was stunned by the arms that wormed their way around my waist from the back.

"Missed you," Evan whispered in my ear.

"Missed you too," I said in a mocking tone. Sadly, those words were true.

He kissed my neck slowly. I stood like a statue, pretending I couldn't feel anything when all I wanted was to kiss him back, to give him the pleasure he was giving me. I wanted to throw my body at him for him to do all he pleased.

I'd done that before. I could lie and say it had been torture, but it had been wonderful. Every move, every kiss, every stroke—everything was imprinted on my mind. We'd made out before but the previous night was etched in every cell of my body. We hadn't been like two rabbits just wanting pleasure. It had been intimate, personal. We had taken time— too much time—yet the desire hadn't diminished. It just kept growing and growing.

It had almost felt like we weren't satisfying a carnal desire, but a deeper one. There had been a connection, an electrical pathway that only existed between us. The image of our entwined hands as he buried his face in my chest was too beautiful. The look in his eyes before he kissed me had *felt* like there was something else.

That was impossible.

I couldn't maintain my statue-form for too long and I knew it. His kisses were so smooth they would make me melt. As much as I wanted that, I also knew it was a dead end. I couldn't be swayed as I'd been the previous night—when I thought maybe he did *love* me. I needed to stop this charade.

"You're so bloody selfish!" I spat.

He stopped kissing me almost immediately. His face emerged from my neck and he walked in front of me so he could look at me properly. I didn't fail to see his confused face. After all, I'd suggested the physical relationship and I was bailing.

I felt embarrassed. If I didn't give a reason for refusing his advances, he would know what was really bothering me— my unrequited love.

"Your dad could con my mom and you're here getting us sidetracked!" I came up with a good save.

"I doubt he's conning her right now," he said taking a seat on the bed and pulling me to it by the hand.

I had a weakness for holding hands. And even an innocent hand holding could be very intimate. And what's more if you're held by someone you loved? I loved the feel of Evan's hand against mine. For a moment, I felt connected to him, but that was only for a moment. I snatched my hand back.

"Did he share with you his plans?" I badgered him. "Do you know something I don't know? Are you in cahoots with him?"

"You're being ridiculous," he said quietly.

I opened my mouth and closed it. I had been about to say I wasn't sure I could trust him. I was angry and it had nothing to do with my mom or Mark. Evan was incredulous! He frustrated me to no end.

He let out a sigh. "Why are on you on edge?"

You! Who else is as chill, gorgeous, and idiotic as you?

"I just need to put this whole Mark thing to rest," I replied.

"We will. Don't worry," he said. "He's going to be out of the house only in the evening. He has a 'business meeting'. I have the keys to the house and I know where he keeps his office keys. We'll find something."

"You're so certain we'll find something."

"I don't see how you being on edge is helping," he commented. "If we could go out, I'd take you somewhere beautiful."

He patted the bed next to him, and I reluctantly sat down.

"Let's talk…," he said.

I raised a brow.

"…about anything. Twenty-one questions…you can ask me anything," he said. "Let's get some food first and just relax, okay?"

He stood up from the bed. I was left with a lot of questions. *Was that Evan or did he have a secret twin brother?* We'd talked in the past, but he'd been so cagey then. He was a celebrity; they were built to be cagey.

* * *

"Do you want to be in the hot seat or shall I?" Evan asked while eating his breakfast burrito. We were still in my room. He'd made himself comfortable on the bed. He was sitting cross-legged, which I learned was his favorite style of sitting.

I was sitting on a chair next to the bed, also eating a burrito.

"You can. No holds barred?" I said.

"Anything...so long as it's off the record."

"I feel so privileged," I said with a mocking voice.

"You are. I rarely answer questions I haven't prepared for."

"Okay, you're on," I said with an evil grin.

"You're scaring me now," he said and chuckled.

"You *should* be scared," I said. "Okay, here we go. What political party do you support?"

He chuckled, almost choking on his burrito. "That's what you want to know?"

"Yes!" I said with a nod. "It's important." I chuckled too, because I wasn't really interested in the answer.

"Uh..."

"Democrat or Republican?" I asked with a serious face.

"What do *you* think?" he said.

"The game is twenty-one questions. I'm the one asking the questions."

"I know nothing about politics," he admitted. "I'm a very ignorant citizen."

"Yes, you are," I agreed. "Okay, question number two, what's your favorite movie of all time?"

"*Pulp Fiction*," he said after a slight pause.

"Really? It's so...bloody."

"Exactly," he said.

"I guess I need not ask what your favorite horror sub-genre is." I said.

He laughed. "I don't like horror movies all that much. I like action."

"What's the last book you've read?"

He laughed, actually laughed.

"What's so funny about my question?"

"It's not you, it's just…the book makes me laugh," he said in between laughs. "It was online. I don't recall the name. All I recall is, I was in it—Cody Wilde was in it. It was slash. There were some really interesting scenes."

"Tell me more!"

"It was mortifying!" he screamed. "Do you know Blake Willow?"

I shook my head.

"He's a fellow model, not important. We get along well and um…in the book we were secretly in love with each other and we denied it but got together when Blake's girlfriend dumped him because he said my name in bed. Basically, the plot was crap and just too erotic. I don't know how I finished it. It qualifies as a book, right?" he explained animatedly. He seemed to be enjoying telling me the story.

"I suppose. Do you just read things that have you in them?"

"I'll have you know I've read all the *Harry Potter* books," he said.

"Okay okay, Mr. Reader. Question…I don't know what number, what do you consider sexy clothing?" I asked. I needed to know that answer.

"You in anything," he teased.

I rolled my eyes. *Why did I think I'd get a decent answer?*

"Moving on, what's your sexual orientation?"

He looked at the ceiling with his lips twisted to the side. "I don't know, and I think I'd rather not label myself."

"You had no trouble with labeling yourself before."

"Yeah, and it turns out I was wrong. So, I'd rather not do it again. I enjoy what I enjoy, and I'm going to leave it at that. I don't want to box myself to fit society's definitions."

I smiled at him. "You're not entirely an idiot, after all."

"My heart just started beating too fast. I think I'm falling in love with you," he said in a mocking tone.

"Ha-ha," I said. I didn't feel like laughing. It was akin to these moments when you know you're in pain but you just laugh it off and say you're fine. I wasn't fine. Why would he say things like that when I desperately wanted him to mean them?

I brushed my hand against my thigh in exasperation. I had to get us away from the last thing he'd said without making it too obvious or awkward.

"Um…am I the first guy you've 'been' with?"

I was an idiot. I was a grave-digging self-burying idiot. I had obviously lost control of my mouth because that wasn't something I wanted to ask. I needn't know that he'd been exploring his sexuality before or after kissing me.

Maybe he and Blake Willow…

"Yes," he said clearly.

Oh.

The answer was kind of nice but it meant nothing. He probably had a long list of guys he was intending on feeling up.

"So…I can be credited for making you discover your sexual fluidity?" I said. It was more of a statement than a question and he picked up on that.

His laugh was melodious. "Yes."

"Don't forget me when you're famous," I joked.

"I don't think I'll ever forget you," he said. The way he said those words made me fall silent. He was silent too. He had this expression on his face that captivated me. For a moment we just looked at each other.

"Uh…next question. Um…" I stammered. My brain had frozen. I couldn't think of what to ask.

"How many times have you been in love?" Evan asked.

"It's not your turn. I'm pretty sure I haven't asked twenty-one questions."

"You sound like you've run out of questions," he told me, letting me know of his observation. "You can answer my question in the meantime."

He'd asked a simple question. I had the answer, but I couldn't tell him the answer. He couldn't know that I was in love with him. Things would be awkward and we'd never recover from it.

"No follow-up questions," I said.

"No follow-up questions until it's my turn."

"In that case I'm not answering," I said firmly.

"Okay okay. I won't ask you any follow-up questions—ever."

I took a deep breath. "I've been in love three times."

"What does it feel like?" he asked, to which I raised a warning brow. "It's not a follow-up question. A follow-up question would be like, 'who'd you fall in love with?'"

I considered him. "I don't know how to describe what it feels like."

"Try," he said.

I put my head in my hands for a few seconds. "They seem... perfect. You know they are not perfect, but you accept their flaws. You see beauty in their insecurities. You want to be there for the good times and the bad. Seeing them smile lights up your day. Your mind knows that doesn't make any logical sense, but your heart...your heart doesn't care because it finds their smile just too exhilarating. It's like... Suddenly this person is worth every sleepless night and those hours you spend watching that goddamn awful movie because every moment with them makes you happy, much happier than you should really be. It's comfortable yet exciting at the same time," I said enthusiastically. "Of course, that is only if it's requited. If not, it's like throwing yourself into a black hole," I finished.

"Ouch!" he said.

"Yeah, anyway I thought of other questions. Do you like animals?"

If I had doubts he knew I had fallen for him, I had no doubts anymore. Evan knew and he was roasting me like the son of Satan he was.

For a moment when I was telling him what being in love felt like, I was picturing us together. I wanted to be there for his good and bad times. My heart jumped beautifully at the sight of him. I also felt like I'd thrown myself into a black hole. The real torture hadn't started but it was beginning to.

"I love dogs. I want one but I'm always traveling," he said.

"Speaking of traveling, weren't you supposed to be in Milan or somewhere replacing a model on the runway?"

"I was but that fell through. There was that public kiss and media attention on me so they thought that'd be a distraction. I was actually glad."

"Oh. That brings me to… do you like what you do? I know I've asked before but…I don't know. Just answer."

He chuckled. "I love modeling and I love acting. When I decided that was the path I was taking, it was an escape but not everything is fake. I enjoy my work and the celebrity life is pretty cool too. There are things I hate about it, but the list is shorter than the things I love…or at least the things I love weigh a lot more."

The things I loved about him weighed a lot more than his idiocy.

"What's your number one deal-breaker in a potential relationship?" he stole a moment to ask.

"It's not your turn," I whined.

"You've probably asked me way more than twenty-one questions," he said. "Answer my question."

"Cheater," I said to which he laughed.

"Besides that."

"Liar," I said. "I don't rate them. It's a long list."

"I gotta hear this list."

"Okay. Off the top of my head: abusive, unhygienic, untrustworthy, racist and sexist, show-off and self-centered," I replied. I'd always thought a casual relationship was a deal-breaker for me, too. Apparently, it isn't anymore.

We continued talking in the room until Evan had to leave for Mark's place. I missed his presence but I thoroughly enjoyed the day. We had only talked but it had felt intimate. I was at ease with him, though his line of questioning bothered me. He'd asked too many questions about my love life.

He hadn't asked me one particular question.

If he asked me if I loved him, what would I say?

CHAPTER THIRTY-EIGHT

EVAN

"Are you in love with anyone?" Zac asks, looking at me with challenging eyes. His voice is quivering with excitement.

"Yes," I say clearly, my heart skipping a beat at the thought of my impending confession.

"Who?" he asks, his ears standing up. He doesn't want to miss this.

"You…it's you Zac," I say without faltering. The butterflies in my stomach run rampant at the smile that creeps up on his face.

Only, he'd never asked the question that I wanted him to. I'd waited with bated breath for that question, but it never left his lips. It was possible it had never entered his thoughts. He deemed me incapable of love, so why would he ask if I was in love?

I'd tried hard to get him to that line of questioning without making it obvious. I thought his curiosity would get to him and he'd ask me the same questions I asked him. Only, he wasn't interested in that.

I'd suggested playing 21 Questions because I wanted to get to know him more and help him get to know me. But while playing, I had the sudden urge to tell him how I felt. I thoroughly enjoyed just being there and talking with him. The way he laughed was beautiful. He was beautiful. The sight of him had my heart beating comfortably fast. He seemed perfect to me, for me.

I was there with him on a dangerous mission not only because I despised my father. I got to be with him, to see more of him.

Though I had the urge to tell him how I felt, I didn't have the guts. I wanted him to ask so I'd be forced to answer. I couldn't tell him outright. It was possible he didn't feel the same way. My first foray into love would be disastrous. He'd justifiably want space and space would turn into distance and distance would turn into complete silence. For the time being, I had him.

I knew we'd be forced to separate soon. I needed to hold onto him just a little bit longer. Maybe I'd get the courage to tell him, but after I left the hotel, there were still pressing matters.

* * *

Dad called to tell me he was leaving the house that evening. That was the window period Zac and I had been waiting for. I left Zac with a kiss and a promise to update him as soon as I could. I raced to the house like a pro-racer.

When I arrived, the house was deserted. I did a thorough check before I retrieved Dad's office keys from his drawer in the bedroom. I called Zac as soon as I unlocked the office and walked in. The room was like the last time, tidy and stacked to the brim. My task was going to be very difficult.

I put the phone on loudspeaker and placed it on the desk.

"I have no idea where to start," I admitted to Zac. I wasn't even sure what I was looking for.

"Start with the drawers," he advised. I could feel the urgency in his voice.

I opened both the drawers on the other side of the desk at the same time. I shuffled through the paperwork, pulling it out and placing it back in. The other drawer only had stationery.

"What's the name of the airline again?" I asked while I sifted through files on the shelves.

"Pacific Eagle Airlines," he said. "Maybe look for a file that contains that?"

"Way ahead of you," I said with a smirk he couldn't see.

I spotted the file on the shelf and pulled it out. There was silence in the room while I read through the pages in the file. Most of them were letters of offers. There were also copies of reports of the accident. There was nothing that looked suspicious, or maybe I just wasn't smart enough to figure it out. There was a lot of legal jargon I couldn't understand.

"Things sound legit here," I said.

"Is his laptop there? Check his emails."

"Okay," I said quickly and pulled the laptop on the desk open. It needed a password. Of course it needed a password and there was no guessing the password wasn't my name or my birthday.

"Needs a password," I said. "I'll look somewhere else. Wait…how much is the settlement amount?"

"A million dollars," I said.

"That's not what I'm seeing here," I said, turning over a page in the file. The letter of offer from the airline stipulated a different amount.

"What do you mean?"

"The airline is offering two million dollars," I said. "This is dated from two months back. I have a feeling the other million is going into my dad's account."

"No…" Zac said and trailed. "The airline will want to publicly announce they have settled the lawsuit and given Mom two million. She would know Mark didn't give her the whole amount."

"Unless he's charging her fifty percent in contingency costs she never knew about but somehow agreed and signed to. If the airline doesn't make the announcement, she'll never know. There's a submission of anonymity here. The airline is obviously dealing with a lot of settlements, each with different offers. Even if they announce it, they can't reveal who they settled with and for how much. If somehow your mom finds out, he'll have a document detailing how he legally took his fees, a document she signed. I just need to find that document," I said.

"You're not dumb after all," Zac said, impressed.

"I sign a lot of legal documents in my life. You learn things," I said. "Now to find that doc…" I said and trailed.

I'd heard movement just outside the office door. My heart almost jumped out of my chest. It was too early for Dad to be back. I had no idea where he'd gone to, but I'd deduced he wouldn't be back that soon. I was wrong.

I stood frozen for a few seconds. If Dad walked in, he'd find me leaning over his desk going through his case files. There was nothing innocent about what I was doing and he wouldn't think there was. Sense returned to me. If he was going to catch me in the act, I'd need to have some evidence ready. I pulled out the letter of offer and stuffed it in my pocket right before there was a knock on the door.

"Mr. Lowe, are you in here?" It was Rosa.

I breathed a sigh of relief that was so palpable it filled the whole room. Rosa would berate me for being in my dad's office but she could keep a secret. At least. I doubted she wanted to see me battered and bruised.

I put Dad's case file back together and shoved it on the shelf before picking up my phone, walking to the door, and opening it.

"Hi," I said with a wide smile to a very confused Rosa.

"Oh, it's you. What were you doing in there?" she asked suspiciously.

"Looking for paper," I said walking out, closing and locking the door.

"Hmm. Paper," she said and shook her head at me.

I grinned and left her to put the key back where I found it. I told Zac I was going to do some more digging and hung up. I found Rosa in the kitchen.

"What're you doing here?" I asked, taking a seat at the kitchen counter.

"I don't live here anymore but I still work here. I occasionally come in to clean, and cook…like last night," she replied.

"Speaking of last night, who was that woman?" I asked.

"No clue," she said putting dishes in the sink and filling it with water. "You shouldn't poke the bear Evan," she said ominously.

"What do you mean?"

"You weren't looking for paper in that office. There are other places you can look for paper besides a locked office. You're looking for trouble," she said firmly. Her back was to me when she said those words.

"What was I looking for?"

"I don't know, but you shouldn't be in there."

"Then help me! I know something's going on in this house. You may not live here anymore but you've lived here for a while. Who is that woman? What's her relationship with my dad?"

"I don't know."

"Look at me and tell me you don't know. You know more than you're telling me."

"I just work for your dad. I don't go poking my nose in his business. You shouldn't, either."

I sighed. Rosa was frustrating. Looking at her, I could tell she knew something. Her words were too ominous. There was a lot behind them. I could sense it.

"Rosa, Dad abused me. He treated my mom like trash. You weren't there to witness it. I know if you were there, you wouldn't have let him get away with it. Right now, Marianne needs your help. You've met her. You've seen how nice she is. That jackass doesn't deserve her. She's a wonderful woman. If my dad is cheating on her, she needs to know," I said.

I already knew the answer. I just needed a corroborating story. Rosa and Zac's mom got along. She'd believe Rosa over me.

Rosa shook her head. "I value my job. It's all I have."

"So, there is something between them. Would you rather Marianne be treated like trash? I thought you were friends," I badgered.

"I..."

"Rosa please! Last time I came here, I wasn't nice to Marianne because I thought she was just like all the other women my dad has been with. But she's not. She's different. She's loving and caring. She didn't treat you like trash like they did. She treated you like a friend. Can your conscience survive betraying someone like that?"

She finally turned to me. She still seemed reluctant to talk but her mouth opened. "The woman from last night is his girlfriend, Rebecca. I don't know when they started but I think it's been six months. She runs some support group or something. She knows Marianne, I mean, she knew her from before Marianne got with your dad. I think she introduced them."

"Wait, Rebecca introduced Marianne to my dad but she is dating my dad herself?"

Rosa nodded.

"So, it's some sort of a polygamous relationship?"

"If only," she said. "Rebecca introduced Marianne to Mark so Mark could con her out of her money. Mark is only pretending to be in a relationship with Marianne. He's after money, money I heard she's about to come into."

Zac and I suspected all along, but it was amazing to hear our suspicions being justified. Zac hadn't been imagining things.

"I thought he has a lot of money," I said, pretending to be surprised.

"When is money ever enough for someone like your dad? Marianne is not the first and probably won't be the last. I've seen people come and go. I've seen people cry for money they lost to him right in this kitchen, and the worst thing is he has some legal thing to back him all the time. Rebecca thinks she's got him, but she'll be replaced too."

I stood up from my chair and walked over to her. "Help me help Marianne."

"Oh no...I don't want to be dragged into this. He'll not only fire me, he'll make sure I'll somehow go to jail."

"Rosa, you don't have to do anything. Just...I think there's something in his office that will expose his treachery before he gets his hands on the money. I need to get it. Just keep guard and tell me when he gets back."

"Evan, he won't hesitate to hurt you again," she warned, shaking her head.

"I need to do this. I let him get away with a lot in the past," I said taking Rosa's hand in mine. "I can't let him get away again. He'll never know you helped me, I promise."

* * *

I called Zac while I was turning my dad's office upside down and told him everything Rosa had told me. We both thought my dad was smooth but didn't think of him as a white-collar criminal. I shuddered to think of how many people he'd

335

conned out of their money by charging exorbitant legal fees or tricking them into signing documents whose contents they did not agree to. He probably did more criminal activities, like fraud and money laundering.

Maybe conning clients who hired him in good faith was just a drop in an ocean of his crimes. It was of utmost importance that I find the document and leave the house before he knew what I was up to.

Zac wouldn't let me get off the phone, but I explained talking to him was causing a delay in my search. He seemed reluctant to let me go. I didn't want to end the call either, but I couldn't talk and read documents at the same time.

It was possible the document I was looking for didn't exist. There were other ways to con Marianne than tricking her to "agree" to fifty percent of contingency costs. Maybe the document did exist but wasn't in the office. My dad did have another office at his law firm in the city.

I was about to give up when I found the golden nugget. The document was conveniently not in the case file. It was placed at the bottom of his desk drawer. I could swear I'd run through the drawer before. True to my suspicions, Dad was charging Marianne fifty percent in contingency costs. That meant half of the money they got in the settlement would go to him. There was also a document that stipulated he was representing her free of charge. Both documents were signed by Marianne. Something told me she didn't know about the first document. I took all the documents and folded them.

When I left Dad's office, he was still not home. The sun had set and the moon was in the sky. I told Rosa I got what I was looking for, but before I could leave, Dad came back. I was with Rosa in the kitchen, my bag on the floor. I had no plans of ever coming back to the house.

I was on the phone with Zac when Dad walked in. He greeted me and looked at the bag. Rosa excused herself to do something in the house.

I put my phone on my shoulder.

"I just...work calls," I explained the presence of the bag.

"Tell them you're spending time with your dad. I'm sure it can wait," he said with a smile. It did not look genuine.

"It can't wait. We're shooting and I'm halting production. Every second that I'm not there is money lost," I said lightly.

"...But you came here to spend time with me," he whined.

"I know. I'll make it up to you," I said with a smile.

I decided to bolt before my acting failed me and I told him what kind of crap he was. I leaned down to pick up my bag. It was a mistake. I'd forgotten about the offer letter I'd stuffed in my jean back pocket. I hadn't done a proper job of stuffing it in because it fell to the floor. Dad and I both looked at it.

This was not going the way I wanted it to.

His fake facial expression changed. He knew what he was looking at. He sized me up before saying callously, "Hand it over, you piece of trash. This is the reason you came back—to go snooping in my office?"

I stood frozen. I could pretend I had no idea what the letter contained or its significance, but I decided not to.

"You genuinely thought you could get away with it, didn't you? I know you intend on conning Marianne out of the settlement money. You lied to her about what the airline is offering."

He didn't deny it. "Congratulations, you have me figured out. The only problem is you can't do anything about it!" he said bending to pick up the letter.

"I don't need that letter to tell Marianne you are planning on conning her of her money!" I said. He didn't know I had other documents.

"And she'll believe you because you're what? Best friends? As far as she's concerned, you're a brat who's out to discredit his dad. It wouldn't be the first time."

"You're unbelievable! How can you con her?!" I yelled.

"Con? No! I'll just be taking my cut."

"She knows nothing about that," I said.

He shrugged. "So?"

"That is obviously a crime!"

"But Marianne agreed to give me a million. Well…" he said and chuckled. "…her signature says she did."

"That is so low! If you wanted to charge her, couldn't you just tell her?"

"She's not smart, but do you think she'd agree to fifty percent when other good attorneys charge only thirty-three percent? And besides, she's my bride-to-be. She needn't know things like that. How will she marry me, then? How will I get access to the other million?"

I was stunned. Was he really that calculating?

"So just tricking her out of a million isn't enough? You want to take the rest of it as well?!"

"Have you seen what she wears? I doubt she knows what to do with a million dollars. I'll be helping her."

"You're a psychopath! It's a crime!" I yelled.

"A crime she'll never know about. If you think of opening your mouth and instilling some doubt in her mind, the world will know about your crime."

His reply was calculated. It stunned me.

"You stole my card and went shopping with it," he enunciated. "It's a crime. It's called fraud."

I groaned.

"That's right boy! You are your father's child. Don't ever do something like that again. You don't even like Marianne."

"You're wrong. I'm not like you, and actually, I like Marianne. And remember you told me no son of yours is filth?

Well, I am filth. I've been with a guy and I enjoy it. Marianne is going to know what you're doing, and about Rebecca too. You can get me arrested. I don't care," I said clearly and finally picked up my bag.

"She won't believe a word you say. I'll invite you to the wedding, but I don't think they'll let you out of jail to attend. You'll be missed," he said with a fake smile.

I smiled too. "I'd rather be in prison than attend your wedding."

I finally walked out of the house. A cold chill hit me as soon as I stepped out. I took a deep breath as I walked to the car.

"Evan?" I heard a whisper. I realized I'd forgotten about my phone call to Zac. I hadn't hung up and neither had he.

I put the phone to my ear. "Hey, sexy," I said playfully. I knew the gravity of the situation, and I didn't want to let it get to me.

"Are you okay?" he asked. His voice sounded desperate.

"Yeah. I'm driving there now. I'll be there in no time. We'll talk then," I said and hung up.

I put my head in my hands. I was shell-shocked at what had transpired in the house. I figured Dad would know someone had been in his office but thought that would only happen after I left. I figured he would know it was me. I didn't even think he'd try and blackmail me.

Choosing to tell Marianne the truth came almost instantaneously. She was a good woman who thought she'd found herself an honest man. She didn't deserve what my dad was doing to her. She was Zac's mom.

I knew my career was on the line. It was yet another scandal. I did care, but I cared about something a lot more.

As I drove towards the hotel room I knew Zac was waiting for me in, I decided it was time he knew how I felt about him. I couldn't keep it a secret anymore. Whatever happens, happens.

CHAPTER THIRTY-NINE

EVAN

My fingers had barely brushed Zac's hotel room door when it was pulled open, leaving my fist in the air. Zac was standing in the room looking worried. He looked like someone who'd been fidgeting before I showed up.

The drive to the hotel had been uneventful, except the butterflies fluttering in my stomach and the way my intestines wound themselves up into a knot.

"Hi," I said sheepishly, pushing my hand down with my other hand.

He sighed, not even trying to hide his sigh. "You're here," he said. The worried lines on his face didn't decrease.

"Well I did say I'm coming here," I said casually.

"I know. It's just…I was worried your dad might try and stop you."

I walked over to him and gently pushed him into the room before closing the door and locking it without even looking at it.

"He didn't. I'm fine," I assured him, pulling him in for a hug. I could feel his breath against my neck.

When he pulled out of the hug he said, "The credit card, that was his?"

I nodded.

"Why?" he asked desperately.

"Because I could, because I thought he deserved a dent in his bank account, because he's a selfish asshole!"

"He's going to get you arrested," he reminded me. He sounded really concerned about the prospect of that. I wanted to assure him I'd be fine.

"I know. I'll be fine. The most I'll get is probably a fine and some community service."

"Your reputation…"

"I can handle it. This changes nothing Zac. He threatened to have me arrested before I turned his office upside down."

"Maybe we shouldn't say anything to my mom. A million is not…"

"…and let my dad get away with it? No, we're telling your mom."

"She won't believe us. Your dad will get you arrested and it will be for nothing," he said.

I put my bag on the bed and pulled out the other documents I had. I hadn't told Zac about them. I put them in his hands. He read through them before looking up at me.

"This…" he said.

"…is proof. Your mom will have no choice but to believe us. We'll tell her about Rebecca, too, and I have a recording of Dad telling me Rebecca is his. Also, I record our phone calls—yours and mine. I have everything he said on record."

"You record our phone calls?" he asked. Obviously, he thought that was more important.

"Not all the time, just some phone calls. I do it for a reason," I said.

He raised a brow.

"Can we get back to the real issue here? I have proof. We need to send it all to your mom before he poisons her against us for her to not want to hear a word we say."

"Right. I'll send her everything now," he said.

I gave him my phone and watched as he phoned his mom. I told him I'd be back, deciding to get out of the room for a bit. I went to my room at the hotel. It seemed like a waste of money paying for a room I didn't even sleep in, but it had been a necessity. I could even sleep in it that night.

I'd made the decision that I was going to tell Zac how I felt about him that night. After everything we'd been through, I realized I loved him more every day. I also realized tomorrow wasn't guaranteed. I had to tell him as soon as possible.

But first I needed to psyche myself up. I chuckled as I paced around in the room. I was not the shy type. I didn't get nervous before photo shoots and interviews. Even when I auditioned for my role in a blockbuster movie, I was calm. Acting in the movie had been smooth, even when I knew I was acting alongside people with degrees in acting, people with big names in the industry.

I certainly hadn't had the butterflies that ran rampant in my tummy. I sat down on the bed to calm myself. That wasn't helping. I stood up again and paced.

I could tell a guy I loved him. It was simple. It *wasn't* simple. Being in love with someone was a big deal. It'd become even bigger if I told him. He could reject me. I mean, *he*'d suggested the physical relationship. What was the point of making things between us awkward?

I had a lot to lose, but a lot more to gain.

I had never been in a relationship, but if Zac loved me even half as much as I loved him, I had a feeling it would be wonderful. I was prepared to compromise, to make sacrifices. It wasn't going to be smooth sailing, but I was determined to make it work.

I could make time for him and give him his privacy. It would be hard to hide our relationship with my celebrity status but we'd try. We wouldn't be able to do everything we wanted to, but I'd make up for that. At least I'd try. I'd shield him from both my fans and my haters and those that stood on the sidelines just waiting for a good story, for drama.

I chuckled when I realized I was already planning for a relationship that didn't exist and was not guaranteed. I looked at my watch. Zac had been talking to his mom for at least fifteen minutes. That looked like ample time to present the proof and possibly argue with her.

I needed to talk to him. I couldn't hold off any longer. I was in danger of bailing.

I walked back to Zac's room and knocked briefly before letting myself in. Zac was sitting on the bed. He was still on the phone.

"I have to go Mom. Love you," he said when he saw me. "Okay, bye," he said after a short pause.

"Mom says 'thank you'," he told me after pulling his phone off his ear.

"So, I guess she believes us?"

"Yeah," he said with a smile. "She believed me in the first five minutes. The rest was me comforting her. She's hurt. She really thought Mark was the man for her. She was just trying to move on with her life."

I nodded. I understood. "So, what now?"

"She's going to get another attorney and decide on a way forward. She's looking into getting your dad investigated. From what Rosa said, it doesn't look like Mom is the only one," he said.

"As long as he pays for his sins."

"What about you? Are you sure you're ready to deal with...?" he said and I joined him on the bed, sitting just next to him.

"I'm fine," I said taking his hand. I massaged it before saying, "I have to tell you something."

My heart was beating way too fast for my liking. It was uncomfortable. *Was this how telling someone you love or have a crush on always felt like?*

Zac's phone chose that moment to ring. Out of all the moments the caller could have chosen, they chose that one. It felt like a scene in a cliché telenovela. It was as if the universe was trying to tell me something.

Well, I wasn't listening.

"Can you ignore it, please?" I pleaded softly.

"It's...Chase," he said.

Even Zac seemed as surprised as I was. *What did that son of a bitch want?*

What if he wanted Zac back? I couldn't give him that chance to wrap his wiles around Zac again. I couldn't let him snatch him in front of me just like that. They had history. We had a few nice memories. I told the world Zac had drunkenly kissed me. He... *lied* and *cheated* on him.

Okay, maybe I was on a better footing than Chase was.

Zac's phone was on the bed next to him. I grabbed it before he could and ended the call. Zac was stupefied. He looked at me in surprise, his eyes much bigger than they usually were.

"I know you and I have a thing, but that doesn't give you..." he said softly and I cut in.

"Could you please just listen to me?" I was desperate and I think Zac sensed it. He gave in. I saw his shoulders relax.

The time was now. Everything had built up to that moment. My heart was going to escape from my chest. Being in love couldn't be healthy. I felt like I was exercising when I was just sitting still.

I took a deep breath.

"The past month we've spent so much time together doing silly and dangerous things and...I've realized something. I...I have fallen in love with you. I love you Zac," I uttered, looking him straight in the eye.

It was out there. I had finally said it. There was a bit of silence between us. I couldn't stand it so I started talking again. "I was livid at Carrie when she leaked that story, but ever since that day, I haven't given her a single thought because…she brought us together. Being with you here has made me realize that I *do love you.*"

He still didn't react. He just looked at me. But then he snatched his hand away from me and stood up. Anger crossed his face.

"Don't do this," he said repeatedly.

"Do what?"

"This! Ruin what we have. You… Don't lie to me. You don't have to lie to me to make me sleep with you!" he yelled.

"I'm not lying!" I yelled back.

"You're doing what Chase did. You're just another Chase. He lied to me and you're doing it, too. You probably think that's how you'll get me to sleep with you, but it's not. I know the terms of our arrangement. I don't expect you to love me, so please don't lie to me."

"But Zac I'm not lying."

"Evan you're incapable of love. I know that much about you," he said.

"I'm *not* incapable of love. I've never been. What I'm guilty of is consciously never letting myself close enough to a person to develop feelings for them. I pushed everyone away. That was, until I met you. I can't say I set out to fall in love with you. It happened and I don't regret anything because you make me happy even when you call me an idiot every time. Believe me."

I stood up and walked to him, pulling out his hands and placing them together under mine.

"It's okay if you don't love me, but you have to believe me." I was pleading. It was also something I never thought I'd do, but I didn't care.

He shook his head. I could see tears welling in his eyes.

"I don't know when I fell in love with you. All I know is, Zac I love…" I said and he cut in.

"No! I get it now. You know I love you! You know I'm hopelessly in love with you. You're doing this to torture me! Is it fun? Are you having fun?"

For a moment everything fell silent for me. Zac's words reverberated in my head.

You know I'm hopelessly in love with you.

He loved me. Somewhere, somehow, he'd fallen too. I could feel my heart swell up with love. Even when I planned an uncertain future, I'd been prepared to deal with his rejection. Hearing him say he loved me was blissful. Zac loved me.

"You love me?" I whispered.

"Now I just hate you," he spat. "Let me go," he said pulling his hands out of my grasp.

I wrapped my hand around his wrist and tightened it. "I'm *not* letting you go," I said firmly.

"What the hell do you want from me?!" he screamed, much louder than before.

"I want you to believe me. I love you Zac. Tell *me* what to do to make you believe me," I said softly.

"Say I did believe you, what do you want me to do with that information?"

"I was hoping we could try being together. A real relationship with all the emotional bullshit and comfort and support and love and moments that drive both our hearts crazy," I replied sheepishly. "And compromises and sacrifices and lots of frustrations that are worth it," I added.

"You don't want to make sacrifices," he reminded me.

"I *didn't* want to make sacrifices. I was caught up in my world," I said and pulled him to me by the arm I was holding. "I want to try…with *you*."

I got a glimpse of a smile forming on his face. My heart fluttered. I felt like just pulling him into my arms and wrapping them around him.

"I love you," he said the words I already knew, but having him utter them sent my heart on a frenzy. But I wasn't out of the woods just yet.

"Do you believe me now?" I asked.

"Yes," he whispered while nodding repeatedly. The smile on his face grew. "Yes, Evan."

I finally pulled him into my arms and wrapped them around him. The feel of his body against me was scintillating yet warm and comfortable. I felt like a burden had been lifted off my shoulders. I was too happy for words.

I pushed slightly out of the hug and cupped his face. "I love you," I whispered before placing a light kiss on his lips.

"You better. I punched the last guy that didn't," he said with an evil grin.

I chuckled. "So…can I call you mine?"

He nodded quickly. "As long as I get to call *you* mine."

"Well, no worries there, because I'm yours," I whispered.

I hadn't even closed my mouth after those words before Zac's lips met mine. I welcomed him heartily. We kissed slowly, guided by the love that existed between us. The kiss was serene yet it was enough to stoke the fire of our love. It wasn't explosive but rather calming. Like our love, it was warm and comfortable, laced with a lot of excitement.

I couldn't believe we were really starting a journey together. It felt surreal. I'd once sworn off love, but there I was, the happiest I'd ever been. My career fulfilled me, but what I had right there was too precious that it transcended what my career could ever bring. Zac loved me. Zac was mine.

"What do you wanna do tonight?" Zac asked after he pulled back.

"Love you," I replied swiftly, placing my lips on his neck.

CHAPTER FORTY

ZAC

The night had turned out to be more than I had expected. It was a night of confessions, one of which made me the happiest guy on earth. After I had believed Evan, that is.

I'd listened in on the conversation between Evan and Mark when he was at the house and it had given me chills. Evan had brushed it aside like he did with everything else. The possibility of getting arrested hadn't convinced him to sweep the proof he had against Mark under the carpet.

Truthfully, I'd considered concealing the evidence. Evan could get arrested. That meant I wouldn't be able to see him or spend time with him. I wasn't ready to make that sacrifice.

I wasn't ready to give him up even though I thought I had to. When he told me he loved me, I desperately wished for that to be true but I couldn't believe him. Chase had told me he loved me when he never did. I didn't want to be lied to again. It was okay if I didn't expect love from Evan. That way I could say he never tricked me.

But...he *loves* me.

But from my experience with Chase, I was warned that I could never be sure if Evan loved me. I could only have faith he did. I trusted his words, and that was enough for me. His deeds would reveal to me whether he loved me or not. For the time being, I was content in basking in the loving look in his eyes and the love cocoon he built around me.

It felt real enough. I was taking the plunge like I'd advised Livy to.

It felt…glorious. I couldn't believe I had been harboring my feelings for him when he felt the same way. I could have been basking in happiness instead of the torture I'd subjected myself to if I had told him sooner.

But maybe the timing was perfect. We'd done some crazy things together and gotten to know each other. We'd built some sort of friendship, and that was important. I couldn't wait to explore where our relationship would lead us. I was too excited my heartbeat couldn't return to its normal rate.

I couldn't believe I was dating a celebrity. I'd never envisioned dating one. My self-esteem wasn't that low that I'd never deem myself worthy. I just had never thought I'd even meet one. They strayed as far away from normal people as they could. Well, that was from what I'd heard at least.

Evan had millions of followers and the world was too interested in his love life. I wasn't sure I was ready for that, but for the time being I shoved that at the back of my mind. We had the next day, and the day after the next day, and the day after the day after the next day…you get the picture.

The petty me reared its head too, wondering what Chase would think. I admit I was ready to show him my massive upgrade, which only made me laugh inside. Another man's trash was clearly another's treasure.

I had no idea why he'd been calling me and at that moment I didn't care. I had a hot guy in my hotel room, whose kisses stoked a wonderful fire in me.

"What do you wanna do tonight?" I asked Evan as he stood in front of me. I hadn't trusted my voice to come out properly after our kiss but it did.

"Love you," he replied quickly and buried his face in my neck.

I leaned my head back and he stepped behind me, attacking my neck. He seemed to love being behind me. He kissed slowly while moving his hands along my hip bones. Slowly, he raised my t-shirt and slid his hands underneath it. The feel of his hands with no barrier drove my senses crazy. He bit a spot on my neck unexpectedly and traced it with his tongue. While distracted by the slight pain on my neck, I wasn't paying attention to the movement of his hand for a few seconds. That was until I felt intense heat and pleasure between my legs. Evan had moved his hand down into my pants, inside my underwear. Stunned by the sudden move, I released a loud moan and threw my head further back. If Evan moved, I would surely fall.

When he moved in front of me and kissed me, our kisses quickly became steamier, more passionate. Evan's lips moved hungrily with mine. With my eyes closed, my other senses were heightened. I could taste Evan's mouthwatering natural taste. I could smell his scent, a scintillating mixture of fragrances that was alluring, fueling my desire for him. I could hear the subtle sounds our lips made against each other and feel Evan's skin as I grabbed him by the waist and pulled him more into me.

Our lips moved in unison for some time until we lost the rhythm completely. Evan pulled back slightly. I took the time to remove his t-shirt. He looked at me with a smile before his lips swooped down on mine. I welcomed him happily. I was starting to get agitated by the separation. The kiss was slower than the last time, but my heart was beating faster.

I traced lines of my own making on his bare back. I loved the feel of my hands against his beautiful skin. I was getting hot everywhere. My breath was coming in short, audible rasps.

I removed my left hand from his back and touched his face just by the lips. I pulled back from the kiss and made sure to put my thumb over his lips just slightly. I had something in mind.

I pressed my lips against the skin of his neck, kissing and licking slowly. All the while my other hand was massaging his back. I moved down slowly, still kissing him. My hand on his back moved up his arm, drawing a subtle line along the way. It finally got to his chest, close to where my lips were. I moved it up and down subtly, barely touching him. Just doing all of that made me excited. It felt nice being intimate with Evan, knowing he loved me.

When I kneeled down so that my head was level with his crotch, I caught a glint in his eyes. I took my time unbuttoning his jeans. I unzipped it slowly, and the act made a loud sound in the stillness of the moment. I thought I was pulling his jeans down until I realized he was doing it for me. I got excited just seeing how eager he was and more so when I saw he was wearing his favorite style of tight-shaping briefs.

He looked very sexy in them, the sight increasing the rate of my heartbeat.

I took them off him slowly and sought to please him. Starting at the base, I wrapped my fingers around him and moved towards his head. He was hard, but I could feel him get even harder underneath my fingers. I started things slow, gradually increasing my pace as I went along. My movements elicited moans, growls, and sounds from Evan that I couldn't decipher.

It wasn't the first time I'd done that, but his moans were different. They felt so pure, so raw. There was just something about them that resonated with me, driving me to give him more pleasure.

I used my hands, my lips, and my mouth. When I felt him move with me, I knew I was definitely doing something right. I welcomed the slight pain I felt on my scalp when he grabbed my hair to keep me steady. I was only too happy to please him.

The initial movements of his pelvis were slow. I got used to the pace, relaxing my muscles in tune. He slowly increased his pace, letting me get used to him. He moved quicker and quicker, finally thrusting with much more vigor. I welcomed him each time, my head kept steady by his hand.

He pulled my hair, and I knew he was close. He stopped moving, pulling away from me altogether. He helped me off the floor and I brushed my reddened knees which hurt a bit. The carpet was well on its way to digging into me.

He pulled me into his arms.

"Now it's your turn," he whispered, his voice raspy and sexy.

* * *

He smiled before pushing me onto the bed. Leg after leg, he removed my jeans. He bent to kiss me but that only happened for a few seconds. His lips found another residence—my chest and abdomen.

Every placement of his lips on my body was exhilarating. He kissed and teased. When he paused and stole a look at me, the look of yearning in his eyes slammed into me. I felt desired. Most importantly, I felt loved. That alone had me clinging to his hair when he kissed along my crotch. My skin was burning, but his lips were hotter. I could feel pleasure mounting.

My body shuddered when he reached his journey. The feel of his mouth on me had me squirming. I was bucking my hips up to meet him. He almost brought me to boiling point, but stopped abruptly. His face was level with mine as he hovered over me. He placed his lips gently on mine.

His kiss wasn't as gentle. It was sweet torture: fast and searing. He pulled back slightly.

"Tell me to stop," he whispered out of breath.

I opened eyes that felt heavy-lidded. "I never want you to stop," I whispered.

Without a word, his lips returned to mine. Passion gripped and overtook us. We kissed furiously. There was so much desire and love around us. My hands roved over any part of Evan I could touch. I almost scratched him but reminded myself his body was his asset. He probably wouldn't mind at that moment, but he wouldn't be pleased in the morning.

He pulled back from my lips slightly and looked at me. I thought I knew what he was asking so I gave him a slight nod.

From then on, it felt like the room was on fire. The preparations were too slow for my liking, but when the moment came, I had to grip the sheets tightly and grit my teeth. Evan held nothing back. The desire had completely taken over. He thrust harder and I moaned louder each time. The pleasure was insurmountable. It was the knowledge that I was doing it with someone I love that increased the pleasure tenfold.

I closed around him and clenched my muscles to give us more pleasure. We rode the wave for a while.

"Fuck," he gasped, a sound that had tremors building in my body.

I could feel the electrical shocks in my toes. I curled them and then the first wave of full-blown utter pleasure slammed into me, rendering my body weak and limp. I released a moan I'd never heard before. I wrapped my legs around Evan, just keeping him in me long enough to ride out the spasm that had overtaken my body.

He entwined my hand with his when I finally let him move. His movements were slow at first, but picked up pace soon enough. Before long they were fast and rough. I could feel him slamming into me. I ran my free hand along his abdomen.

"Fuck!" he screamed. His body jerked and pulsed. He'd reached his climax.

I looked up at his face. His eyes were tightly closed and his nose scrunched. I watched his face slowly relax. I steadied myself and sat up slightly so I could kiss him. He welcomed me with no resistance, even though I gave him short repeated kisses that couldn't amount to anything.

"I love you," I whispered.

I watched as he smiled. "I love *you*."

My heart could have exploded just hearing that. I was happy. I was truly happy.

* * *

Evan and I lay on the bed after that. For a moment, we lay in silence. I was just listening to my heartbeat, which was still considerably too fast. Evan turned to lie on his tummy, putting his arm around me. At least I thought that was what he was doing, but I realized he was taking his phone from the nightstand.

I was irrationally disappointed and it showed. He lay on his back, putting his phone up in the air.

"What're you doing?" I drawled, and then I realized my face was looking back at me from Evan's phone.

He was taking a picture.

"What? No! My hair is a mess. Delete it," I said trying to grab the phone.

"You look fine," he said taking his phone out of my reach.

"I look like I just came from a battle."

"You look sexy," he said bringing his phone close to my face so I could see the picture.

It was of the two of us shoulder to shoulder. I was looking lovingly at him. Of course, he looked gorgeous. I, on the other hand, looked like I'd been in a fight with a bear. The bear won, in case you're wondering.

I had been planning to press the delete button on Evan's phone before my phone rang on the nightstand. I rued my missed opportunity before grabbing my phone. I remembered that Chase had called me earlier but it wasn't him. It was Livy.

"Hey," I said brightly when I answered.

"What's wrong with you?!" she barked.

I groaned. "I'm okay, how're you?"

"Zac, where are you? You missed class and you're not in your room. I thought you were in hospital or kidnapped."

You really do have to appreciate the friends that care about your education and your well-being, but sometimes they have to let you be a bit crazy.

"I'll explain when I come back."

"We have a new assignment and a test in two weeks. Thought you'd like to know," she said. "Are you okay, though?"

"Yeah, I'm fine, Liv," I replied. "I'm in Sapphire Beach Town. It's a long story."

"As long as you're okay."

"Hold on," I said quickly and placed my phone against my shoulder.

"Best friend," I whispered to Evan, pointing at my phone. "Can I tell her about you?"

His smile made me feel like he was making fun of me. We hadn't talked about just how much we'd be private, but there was no way Livy wasn't going to know. I couldn't hide my relationship from my best friend. It might as well not exist if I couldn't talk to anyone about it.

He nodded.

I put my phone to my ear. "Liv, I'm about to tell you a secret. You cannot breathe a word of this to anyone, not even Sean."

"I give you my word."

"So…I'm in Sapphire Beach Town with Evan. We…" I said but was interrupted by her squeal.

"Sorry, sorry. Go on. I'm listening," she said excitedly.

Her excitement made me chuckle. "We are…we are officially dating."

Livy gasped. Trust her to be dramatic.

"Are you…" I said, but she interrupted.

"So, he's gay?"

"No. He…has no preference."

"Oh my God! So…tell me everything! Did you finally talk? Are you happy? How did it happen? He better not hurt you. Tell him I may be short but I can throw him down," she said.

"I'll tell you everything when I see you. And don't worry, if he hurts me, he'll probably never model again." I chuckled.

"You sound so happy. I'm happy for you. But come back, you're missing important lectures."

"I will," I told her before I hung up.

"…I'll never model again? What have I turned you into?" Evan said as soon as I put my phone down.

I shrugged. "Someone told me harbored anger consumes people."

"Didn't mean you should end careers," he said with a chuckle.

"Then don't hurt me baby," I said and moved slightly so I could lie on his chest.

He put his arm around me this time, but that didn't last long. His phone rang. *Was the universe just against him putting his arm around me?*

He answered and got off the bed. He paced around the room. I paid attention to his body more than his conversation. He was just wearing his briefs and he looked mouthwatering. His contours were perfect. His skin begged to be touched. His six-pack was too exquisite.

This was definitely an upgrade. Luckily, his personality was too.

"You're fired!" he uttered words that brought my attention to his phone call. He hung up seconds later.

His phone rang while he was still holding it. He answered and listened to the other person before saying, "You're hired. I'll call you later." He hung up again.

The situation was amusing. "Did you just fire and hire the same person?" I wanted to know.

"No. I fired my manager and hired Rosa," he said.

I sat up on the bed. My eyes narrowed. "You hired Rosa as your manager?"

He laughed. "God no, Rosa is an amazing soul but she's no manager. I doubt she knows anybody in the industry. I hired her to be my helper…domestic stuff."

"Oh."

"Yeah, my dad fired her. She needs a job, and I'm a slob. Okay no, I'm not that bad. I need a chef more than I need a cleaner," he explained. "I'm not at the apartment all that much but she'd never just take my money even though I have enough."

"That's…nice of you. So, the manager thing…did you really fire your manager?" I asked.

He nodded. "I've had enough of her shouting in my ear. She knows what she's doing, but I need someone who understands me, someone who knows me and doesn't try to embellish me."

"Any ideas?"

"No. For now I manage myself," he said.

"I can see how that can be disastrous," I joked.

"Hey! I have learned things. I can do this. For instance, I'm going to call David Markham personally and fix things. I'm going to tell him the truth about me and if he doesn't want me, he can scram."

I stood up from the bed and walked to him. Wrapping my arms around him I said, "I don't know much about your work but I'm your biggest fan. I'll support you, and call you an idiot when I think you're being an idiot."

He smiled. "I appreciate that."

"Can you really survive without a manager?" I was curious to know. I was still unsettled by him firing his manager. It had been so sudden.

"A manager is a luxury baby. I still have a team of people. Well, I'm going to fire my PR manager, but I still have all the necessary people. And I'm quite capable of negotiating my own deals," he said.

"You take nothing seriously!" I reminded him.

He shook his head. "I *seem* like I don't take things seriously. Well, two-thirds of the time I don't, but when it comes down to it, I give it my all. Getting you is an example."

I chuckled and swatted him on the arm. For a few seconds, he pressed his phone, his finger moving on the screen quickly. He gently removed my arm from his waist so he could put the phone in my hand.

"It's your decision," he said.

His words confused me, but when I saw what was on his phone screen, I understood. He was on the Instagram app, on the 'Upload' page. There was a picture of us, the one he'd taken earlier. It was captioned: "*My happiness*". There was no going around that picture. It was clear. Though our faces took up most of the frame, you could still see the background of pillows. There was no twisting the story this time. It wasn't the best picture I'd ever taken, but I looked really happy.

I had only to click 'Share' and it would be shared to all of Evan's followers and everyone who comes across his page.

"Are you sure about this? It's another trending opportunity. This time you'll be labeled a liar. You went on national TV and said…"

"Shut up. There's always a way to twist something. I didn't know then that I loved you and that's the truth. I can tell the world that without backtracking on the story I told. You kissed me that first time and though I was shocked, I realized after the whole interview that I felt something. I wouldn't entirely be lying," he said.

"David Markham..." I said.

"If David Markham doesn't want me to be happy, then he can go to hell. I've oppressed myself for too long," he said.

I smiled. A bird of happiness was taking flight when I pressed the share button. I knew my life was about to take an amazing turn. The spotlight was going to be on me. I was not built to be in the limelight. I was just going to be me...but I'd make some compromises and sacrifices for him.

I hoped Evan really knew what he was doing.

I didn't have a problem not appearing on his social media but his decision had me squirming happily. He didn't want to hide me. He didn't want to hide our love.

"Okay. The pic is up," I said breathlessly. I felt like I had just done the most dangerous thing.

He walked away from me to get onto the bed. "Are you still on Instagram? I want to follow you, so while you're on my phone, press the "Follow" button on your account—if you don't mind, of course. I promise I'll fight the urge to tag you on some ridiculous posts"

I pressed the search button and typed in my name. While I was typing, my phone rang. It was on the bed so Evan grabbed it. He was about to hand it to me when something on it caught his eye. He pressed a button on it and raised it to his ear.

He'd just answered my phone. Apparently, we were at that level already. I chuckled while shaking my head.

"Hi," he said.

He didn't even bother saying that wasn't his phone.

"No, this is Cody," he said. "Yeah, Wilde. Cody Wilde."

"I wouldn't be laughing if I were you. Why would I lie? Anyway, what do you want?" he said.

"I'll tell him you called," he said and hung up.

I raised a brow.

"Your ex wants you to call him when you can. Can you believe he laughed when I told him who I am? He doesn't believe me," he said.

"Look at you…staking your claim," I said looking at his lovingly.

"That's not what I did," he said quickly.

"Of course," I said with a grin as I walked over and placed my lips on his.

"Aren't you gonna call Chase?"

"He can wait forever if he wants to," I said before placing my lips on his again, biting his lower lip slightly.

We kissed slowly. I climbed on the bed to join him, and he pulled me into his arms immediately. I caught a glimpse of his eyes. There was a sparkle in them. They looked so beautiful. He looked so beautiful and happy. My heart soared.

I couldn't believe I was really there with him, in his arms. We'd found our way to each other, amidst a lot of scandals and con artist fathers. We'd found our love. Now we just had to water it and watch it grow. It wasn't going to be easy. Evan was famous and travelled all over the world. I was just a guy whose life consisted of a lot of studying and assignments. Being in a relationship while living in different worlds was going to be hard. We planned to cherish every moment we had together…well, I did.

I hoped he did too.

"I don't know how I'm going to survive when you're in jail," I told him while lying in his arms.

"I hope I'm allowed conjugal visits," he joked.

"I love you," I said.

There was a slight pause. "I love you, a lot."

EPILOGUE

ZAC

I scratched the back of my hand nervously. I didn't realize I had been doing it for a while until I realized my hand had turned slightly red. I stopped my movements immediately and nearly laughed out loud at myself. I couldn't laugh though. I didn't want to draw attention to myself. I was self-conscious already.

I raised my head slightly to look around me. I was particularly interested to see if anyone had been looking at me while I scratched myself like I had some sort of contagious skin disease. No one seemed to be interested in me.

In retrospect, I was a nobody sitting amongst the famous and wealthy. Everyone had a role in the entertainment industry—musician, actor, fashion designer, photographer, model. While I was a college student majoring in psychology. I didn't belong there. No one was focusing on me; they were either interested in themselves or chatting with someone from their world. My only claim to fame was dating a world-famous model.

The night was a bit chilly outside. We were slowly nearing winter. The ballroom I was in kept the chilliness outside.

"Are you okay?" someone asked next to me.

I nodded.

"Are you sure?"

"I'm just…nervous, I guess. Everyone is famous here. It's hard to wrap my head around it all. It's a bit overwhelming," I said.

I looked around at the famous faces in the room. They had all gathered together in the ballroom of one of the biggest hotels in Miami. It was a luxurious room filled with the scent of opulence and fame. There were dozens of stylish tables and chairs adorned with the fashion industry's elite. I had a table I was sharing with three other people, who bore names well-known in the modeling industry.

"Just pretend you don't know who they are," another voice chimed in.

"That will be easy. I don't really know who most of the people here are. I just know they are famous," I said looking at the person.

I had been introduced to him only a few minutes prior. He was a model, one of the many people Evan had worked with.

Evan had done his best to tell me who was who in the industry and who was dating who. There were only a few names you could cram into your head before you get bored. I couldn't keep track of it all. I wondered how he did it.

I had met and befriended some of his acquaintances. Cullen McCarthy was a friend he made on the set of his movie and he shared his apartment with Clive. I got along with Clive very well. He was a very curious guy but down-to-earth too. He wasn't at the event, though.

I resumed touching my hand unknowingly until I was interrupted by my phone vibrating inside my pants pocket. I removed it slowly, careful not to rip the seams of my expensive navy blue suit. It was made of what Burberry called a blend of heritage wool, mohair, cashmere, and lightweight cotton tailored for a slim and modern fit. It cost more than most of my items of clothing. The last time I had worn a suit was at my dad's funeral. Evan had picked it after I stared at all of them with a blank face. When I fit it, I knew it was the one. It just fit my body perfectly. Tonight, I paired it with a white open-neck t-shirt and black shoes.

I looked at the text I had just received.

"Bathroom break? I have just the right remedy to cure your nervousness." It was Evan.

I smiled to myself and typed back.

"As much as I'd love that, you have to go up soon. This night is yours."

I got a sad face emoji in reply. I smiled at my phone and looked at the person sitting next to me. He looked as though we weren't texting each other.

Evan and I were still together. Four months had passed since we formally became boyfriends. He hadn't taken any modeling jobs in that timeframe so we spent a lot of time together. I was on summer break and an honorary guest at his apartment. In between talking, making love, and teasing each other, we had time to work on a project Evan decided to take on.

His own past with his dad had taught him the value of having some form of parental guidance in life. He wanted to offer that to underprivileged kids whose parents were no longer there or had abandoned them. Losing his mom to cancer also made him passionate about healthcare and making sure it was affordable. Evan, goodhearted as he was, was definitely not someone to offer guidance, so his plan was to put the pretty faces in his industry to good use, and get them to join him in making a difference.

We started and registered a foundation, getting experienced people to manage it. Evan donated a large amount of his money to get it started, and I helped out with setting objectives. We were starting small and hoping it would grow big enough to support more charitable causes.

That night, we were formally launching it. I was excited. I'd worked my ass off on it and I was glad we were finally letting the world know.

We'd named it Genesis—the beginning—and we both hoped it was the beginning of something great and beautiful. At that moment, the name "Genesis" was staring at me from the front of the room. It was big and bold, commanding attention.

Our relationship was great. After Evan's Instagram post, my life had become a whirlwind for a while. My phone rang numerous times a day from journalists who wanted an interview. I politely declined all of them, but it got annoying. Evan did one with Cecilia dos Santos focusing on our relationship and his outburst about his dad.

My life didn't just get disrupted by journalists, though. My classmates wanted details too. Random people sent me follow requests. A walk to the store turned into a run because people were just waiting to take a picture of me. It got unsettling, but I got used to it. I even basked in it. Even the *Zack & Cody* jokes were funny. Over time, it died down. People forgot about me, and I couldn't say I was sad.

Luckily, Evan didn't forget about me. He showered me with love every chance he got. We were taking beautiful steps in our relationship. He was more open and just down-to-earth. He occasionally posted pictures of us doing all sorts of crazy stuff on his social media.

David Markham had decided to keep him on even without Jennifer. He'd finally put pen to paper. Being the brand ambassador involved shooting a short advert for the brand. It was going to take place on a Brazilian beach two weeks after the event and I'd been invited to tag along. Seeing a certain Bosnian beauty by the name of Emilia Pjanic draped all over him wasn't going to be great, but the nighttime beach strolls sure were.

I was looking forward to going to Brazil, but before that, I had to go home to spend some time with my mom. After Mark, she was heartbroken, but she was doing well.

Investigations into Mark's dealings were well underway and Mom had gotten herself another lawyer to represent her in the settlement negotiations. Word was Mark was entitled to some money but it meant nothing. His claws were off my mom, and that made me happy.

Speaking of Mark's claws, he still hadn't said anything about Evan stealing his credit card. Maybe he was waiting for the right moment to strike. That was unsettling, but for the time being, everything was perfect.

Evan was sitting next to me, beaming. That night he was wearing a slim fit check wool travel tailoring dark grey suit with a white shirt and a black tie. It suited him perfectly. He was radiant.

My phone vibrated, interrupting me from staring at the Genesis sign. It was a text from Livy.

How does it feel to dine with the rich and famous?

I grinned and texted her back. *Still overwhelming. Wish you were here.*

Livy was doing great. She and Sean were still an item. He treated her like a princess, and she glowed every time I saw her. Avery and Claire hadn't decapitated her like she thought they would. In fact, they were eerily quiet.

Chase. I never got to know what Chase wanted. I'd largely ignored him when I was in Sapphire Beach Town but when I got back to college, I met him in the dorm hallway one day. My curiosity had gotten to me and I'd asked but he'd just brushed it aside and said it was nothing. He'd called me twice. I wasn't dumb. It wasn't just "nothing".

Regarding what he wanted, your guess is as good as mine.

Bruce. Well, I found out Bruce was definitely a skirt chaser. There were rumors he and Chase had broken up. And then there were rumors they were still together in spite of Bruce's shenanigans. I didn't follow the rumors too closely. I was too busy dodging the paparazzi.

When I raised my head from my phone, Evan was no longer sitting next to me. He was at the podium, commanding everyone's attention. I could swear I had looked at my phone for a few seconds. How did I miss that part?

"Good evening everyone…" he started.

Even from where I was sitting, I could see how confident he was. He was exuding confidence with every word and every slight look he gave the crowd as he gave his speech. He was actually a good speaker. He made a few jokes and flashed his pure white smile. Every word was said eloquently.

"… and Pentech Industries. I couldn't stress more how grateful we are for the contributions we already have. I'd like to take this opportunity to thank one person who made this all a reality. Please stand up Zac."

Huh? We had not talked about this!

The guy across from me looked at me. I think everybody else looked at me. *By chance, wasn't there another Zac in the room? Zac Efron? Zach Braff?*

I stood up slowly, still unsure if Evan meant me. It was possible Zach Galifianakis was in the room.

"Zac is the brainpower behind the Genesis Foundation. We came up with the idea together but I was clueless on how to set everything up. He took care of everything, from the planning to the execution. Zachary Nielsen everyone!" Evan said.

People clapped while looking at me. I was the center of attention. It wasn't as bad as I thought it would be. A few flashes went off as people took my picture, before I sat back down.

The clapping died down.

"I would like to thank you personally Zac for working tirelessly so we could reach this day, for pushing me and helping me see other people besides myself. Thanks, babe."

I smiled, but deep down I wanted to kill him. He'd made me the center of attention. It wasn't terrible but he needn't know that.

"Thank you for your attention," he said to the audience. "I know parts of my speech were boring," he joked.

He left the podium and someone took his place. He walked straight to me. I turned to face him before he got there, and he did something I hadn't expected. My lips had parted to say something, and his lips went straight for mine.

It was a light kiss, something very subtle yet it garnered the attention of almost every soul in that room.

Evan pulled back.

"Thanks," he mouthed.

Chatter resumed in the room.

Evan crouched to my level. "If you want to punch me babe, best not to do it here."

I smiled slowly. "I *will* definitely punch you when we are alone. A heads-up would have been nice. I don't like being the center of attention, you know that."

He grinned. "Be careful where you leave marks, someone might just think you are a rough lover."

"Well, you do have makeup," I said. I liked teasing him about makeup.

He got up and resumed his seat next to me. He intertwined our hands underneath the table and faced the front, where one of the foundation's trustees was giving a speech.

"I have two interviews after this and then we can go. Think you can wait that long?" Evan whispered after leaning towards me.

"I don't think so. I'm already tired."

"I'll wake you up when I come up. I will do it even if you protest, so don't. I'll be back before you know it," he said.

I looked at him lovingly. We were no longer paying attention to our own event.

"I love you," I mouthed.

"I love me too," he said.

"I would be surprised if you didn't."

*   *   *

EVAN

Zac was pure perfection. And Zac was all mine. Just seeing him there made me really happy. He'd poured his heart and soul into the foundation while juggling his college exams. It didn't feel right not to acknowledge him.

I knew if I'd let him know before, he would have said no. He didn't like being the center of attention. Being at the event surrounded by egos and wealth was unsettling enough. I hoped he would forgive me just that once.

I had to flaunt his beauty, brains, and heart to the world. Or maybe only so I could get a view of his beautiful butt.

The event ended, and Zac left. I did my scheduled interviews related to the foundation. A few minutes later I made the trip to my room. I was excited that Zac would be there. I hoped he wasn't asleep. Though I told him I would wake him up, it wasn't as easy for me as I made it sound. It didn't feel right disturbing his peace.

When I got to the room, I knocked.

He wasn't asleep, or at least he didn't look like he'd been sleeping when he came to open the door.

"Hey," he said seductively and grabbed my jacket to pull me into the room.

The door was barely closed before he planted his lips on mine. We kissed for a few seconds before I decided to close the door. There was no telling who was out there.

Zac walked to the bed.

"What have you been doing besides missing me?" I said.

"Talking to Livy."

"How's that fireball?" I asked.

"She's okay, although she's not quite happy she wasn't invited to your event."

"Tell her I'll take her as my date to the next carpeted event I'm invited to," I said. "…since you're camera shy."

"I'm still mad."

"How can I make it up to you?" I drawled seductively.

"Well…" he said, walking to me and pulling my tie. "There are ways."

Before I knew it, he'd already drawn me close, his hot breath fanning my lips as he unbuttoned my jacket. I put my finger under his chin and raised it, bending my head slightly to plant my lips on his. At that, Zac bit my lower lip and smiled into the kiss. I grabbed his lower lip then, kissing him fiercely. It turned our kisses erotically painful, and they were strangely more satisfying.

I stopped kissing him, leaning over to bite his neck before whispering, "Remember those marks we talked about?"

He nodded.

"Shall we get on with it? I do have makeup."

The End.

BOOK YOU MIGHT ENJOY

KISSING OLIVIA WINCHESTER
Athena Simone

Joey Montgomery, a simple and shy girl, was forced to volunteer at the carnival her mother's elite country golf club had organized. Her job? Just taking in-charge of the kissing booth and being paid to kiss random strangers.

In every kiss, Joey was either feeling neutral or utterly disgusted. But everything else didn't matter when the most popular girl in town paid a visit to the booth to get a kiss from her.

Olivia Winchester, a bold and outgoing bisexual gal, went to the carnival with her friends. There, she met the girl whom she has never noticed before; the girl who made her feel a rollercoaster ride of emotions; the girl whom she had shared a kiss with.

What's in store for Joey and Olivia after that one kiss? Will it ignite a spark between them? Will it bring them closer?

BOOK YOU MIGHT ENJOY

ALL IT TOOK WAS ONE LOOK
T. Lanay

"My mate's a guy!"

Aiden is your average seventeen-year-old senior with crazy best friends and a supportive family… unless you count the fact that he's got a big secret to tell. Aiden is what most people would call a "closet gay," something he believes he can't let his school know. And the secrets don't stop there.

Aiden goes through high school the best way he knows how—being invisible. But his perfect survival plan comes to a screeching halt when his cousin, the big bad bully himself, gets dropped off at his home to stay for a few months.

In a drop of a hat, Aiden finds himself falling straight down the rabbit hole he once managed to escape from, and the only person that can help is Liam Moore, the star quarterback, the most popular and definitely the straightest guy in school. There is NO WAY!

But what Aiden doesn't know is that Liam has his own share of secrets. He's trying his best to fight it, but his eyes that glow bright yellow in the most in-convenient of times betray him.

The full moon is fast approaching, and the pull gets stronger and stronger. How long will Liam and Aiden last? Is the big bad soon to be alpha wolf corrupting poor innocent little sheep? Will Aiden finally learn to stand up for himself?

All It Took Was One Look is all about acceptance, unconditional love, and embracing your sexual identity—no matter if you're human or not. Don't miss this one of a kind LGBT slash werewolf read! Grab your copy now!

ACKNOWLEDGEMENTS

This book has been a journey, not only for the characters but for me as well. I've learned a lot about myself and the people around me. I've learned that with the right amount of support and encouragement from the people around you, you can do anything – well almost. You can definitely write a book!

To Lu, who made me believe in love again and has to deal with me talking to myself, thank you for always wanting to know what goes on inside my head. You are the reason this book even got an ending.

To Lin, thank you for being a supportive friend who encouraged me to continue writing and even offered to look through the book edits for me when I was too lazy to look at them. You were more excited than I was when you learned I was getting published. Oh friend!

To my editor Shem, thank you so much for your patience with me and dedication to the book.

To Olli and Dukey, thank you for keeping your barking to a minimum. To Kyra, thank you for keeping the pups in check.

To everyone who has ever read any of my books, voted or commented on them; you probably already know but I have to remind you, you motivate me to write more and more.

AUTHOR'S NOTE

Thank you so much for reading *The Forbidden*! I can't express how grateful I am for reading something that was once just a thought inside my head.

Please feel free to send me an email. Just know that my publisher filters these emails. Good news is always welcome.
dante_cullen@awesomeauthors.org

Sign up for my blog for updates and freebies!
dante-cullen.awesomeauthors.org

One last thing: I'd love to hear your thoughts on the book. Please leave a review on Amazon or Goodreads because I just love reading your comments and getting to know you!

Can't wait to hear from you!

Dante Cullen

ABOUT THE AUTHOR

Animal lover. Adventure seeker. Night owl. Music 'appreciator'. Terrible dancer. I still dance though, a LOT. I started reading and writing from a young age. If I'm not reading, I'm probably writing…or dancing. A lover of mystery, I have a penchant for complicated plots and dramatic twists. The psychology behind a character's actions is also something I find intriguing.

Printed in Great Britain
by Amazon